Lesley ▮▮▮▮▮▮▮▮▮▮▮▮▮▮▮ rofessor
of Chi▮▮ ▮▮▮▮▮▮▮▮▮▮▮▮ on Asia.
But it ▮▮▮▮▮▮▮▮▮▮▮▮▮▮ lluring.
She lived there for a total of fifteen years.

Her books on Japan include *On the Narrow Road to the Deep North*, which was made into a Channel 4 documentary, ▮▮ a Lost Japan; the best-selling *Geisha: The Secret ▮ory of a Vanishing World*, for which she spent half a year living among geisha; and *Madame Sadayakko: The Geisha who Seduced the West*, on Puccini's model for Madame Butterfly. She is the author of two previous novels, *The Last Concubine*, shortlisted for the Romantic Novel of the Year ▮ard, and *The Courtesan and the Samurai*.

▮▮sley has presented television programmes on Japan for Channel 4, the BBC and NHK. She lives in London with her husband the author Arthur I. Miller, and goes to Japan every year.

www.lesleydowner.com

Praise for *The Samurai's Daughter*, published in hardback as *Across a Bridge of Dreams*:

'Tensions between modernity and tradition, love and death, duty and desire are powerfully drawn against the backdrop of an era hurtling towards its inevitable end . . . The book's real strengths are in drawing the reader convincingly into an exotic world and moving the plot along at an exhilarating pace, which it does with satisfying results'
Times Literary Supplement

'This engrossing new novel from geisha expert and historian ▮▮ Downer . . . Like the era she describes, Downer has ▮ted two contradictory themes: love and war. Fans of period romance should be sure to pack *Across A Bridge of Dreams* this summer, but those wh▮ ▮▮▮▮ ▮▮▮ ▮▮▮▮ ▮▮ historical fiction will also ▮▮▮▮'
Independ▮

www.transworldb▮ ▮▮▮▮▮

'A really good novel, suffused with the atmosphere of Japan in the late nineteenth century – when westernising influences were beginning to penetrate its traditional culture – and populated with believable characters, whose fates are not settled until the last few suspenseful pages . . . Lesley Downer has hit the bull's eye as a novelist'
Spectator

'A gripping narrative of star-crossed love as the civil war years reach their dramatic endgame'
Japan Times

'A magnificent, sweeping tale of love and war in nineteenth century Japan. No one writes about Japan with more mastery of historical and cultural detail than Lesley Downer. I was enthralled by this wonderful novel'
Katie Hickman

'Against the backdrop of civil war, Lesley Downer has created a rich epic of love, confusion and loyalty. Her deep knowledge, powers of description and meticulous attention to detail draws us into the hopes and fears of nineteenth century Japan in such a way that you will taste the food, watch the fashions, smell the streets and live through the personal tumult of a society on the edge of change. With *Across a Bridge of Dreams*, Ms Downer shows she is a writer at the very top of her game'
Humphrey Hawksley, BBC World Affairs correspondent

'This tale of a forbidden love, set during the era of the Last Samurai, completely captivated me. I was swept along by Taka and Nobu's struggle to be together in the face of family opposition, social difference and, ultimately, war. The world of the book – 1870s Japan – is vividly evoked. But most of all this is a compelling and intensely romantic story, beautifully told'
Isabel Wolff, author of *The Very Picture of You*

'An epic tale of love and war, full of colour'
Choice

The Samurai's Daughter

Lesley Downer

CORGI BOOKS

The quotation on p. 15 is from John Pierre Mertz, *Novel Japan: Spaces of Nationhood in Early Meiji Narrative, 1870–88*, Michigan Monograph Series in Japanese Studies Number 48 (Ann Arbor: Centre for Japanese Studies, The University of Michigan, 2003), p.1. Copyright 2003 The Regents of the University of Michigan. Used with permission of the publisher.

Every effort has been made to obtain the necessary permissions with reference to copyright material, both illustrative and quoted. We apologize for any omissions in this respect and will be pleased to make the appropriate acknowledgements in any future edition.

This book is a work of fiction and, except in the case of historical fact, any resemblance to actual persons, living or dead, is purely coincidental.

A CIP catalogue record for this book is available from the British Library.

Addresses for Random House Group Ltd companies outside the UK can be found at: www.randomhouse.co.uk
The Random House Group Ltd Reg. No. 954009

The Random House Group Limited supports the Forest Stewardship Council® (FSC®), the leading international forest-certification organisation. Our books carrying the FSC label are printed on FSC®-certified paper. FSC is the only forest-certification scheme supported by the leading environmental organisations, including Greenpeace. Our paper procurement policy can be found at www.randomhouse.co.uk/environment

Typeset in 11/13.5pt Sabon by Falcon Oast Graphic Art Ltd.
Printed and bound by CPI Group (UK) Ltd, Croydon, CR0 4YY.

2 4 6 8 10 9 7 5 3 1

To Arthur

Haru no yo no	On a spring night
Yume no ukihashi	The floating bridge of dreams
Todae shite	Breaks off:
Mine ni wakaruru	Swirling round the mountaintop
Yokogumo no sora	A cloud drifts into the open sky

Fujiwara Teika (1162–1241)

The Gion Temple bells toll the impermanence of all things; the sala flowers beside the Buddha's deathbed bear testimony to the fact that all who flourish must decline. The proud do not endure, they vanish like a spring night's dream. The mighty fall at last like dust before the wind.

The Tale of the Heike (compiled around 1371)

1870s' JAPAN

200 km
200 miles

TONAMI

Sendai

Mt Bandai
Aizu-Wakamatsu
AIZU
Lake Inawashiro
Nikko
Great North Road

Sea of Japan

Edo/Tokyo

Mt Fuji
Yokohama

Honshu

Lake Biwa
Nagoya
Kyoto

Osaka

Eastern Sea Road

CHOSHU
Hiroshima
Hagi

Kochi
TOSA
Shikoku

HIZEN

Kumamoto

Nagasaki

Kagoshima
Mt Sakurajima
SATSUMA

Kyushu

Pacific Ocean

N

PART I

The Black Peony

1

Tenth month, year of the rooster, the sixth year of the Meiji era (November 1873)

A savoury aroma seeped through the curtained doorway and around the window frames of the Black Peony, the most famous restaurant in the entire city of Tokyo. Taka gripped the rim of the rickshaw to stop herself shooting forward as it jolted to a halt and the boy dropped the shafts to the ground. She sat back in her seat, closed her eyes and took a long deep breath. The smell filled the air, akin to the tang of grilling eel but pungent, oilier, richer. Beef, roasting beef: the smell of the new age, of civilization, of enlightenment. And she, Taka Kitaoka, at the very grown-up age of thirteen, was about to have her first taste.

Fujino, her mother, had already clambered down from the rickshaw in front and disappeared through the doorway with a shiver of her voluminous dove-grey skirts. Aunt Kiharu bobbed behind her, tiny and elegant in a kimono and square-cut haori jacket, like a little ship after a huge one, followed by Taka's sister, Haru, in a pale yellow princess-line dress, her hair in a glossy chignon.

Taka too was in a western-style dress. It was the first time she'd ever worn one and she felt proud and self-conscious and a little nervous. It was a rose-pink day dress with a nipped-in waist and the hint of a bustle, brand new and of soft silk, specially commissioned from a tailor in Yokohama. She'd told Okatsu, her maid, to pull her corset so tight she could hardly breathe, and had put on a jacket and gloves and a matching bonnet. She lifted her skirts carefully as she went through the vestibule, past rows of boots smelling of leather and polish.

Inside the Black Peony it was hot and steamy and full of extraordinary smells and sounds. Smoke from the cooking meat mingled with the fug of tobacco that blanketed the room. Above the hubbub of voices and laughter, slurps and the smacking of lips, there were hoarse shouts of 'Over here! Another plate of your fine beef!' 'The fire's going out. Bring more charcoal, quick!' 'Another flask of sake!' As a well-brought-up young lady, Taka knew she was supposed to keep her eyes modestly fixed on her mother's skirts, but she couldn't help it. She simply had to look around.

The room was crammed with men, big and small, old and young, sitting cross-legged around square tables, each with a charcoal brazier sunk in the centre, dipping their chopsticks into cast iron pans in which something meaty sizzled and bubbled as if it were alive, changing hue from red to brown. They were dressed in the most extraordinary fashions, some like traditional gentlemen in loose robes and obis, others in high-collared shirts with enormous gold timepieces dangling from their breast pockets and with stiff-brimmed hats and furled black bat-wing umbrellas laid on the floor beside them. Sheets of paper were pinned along the walls with words brushed in the angular *katakana* script which marked them as foreign: *miruku*, *cheezu*, *bata* – 'milk', 'cheese', 'butter' – words that anyone with any hope of being seen as modern had at least to pretend to be acquainted with.

Taka had never before been in such an exotic place or seen such an assortment of terrifyingly fashionable people. She gazed around in wonder then flushed and quickly dropped her eyes when she realized that the men were staring back.

'Otaka!' her mother called, using the polite form of Taka's name.

Picking up her skirts, Taka raced after her down the hallway and into an inner room. It was filled with heavy wooden furniture that cast long shadows in the flickering light of candles and oil lamps. Maids slid the door closed behind her but she could still hear the raucous shouts and laughter. She settled herself on a chair, smoothing the swathes of fabric, trying not to reveal how awkward she felt with her legs dangling instead of folded under her in the usual way. Her mother had spread herself over three chairs to support all the ruffles and layers of her tea dress. Maids fanned the charcoal in the braziers then carried in plates of dark red, shiny meat and laid slices on the hot iron griddle. As the smell of burning flesh filled the air, Taka wrinkled her nose in dismay.

'I don't think I can eat this,' she whispered to Haru.

'You know what Mr Fukuzawa says.'

Taka looked admiringly at her sister's gleaming chignon, envying the way she was so perfect and never had a hair out of place. Two years older than Taka, Haru seemed grown up already. She was always smiling and serene, ready to accept whatever came her way. She picked up her chopsticks and leaned forward.

'We have to eat meat to nourish our bodies if we're to be tall and strong, like westerners.'

'But it smells so . . . so peculiar. Will I still be able to pray to Buddha and the gods if I eat it? Won't it make me smell like a westerner? You'll be able to smell it wherever I go.'

'Just listen to you girls,' trilled Aunt Kiharu, putting her dainty fingers to her chin and tilting her small head. 'Haven't you read *Cross-legged round the Stew Pot*?'

'Of course not,' said Fujino primly. 'They don't read such nonsense. They're well-brought-up young ladies. They go to school. They know far more already than you or I ever will. History, science, how the earth began, how to talk properly and add up figures . . .'

'Ah, but, my dear Fujino, I wonder if they're acquainted with the important things – how to please a man and entertain him and make sure he never leaves your side!'

Fujino folded her fan and tapped her smartly on the arm, clucking in mock disapproval. 'Really, Kiharu-*sama*. Give them time.'

Aunt Kiharu was Taka's mother's closest friend. They had been geishas together in Kyoto and Taka had known her ever since she was a little girl. Now she tipped her head coquettishly and gave a knowing smile, then pursed her lips and recited in a high-pitched lilt:

'Samurai, farmer; artisan or trader;
oldster, youngster; boy or girl;
clever or stupid, poor or elite,
you won't get civilized if you don't eat meat!
Meat for the winter months – milk, cheese and butter,
   too;
Scrotum of bull will make a man out of you!'

Fujino hooted with laughter. She dipped her chopsticks into the simmering pan, lifted out a slice of greying meat and placed it neatly in Taka's bowl. 'We don't want to turn you into a man, but we certainly want you to be civilized!'

Taka chewed the morsel thoughtfully, turning it round and round in her mouth. It was stringy and there was something rather nauseating about the taste but she would have to get used to it if she was to be a modern woman. She thought of the rickshaw boy waiting outside, smoking his pipe, and the grooms squatting in the antechamber. It was a shame they would never have the chance to be civilized, but that was just the way it had to be.

That year Taka's body had changed more than she could ever have imagined possible. She'd grown long and slender like a young bamboo, she'd seen breasts swelling under her kimonos, she'd had her first bleed – she'd become a woman. If she'd stayed in the ancient capital, Kyoto, where she was born, she'd be finishing her geisha training by now and preparing for her ritual deflowering. But instead here she was in the bustling city of Tokyo, learning to be a modern woman.

For the world was changing even faster than she was. She'd spent the first years of her life in the geisha district of Gion in the heart of Kyoto, in a dark wooden house with bamboo blinds that flapped and creaked in the breeze and a flimsy door that wobbled and stuck in its grooves. Her mother was a famous geisha there. When she strolled the narrow alleys of the district, the passers-by inclined their heads and sang out, 'Good morning, Fujino-*sama*, how are you today?' in high-pitched geisha lilts.

In the daytime the plaintive twang of the shamisen echoed through the house as Fujino practised the per-forming arts that were her trade, for geishas, as everyone knew, were entertainers, artistes; the two characters *gei* and *sha* mean 'arts' and 'person'. In the evening she and her fellow geishas appeared at parties. They served food, topped up sake cups, performed classical dances and songs, teased, told jokes and stories and played games. Some of their customers were merchants, old and jowly, others young and handsome samurai. But whoever they were, if they had worries the geishas were ready to lend a sympathetic ear. They were the men's best friends and some were also their lovers.

From when she was a little girl Taka helped out at geisha parties, absorbing the geisha ways, running around with trays of drinks and listening to the geishas' witty chat, learning to speak their special dialect with a coy Kyoto lilt. Her mother and Haru taught her to warble geisha songs and dance prettily and play the shamisen. Her older brother, Ryutaro, had been sent to live with their father and learn how to fight. He had been killed in battle, so long ago that she barely remembered him. But the younger, Eijiro, stayed with the family and was always around the house, tormenting her.

Ever since she could remember the streets had been full of samurai, milling about, brawling. There were regular clashes between men of the southern clans who were determined to depose the shogun and his government and the northerners who formed the shogun's police force and supported him. When she was very small, samurai of the southern Choshu clan had set fire to the imperial palace, where the emperor lived. One of her earliest memories was of standing in the street, gazing in excitement, while smoke billowed and people ran about in panic, afraid that the fire would spread through the wooden city.

More than once the shogun's police had come hammering at the door, demanding to see her father. She'd be bundled off to the back of the house and would watch open-mouthed, her heart pounding, through the crack in the sliding paper doors while her mother barred their way, swearing he wasn't there, though Taka knew perfectly well he was.

She'd always known that her mother and her geisha friends loved the men of the southern clans and that the shogun's police and the northerners were the hated enemy. Every night southern samurai congregated in the teahouses to discuss and plot or just talk and laugh. Her mother played the gracious hostess while they drank and argued, keeping an eye out in case the shogun's police suddenly appeared. And of all the gallant, brilliant samurai, the most gallant and brilliant of all was her father. People addressed him as 'General Kitaoka'. Big and bluff and rather serious, he presided over the gatherings. He'd sit quietly, then start to speak and the others would fall silent and listen. Taka felt proud to be the daughter of such a man.

He was often away. Sometimes she would find her mother weeping and guess that he was at war and that she was afraid for him.

When Taka was eight there was a huge battle right outside the city. She heard the boom of cannons and smelt the smoke that drifted across like a cloud.

Then there was rejoicing. The southerners had won. A few months later the shogun was overthrown. His capital, Edo, was taken and Edo Castle, where he had lived, handed over to the southerners, who were to form a new government in the name of the young emperor. Her father was one of the leaders. A few months later news came that the emperor would leave Kyoto and move to Edo.

Taka and her family had to move too, to join her father, and suddenly her life turned upside down. She'd never left the geisha district before, let alone been out of the city, certainly never travelled in a palanquin. Now she spent twenty days on her knees in a cushioned box jolting along the Eastern Sea Road. When she peeped out of the small window or stepped out to stretch her legs, all she could see was an endless line of people and palanquins escorted by attendants and guards and porters and horses laden with baggage. She crossed forests and mountains and saw the sparkling waters of the ocean for the first time.

Edo, their new home, was the biggest, richest, most exciting city in the world. Not long before, it had been a place of daimyo palaces and samurai residences, of narrow streets crammed with artisans and merchants, depicted in innumerable woodblock prints. With the emperor here, it became even more exciting. It was declared the new capital and given a new name: To-kyo, 'the Eastern Capital'. Kyoto had been just 'the Capital'.

Even now Tokyo was barely five years old. It was a young city, bursting with noise and energy, where people hurried about, gazing at the extraordinary new buildings rising around them. When Taka first arrived, the Ginza, where the Black Peony was, had been a nondescript neighbourhood of shabby wooden shops selling chests or cabinets or fabric. The previous year there had been a huge fire and the district had completely burnt down. Now it had risen again. It was a magical place lined with splendid brick and stone buildings, with colonnades and balconies where men in Inverness capes and ladies in voluminous western dresses gazed at the rickshaws and horse-drawn omnibuses careering by, as if the whole world had suddenly come to life.

People said, and perhaps it was true, that for the first time ever they felt they could change their destinies. Under the rule of the shoguns, everyone's clothing and hairstyle had been decreed by law. A man of the samurai class had to dress as a samurai, a man of the merchant class as a merchant. But now, if they had the money, anyone could don the costume of the new age, and no one would have any idea what class they had once belonged to. The new government positively encouraged it. If people wanted to be really modern, all they had to do was eat a little meat.

And now there were westerners walking the streets. Taka's mother had told her how when she, Fujino, was a child, before Taka was born, Black Ships had steamed into Edo Bay, bringing pale-faced barbarians with grotesque features and huge noses and terrifying weaponry. Now they were everywhere, installing western-style buildings and lighthouses and telegraphs, though people still stared wherever they went.

Taka often saw them on the streets. There was even a barbarian who came and taught her English. They looked very strange, barely human, in fact, but she knew they were to be admired, for they held the key to civilization and enlightenment. The government encouraged men at least to dress western style, eat meat as the barbarians did and learn western languages so that Japan could join the outside world and be the equal of the western nations. Fewer women took up the new fashions but geishas had always been trendsetters and Taka's mother in particular was always ahead of the times.

Even the calendar had changed. The previous year had been the fifth in the reign of Emperor Meiji, a yang water monkey year according to the traditional calendar, which should have been followed by the sixth, a yin water rooster year. But then the government had made the extraordinary announcement that the year would end on the second day of the twelfth month. The following day was to be known as 1 January of the new year, numbered 1873 by the western calendar.

The old calendar had made sense but the new one made none. As far as anyone knew, 1873 was just an arbitrary number. After all, who could possibly remember one thousand, eight hundred and seventy-three years ago or have any idea why the calendar should start then? Most people simply ignored the official calendar and continued to use the old one, just as they ignored the new name, Tokyo, and thought of the city as Edo and themselves as Edoites.

The only practical change was that New Year had come too early. It felt completely wrong to be observing New Year rituals and enjoying New Year dishes at the height of winter, rather than when the plum blossoms were coming into bud. In previous years the children had gone out to play battledore and shuttlecock and watch the strolling players but that year it was far too cold.

Taka's father had been there when the calendar changed. His work often took him away but she loved it when he was at home. She was a little in awe of him. He was huge, as big and tall as a sumo wrestler, and round like a bear – like Fujino, he was larger than life.

He had written a poem to mark the change of calendar and took her on his large knee and gave it to her:

Since times long gone this has been the day we greet the
    New Year.
How will the western calendar reach the distant
    mountain villages?
The snow announces the coming of a fruitful year and
    families treasure their elderly.
How joyful are the shouts of the village children.

*

21

'So Oharu's getting married and you'll be a grand-mother soon,' Aunt Kiharu was saying with a high-pitched laugh. Haru's cheeks turned bright red and she stared fixedly at the glistening meat in her bowl.

'And next we have to get Taka off our hands,' boomed Fujino.

It was Taka's turn to cringe. If only her mother didn't have to speak quite so loudly, she thought, valiantly struggling with another piece of meat. It was horribly chewy but she refused to admit defeat.

Suddenly she noticed that something had changed. The voices and clatter of chopsticks, the rustle of sleeves and patter of feet in the next room had stopped. There was utter silence, as if everyone was holding their breath, then a terrifying bellow followed by crashes as the diners scrambled to their feet and rushed for the door.

There was another sound too – footsteps, padding towards their private room. Taka felt a shock of fear. She stared around. They were trapped, there was no other way out. She rushed to the back of the room, knocking against a table as she ran. Fortunately it was big and heavy and didn't fall over. If the glowing charcoal had spilt it would have set the whole place alight. She tried to hide behind Haru and the maids, crouching so close against the wall that she felt the sandy grain of the plaster pressing into her skin.

Her mother's three chairs crashed over. Fujino was on her feet, her dagger flashing in the candlelight. Now that she was the mistress of one of the country's leading samurai, she'd taken to carrying a dagger, as samurai women did. Aunt Kiharu was beside her and she too had a dagger in her hand.

Breathing hard, Taka watched as the door slid open. A face appeared in the dim light of the hallway, swathed in a scarf like a brigand. Black eyes glinted from between the folds of cloth. It was a man, big and burly, in shabby leggings, the wide sleeves of his jacket tied back ready for a fight. He had a sword in one hand.

Taka knew exactly what he was – a ronin, a lordless samurai, impoverished and embittered, accountable to no one. When she was little, the streets had swarmed with men like him, swaggering about, looking for trouble. Memories flooded back, memories she'd done her best to suppress – of shouts echoing down the streets, fists pounding at the door, her mother confronting angry intruders. She remembered peeking through the shutters and seeing bodies right outside their house.

Fujino stepped in front of him. Taka had often wished her mother were more like her schoolfriends' mothers – wispy, tight-lipped, nervous, not so huge and flamboyant. But now her heart swelled with pride.

'What a commotion,' Fujino said softly. It was her geisha voice, the icy tones she had used when men grew unruly from too much drink, when a glance from her narrowed eyes could make them tremble like children. 'And all for one man!' She drew out the syllables with scorn. 'I'd put that sword away if I were you. Money, is that what you're after?'

The man hesitated as if taken aback by her boldness. He glared at her defiantly.

'Where is he, that traitor?' he growled. 'I know he's here.'

He spoke in the broad vowels of a southerner. So he was a man of the Satsuma clan, like Taka's father. It was her father he was after. She knew her father had enemies, it was far from the first time someone had come looking for him. The man must have spotted the family crest on their rickshaw.

'What do you think you're doing, a Satsuma man, waving your sword like a thug? You should be ashamed. The police will be here any moment. You'd better leave quickly, while you have the chance.'

'He's here, I know he is, that traitor Kitaoka.' He spat out the name.

Fujino drew herself up. In her voluminous skirts she filled the room. The man seemed to shrink before her.

'Be careful how you speak of my husband, fellow,' she boomed. 'He's a far greater man than you'll ever be.'

The man raised his sword a little, keeping the blade pointing down.

'Your husband?' he sneered. 'You're no samurai wife. I know a geisha when I see one. You're that fat Kyoto whore, that precious geisha of his. You've certainly come up in the world since you were swanning around the pleasure quarters, haven't you, Princess Pig! Well, I'll spoil your pretty face.'

Fujino raised her dagger.

'Coward. We're all women and children here.'

'Women and children. I've got women and children of my own to support. Shame on you, with your fancy barbarian clothes, filling your stomachs with barbarian

24

food. We didn't fight and die to see our women aping stinking barbarians. My name is Terashima Morisaburo,' he added, tearing off his scarf to reveal a swarthy face with a scar puckering one cheek. 'You can tell Kitaoka one thing. He thinks he can take our swords, he thinks we're going to hand them over just like that and leave ourselves defenceless. He thinks we're going to stand by while he disbands the army and recruits peasants – peasants! – to do the work of samurai. And what are we supposed to do, we samurai, how are we supposed to survive when we have no work and no stipends? Well?' The man took a step further into the room. 'Answer me that!'

He reached his sword under Fujino's skirts and jerked the blade upwards. She stepped back out of the way but Taka heard the fabric rip.

'That's what I think of your western finery.'

There was a swish as the man swung his sword. Taka gasped in horror. Fujino raised her dagger to parry the blow, but instead of the clang of steel on steel, there was a dull thud. Peeking from behind Haru's skirts, Taka saw that the man had misjudged the height of the room. The sword had lodged in the low crossbeam of the ceiling and stuck there, quivering.

Then she noticed a movement in the hallway outside and caught a glimpse of dark skin and the flash of eyes, slanted like a cat's. There was someone else there – not the rickshaw boy, not the grooms, but another attacker, even more fearsome than the first. The restaurant was totally silent. Everyone had fled. There was no one to protect them from these villains.

Sawdust showered from the ceiling and there was a

splintering sound as the samurai wrenched his sword free. He raised it again, holding it in both hands, preparing to bring it down in a death blow.

Suddenly a thin arm snaked out of the shadows behind him and wound around the man's neck. Taken by surprise, the samurai stumbled backwards. His head jerked back and he grabbed at the fingers as they tightened around his neck. His face turned purple and his sword fell from his grasp. Fujino lunged forward and snatched it up. Bellowing with rage, the samurai thrashed with his elbows, prised the fingers off, spun round and started pummelling his assailant.

Taka caught a glimpse of the new arrival's face and her jaw dropped as she realized he was just a boy, a scrawny boy. His eyes were wide with fear in his sunburnt face, but he was scowling with determination. He'd had the advantage of surprise but now it was obvious he didn't have a chance against the brawny samurai.

Fujino was chewing her lower lip and frowning in concentration. She handed the sword to Kiharu, raised her dagger and paused, her arm above her head. Fearless though her mother was, Taka had never known her draw blood. Fujino took a breath and brought the dagger down, straight into the samurai's exposed shoulder. As she wrenched it out, blood spurted, staining her lavish skirts. She was quivering with horror.

The man yelped and grabbed at his shoulder; the blow had slowed him down but hadn't disabled him. Fujino jerked her head imperiously and the boy leapt out of the way, then she threw herself on top of the samurai, shoved him to the ground and plumped down on his back in all her enormous bulk. Tiny Aunt Kiharu sat on his legs. The two women were panting and their cheeks were flushed but their eyes were afire. The samurai writhed and pounded the floor and emitted muffled yells, but to no avail.

Anxious faces appeared at the door – a tubby officious-looking middle-aged man rubbing his hands nervously, and two burly policemen with stern faces and smart buttoned uniforms. In the hubbub no one had noticed them approaching. The policemen pinioned the samurai's arms and Taka heard him gasp for breath as Fujino heaved herself to her feet. She smoothed her skirts, examining them ruefully.

'So sorry, your ladyship, so sorry,' said the tubby man, whom Taka took to be the restaurant owner, wringing his plump hands. He fell to his knees, bowing again and again. Other faces appeared, peeking round the door, eyes huge like frightened rabbits – the rickshaw boy and the grooms. They threw themselves to their knees in front of Fujino and blurted excuses, beating their heads on the ground.

Their rescuer was standing uncertainly in the hallway. He was a thin-faced urchin, not much older than Taka, tall and gangly, with a long neck and prominent nose. His face was blackened as if he'd been working in the rice fields and there was fuzz on his upper lip. He was wearing a most peculiar assortment of clothes. Taka had to stop herself smiling as she realized he was wearing a girl's kimono jacket with the sleeves shortened. His narrow black eyes darted curiously. Taka looked around, following his gaze, and saw the overturned chairs and mounds of meat scattered on the floor. The tables with their buckets of glowing charcoal were miraculously still upright.

Fujino turned to him.

'You came just in time, young man,' she said gravely, settling herself on her knees. 'We are in your debt.' The boy dropped to his knees too and bowed, shuffling uncomfortably.

'Excuse me,' he said, staring at the ground. 'I didn't do much of a job.' There was a rustic twang, a hint of a dialect of some sort underlying his Edo speech. He glanced around as if he was eager to escape.

'Nonsense,' said Fujino briskly. 'You saved us.'

'He was just passing by, your ladyship,' said one of the rickshaw boys, bowing frantically and baring his teeth in an embarrassed grin. He grabbed the boy's arm and gripped it firmly. 'It was us, we stopped him. Our ladies are in trouble, we said, and told him to go for help. A robber's burst in, we said, one of those ronin, a Satsuma man by the looks of it. We hadn't dared ask any of the diners, they all looked too important. But he just pushed us aside and rushed straight in.'

'I didn't do anything, your honour,' the boy mumbled. 'There was only one of him and I couldn't even hold him back on my own. I'm sorry I failed you. Anyway, I'll be on my way.' He bowed again and backed on his knees towards the door.

Fujino put her hand to her waist where her obi should have been, as if she'd forgotten she was wearing a western dress. She reached for her purse then looked at the boy and put it aside. It was obvious that he was far too proud to accept money.

'Your name, young man?' she asked gently.

'Yoshida, Nobuyuki Yoshida. Glad I could be of service.'

His skinny arms were like sticks poking out of his tattered sleeves. Taka could see her mother's brows knit as she tried to sum him up. He was far too shabby to be of samurai or merchant class, but he didn't carry himself like a servant either. He was impossible to place.

'Wait,' Fujino said, putting a serviette over the bloodstains on her skirts. 'Master, take this boy to the kitchens and give him some food. And provide him with a decent set of clothes, too.'

The restaurant owner's round face was shiny with sweat. He raised his eyebrows as he looked at the boy then gave a sigh, put his hands on the ground and bowed deferentially. 'Whatever you say, your ladyship. The young man certainly deserves a reward. We'll make sure we send him off with a full belly and a good cotton robe.'

'I'll be on my way,' the boy muttered again.

'What house do you belong to?' Fujino persisted.

The boy stared at the ground. 'I've only recently arrived in Tokyo, madam. I have relatives here but . . . er . . . I've been staying with a man called Shigehiro Iinuma, a middle-ranking official from the Omura domain in Hizen. I was in service there.'

He hadn't mentioned his family.

'You were, you say. And now?'

The boy's tawny cheeks flushed. 'I'm looking for work.'

'What about your family?'

Taka cringed. Her mother was a geisha. Where others would have hesitated, she was always shockingly direct.

The boy hesitated. 'I have a father and brothers, your honour. They're far away.'

'So you have no work?' Fujino had the ability to prise information out of anybody, no matter how reluctant they were.

'To be honest, madam, I've just been to see a man. I was hoping to get a job as an errand boy. Hiromichi Nagakura gave me a letter for him. But his house is full already and he says he can't afford any more servants.'

The words came out in a rush. Taka shivered, trying to imagine a world so harsh that people couldn't even afford an extra errand boy. They had so much and he had so little and he'd saved their lives. Their house was full of people already. Surely one more wouldn't make any difference? She spoke up. 'Can't we give him a job, Mother? I need a footman to carry my books when I'm going to school.'

The room fell silent. As she squeaked out the words, everyone turned to look. Haru nudged her to tell her to be quiet but it was too late. The boy had been staring about him like a cornered bear but he too swung round.

Taka felt heat rise to the tips of her ears and lowered her eyes. Fujino frowned, then her face softened and she smiled indulgently. When she turned back to the boy she was looking thoughtful.

'Hiromichi Nagakura, you said, the ex-vice governor of Aomori? You carry a letter from him? Show me.'

The boy scowled, as if to communicate that he had no need of anyone's pity. Fujino held out her hand coaxingly. When she wanted something no one could deny her, Taka thought admiringly. The boy pulled a scroll out of his sleeve. Fujino unrolled and read it, frowning.

As her mother scrutinized the scroll, Taka saw the boy staring at the ground, shoulders hunched, struggling to maintain his look of fierce indifference. His eyes widened and he squeezed his thin hands tightly together as if forbidding himself to hope.

'Well, Nobu,' Fujino said slowly, turning to him. 'You're obviously an honest, strong boy. We need someone like you. You'll be better than these good-for-nothing grooms who abandon us to be attacked by madmen. We need an extra hand. Let me know who to speak to and we'll give you a job.'

Nobu looked at her and, for the first time, he smiled.

2

In the antechamber of the Black Peony darkness was closing in. Lanterns sputtered into life as lamplighters touched tapers to wicks and an acrid fug of burning tallow mingled with tobacco smoke and the powerful odour of roasting flesh.

Nobu had followed the rickshaw pullers and the grooms out and was squatting on his heels, chewing the stem of his pipe. Where he came from, good plain food – rice, tofu, vegetables, fish – was what people ate, he thought, not slaughtered animals.

Shouts and laughter boomed from the inner room. Everyone seemed to have forgotten the disturbance already. Nobu wrinkled his nose and stared under his eyebrows at the dandies in their outlandish tight-sleeved outfits sauntering in and out, waving their hands and flashing their teeth, talking at the tops of their voices. They were like creatures from another world.

Ever since he'd woken that morning he'd had the feeling that something was in the air. It might have been the icy wind blasting through the crack in the door or the squawks of the crows or the creaks of carts as vendors passed by, singing out, 'Roasted chestnuts!' 'Sweet potatoes!' 'Tofu!'

He'd been gulping down a bowl of miso soup in the Iinuma family's cramped tenement at the end of a narrow alley in the 'low city', Tokyo's run-down East End, when the master of the house, a stooped beaten-down man with a freckled pate, had told him, shaking his head miserably, that they simply couldn't keep him any longer. They could barely afford the food to put in their own mouths. Nobu knew that was true. The house was overrun with children and they made a miserable living cutting dried tobacco leaves. He'd been moving from house to house for years now. That was what happened when you had to depend on charity.

Iinuma-*sama*'s faded wife had wiped her hands on her apron, pressed a few coins into Nobu's hand and stood waving from the doorway as he set off into the labyrinth of alleys. He'd turned a few corners then, at a loss for what to do, had gone in search of Hiromichi Nagakura, the ex-vice governor of the northern province of Aomori and an old friend of his father's. Nagakura, a thin man with a gentle face and perman-ently bemused expression, still dressed like a samurai and did his best to live as though nothing had changed. He had fallen on hard times too but he'd helped Nobu out in the past. He'd given him a letter for a man called Tsukamoto who he said might have an opening for an errand boy.

Nobu had walked halfway across the city, tramping through piles of fallen leaves, but when he finally found the house, Tsukamoto, a heavy-browed man with a sour expression, had taken one look at him and said, 'Be on your way. There's nothing for a scarecrow like you here.'

'A scarecrow like you . . .' Nobu felt the blood rush to his face and clenched his fists at the affront. The words thundered in his ears as he stumbled off, barely aware of where his feet were taking him. He was pushing his way through a crowd of people, hearing voices and laughter roaring around him, when a wild-eyed man with his face half hidden in a scarf and a couple of sword hilts poking from his sash barged past, shoving him roughly aside. Nobu recognized him straight away – a southerner, a member of the Satsuma clan, the source of all Nobu's woes.

Nobu was sure of one thing: his enemy's enemy was his friend. Whoever this fellow was out to attack, he would defend them and land a few punches on an enemy jaw at the very least. He'd dashed after him blindly, barely aware of the antechamber full of panicking servants and the diners pushing back their tables and fighting to get out of the intruder's way.

And now it seemed he'd won himself a job.

'Quite the hero,' said a nasal voice. A scrawny fellow with watchful, close-set eyes and the sun-baked pate and sinewy calves of a rickshaw puller prodded him in the ribs. He'd thrown his indigo-blue happi coat wide open to show off the splendid tattoo adorning his bony chest.

'Just charged in without thinking,' Nobu muttered, staring at the scuffed wooden floor. It wouldn't do to incur this fellow's enmity, which he might if the man thought he was trying to show him up.

'You're the lucky one, aren't you?' said the rickshaw puller, tapping out his pipe in the ash box. He narrowed his eyes and peered at him, then gave a gap-toothed grin. 'Gonsuké's the name. No belongings to fetch, I can see that.'

If he had he wouldn't have been wearing a girl's kimono jacket, Nobu thought ruefully. Gonsuké's splendid livery made him feel self-conscious. The plump lady in the grey dress had told the restaurant owner to give him clothes and a meal, then offered him a job instead. At that moment he wished he could have had the clothes and food. The apprentices and grooms lounging around the antechamber were all staring at his outlandish costume and he could feel hunger gnawing at his stomach.

He'd been lucky, he reminded himself. If he hadn't met these ladies he'd have been sleeping out that night and it was turning very cold.

'Live round here, do they?' he asked, as casually as he could. He didn't want this man to guess how desperate he was for a job.

'Shinagawa, on the edge of the bay, by the execution grounds. Where the Eastern Sea Road starts. You know it?'

'You mean . . . the Satsuma mansions?' Nobu stared at him wildly. It had never occurred to him that these people could have anything to do with the southerners. After all, Gonsuké spoke with a low city accent and, as for the ladies, Nobu knew a geisha when he saw one. In the rough neighbourhoods where he usually spent his days and nights they were everywhere, though these ladies were obviously geishas of a much higher rank. They carried themselves with all the airs and graces of the Kyoto entertainment district. The large plump one with the pearly complexion and classic geisha features had been wearing one of those modern western-style dresses, puffed out like a temple bell, as many geishas did. As for the smaller one, it was obvious what she was by her shiny green-tinged lips and the provocative way she tugged her kimono collar down at the nape of her neck and swept her hair up to show off the skin there.

The two young girls had certainly looked a little classy for geishas' daughters. But Satsuma . . . ? The women could be the concubines of one of the Satsuma leaders, he supposed. But still it made no sense. Why was a Satsuma ronin attacking Satsuma ladies?

And supposing they were connected to the Satsuma, how could he possibly take a job with them? No matter how desperate he was, he'd never in his life sunk so low as to work for the enemy, the 'potato samurai' who'd come swarming up from their sweet potato fields in the deep south to snatch control over the country. There was not a government position now that they didn't monopolize.

It was bad enough being a servant but at least he'd always managed to find work among his own people. Even impoverished northerners needed servants. Usually they couldn't pay him, they just gave him his meals and somewhere to sleep in exchange for cleaning and tidying, and after not very long they'd realize they couldn't afford even that. He'd always ended up back on the streets, knocking on the door of the next person he'd been recommended to, begging for work or at least somewhere to lay his head.

'I tell you, the gods were smiling on you. Don't you know who our master is?' Gonsuké swivelled round importantly to show Nobu the crest emblazoned in white across the back of his happi coat. It was a feather in a circle. Nobu stared uncomprehendingly and Gonsuké raised a scraggy eyebrow. 'Don't you recognize it? Kitaoka – our master is General Kitaoka, the greatest man in the whole of Japan. Even a beggar like you must have heard of him.'

Nobu recoiled in horror.

'General Kitaoka . . . ?' Kitaoka – the most hated southerner of them all, commander-in-chief of the southern forces, who'd persuaded the shogun's men to hand over Edo Castle to the enemy without even a fight, the murderer who'd been responsible for the deaths of half Nobu's family, the destruction of his domain and the dispersal of his whole clan. The very thought of Kitaoka made him shudder. He hated him from the very depths of his soul. Every Aizu knew his name. He had Aizu blood on his hands.

Gonsuké grinned. 'No need to look so worried. You're wondering why such a great family would look twice at a scarecrow like you. I wonder that myself. All they had to do was give you some money, not offer you a job. You must have done something in one of your previous lives to have had such good luck.'

A chill ran down Nobu's spine. He'd been about to walk blithely right into the enemy's grasp. He needed work, but not so badly that he'd grovel in front of the Satsuma butcher. He'd rather starve than that.

Panting in horror, he shoved his pipe in his sash, leapt to his feet and barged through the mob of men in their medley of ill-fitting western clothes and Japanese garments, grinning and gabbling like monkeys. He'd reached the doorway and was breathing fresh air and was about to rush into the street when there was an explosion of shouts and laughter and swirling smoke behind him as the door to the dining room slid open. A girl appeared, the one who'd asked her mother to give him a job.

She glanced around the room, frowning as if she was looking for someone. As she darted through the crowd who leapt aside to let her pass, he realized with a shock that it was him. She grabbed his sleeve and held it tight. 'Don't go,' she pleaded. 'Please don't go. Come with us. It's a good house, you'll be happy there.'

Nobu stopped in his tracks. He'd seen plenty of women in his young life – the samurai matriarchs of his childhood, the geishas, courtesans, musicians and foul-mouthed whores who populated the East End and the wives and concubines of the impoverished northerners he'd been in service with – but never anyone like her. Halfway between a child and a woman, she had the sweetest face he'd ever seen, with skin like porcelain and wide brown eyes with a fleck of gold and an air of innocence that was irresistibly appealing. He realized that he was staring but it was hard to turn his eyes away. He forgot his urge to flee. It was unimaginable that such a girl could be related to the monstrous General Kitaoka.

She seemed blithely unaware of the fears and misgivings clamouring in his mind. Her face lit up. 'So you'll stay then. I'm so happy.'

The rickshaw pullers and grooms leapt to their feet, bowing deferentially, as her mother, large and regal, swept into the antechamber, her skirts rustling, followed by the lady in the kimono and the older girl in the pale yellow dress.

Nobu had been so determined never to work for them but now he saw them he thought it couldn't be that bad. They seemed kind and the girl in the pink dress smiled at him so winningly, as if he was the one doing them a favour. He was intrigued by them. He knew if he went with them he'd have to watch his step. It was sheer folly going to live in the house of the enemy. But he had nothing left to lose, and at least it was a job.

The Satsuma section of town was right at the edge of the city, in the no-man's-land where the shoguns had had their execution grounds. It was at the Tokyo end of the Eastern Sea Road, along which the Satsuma delegations used to march when they came up from their home at the tip of the island of Kyushu way down in the south-west. The powerful Satsuma clan had been among the chief of the shogun's enemies and it was there that they had been ordered to build their mansions, a good distance from Edo Castle, where they could cause the least trouble. It was also where the foreign legations had been located when the barbarians arrived, for the same reason.

Nobu ran with the grooms in the cloud of dust kicked up by the rickshaws rattling along ahead of them. When he looked around he saw that they were on a broad road lined with shadowy temples separated by dried-out rice fields and dusty mulberry plantations. Trees rustled and swayed and the last of the leaves floated down, russet, orange, dark red and gold, as they had on the meadows and mountains of his childhood home. The sudden memory brought tears to his eyes and he slowed his pace, kicking the leaves aside, as he thought of Aizu's gracious streets and thick-walled black-painted houses and the jagged peaks glistening on the horizon. He wished life didn't have to be so harsh, that his home still existed and he could go back there, instead of wandering this hostile city, watching out for any chance to survive.

He had had to grow up so quickly. One moment he had been a child, running to school with his satchel full of books, the next the city had been in flames and he'd been tramping along in a line of refugees, barefoot in the snow. Sometimes he felt so tired he wished he could curl up somewhere and never wake again.

He thought of his brothers – the oldest, Yasutaro, badly wounded in battle; Kenjiro, the second son, the brilliant one of the four, but always sickly; and Gosaburo, the third son, who had given up his own future prospects to take care of their father – their brave, proud father, exiled from their domain, forced to live a life of poverty on the salt flats of the far north. He shook his head, filled with shame at his own self-pity.

Concerned for his schooling, Yasutaro and Kenjiro had brought him with them when they came south to Tokyo to look for work. But they had quickly discovered that northerners of an age to have fought in the war were treated with suspicion. It was easier for a child like Nobu to make a living than for them. Kenjiro, who'd mastered English, found the odd job interpreting for westerners in obscure parts of the country, but Yasutaro had ended up drifting north again.

Nobu was the lucky one. He hadn't acquired an education but he had at least succeeded in surviving here in Tokyo, where there was a chance of work; he had food in his stomach or he would have soon; and now he had a job, though he could never confess to his family who his employers were. He might even manage to earn a little money to send to them.

It was dark by the time the line of rickshaws and grooms rounded a corner. A stiff breeze brushed Nobu's cheeks and he smelt salty air and saw the glitter of water, bobbing with sails and ships. Squares of yellow light patched the ground in front of a row of open-fronted stalls. The moon was rising pale over the sea. Seagulls flapped their wings and shrieked. Nobu stopped, panting, and wiped his brow. 'Tokyo Bay,' said one of the grooms. 'We're nearly there.'

Nobu's heart sank as he wondered what sort of place this would be.

They followed alongside a high wall that seemed to go on for ever, with a ditch at the foot overflowing with leaves, then came to a gateway as big as an East End tenement with carved lintels and a heavy tiled roof. Nobu followed the grooms through the gate and across an expanse of raked gravel, along pathways between moss-covered gardens with pine trees swaddled in straw for the winter. He turned a corner and saw in front of him a cluster of buildings looming in the darkness, with sweeping roofs, verandas and porches, linked with bridges. Threads of light glimmered through the cracks in the rain doors. At the front was a huge main entrance where palanquins and rickshaws could pull up, with gold screens faintly visible inside. Uniformed guards paced to and fro, rifles resting on their shoulders.

Nobu stared in consternation. It was too grand, too huge. He didn't belong here. He should leave while he still had the chance. But the gates had closed and the rickshaws were trundling around to the side of the house. The servants were lined up already, bowing, to greet the ladies and help them down.

'Gonsuké, show Nobu to the servants' section.' The leading rickshaw creaked as the large lady put one pale silk-shod foot, then the other, on the step which one of the servants had set in place. 'Make sure he gets a good meal and a decent set of clothes.'

Nobu was following Gonsuké towards the house when the door slid open and a tall, heavyset young man strode out. The servants bowed and stepped back, falling over each other to let him pass. His hair was cropped short and he was wearing expensive western-style clothes. Nobu's heart sank as he saw his supercilious air and the arrogant way he held his shoulders, and he shrank back and tried to lose himself among the grooms and rickshaw pullers. He had heard that General Kitaoka was a giant and this fellow was huge; his son, he guessed. The young man barked at the grooms then swung round and fixed Nobu with his large black eyes, hands on his hips. Nobu stared stubbornly at the ground.

'What have we here? Who's this surly character? Not taken on a new servant, have you, Mother? What would Father say? We can't even afford the ones we have.' The young man stepped closer and poked Nobu in the chest. 'You. What do you have to say for yourself?'

Nobu scowled and clenched his fists. He was panting with rage. It was all he could do to hold back and not do anything foolish. He hated the way the potato samurai had not only defeated his people but turned them into slaves, made them creep abjectly while they ground them under their heels. His fortunes might have fallen and this jumped-up peasant's risen but Nobu was not one whit inferior to him. But this was not down-town Tokyo and besides, this man was twice as big as he was and burly too. He wouldn't stand a chance if he tried to fight him. He'd have to bide his time. That had become the lot of the Aizu. One day their moment would come and they'd avenge themselves. He took a breath, got a grip on himself and bowed his head.

'Don't be a bully, Eijiro. Leave him alone!' The girl in the pink dress had jumped down from her rickshaw and raced over to them, holding her skirts high, her small feet crunching on the gravel. 'He can do plenty, a lot more than you.'

'We had some trouble at the Black Peony,' said the large lady calmly. 'Someone tried to attack us – a mad ronin, waving his sword around. He could have killed us. This lad appeared out of nowhere and helped us, so I offered him a job. It was the least I could do.'

'He saved our lives,' said the girl. 'He's going to carry my books for me when I go to school.'

The young man drew himself up and his face darkened. He should have followed his instincts, Nobu thought. He was going to have problems if he stayed. Then he stole a glance at the girl, who was glaring defiantly at the young man. No one had ever stood up for him before, certainly not someone as pretty as her. He wouldn't leave just yet, he told himself.

3

One afternoon, a month or so after the new servant had arrived, Fujino summoned Taka, Haru and a few of the maids and they trooped out to the storehouse in the grounds of the mansion. It was cold inside the whitewashed earthen walls and Taka's breath puffed out like steam. She had swathed herself in layers of kimonos and put a padded haori jacket over the top but she still rubbed her hands together and pulled them into her sleeves to keep them warm. The tatami was like ice under her feet.

She wrinkled her nose. The storehouse smelt of age and damp and mouldy plaster. It was full of dark corners that no amount of lantern light ever reached, where all sorts of monsters and ghostly presences seemed to lurk. Family heirlooms, priceless antiques, things no one would ever use were stored within these fireproof walls. Even if the great house burnt to the ground and the whole family perished, these mouldering treasures would survive.

As they stepped further in, the trunks and chests cast enormous shadows that swayed menacingly in the light of the swinging lanterns. They brushed the cobwebs off some of the chests and started to open them up. Fujino pulled out kimonos in paper wrappers, boxes of porcelain, dolls and ancient books, lacquerware, scrolls and tea-ceremony utensils, shaking her head distractedly and groaning, 'This won't do. No, not this either.' She was supposed to be planning Haru's trousseau, but she seemed quite overwhelmed by the task.

Okatsu, with her round face and pretty smile, was on her knees, putting things away as quickly as Fujino pulled them out. She was Taka's special maid and had been ever since they'd come to Tokyo five years earlier. She was ten years older than her. When Taka's brother's friends came to visit they teased her relentlessly and Taka often had to rescue her as they chased her around the house, grabbing at her and trying to tickle her. Once one of them had knocked over a lamp while he was grappling with her and broken the paper shade and soaked the tatami mats with oil. She put up with it all with cheerful good humour. Good humour was her speciality. Whatever chaos might be going on around her, Okatsu could always be relied upon to sort it out.

'Here's the one I was looking for.' There was a rustle of paper as Fujino folded back a wrapper and lifted out a kimono. Taka held her breath and stretched out her hand to touch it. In the dim light, wild chrysanthemums embroidered in gold, pink and indigo scrolled across the pale mauve silk of the sleeves, shoulders and hem.

'And this one.' Her mother held up an over-kimono with a thick quilted hem and a design of bamboo leaves woven into the pale ivory silk. It was embroidered with olive-green bamboo fronds, and a little green heron with an orange beak peeking from the foliage. The cuffs and shoulders and hem were a glowing shade of persimmon orange. 'They're heirlooms. I haven't seen them for years.'

Taka lifted the soft fabric reverently. It was smooth and heavy.

'These were my mother's too.' Dabbing her eyes, Fujino reached into another chest and brought out ancient tea-ceremony bowls, tea caddies in woven silk bags and bamboo tea whisks and ladles. She took a tea bowl in her plump hands, feeling the weight of it, then passed it to the maids. 'Your grandmother was the most famous geisha in all Kyoto. The imperial princes used to come down from the palace to be guests at her tea ceremonies and see her dance.'

Taka and Haru nodded. Their mother had told them many times how one of the princes had fallen in love with their grandmother and wanted to take her as his concubine. But the palace authorities had forbidden it and to defy them would have meant exile and disgrace, maybe even death. Their grandmother had been in love with the prince too but as a good geisha she put his well-being before her own and forbade him ever to see her again. Later she had been the mistress of merchants and sumo wrestlers and then had had a long relationship with a famous kabuki actor, but she never forgot the prince. When the mistress of her geisha house died, she was given the keys and became the mistress herself, and so achieved what was every geisha's dream in those days – financial independence.

Taka had been terrified of her. She remembered her as a small, stern woman who had seemed very, very old. She held herself very straight and used to clamp her bony fingers around Taka's arm and fix her with her piercing eyes whenever Taka did anything wrong. The skin of her wrists was so thin it was almost transparent. She ran the geisha house with a rod of iron but was kind to her grand-children and used to tell them stories in a husky whisper.

Haru was on her knees, her hands folded in her lap, her chignon perfectly oiled. She gestured at the pile of kimonos and pottery and lacquerware. 'I don't need these, Mother. I'm going to another house, they'll be lost to ours. You keep them.'

' "Going to another house".' Their mother shook her head and laughed sadly. 'The daughter of Fujino of Gion, getting married. Whoever would have imagined that? Some of my friends married their lovers but not me, your father never chose to take me as his wife. I'll always be a geisha. But my Haru a bride, imagine! And you too, Taka. You're going to school and you will be a bride too. Soon no one will ever know we're of geisha stock.'

Kneeling with her back gracefully rounded, Haru looked more like a great lord's daughter than a geisha. Taka couldn't believe she could be so grown up, so calm and collected. 'If it was me going off to be married I'd be desperate to know what my new husband was like!' she cried.

'They're a respectable family, they're of the highest rank and he's an upright man with excellent prospects. The go-between assured me of it.' Fujino savoured the word 'go-between'. Taka knew how proud her mother was that she'd had Haru's marriage properly arranged, just as respectable samurai families did. It was a union of families, not a spur-of-the-moment geisha alliance.

'He's had the family thoroughly investigated, through several generations. There are no financial problems, no hidden scandals, no insanity, no reasons for worry.'

'I'm looking forward to putting on my wedding kimono and going off in my lacquered palanquin,' said Haru quietly. 'Though I am a little worried that I might not meet the family's expectations. I hope I'll be able to satisfy my mother-in-law.'

She twisted her small hands. She was actually very nervous, Taka could see that now. To be sent away to marry a man she wouldn't even meet until her wedding day . . . Taka knew that her mother had only the best of intentions for both of them but it was a terrifying prospect all the same.

Secretly, in her heart of hearts, Taka wished her own life might turn out more like her mother's, or like the lives she read about in romances and the diaries of court ladies of long ago. She daydreamed about exchanging verses with a mysterious gentleman on a moonlit night, as Lady Sarashina had done hundreds of years ago, or having a secret tryst in the overgrown grounds of a ruined mansion, like Ocho and Tanjiro in *The Plum Calendar*, or being consumed with forbidden passion like the lovers in kabuki plays who killed themselves because it was the only way they could be together.

Or perhaps she would run away with one of the imperial guards, the dashing young men with their cropped haircuts and uniforms with shiny buttons who had filled the house when her father had been here. She used to admire them from a distance. There was one in particular who'd been tall and quiet and rather intriguing. She could see that he was her father's special confidant, though he was far too grown up to pay the slightest attention to a child like her.

She knew that in reality geishas were no happier than wives, that her mother was often lonely and missed her father and wished she could go back to Gion. But at least she and Taka's father cared for each other. From what Taka's schoolfriends said, samurai wives hardly ever saw their husbands. But in the end it made no difference what Taka wanted. Her life was not in her own hands. Soon she too would be sent away, like Haru, to marry a man she didn't know. That was what happened to samurai daughters, which was what she'd now become.

'I'm going to miss you, Haru-*chan*,' said Fujino, sighing. Her eyes swam with tears. 'It's going to be so quiet when you leave. First your father, now you. I don't know how I'll bear it.'

'Will Father come back for Haru's wedding?' Taka asked softly. She knew the answer. Of course he wouldn't.

It seemed so long since she'd seen her father. She did her best not to think about it, to forget his absence, but now, unexpectedly, she remembered his big comforting hands and bulky body and large square face, as sharp and clear as if he were there. She saw him prowling the empty rooms, smoking pipe after pipe, talking in his gruff voice with his colleagues, laughing his booming laugh. Sometimes she'd peek into his quarters when she knew he was alone and find him kneeling at his table in front of a pile of papers, his brow furrowed. He'd scowl and tell her he was busy; but then he'd break into a grin and beckon and she'd run in and perch on his huge thighs. She remembered the rough feel of the cotton robes he wore at home. Cocooned in the curve of his arm, she'd felt protected from anything.

She'd tell him about her day, what she'd read, what she'd done, and he'd listen and nod and say gravely, 'Is that so, little Taka? Is that so?' Then he'd tell her about his own childhood, growing up far away at the very tip of the distant island of Kyushu, in the city of Kagoshima among palm trees and blue skies, with Sakurajima volcano rising in the middle of the bay, rumbling and belching smoke. Thinking of him made her feel empty inside.

When her father had been there, people had crowded the house night and day, filling the public rooms and hallways. She remembered soldiers standing around in knots, heads pressed together, discussing earnestly, petitioners lined up with gifts to give and favours to beg and people arriving to ask advice. Everyone, it seemed, was eager to meet the great general.

In the evenings stern-faced men with moustaches, in full pleated hakama trousers and knee-length haori jackets elegantly knotted at the front or crisp western-style uniforms, would drive up to the great main entrance by rickshaw or carriage. Taka's mother hired geishas to entertain them and many of the men brought geisha mistresses. They didn't bring their wives. It would have been unthinkable for a samurai woman to mingle with men other than family members. That was the role of trained professionals like geishas; and Taka's mother was one of the most famous geishas of all.

The men drank, talked and dined and, when enough sake had been consumed, the geishas played their shamisens and danced and sang and the guests too rose unsteadily to their feet to show off their dancing and musical skills and later still played drinking games, just like in the old days in Kyoto. Taka's father, handsome and gallant, freshly shaved and invariably in traditional haori and hakama, would hold court.

Taka loved hearing his low voice and booming laugh when she peeked into the lamp-lit banqueting hall, though now she was no longer being trained as a geisha she was seldom called upon to serve the guests. When she did have a chance to take in drinks or food, she was supposed to behave like a proper samurai lady – keep her eyes modestly lowered, place the trays before the guests, bow and slip away. It was depressingly unlike the old days when she'd been encouraged to sit with the guests and charm them with her girlish chat. The life of a samurai lady, it seemed, was going to be a lot less fun than life as a geisha had been. In fact she was beginning to suspect that now her status had changed, fun would no longer come into it at all. From now on life would be all duty and obligation.

Then one day, shortly before they went to the Black Peony, her father had stormed in early from work and she'd heard him and her mother talking in low voices. The imperial guards in their splendid uniforms had arrived shortly afterwards, fifty or sixty of them, and she'd heard talking and shouting and the clang of steel. For five days there had been impassioned meetings, day and night. Then the servants had packed her father's bags. When Taka asked, her mother had snapped, 'Your father's going to Kyushu,' in a tone of voice that forbade further questions. She'd looked pale and tense, even though he often went away.

They'd lined up to say goodbye. When her father came to Taka, he took her chin in his big hand and looked at her hard and she saw tears in his eyes. 'Well, little Taka,' he'd said. 'Take care of your mother.'

Then he was gone, along with all the young men, in a long line of rickshaws kicking up dust. Suddenly the house fell utterly silent.

Taka wondered why her father hadn't taken them with him. In the Satsuma capital, Kagoshima, down at the tip of Kyushu island, he had a wife and children, that was no secret, but he could perfectly easily have set Fujino and her children up in a house there too. Most people's fathers kept several households. But he'd chosen not to, perhaps because he'd left in such a hurry. Besides, Fujino would have been bored to death in the countryside.

Geishas were used to their men being absent. They all knew their lovers had wives and children, which made it all the more vital to obey the first rule of the demi-monde – never to forget that love was a game. Taka had had it drummed into her from a young age. Geishas twisted men around their little finger and made them fall hopelessly in love with them – that was their job – but they always took care never to be swept off their feet themselves. Most geishas juggled several men, who all thought they were their sole lover and supported them, and as a result the women enjoyed handsome livings.

But Taka's mother didn't play-act as a geisha was supposed to do. She really was devoted to General Kitaoka. She relied on him to support her and her children. There was no second lover. She paid no attention to that most fundamental tenet. That made Taka afraid for her. It was all very well being a geisha, but only if you were careful never to lose your heart.

The maids were packing away vases, kimonos and lengths of silk for Haru's trousseau when the storehouse door slid open, letting in the darkness, along with a blast of icy air that whipped around the room. The lantern flames flickered and went out, loose kimono wrappers skittered across the floor and lacquer tea caddies rolled around, clattering. It was Eijiro, his kimono flapping. He brushed aside Okatsu and the other maids and stood over Fujino and the two girls, a triumphant grin on his large face.

'I told you so!' He paused dramatically. Taka groaned inwardly, wondering what trouble he was brewing up now. Ever since their father left he'd been strutting around the house, playing the lord and master, telling everyone what to do. 'You know the sword with the gold inlay hilt that I brought back from Aizu, that I keep in the alcove in the men's living quarters?'

'The Matsudaira sword?'

'I had my suspicions about that Nobu of yours from the very start. He does his best to hide his accent but I pick up the northern twang every now and then. You're so fond of him I knew I'd need solid proof so I called him in and said, "I have something for you to polish." Then I showed him the sword. You should have seen his face. He clenched his fists. He was shaking. He looked like he'd seen a ghost. He knew exactly what it was and where it came from and how I must have got it. I thought he was going to rip it out of its scabbard there and then and have a go at me, the way his eyes were flashing. I'd finally broken through that servile pretence of his. I knew then for sure.' He put his hands on his hips. 'I must say, I wasn't surprised. I never liked him from the moment you brought him into the house. He's a surly fellow. The way he swivels his eyes, taking it all in from under that heavy brow of his.'

'So what happened?' asked Haru. 'Did he refuse to polish it?'

'Of course not. He polished it so thoroughly I thought he was going to wear it down to nothing. He has to keep up the pretence. So there's your proof. He's an Aizu to the core. You brought an enemy into the house! What do you think Father would say? I'm going to throw him out right now.'

Fujino lowered her head and stared at the kimonos in their wrappers piled on the floor. Taka wondered what she was thinking.

It was hard to see Nobu as one of the hated Aizu. Of all the northern clans who had fought for the shogun, the Aizu had been the most stubborn and the most feared. It was only when they were defeated that the war finally came to an end. Her father had told her that the shogun and his supporters had wanted to stop Japan moving forward, that if they hadn't been driven from power, their country would never have had the chance to acquire civilization and enlightenment like the western nations.

Taka remembered the shogun's police, thin intense Aizu men with ferocious scowls and burning eyes, hammering at their door in Kyoto while her mother blocked their way, swearing her father wasn't there.

Eijiro had actually fought in some of the battles, it wasn't surprising he felt strongly about it. But it had all been so long ago – well, five years ago, which to him might not seem so long but to her was almost half her life. She'd been a child then, it hadn't seemed frightening to her so much as exciting.

Ever since Nobu arrived Eijiro had taken a dislike to him. Taka saw him every day, sweeping the gardens, scuttling up and down the huge rooms wiping the tatami, taking his turn to serve meals along with the other servants. He was always behind the rickshaw when she and Haru went to and from school. He behaved impeccably, did his work quietly, didn't give himself airs, but there was something about him that set him apart from the other servants. The family all felt it. If he'd been like the others, Eijiro would have treated him as he did them, ignored him except to bark orders. But for some reason he seemed to see him almost as a rival.

She narrowed her eyes. She was still not sure that Nobu really was an Aizu. Eijiro's proof wasn't convincing at all. But if it was true, if he really was, then the Aizu couldn't have been so bad after all, she thought.

It wasn't her place to speak but the words burst out before she could stop herself. 'Father's fair and just,' she said. 'You know very well what he would say. I don't believe Nobu is an Aizu, but even if he is, he was little then. He didn't fight in the war.'

'He had plenty of family who did. He's a degenerate like the rest of them. Walks around with a scowl on his face, never says a word. You can't tell what he's thinking. Nothing good, you can be sure of that. You told me what he did to that Satsuma samurai at the Black Peony.

He'll do the same to us one of these days – slit our throats while we're asleep if we don't watch out.'

Taka would have laughed if Eijiro hadn't been so determined. He hadn't even been there. Nobu had been no match for the samurai at all. 'He's not like that,' she protested. 'He's good-tempered and hard-working, isn't he, Mother?'

'You've been kind to him long enough. You've more than paid him back for helping you out at the Black Peony. You don't owe him anything. He has to go.'

Eijiro set his shoulders. Taka knew women were supposed to obey men, that a woman had to obey her father, then her husband and, when he died, her oldest son. But there was nothing about obeying your brother, especially when that brother's orders made no sense.

'You shouldn't have sent her to that school, Mother,' Eijiro snapped. 'Filling her head with silly ideas. Girls should know their place. We should be training her to be a good wife and wise mother. She doesn't need an education.'

Fujino frowned. She had taken out her fan and was tapping it thoughtfully. 'Poor Nobu,' she said. 'He's only a child. Taka's right. Even if he is an Aizu, he's an honest lad. Your father would agree we should be charitable.'

Taka could tell by the faraway look on her mother's face that she was thinking of Ryutaro. He would have been only a few years older than Nobu when he died. The firstborn, Ryutaro had been their mother's favourite. Taka had hardly known him. By the time she was old enough to remember, their father had sent for him, and she was only eight when news came that he'd been killed in one of the last great battles of the civil war. Geishas were used to giving up their sons and were expected to be proud when they died in battle, but for their mother his death had come as a terrible blow.

'Ryutaro would say so too,' Taka said firmly. She knew how to win her over.

Fujino nodded. 'Leave him alone, Eijiro,' she said. 'You're not dismissing any of the servants without very good reason.' She sniffed quietly and dabbed her eyes with her sleeve.

Eijiro scowled. 'I'll find one.' His brow darkened and he turned on his heel and left.

Taka allowed herself a smile of victory. She didn't know why she'd championed Nobu so vigorously. Perhaps it was because Eijiro was set against him and anything Eijiro opposed she defended. Or perhaps it was because Nobu was young, like her, and she could see how hard his life was, much harder than hers. She was just a thirteen-year-old girl, she didn't have any power at all, but she knew unfairness when she saw it. If she caught Eijiro bullying him she'd stand up for him, she told herself. Eijiro might be out to cause Nobu trouble but she could be just as stubborn. She vowed to herself that from that moment on she would do all she could to protect him.

4

In the days and weeks that followed, everyone was so busy preparing for Haru's wedding that even Eijiro had no time to worry about the new servant.

Once again New Year came early, when there was still snow on the ground, long before the first aubergine-coloured buds brightened the gnarled branches of the plum trees. Taka tried to forget that this was the last New Year she and her sister would ever spend together. They played the poem card game and the flower card game and Haru won every time. And so began the 7th year of Meiji, a wood dog year, 1874 by the new calendar.

One spring day, a couple of months later, when the cherry trees were coming into bud, Haru stepped into her wedding palanquin. Taka had helped with her make-up and formal black kimono with the family crest on the sleeves and collar and thought she had never looked so lovely, like a porcelain doll. Once she was settled on her knees inside and the go-between, hair-dresser, attendants, porters and trunks were all lined up, the bearers lifted the litter on to their shoulders and the procession set off. Taka and her mother and the maids and servants watched from the gate as the line of people grew smaller and smaller until they disappeared under the trees. Tears ran down Taka's cheeks and she could hear her mother sniffing. Haru wasn't going far – her new family lived in Tokyo, close to the imperial palace – but she wouldn't be able to come back to visit until her mother-in-law allowed her to.

A few days later a letter arrived. Taka read it over her mother's shoulder. 'Greetings,' Haru had written. 'I hope you are keeping well in this changeable weather. Just to let you know that I am in good health and fine spirits. The Fukuda family take care of me and my husband is kind.' The letter ended, 'I am very busy about the house and grateful to my mother-in-law for her patience in enduring my stupidity and clumsiness. Your daughter, Haru.'

Tears came to Taka's eyes, thinking of Haru, dear Haru, in a house among strangers. She must be so lonely. Taka sighed. Soon she too would be writing just such a letter, full of empty phrases, giving away nothing, for soon she too would be sent to another house.

The cherry trees in the gardens were heavy with blossom when Fujino announced that some of her geisha friends were coming to visit the following day. A famous dance master was in town and he was going to teach them some new dances and then they would have a tea ceremony and a meal.

'Don't bother us,' she told Taka. 'Take care of yourself for a few hours when you get back from school.'

Next day Taka was up well before dawn. The sky was streaked with pink and the air was fresh when she came out of the house and saw Nobu standing beside the rickshaw, holding her books and lacquered lunch box. Washed and shaved and with his hair oiled into a top-knot, wearing the striped robe and narrow sash her mother had given him, he looked really distinguished. All the girls at school had footmen to carry their books but theirs were stunted, bandy-legged Edo lads, like Gonsuké, the rickshaw boy. None was handsome like Nobu. As Taka climbed in and they set off, rattling and bouncing along, she looked back at Nobu running behind in the dust. It seemed terrible that he would never have the chance to go to school himself.

The school Taka went to was in a building that had been a Buddhist temple, with dark corridors running alongside musty rooms where girls sat on their knees at low desks, studying in the faint light that glimmered through the paper shoji screens.

Most girls, as Taka's mother regularly reminded her, were just taught the basic alphabet and a few *kanji* characters and had to learn by heart books such as *The Greater Learning for Women*, *The Classic of Filial Piety* and *One Hundred Poems by One Hundred Poets* before being sent off to needlework school at the age of thirteen to learn to make clothes. The theory was that girls were simple-minded creatures, weak of body and weak of mind, who didn't need to be able to read or write much more than the slip to tell the dyer how to colour the yarn. But Taka's was a school for the daughters of the elite. They had to learn seven to eight thousand *kanji* characters so that they would be fully literate. They studied poetry-writing, arithmetic and the use of the abacus, memorized the Confucian and other classics and even learned English, all subjects usually restricted to boys.

Taka knew how privileged she was to be going to such a special school. But as the rickshaw boy lowered the shafts she felt a rising sense of panic, as she did every day. She went in, turned her wooden nameplate face up, helped unstack the desks and took her place with her writing box in front of her, but she still had a gnawing sense of foreboding.

Most of the girls were of samurai stock, the daughters of her father's colleagues. While Taka had spent her early years learning to be a geisha, they had been studying reading and writing and samurai arts like horse-riding and sparring with the halberd, the women's weapon. Taka had soon discovered that singing and dancing were skills practised by vulgar townswomen or, worse still, geishas, who were so low class they didn't even feature in the class system. Such skills were certainly not practised by well-brought-up samurai girls, who wouldn't have dreamed of behaving like performing monkeys, which was what they considered entertainers to be. Taka had done all she could to lose her Kyoto accent and geisha ways, but it didn't matter. Everyone knew perfectly well that her mother was a geisha.

While her father, the famous General Kitaoka, had been in town, no one had said a word, added to which Haru was so cool and dignified that no one would have dared question her samurai credentials. But now everything had changed. Taka had thought that, with Haru gone, she might make friends at school, but she was too different from the others.

The day began with morning recitation, in which the girls all read aloud at the tops of their voices. They all read different passages, whatever they were working on, so there was quite a noise. Then came writing practice. The teacher brushed a character for Taka and she wrote it again and again till she'd mastered it, then moved on to the next. Her hands were soon covered in ink.

That day they started on a classic text. The others all read confidently but when it came to Taka's turn she was stumbling.

Later, as they collected their books to go home and ran up and down, sweeping the classroom, the girls were talking about the cherry blossoms that hung low over the streets and temple grounds.

'We're taking a picnic and going cherry-blossom viewing tomorrow,' said tall, slender Ohisa. She carried herself with an aristocratic air and was so fashionable she wore western clothes even to school.

'Yes, today's the day,' said short, bespectacled Yuki. 'My mother says the cherry blossoms are at their height.'

'Wasn't there a song about cherry blossom?' asked Ohisa, glancing round at Taka. Taka smiled and nodded, pleased to be included in the conversation, and hummed 'Sakura, Sakura', the famous song that the geishas sang at this season, letting her hands rise and fall to the rhythm of the tune. She half thought the others would join in but instead they stared at her and burst out laughing. Too late she realized she'd fallen into a trap.

'You would know it, wouldn't you?' said Ohisa, drawling out each word in slow deliberate tones. 'What did they say your mother was? A geisha, wasn't it?'

Taka fell silent and dropped her head. She'd been shown up for the fake she was. Cheeks burning, still smarting from the sting of the words, she ran out to the rickshaw, her eyes brimming with tears. Even the sight of Nobu waiting there with Gonsuké couldn't lighten her mood.

Back home, her mother's party was in full swing. The tinkle of shamisens and the geishas' shrill laughter made Taka feel a hundred times worse. She swung on her heel and headed out into the grounds. She would walk under the cherry trees. That might make her feel better.

She heard her maid Okatsu's high-pitched voice behind her. 'Madam, madam, where are you going? It'll be dark soon. There might be snakes or foxes. You can't walk alone.'

'Walk with me then.'

Taka's mother's voice floated out from the house. 'Okatsu, where are you? I need you, right now.'

There was silence. Taka was already well away from the house. Okatsu's voice rang out. 'Nobu, you lazy fellow. What are you doing? Go with the young mistress.'

Feet came running after her. She paid no attention.

In the five or six years they'd lived there Taka had explored every corner of the estate. It was huge, like a chunk of countryside on the edge of the city, large enough to get completely lost in. It took an army of gardeners to keep it all in perfect shape. Parts were landscaped, modelled after scenic places in Japan, complete with hills and lakes, arbours, bridges and winding paths, with stone lanterns and teahouses cunningly tucked away so that the stroller came upon them unexpectedly, with a pleasing sense of surprise. Other parts were deliberately left wild. At the back of the grounds paths led past bamboo groves into woodland. Pale pink cherry blossom drifted like snow, forming piles along the paths and heaping up against rocks and tree trunks.

Taka kicked through the blossom sulkily, barely aware of Nobu following behind her. Now that she was supposed to be a samurai girl, she wasn't allowed to mix with boys any more. But servants were different, they didn't count as boys or men, they were another species.

'I hate school,' she said fiercely. She was well away from the house, tramping up the slope that led to the woods. She could see the trees ahead of her, an enticing tangle of foliage. A breeze rustled the leaves. 'I'm never going back.'

'You must.' She turned in surprise. She hadn't been expecting a reply. 'It's the only way you'll learn. You're so lucky to be going to school.' Nobu stopped when she stopped, keeping a proper distance between them.

A wind had blown up and bats flittered under the trees. A bird sang out forlornly.

Taka looked at the boy appraisingly. He had dark intelligent eyes and a rather prominent, strangely aristocratic nose. He was a servant but not a servant. She couldn't be sure where he belonged. The other servants would never understand what her life was like, but there was just a chance that he might.

She sighed. 'All the others are good at history and arithmetic and know the classics. They've all been studying ever since they were little but all I did was learn to sing and dance and play the shamisen. When my father was here they kept their mouths shut but now he's gone they don't care. Today we started *The Tale of the Heike*. Everyone knew it except me. They were whispering behind their hands, laughing every time I made a mistake. And then ... And then ...' She couldn't bear to recount the humiliation of how she'd forgotten herself and begun to sing and dance. Her eyes filled with tears.

There was a silence, then Nobu murmured something. At first Taka didn't catch his words. His voice was so soft she hardly heard him. Then she realized what he was saying. ' "The Gion Temple bells toll the impermanence of all things; the sala flowers beside the Buddha's deathbed bear testimony to the fact that all who flourish must decline. The proud do not endure, they vanish like a spring night's dream. The mighty fall at last like dust before the wind." ' He was reciting the first lines of *The Tale of the Heike*, the ancient epic that she'd been struggling with that morning.

He didn't repeat mechanically, by rote, as they had at school. They were not just characters to be learned. He spoke with feeling, as if the words were wrenched from his soul. Suddenly, for the first time, Taka understood the meaning. 'The mighty fall at last ...' Now she and her people were the mighty ones, but once, maybe, Nobu's had been. In any case, all were destined to fall at last 'like dust before the wind'.

She stopped, hardly daring to breathe, waiting for him to continue. The faint notes of shamisens and the sound of singing drifted across from the house on the other side of the grounds.

'How do you know that?' she asked, astonished.

He scowled and hung his head. 'I learned it when I was little.'

'You mean . . . you can read?'

His scowl deepened. 'I haven't studied for years. I just remembered it.'

Taka stared at him, her heart touched. He was probably a couple of years older than her, tall and gangly with dark hair sprouting on his cheeks. He shifted from foot to foot. There was so much she wanted to know about him – about his life, his childhood. But now that Eijiro had told her he was an Aizu she hardly dared ask. She felt he had a dark secret she ought not to probe.

She remembered when he first came to their rescue. He had seemed part of another world. Now he was just one of the servants, yet she could see that, like her, he was different. She was different from the other girls, he was different from the other servants. She chewed her lower lip thoughtfully.

'I'm so behind,' she said. 'Will you help me? I need to practise my writing. Why don't we find somewhere to sit and I'll show you the characters I learned today.'

She didn't want him to feel patronized. He seemed so touchy, she knew it would be all too easy to offend him. She had the feeling he'd just disappear one day. He'd flit away and be gone and no one would know where he was, they'd simply never see him again.

He looked at her and his face lit up. She could see his black eyes shining in the gloom. He was completely transformed. Then he frowned. 'But it's wrong for you to be alone with me. I'm a man.'

'I'm allowed to be with servants.' They both knew

that wasn't quite true. Again she was afraid she'd offended him but he didn't seem to notice. 'Come. I'll show you my secret place.'

Taka led the way, pushing aside branches and brambles and stepping over fallen tree trunks. Deep in the woods there was a hidden grove where she and Haru used to play. They'd dragged out logs to sit on and made a little roof to creep under when it rained.

They sat side by side on a tree trunk. Taka cleared away pebbles and gravel and smoothed out a patch of ground while Nobu sharpened a stick.

'Write "man",' Taka said. It was best to start at the beginning.

Now he really was offended. 'Every child knows that,' he snorted. He drew two strokes on the ground to make a stick body above a pair of forked legs.

'Now "big".'

He smoothed out the ground, then drew another stick man with an extra horizontal stroke like arms stretched out.

' "Mother".' He frowned. A shadow crossed his face as he bent and wrote the character. They went on till they came to one he didn't know.

' "Purity".' She wrote it for him then he copied it, writing it again and again, stroke by stroke. They did ten new characters then she tested him on the first one. By now it was so dark they could barely see the characters scratched on the ground.

Taka jumped up, suddenly aware that they would both be in dreadful trouble if they were found out. Nobu would be in more trouble than her. He might be beaten or dismissed or worse.

'We must go.'

'Thank you,' he said. 'For helping me.' She flushed, aware of his eyes on her. As they scrambled through the bushes and ran back to the house she realized she hadn't felt so happy since Haru had left.

That evening she sorted through her books. There were simplified versions of the classics – the poems of Ariwara no Narihira, *The Tale of Genji*, *Yamato Library: Teaching One Hundred Poems by One Hundred Poets* and *Crimson Brocade: A Great Treasury of One Hundred Poems by One Hundred Poets*. There were books listing the eight celebrated landscapes with the poems associated with each, including Narihira's famous poem on Mount Fuji. Then there was *A Japanese Fabric of Selected Practices for Women*, *Old Courtly Practices for Women: A Thin Pocketbook* and *A Treasury of Precepts for Women*. She picked out the ones she'd finished with, that she thought would be the most useful. Then she dug out a spare writing set – an ink block, stick of ink, water dropper and brushes – and a new workbook. She was already planning a whole learning programme for him.

The problem would be to get him away from the other servants and out of her mother and Eijiro's sight so she could teach him. She knew her mother would never approve and Eijiro would be outraged if he found out. Taking a servant away from his work, spending time alone with a young man – it was utterly scandalous. It would be Nobu who would suffer. Eijiro would beat him or dismiss him, maybe even kill him. He was a mere servant, their property, Eijiro could do as he pleased with him.

She gazed thoughtfully at the screens painted with landscapes and birds and animals that formed the walls of the room, at the oil lamps glimmering inside their shades, at her small writing desk piled with books she'd chosen, at the alcove with a few flowers casually arranged in a vase and a scroll hanging behind on the wall, at the delicate shelves and great wooden chests, at the tobacco box and the brazier with the kettle on its iron hook hanging above it and the teapot and cups on the edge, at her own shadow moving fitfully with every breeze that shivered the lantern flames.

Then she started to smile. Okatsu. That was it. She would take her maid, Okatsu, into her confidence. Okatsu would be their chaperone. She could always say she needed Nobu to help her with such and such a task. She was a resourceful girl, she'd think of something. Best of all, Taka knew her brother had a soft spot for Okatsu. If anyone could twist him round her little finger, she could. She could keep an eye out and distract him if he started asking questions or nosing around.

Taka knew she was breaking all the rules but that only made it all the more thrilling, most of all the fact she was defying Eijiro. She was full of excitement. She had a project at last.

5

Summer was at its height, when people ate oily dishes like grilled eel and braised aubergine and kept cool by going to the kabuki theatre to watch gruesome ghost stories that sent shivers down their spines. The servants had taken out the wooden rain doors that formed the walls of the house and the painted fusuma doors between the rooms, turning the mansion into a vast pavilion floored with cool tatami smelling faintly of rice straw, with nothing but slender wooden pillars to mark where one room ended and the next began. From time to time a breeze wafted through. Fujino lounged inside, mopping her brow and flapping her fan.

Nobu was out in the grounds, helping the gardeners put up a trellis to support the overgrown branches of an ancient pine. The ear-splitting buzz of cicadas filled the air – *min mi min mi* droned from one tree, *wa wa, tsuku tsuku* from another. He took off the rolled-up towel he'd wrapped around his head and wrung it out, sending sweat splashing on to the dusty ground. He'd knotted his happi coat around his waist and pine needles scratched his skin. Mosquitoes buzzed around his face.

He hummed as he tied the bamboo frame in place and

looped rice-straw ropes around the branches. He was happy, happier than he'd ever been since he left his home country. He'd found a new home. Fujino was kind to him, the other servants were friendly and he had a roof over his head and decent clothes to wear. Above all he was studying. His reading and writing were coming on apace.

Whenever Okatsu had a chance, late in the afternoon when Taka was back from school and Nobu was in the kitchens or sweeping the gardens, she would appear and say, 'Nobu, we need to pick something for dinner.'

Taka had discovered that Nobu knew all the wild plants that grew in the grounds. One day, not long after they began their studies, they'd sneaked off to the woods with their books. He kept half an eye on the ground, as he always did, looking out for edible roots, shoots, buds and leaves springing up in the moss and under the pines. They were stepping across the stream that meandered between the trees when he spotted a delicate beige shoot peeking out from the fringe of grass and wild plants along the edge.

He pushed the undergrowth aside, reached down to the base and snapped it off. It was moist and shiny with a honeycombed oval head and fronds around the tiny stem. He put it to his nose. The faint earthy smell reminded him of his northern home, of saucepans simmering on the soot-blackened stove. He held it out to Taka, beaming as he looked around and saw tiny pale shoots poking up everywhere.

'Horsetail shoots! I didn't know they grew here. We must get something to put them in. The cook can fry them up for dinner.'

Taka sniffed the frail stem then wrinkled her nose. He laughed aloud. 'Up north we eat everything – fiddlehead ferns, coltsfoot, burdock, butterbur. There are so many delicious things that grow in the woods and mountains.'

'I don't believe you,' she said with a giggle, looking at him wide-eyed.

He nodded as seriously as he could. 'We eat bee grubs too, and locusts, and bear meat when the hunters manage to catch one and bring some back.' He licked his lips at the thought. 'But that's for special occasions. Of all the spring foods, horsetail shoots are the best. You sauté them with soy sauce and a bit of sake. They're really tasty. We'll need lots.'

They went back to the house for containers and later in the day brought a basketful back to the cook. He was soon eagerly experimenting.

After that, Okatsu was put in charge of finding wild vegetables and Nobu went with her because only he could identify them.

It was the perfect excuse. Nobu and Taka would meet in their secret place in the woods and sit side by side to pore over their books. There were always new characters to learn and text to read. Taka was a strict teacher, testing him and telling him off when he forgot something.

Whenever he had a spare moment he'd practise the latest characters, scratching them on the ground when he was working in the gardens then quickly smoothing them over, writing them with his finger on his hand again and again as he cleaned the house. At night in the servants' quarters he'd take a lantern, bury his head under the bedclothes and work through the books Taka had given him. Even if it was instructions on how to be a good housewife, every new word added to his vocabulary.

He'd begun to discover there were things he could teach her too – old stories his mother had told him, tales from ancient history that she didn't seem to know. And sometimes they just talked – about the house, the family, her teachers, her school, her hateful school-mates, about history, geography, poetry, painting, the Chinese classics and the English books she was starting to read.

'I'd like to be a poet or an artist or a scholar,' she told him one day. They were sitting side by side, leaning against a tree. She wriggled closer to him and rested her shoulder against his arm. He sat as still as he could, feeling her warmth and smallness, her body touching his. 'I can't think of anything worse than to be sent off as a bride, like my sister Haru was,' she whispered, looking up at him. 'I'd rather stay here with you.'

And once, to his intense delight, she danced for him, singing softly, moving to her song, telling a story with her hands – reading an imaginary letter, wiping away imaginary tears. When he applauded she blushed and laughed and threw herself down next to him on the leaves.

Okatsu kept watch and on the way back to the house they looked for fern heads or butterbur to fill their baskets with. No one challenged them or seemed suspicious and they started getting bolder. When Fujino and Eijiro were out, Taka and Nobu sometimes sat swinging their legs on the veranda outside the large airy room where Taka did her writing and painting, looking out at the trees and rocks and flowers shimmering in the heat, kicking their feet together.

It was not all good. Nobu still didn't get paid so he had no money to send to his family, though he heard from them from time to time. When he had a day off he tramped across town to visit his mentor, his father's old friend Hiromichi Nagakura, who had given him the fateful note and sent him off on the journey that ended at the Black Peony. There were letters waiting for him there.

He read them himself now, Nagakura didn't have to read them to him. His two eldest brothers were doing well, they wrote, he had no need to worry about them. He could see they wanted to reassure him. Yasu, the oldest, was still out of work but Kenjiro, the brilliant one, who spoke and read English, had found a job interpreting for some foreign technicians in some remote area, though his health was still poor. Both, being older than Nobu, had had time to complete their education before they found themselves out on the streets. They were hoping to get back to Tokyo and find somewhere to live so they could see him from time to time. There was no word from Gosaburo or Nobu's father, living in poverty in the far north of the country. Nobu had to assume that they were all right, that if they hadn't been his brothers would have told him.

Eijiro was a worry too. He was almost always out, doing whatever it was spoilt young men of twenty did. But when he was around he made Nobu's life a misery. He'd come into the kitchens shouting, 'Nobu, you lazy dog, where are you? The shoe cupboards need cleaning,' or 'The toilets are disgusting. Give them a good wiping out.' Nobu did whatever he wanted, trying not to give a hint of resentment, to make sure Eijiro had not the slightest excuse to throw him out. They both knew where they stood. Eijiro was a Satsuma, Nobu an Aizu, and the Satsuma were at the top of the dung heap, for the time being, at least.

He frequently reminded himself that his life here was too good, it couldn't last, but he might as well enjoy it while he could.

He tied the last branch of the pine to the trellis, made sure it was firmly in place, straightened up and wiped his sleeve across his brow. Tomorrow, the seventh day of the seventh month of the old lunar calendar, was a holiday – Tanabata, the festival of the weaver princess and the cowherd. Even inside the high walls of the estate he felt the excitement and heard the noise from the road outside where people were putting up lanterns and hanging out huge paper streamers.

That evening Nobu strolled out into the grounds. The trees were like ghostly black sentinels. He walked away from the house until he was swallowed up in the silence. A lone cicada let out a piercing whirr and mosquitoes whined around his head. He found an open space beside the lake and gazed up at the sky. The moon had not yet risen and a band of stars swirled across the vast black dome, from one side to the other: the River of Heaven. He thought of another moonless night and remembered his mother's voice. He could almost hear her talking to him.

Usually he tried never to think about it but now, despite himself, memories came flooding back. It had been a balmy night, though summers in the northern mountains were never as hot and sticky as in Tokyo. He'd been a little boy then, standing with his mother in the garden of their big house with Aizu Castle rising above them, huge and black, filling the sky, blotting out half the stars.

'Look, little Nobu,' his mother had said. He could almost smell her perfume and hear her cool northern tones. 'Up there, all those stars – that's the River of Heaven.' He'd looked and seen a shimmering ribbon of stars cutting across the sky, even brighter up north than here in the south. 'See those three big stars?' He'd tipped his head right back and looked and looked until he made out three points of light marking a vast triangle to each side of the river, right at the pinnacle of the great dome.

'The brightest one is the weaver princess,' his mother had said, pointing. 'And there in the opposite corner, across the River of Heaven?' He'd followed her finger and picked out a star sparkling on the other side of the crowded swathe of stars. 'The cowherd.'

'What's the third one?' he'd asked.

'That's not part of the story,' she'd said, laughing.

'Tell me, tell me!' She knew how he loved stories. Kneeling down, she took him on her lap and began, 'Once long, long ago . . .'

Once long, long ago, so his mother's story went, the weaver princess lived in the celestial palace. She was the daughter of the king of heaven and spent her days sitting by the bank of the heavenly river weaving silks in all the colours of the rainbow to make clothes for the gods. Then one day her eyes fell on the handsome young cowherd who herded his cows on the opposite bank. They fell in love and married. But they were so engrossed in each other they had no time for anything else. The princess stopped weaving her beautiful cloth and the cowherd let his cows stray all over the skies. Finally her father, the king of heaven, had had enough. He decreed they should be punished. Henceforth they would be separated for ever, made to live on opposite sides of the River of Heaven and never see each other again. Then he relented. Perhaps the princess's tears touched his heart. They could cross the river and meet just once a year, he said, on the seventh day of the seventh month.

The lovers pined and yearned for the day they could be together. But when that day came they discovered there was no bridge. They gazed at each other across the river of stars, weeping. Just then a flock of heavenly magpies flew by. Seeing them weeping, they felt sorry for them and made a bridge with their wings so the two could meet.

Every year thereafter they did the same. But when it rained the magpies could not come and the lovers had to wait another year before they could meet again. And that was why everyone prayed for fine weather at Tanabata. When it rained, his mother told him, that was the tears of the star-crossed lovers.

Every Tanabata Nobu had laboriously written wishes on strips of paper in his childish hand and gone with his mother, sisters and brothers to the local temple. There they knotted the papers around swaying bamboo branches to make the wishes come true.

Nobu wrenched himself back to the present. Six years

had passed since then. He looked up through a blur of tears at the brilliant stars and dashed his hand across his eyes and blinked hard. The pain of the memory was almost too much to bear. Then the moon began to rise and flood the gardens with light and he couldn't see the weaver princess or the cowherd any more.

Early next morning Nobu was tidying away the last of the breakfast dishes when Okatsu came running into the kitchens, her cheeks flushed with excitement. 'Madam wants you to find some taro leaves and collect the dew on them.' She gave him a flask.

Nobu smiled. He knew the old Tanabata custom of writing wishes with ink made using the dew that collected on taro leaves. He washed his hands and went outside. The cicadas were shrilling and trees and rocks and flowers shimmered in the heat. It was going to be another stifling day. He found a patch of taro plants. The huge heart-shaped leaves, like great cups or out-stretched hands, were brimming with dew. Carefully he tipped the dew off till the flask was half full.

Taka was on her knees on the veranda, dressed for summer in a simple blue and white cotton yukata. With her hair knotted away from her face and her fresh young skin, wide-spaced eyes and delicate features, she was utterly bewitching. Nobu caught his breath. He felt his face burning. He lowered his eyes and scuffed the ground with his foot. He shouldn't be looking at her like this, he told himself. She was his mistress and teacher and to think of her in any other way, even for the space of a breath, was utterly disrespectful. Such a girl was not for the likes of him.

Forcing himself to concentrate, he tipped the dew into the well in the ink stone, took the ink stick and started to grind. For the rest of his life, he thought, whenever he smelt the sweet fragrance of fresh-ground ink he would always remember this day. Taka picked up her brush, dipped it in the ink, wiped it off on the edge of the stone then wrote in an elegant scrawl down the paper.

'Nobu, you must make a wish too,' she said, smiling at him as she laid the brush down on a rest. 'Then we'll all go to Sengaku Temple and tie them on the bamboos.'

Nobu picked up a brush. His studies had come on so well that he didn't need help any more with his writing. Boys were supposed to ask for success in their school-work and girls that their needlework be as beautiful as the weaver princess's, but he had something different he wanted to wish for. He put his brush to the paper, covering it with his hand so no one but the gods who grant wishes would be able to read his words. Then he folded the paper in half and in half again, into a long narrow strip.

Suddenly Nobu heard heavy footsteps running across the big empty rooms towards them. Engrossed in their writing, they hadn't noticed the commotion inside.

'Mother, come and see.' It was Eijiro. There were bangs and thuds. He was kicking tables out of the way, sending lanterns, teapots and teacups flying.

Nobu looked around, frozen with horror. He thought of jumping off the veranda and hiding under the house but there was no time. Eijiro would have been able to see them from halfway across the house through all the open rooms. He had been out last night. How could he possibly be back at this hour? They'd become so relaxed they'd almost forgotten they were doing something forbidden. They hadn't even bothered to keep watch.

A moment later Eijiro came charging out, his face flushed. A stale smell of tobacco and sake wafted along with him. He stood, catching his breath, glaring down at them. 'I've been waiting to catch you. I've had my suspicions for a long time.' Nobu, Taka and Okatsu sat, unable to move. They'd been caught in the act, no amount of excuses would save them.

Eijiro lashed out with his foot. The flask that Nobu had collected dew in flew off the veranda and smashed on the gravel.

Fujino was panting across the tatami behind him, her plump face dripping with sweat, dark stains on the front and under the arms of her cotton kimono. 'Eijiro, by all the gods . . . Whatever are you thinking of? You're a grown man.'

'Aizu dog. You've overstepped the bounds,' Eijiro shouted. 'I always said we shouldn't bring people in off the street. We've repaid our debt to you a thousandfold. You're not hanging round my sister a moment longer.'

Fujino stepped out on to the veranda. As she saw Taka, Nobu and Okatsu sitting together, her eyes widened and her shaved eyebrows shot up. Like all adult women, she shaved her eyebrows and painted her teeth black using a polish made of gallnut powder and iron dissolved in vinegar or tea. It would have been eccentric beyond belief if she hadn't. That day it was still so early that her maid hadn't painted her face yet. She was entirely without eyebrows, which made her look even more surprised. She took her fan from her obi and started flapping it very fast.

Taka was staring down at the floor. She set her jaw. 'We were just writing our Tanabata wishes, Mother. Nobu rescued us, didn't he? He's one of the family. You're fond of him too.'

Eijiro snorted. 'The gods know what you've been up to. What will people think? What are we going to do when we need to find a husband for Taka, when people start saying this precious sister of mine spends all her time with a servant boy and an Aizu? We'll have her on our hands for ever.'

Nobu bent his head and tried to pretend he wasn't there. He knew he'd committed an unforgivable offence. Then he realized he was still holding the paper with his wish on it. He crumpled it up as small as he could and furtively tried to slip it into his sleeve. Eijiro must have seen the movement. He grabbed Nobu's wrist and snatched it from his hand. It nearly tore but he managed to get hold of it. Nobu's heart plummeted. He wished he could disappear through the floorboards, jump off the veranda and race away and never come back again.

'So the dog can write,' said Eijiro, unfolding it. As he read it his lips began to curl. A strange look – triumph mingled with glee and contempt – crossed his face. 'Just listen to this. "May I stay in this house near to Taka-*sama* for ever."' Nobu's face was burning. How could he have been so stupid as to write such a thing? He glanced at Taka. She was avoiding his eyes, gazing studiously at the floor.

'Here's what I think of that,' said Eijiro, ripping the

paper into pieces and tossing them out into the sweltering heat. 'You heard, Mother. We have to get rid of him
right now.'

Taka appealed to her mother, her voice rising sulkily.
'It's not fair. We've done nothing wrong. I've been
teaching him to read, that's all. I admit I shouldn't have
interfered with his work, but I wanted to help him. He's
very clever, he shouldn't be a servant. Don't blame
Nobu. It was my fault, not his. You know Eijiro's been
after Nobu ever since Nobu got here. He's been looking
for a way to catch us out. He's a trickster.'

'Insolent girl! How dare you speak of me like that?'
Eijiro raised his large hand and gave Taka a resounding
smack on the head.

'Children, children. Enough!' barked Fujino.

Nobu heard the blow and saw Taka rock on her knees
and go pale. She put her hand to her head and tears came
to her eyes. She was glaring at Eijiro, her lips trembling.

There was nothing strange about Eijiro hitting his
sister. Women were property, along with servants, and
their menfolk could do as they liked with them – punish
them, beat them, even kill them. That was the way it
had been in Aizu too. Taka was just a chattel, to be sent
off to another house. But even though Nobu knew all
this in theory, somehow he just couldn't see it like that.
It was all he could do to stop himself lunging at Eijiro,
though he knew once he touched him he was finished.

'And you, Okatsu,' said Fujino. 'You should know
better. You're a grown woman. You should have
stopped Taka. That's what we employ you for! We'll be
looking for someone else if you're not careful. I'm disappointed in you.'

Okatsu was on her hands and knees, her face pressed to the ground. She looked up. 'It's not what you think, madam,' she whispered, her voice shaking. 'I've never left them alone together. I can vouch for them. They weren't doing anything wrong.' She wept, bowing again and again. 'I'm sorry, I'm sorry.'

'It's not your fault, Okatsu,' said Eijiro. He swung round. Taka still had her hand to her head. 'But you, my girl – mixing with men, consorting with a servant and an enemy. You've brought shame on this house!'

He picked up the ink stone, spattering Taka's kimono and splashing ink across the veranda, and drew back his arm as if he was going to hit her round the head with it. Nobu gasped in horror. He leapt to his feet and grabbed Eijiro's wrist. Even as he did so he knew he'd destroyed any chance he might still have had of staying at the house.

There was a gleam in Eijiro's eye. He'd goaded Nobu into doing exactly what he wanted – behaving so badly that he'd have no choice but to throw him out.

Nobu had nothing to lose now. Blind with rage, he could hardly see or think. His heart was pounding and his breath came in sharp pants. He was ready to kill Eijiro. The old samurai adage flashed through his mind: 'Let the enemy cut your flesh so that you can cut his bone.'

Eijiro was bigger and stronger but Nobu pulled him towards him and swung a punch. He would have liked to grip him round the neck but even at this moment of madness he knew that would be going too far.

The next thing he knew, he was flying backwards off the veranda. As he crashed on to the gravel, Eijiro landed on top of him and started pummelling him. Nobu smelt sweat and blood. He could see nothing but a bloody haze. He swung his arms desperately, trying to get in another blow, and his fist made contact with something hard. Eijiro gave a yowl.

Fujino shouted, 'Help, help! Come quickly, stop them. He's killing my son.'

Her words sent a shock of misery through Nobu. So it was only her son she cared about, not him. He'd been wrong, he hadn't found a new home, this wasn't his home at all. All the fight went out of him. He was too overcome by despair even to try to stop Eijiro getting in a couple more punches before the servants raced over and wrenched them apart.

Eijiro stood looking down at Nobu, his hands on his hips. 'Ungrateful bastard. You're lucky I didn't kill you. We take you in and look how you repay us!' He was scowling but there was a hint of a smirk on his face. 'Get out, now.'

'Let him take his belongings.' It was Taka's voice. She was sobbing.

'Belongings? He has nothing, just what we've given him.'

Nobu sat up slowly. He put a hand to his face. It was red with blood.

'Aizu cur. Never set foot on this property again,' Eijiro barked. 'Gonsuké, Chubei. Get him out of here.'

The servants hauled him to his feet. He heard Eijiro's voice. 'No need to be so gentle. He's a criminal, mind, and an Aizu.' They marched him round to the front of the house. He stumbled across the gravel, through the moss-covered gardens, under the pine trees. The great gate with its carved lintel and heavy overhanging roof loomed in front of him.

Then Okatsu appeared from nowhere, running across the gravel. She thrust a purse and a bamboo travelling case into Nobu's hand. The servants didn't seem to care. They didn't try to stop her.

They pushed Nobu towards the small side gate and slid it open and Nobu stumbled into the road. He sank down on his knees. People walking by in their festival clothes stepped back in alarm and gave him a wide berth.

The gate slammed behind him. He sat dazed in the road. It had been a brutal awakening. A phase in his life was over. He was back on the street again, broke, with nothing – almost nothing; he had the purse and the bamboo case. Pain, despair, poverty, misery were all familiar companions. The only thing that was new was an aching feeling of emptiness. The certainty was like a blade, cutting him to the bone: he would never see Taka again.

Slowly he got to his feet and limped away. He didn't look back.

PART II

The Weaver Princess and the Cowherd

6

Seventh month, year of the rat, the ninth year of the Meiji era (August 1876)

It was going to be another sweltering day. Taka put down her brush, took her handkerchief from her sleeve and dabbed at the sweat that prickled her face and arms. From the garden came the tinkle of wind-bells and the dry clack of a bamboo pipe, pivoting down to strike the edge of the stone basin with a monotonous 'tock, tock'. Cicadas erupted in an ear-splitting whine. How odd, she thought, that such tiny insects could make such an enormous noise. The sound throbbed in her ears. It seemed the embodiment of summer.

Servants bustled around, scuttling up and down the tatami pushing damp rags or dusting and polishing the delicate wooden frames of the shoji screens. Muted light glimmered, falling across her paper.

She tipped a little more water on to the ink stone, took the ink stick and began to rub. Then the sweet scent of freshly rubbed ink brought a surge of memory so intense that tears sprang to her eyes. She took a sharp breath, put down the ink stick and buried her face in her hands. It was nearly two years ago now, that dreadful day when she'd seen Nobu for the last time.

It had been on a day just like this, hot and close, that Nobu had left, walked out of her life and never come back. She'd cried for days and even now, when she went to her secret place in the woods to sit and think, she'd remember being there with him and the sting of the memory would make her cry again. He'd just been her servant and her pupil, she told herself, there was nothing more to it than that. She'd been lonely and he'd come to seem like a friend. It was the way Eijiro had treated him, the brutality of it, that had made her so upset. Since he had gone, her life had felt terribly empty.

She'd never heard from him, of course, not a whisper. She didn't expect to. He'd simply disappeared, been swallowed up in the great city of Tokyo. Or perhaps he'd gone back to Aizu. She'd never know.

These days she didn't think about him much any more – only when she smelt ink or the rickshaw wheels creaked in a certain way or she saw a clump of horsetail shoots sprouting beside the river.

She was going to a new school now – Kijibashi, the first-ever high school for girls in Japan. Before her father had left she had begged him to put her down for it. It was quite different from the old one. There were girls like her there, girls she could get on with – Kyoto girls, including some who'd started their lives as geishas, as she had. She no longer had to be ashamed of her dancing skills.

Taka loved her new school. She knew how privileged she was to be there. Like the others, she dressed in outrageously daring hakama skirt-trousers, such as a boy would wear, over a maroon kimono with a mannish square-shouldered haori jacket on top, and stepped out with her western books feeling like a true member of the modern age. She worked hard at her studies – singing, maths, sewing, calligraphy, art and English, her favourite.

They'd just started a romance, like *The Plum Calendar* or *The Rustic Genji* or *Tales of the Macabre*, but written entirely in English. *Gu-rei-tsu Ekku-supeku-tei-shi-onzu* was the title. If she read the syllables quickly enough she could make them sound as they did when her teacher, a sweaty red-faced barbarian called John-*sama*, said them: *Great Expectations*. It was the story of a boy called Pippu, he had told them, and the title meant 'huge dreams'. It seemed a good book for her to study. She too had huge dreams – though she was a girl, not a boy, so whether they'd ever be more than dreams was something she didn't dare even to think about.

The disastrous events of two summers ago had led to one good conclusion. After Nobu left Fujino had stopped mentioning marriage, though Taka could never let herself relax completely. She knew that her reprieve couldn't last for ever. Her mother never spoke of Nobu and Taka sometimes wondered if she too felt sorry about the way they'd treated him.

She focused her mind. Her painting master was due to visit that morning and of all her teachers she was fondest of him; and in the afternoon she and her mother would be whirling through the streets to a dance performance given by one of Fujino's geisha friends.

Humming quietly, she dipped her brush on the ink stone, wiped off the excess ink on the edge, then brought it down firmly. She pressed it then lifted it so it danced across the paper, making the stroke first heavy, then light, then sat back on her heels, checking the way the ink faded and dissolved at the edges of the stroke. It was the hundredth bamboo she had painted that day, and the first that satisfied her.

Footsteps came whispering across the tatami towards her. She looked up, startled, as Fujino swept in and settled herself on a cushion, tucking her kimono skirts under her knees like a mother hen smoothing her feathers. At home, especially in this hot weather, even she wore Japanese robes rather than the cumbersome western skirts she usually favoured.

Taka pursed her lips. Her mother didn't usually drop in to see her so early. Her eyes were sparkling and she'd compressed her full mouth into a tight little knot, as if she had some news fairly bursting out of her but was nervous about how it would be received.

Taka rinsed her brush and dried it on a cloth. 'I'm just finishing, Mother.'

Fujino took out her fan and flapped it, her plump cheeks glistening with sweat. 'It's so unkind of your father to go away and make me do this all by myself,' she sighed. 'It's a heavy responsibility.'

Her teeth were shockingly white. A few months ago she'd stopped blackening them and now, instead of being discreetly hidden inside her mouth, as everyone else's mothers' were, they gleamed like pearls, like a virgin girl's or a man's. It was hard to get used to this new face of hers. Taka tried to stop herself staring.

She knew her mother had an important role in Tokyo society. Admittedly she didn't get invited to many formal parties any more now that Taka's father was no longer here, but everyone still remembered and revered him. People bowed low when she bowled past in her rickshaw or carriage and she liked to keep up appearances.

The empress had announced some time ago that henceforth she would stop blackening her teeth. Hard though it was to believe, foreign women, it seemed, did not use black tooth polish. Taka remembered giggling helplessly at the very idea of unblackened teeth. Nevertheless it was imperative that members of Japanese high society should follow their lead if the country was to become truly civilized and enlightened. The ladies of the court had quickly followed suit. As a geisha and a member of Tokyo society, Fujino simply had to keep up with the fashions.

All the same Taka sometimes wished her mother didn't have to be quite so progressive. She had even stopped shaving her eyebrows, which now sprouted bushy and black like two caterpillars above her eyes.

'I've been watching out for a position for you for several months,' Fujino said, leaning forward and looking at Taka in that disconcertingly direct way of hers. 'I'm sure you've noticed all the neighbourhood women coming by. It's not to visit me, it's you they want to look at. I've interviewed a lot of candidates and I'm proud to say I've been exceptionally fussy. I've received ten or twenty proposals and thought them all through and rejected them. It's not something I ever expected to have to do on my own.'

A mosquito droned around the room and Taka batted it away.

'I've done my best, and I'm sure I have the right candidate. I thought about it all night. This is the man your father would want you to marry.'

'To marry . . . ?' Taka shivered despite the heat of the day. 'But, Mother . . .'

Taka had suspected this was what Fujino had been leading up to but she'd pushed the thought away. She bowed her head. She'd seen her friends one by one say goodbye and leave school, their faces frozen into rigid smiles as they contemplated a future they couldn't imagine, with a man they had yet to meet. But she'd always told herself that she'd be the one who'd escape.

Fujino laughed her tinkly geisha laugh. Taka hated it when she put on her geisha face. It meant she was about to wheedle her into doing something she didn't want to do.

'Come, come, young woman,' she said. 'No need to look as if you've seen some dreadful wailing ghost tearing out its hair in clumps. You know how modern I am. It's not like in the old days. When I was a girl – younger than you, a lot younger – your grandmother just packed me off. She didn't even tell me what she had planned.'

Taka knew exactly what she was talking about. Packed her off to be deflowered, she meant.

Taka remembered her last days at the geisha house in Kyoto. When she complained about having to move to Tokyo, Haruyu, the withered old geisha who worked there, had told her how lucky she was. It meant she would never end up as Haruyu had. When the old lady was thirteen, as soon as she was an adult, she'd had to line up to be chosen by a customer. Haruyu had hidden a comb, she told her, turned backwards, in the back of her hair. It was supposed to be a charm against being chosen but there was no guarantee it would work. In any case, even if the ancient jowly silk merchant or the sweaty-palmed purveyor of lacquerware chose another girl for the night, her virginity would still have to be sold to someone. After all, she had a debt to repay. Haruyu didn't bewail her lot. She was perfectly down to earth about it. It was what happened to women like them.

'Marriage is not such a terrible fate as what I had to put up with, I can promise you that,' Fujino said, smiling her superior smile as if she'd settled the argument. Taka was not at all sure about that. She suspected that marriage would not be all that different from what had happened to her mother and to Haruyu. She too would have to lie with someone she didn't know.

Her mother glanced at the servants, who moved discreetly away. She moved closer to Taka and lowered her voice. 'The offer came through a Hiroyuki Hashimoto, a gentleman of excellent standing and very suitable to broker your marriage. He met your father when Father was still in government. He's the head clerk of the Shimada company.' She paused and looked at Taka with a knowing smile. Taka knew her mother was expecting her to be delighted. The Shimadas were of the lowly merchant class but they were enormously rich and successful and, from all Taka had heard, practically ran the government.

Fujino took a breath and fluttered her fan as if the

very thought of these people filled her with excitement. 'The Shimada house would like to make an alliance with us, even though your father is in retirement.'

'In retirement . . .' It made it sound as if her father had taken holy orders, not stormed off in disgust at his government colleagues and gone home to his base on the island of Kyushu. But her mother preferred not to mention such thorny matters or, if she had to, referred to them only obliquely.

'The Shimadas have already carried out a thorough investigation and of course everything is in order,' her mother continued. 'They're very impressed with everything they've heard about you – your character, your accomplishments.'

Taka stared at the spreading sweat stains under Fujino's plump arms. She was dizzy from the heat. The whirr of the cicadas drummed into her brain. I'm not as naive as all that, Mother, she thought to herself. They want to make an alliance with the second family of General Kitaoka. It has nothing to do with me.

'Please, Mother,' she said plaintively, trying her best to keep her voice from shaking. 'Can't we wait a while? My . . . My studies. I haven't even completed them yet.'

Fujino snapped her fan shut and glared at her.

'You're already sixteen. Do you want to end up an old maid, like one of those shrivelled old women who live with their parents for ever, without ever knowing a man or having children of their own? It's a woman's job to bear children, that's what women are for. You're lucky anyone's prepared to take you. Your father was so eager for you to attend this fancy high school of yours. I knew they'd put silly ideas in your head. I warned him no respectable household would want a girl with education. They'd think you were disobedient and headstrong and not well trained in wifely skills. And they'd be right.'

She unfurled her fan and flapped it imperiously at the mosquitoes whining around their heads. Okatsu, Taka's maid, slid silently across on her knees, pushing the mosquito burner closer. The sharp sweet smell of smouldering chrysanthemum petals tickled Taka's nostrils. Fujino smoothed her skirts impatiently.

'Don't you want to know about your husband-to-be? He's a very attractive proposition.' Her face was stern still but there was a dimple puckering her plump cheek. 'He's Mr Shimada's adopted son and chosen heir, no less,' she cooed. 'Mr Hashimoto confided that he's said to be a genius – a banking genius. He's working with Mr Shibusawa at the moment, helping him develop a western-style banking system here. His name is Hachibei Masuda.' She leaned forward, a gleam in her eye. 'Mr Hashimoto assures me he'll be worth many thousands of yen – even millions – in years to come.'

Taka scowled. Fujino was using her most honeyed tones, as if seducing a particularly intransigent customer; but Taka was not a customer, nor was she seduced. How could her mother imagine that any self-respecting samurai daughter would be impressed with a man who soiled his hands with money? She knew geishas saw things differently, geishas liked money – though she'd always thought her mother, at least, was above such things. And times had changed, she had to keep reminding herself of that.

She wondered if that was the problem. Her father had

been away for nearly three years now and she didn't know how her mother managed to continue to support the household. She'd always assumed her father's stipend covered all the bills but she wasn't sure. Maybe that was why Fujino was so eager to make an alliance with a wealthy family?

'And how can it be that such a desirable young man is still available?' Fujino flashed her disconcertingly white teeth. 'You may well ask. The answer is because he's been abroad, studying in America. He only came back a few days ago. And what do you think he needs now? A wife, of course, from among his own people. Naturally only the best will do, so they've come to us. I've been waiting and waiting for the perfect proposal, Taka, and this is it. You're to be mistress of the House of Shimada. You'll have a huge house and a bevy of servants.

'So you see? He's a man after your own heart – a man of the world, who'll appreciate an educated wife. He's exactly what you want. He's the perfect choice.'

Taka said nothing. She didn't know why her mother even bothered to talk to her about it. After all, everything was already decided.

'I've met his parents, of course, and him, too,' Fujino added. She flapped her fan furiously as if flustered at the very thought of him. Her plump cheeks had turned quite pink. Taka stared gloomily at the ink drying on the ink stone and the curling sheets of paper painted with bamboos. The more she heard, the less she wanted anything to do with this man. 'He's very nice-looking indeed, I might even say handsome. His manners are impeccable, he's very accomplished and he's just the right age – twenty-five. All in all, a delightful young man. So you see, there's no need to look so glum. I care about my Taka, I wouldn't do anything to make her sad.'

She had the same look on her face that she wore when they played the flower card game, when she held the winning hand. Taka sighed. She had no choice.

'Let me remind you, my girl, you're the second daughter of the second house. There's the present number one wife, Madame Kitaoka, in Kagoshima, and she has children. I don't even know what other concubines your father has. I just have to assume I'm number two.' Her mother allowed a look of sadness to flicker across her face. Then she rounded on Taka. She was playing a complicated game. 'So you see? You're very lucky that anyone at all will take you, let alone a man with as bright a future as Masuda-*sama*. It'll be at least as brilliant a match as we made for Haru. Your father will be most pleased.'

Taka sighed. Haru, her dear sister Haru. How she missed her! She remembered how they used to kneel side by side, working together at their paintings. And now Haru was gone, erased from the family register, the property of another house.

She remembered how she'd gone off so bravely in her wedding palanquin with attendants running behind. The last time Taka had seen her had been more than a year ago, when she had come home to have her first child, her belly huge, groaning as she heaved herself up from the floor. At night when they lay side by side in their futons she had whispered that her days had become terribly long and dull. 'I sew,' she'd said. 'I look at the garden. I can't shut myself in my room any more and read. Time passes so slowly.' Her husband was kind enough, but she seldom saw him, and she had to do whatever her mother-in-law instructed.

And then the day of the birth had come. Taka would never forget that, not as long as she lived. She could still see Haru's face, as clear as if she was there next to her – parchment white, her lips squeezed together as she struggled to maintain the composure expected of a samurai wife. Taka had run back and forth carrying basins of hot water, following her mother's instructions, then knelt beside Haru and gripped her hand tight as the spasms racked her, praying to every god she could think of that her sister wouldn't die, as so many women did.

And finally Haru could hold back no longer and let out shriek after piercing shriek as a tiny creature pushed out, first a livid crumpled head with a thatch of black hair slicked with slime, then a small purple body. Haru had grasped him in her arms and held him tight, panting and proud, as if she had found a reason for living at last.

Taka was not ready for that at all. Not yet, she thought, not yet.

'I know you love your studies,' said her mother, patting her arm. 'But there's nothing to stop you continuing once you're Masuda-*sama*'s bride.'

'What about Eijiro? You're not forcing him to marry!' Suddenly it all seemed so unfair. Her brother had turned into a wild young man who frittered away his days and showed no signs of growing up, let alone settling down and getting married.

Her mother's face softened. 'All in due course, my dear, all in due course. He's a man, my dear, what do you expect? That's what men do. You'll learn that when you have sons of your own. They have their wild phase when they're young, but then they settle down and take over the household, just like their fathers.'

'But you weren't forced to marry a stranger, Mother. You and Father . . .'

General Kitaoka had never been a stern patriarch, aloof and distant, like other girls' fathers. When he'd lived there with them she'd seen him stroke her mother's hair when he thought no one was looking, and pillow his great head on her bosom. She knew how much they cared about each other.

It was nearly three years now since he'd fallen out with his colleagues, resigned his government positions, packed his bags and disappeared in a cloud of dust at the head of a train of rickshaws. Every now and then a letter came. He was a gentleman farmer now, he wrote. He hunted, he fished, he walked in the hills with his dogs, he practised swordsmanship, he read books, he wrote poetry. Sometimes Taka tried to picture his new life. She knew he lived with his samurai wife in the city of Kagoshima in Satsuma province, at the southernmost tip of the island of Kyushu, so far away it seemed like the end of the world. How dreary it must be, she thought, after the culture of Kyoto and the excitement of Tokyo.

When he'd left she'd wished he'd taken them with him to Kagoshima. It would have been so easy just to set them all up – her mother, her brother and her – in a separate house, away from his wife. But now she was relieved he'd left them behind in Tokyo. She couldn't imagine a worse fate than to be exiled to such a place.

Nevertheless, no matter how strange and inconsistent his behaviour, she knew he would not have forced her into marriage. He was too unconventional and he loved her too much.

'I'd rather be a geisha, like you.' She'd blurted out the words before she could stop herself. Her mother bristled.

'That's quite enough. We're the subordinate family of General Kitaoka and don't you forget it. We've all come up in the world and I'm certainly not going to let you bring down the family name. You'll do much much better than I ever could. And that's an end to it.'

'But why did you spend all that money to have me educated if all you intended was to marry me off and have me spend my life locked away in someone's house?' Taka wailed. 'It's no better than being a servant. Why can't I work? I'll teach poetry, or painting.' Her mother raised her caterpillar eyebrows. 'I know I'm just a woman, but I can be a scholar, a good scholar,' Taka added miserably, trying to drive the mocking smile from Fujino's face. 'I'll be the first woman scholar. You wanted me to be progressive. That would be very progressive.'

Her mother flapped her fan impatiently.

'I knew all that education wouldn't do you any good. I told your father so,' she sighed. 'You've turned out just like him, dear, and, I have to confess, like me, too – headstrong. I suppose I couldn't have expected a geisha's daughter to be as well behaved as a samurai girl. But you'll do as you're told all the same.'

The maids had brought in tea and she poured out a cup each for Taka and herself, then leaned forward and patted her hand.

'But you're right, my dear. This is the age of civilization and enlightenment and we do things the modern way. Masuda-*sama* is eager to see you so I've invited him over to meet your brother. You'll welcome him and serve tea. I can assure you, you'll be won over. Such a charming young man. You see, I have no terrible secrets to conceal.'

Taka was startled. It was quite unheard of for a man to look over his bride before the wedding day. If her father had been here he would never have allowed it. It was only because her mother was a geisha and had no idea of the way respectable people behaved, she thought.

'In fact he's coming this afternoon. I only wish your father could have been here too.' Fujino's voice had changed and to her horror Taka saw her eyes fill with tears. She looked away. She didn't want the slightest hint that her mother might have feelings too, like her.

'Just as we thought the war was over and our lives were going to be peaceful again, off he storms,' her mother wailed. 'Him and his precious principles. There he was, the most powerful man in the entire country and he throws it all away. The gods alone know what he can be thinking of, with his farming and his hunting.' She dabbed her eyes with her sleeve and gave Taka a wan smile. 'Just look at you. You've got ink all over your face! You'd better tidy yourself up if you're going to be a rich man's wife.'

Perhaps that was why her mother was so eager to find

a husband for her, Taka thought, as the whisper of stockinged feet disappeared into the vast expanses of the great house. Perhaps she needed to keep herself busy to fill the emptiness in her own life. She seemed a little too bright and cheerful. If only she hadn't been a geisha. Geishas and samurai were two sides of the mirror and Taka felt eternally torn between her mother's geisha ways and her father's fierce samurai spirit.

And the worst of it was, there was no escape. She could already feel the prison walls closing in around her.

7

'Otaka-*sama*,' Okatsu hissed, panting with excitement.

Ever since Fujino had burst in with her extraordinary announcement, Okatsu had been rushing back and forth, pulling out armfuls of dresses. They hung around the walls, stiff and flouncy and brilliantly coloured, like exotic birds – day dresses heavy with ruffles and ribbons, shaped gowns with bodices and draped and trimmed skirts, floaty frocks with trailing overskirts, and a couple of thoroughly uncomfortable whalebone corsets, purchased direct from Mr Kawakami of the Ebisuya emporium, who had brought trunkfuls of them to the house.

'I'd knock over the teapot in one of those,' Taka said, laughing, opting for a simple pale blue kimono with a subtle design of gentians across the sleeves and hem.

'You'll look like an old lady in that,' Okatsu complained as she helped her tie the under-kimono and collar in place. 'Why not something more bright and girlish?'

'He's been in America, he won't even notice,' said Taka. The truth was, she half hoped someone as progressive as this Masuda-*sama* would turn his nose up at a woman dressed in traditional costume.

Now Okatsu was on her knees, her face pressed to the

shoji screens that closed off the room, hiding them from view. She'd pushed the screens apart just enough to peek through. 'Taka-*sama*. The honourable guest is arriving!'

'Okatsu, don't peek. It's not dignified.'

'He looks like a real gentleman,' Okatsu squeaked breathlessly. 'And his clothes – just like a barbarian's. Madam, come and see. You know you won't be able to once you're serving tea.'

She was right, it would be quite unseemly. Taka hesitated, then took Okatsu's place. She held her breath, closed one eye and pressed the other to the crack between the screens. Her heart was pounding. It must be because she would be mortified if this unknown youth were to catch a glimpse of her, she told herself.

In the dazzling afternoon sun, the footmen were closing the gates and servants clustered around three splendid upholstered rickshaws with painted wheels and the hoods pushed back, emblazoned with the circle and half moon of the Shimada family crest. A young man was stepping down from one. He turned towards the house and for a moment his face was in full view. Light sparked off something metallic – a watch chain. Taka drew back, fearful he would see her, then took a breath and put her eye to the crack again.

It wasn't so much his face she noticed as the lordly way he carried himself, as if he owned the world. He stood very straight, looking around with a disdainful air, his eyebrows arched and a distinct downward curl to his mouth, as if to suggest that this sort of place was really rather below him. His hair was glossy, cut in the modish *jangiri* style, cropped short with a side parting like a westerner's and sleekly combed. While her brother and his friends mixed Japanese and western – a western jacket over flowing hakama trousers or a Japanese robe topped with a bowler hat, Masuda-*sama* was western from head to toe. He was wearing a suit that looked very expensive, with a waistcoat, a neatly folded handkerchief poking from his top pocket, a necktie and shiny leather shoes, and seemed perfectly at ease in it all.

The cicadas droned, the sun beat down and the court-yard shimmered in the heat. Beads of sweat were trickling down his face. He scowled and took a big handkerchief from his trouser pocket and wiped them away with the ferocity of a warrior beating back the enemy.

'He must be sweltering in all those clothes,' Taka whispered to Okatsu. She could see he was the sort of man her mother would think quite perfect – young, cocky, well dressed and extremely rich.

Besides Masuda-*sama* there were a couple of bewhiskered men who Taka guessed must be the marriage broker, Hashimoto-*sama*, and Masuda-*sama*'s father, and a broad-faced younger man with a determined expression who, according to protocol, was probably his brother. She was taken aback to see a woman too. Women didn't usually attend these formal events. It showed the family must be really very progressive indeed. The woman was in her middle years, a forbidding-looking dowager with a scowl, a noticeably receding chin and a pair of glasses on a stick which she held to her eyes as she looked around. They were all dressed in formal western clothes, the men in high-collared suits, the woman in a day dress with a train and a large bonnet.

Taka knew very well that once she was married to this

youth, it would be his mother, not him, whom she would see on a daily basis. She would have to serve her until the day one or other of them died. If she was kind, Taka's life would be easy; but most mothers-in-law were far from that. Taka watched, her heart sinking, as the woman swung round and snapped at a servant who apparently wasn't holding the parasol precisely where she wanted it.

As for Masuda-*sama*, it really didn't matter what he looked like or what sort of person he was. Of course, it would be a brilliant match. Her friends would be eaten up with envy. When they left school, they all bragged about the wealthy young men they had captured and their expensive wedding kimonos and lavish palanquins; and she, Taka, it seemed, was to marry the wealthiest and most eligible of the lot.

But once they were married she'd hardly ever see him any more. Somehow they would produce children, but other than that he'd amuse himself in the pleasure quarters and geisha districts and no doubt keep a flotilla of mistresses, as men of his wealth and standing did – as her own father did. That was why all the other girls accepted whatever husband their parents chose for them, partly because it was what they were expected to do and also because in the end all that mattered was that he should be a man who could support a wife in the proper style. His character was irrelevant. Their relationship would be purely formal.

But in that case she could make the same compromise – except that while he was busy with his work and his mistresses, she would be imprisoned at home with his mother. That was the future she dreaded – and there was no escaping it.

Peeking through the screens, she felt such a sense of in-evitability that she sank back on her heels, speechless. She was utterly trapped. Before, her life had stretched ahead of her, full of possibilities. Now that freedom, those possibilities, had all come to an abrupt end.

The little group was walking across the courtyard, servants scurrying alongside, holding parasols over their heads.

'Okatsu, go and welcome them. I can't,' said Taka. She'd suddenly had a wild idea. Her brother and his friends all seemed to find Okatsu irresistible. Whenever she went to serve them, all eyes turned on her. She had to endure endless teasing and occasionally wriggle out of their clumsy embraces. Maybe she could work her magic on this young man too.

Okatsu covered her mouth with her hands and squealed with laughter. 'That's absurd, madam. I can't do that.'

'You'll do it so much better than me. Anyway, it's not proper for this Masuda-*sama* to see his bride before the wedding day. It's not the way things are done.'

'But that's why he's here, madam, to see you. Isn't that what your honourable mother said?' Okatsu might be her loyal maid, but she knew where the real power lay – with Fujino.

'Can't you tell Mother . . . Please, tell her I'm ill,' Taka said, beginning to panic.

Okatsu laughed till her shoulders shook and remained firmly on her knees. Taka gave her a last beseeching look and rose reluctantly to her feet. She hadn't felt so nervous since her entrance examination for Kijibashi. This was far worse. This was how condemned men must feel when they were on their way to have their heads cut off, she thought.

The doors at the great front entrance had been pushed right back and a large screen painted with a tiger filled the space. Gold eyes glinted in the gloom. Taka knelt behind her mother, pushing herself as far back into the darkness as she could and keeping her eyes fixed firmly on the ground as the young man stepped out of his shiny leather shoes and up into the cool shadows of the entrance hall. An unfamiliar foreign scent mingled with the distinct whiff of sweat as a pair of feet, clad in fine silk socks, stopped before her. She flushed till her ears were on fire.

'Apologies for the short notice,' he said. His voice was rather high-pitched, with a hint of a drawl, reminding Taka that he was just back from abroad and probably not used to speaking Japanese. 'You'll have to forgive me, I know this is all rather sudden. I haven't been back for long and I guess I've acquired foreign habits. Your mother's told me all about you.'

Taka's mother answered for her. 'Welcome. Our house is small and dirty but please come in.' It was the most conventional of phrases and she would have said it whether they lived in a hovel or a palace. The fact was that their house was not that small but not overly large either, rather modest in fact for the house of the second family of General Kitaoka.

In the kitchens, the maids had laid out tea utensils. Taka had learned tea ceremony as a child in the geisha district in Kyoto. Now that everyone was modern and progressive, it was considered laughably old-fashioned but she still loved it. Fujino had insisted that Taka perform just a simple summer tea ceremony, enough to show that she had all the traditional accomplishments but was not at all old-fashioned. It was a difficult balance to maintain.

'Hurry,' said her mother. 'I don't know why you're wearing such a dowdy kimono. I can't imagine what Madame Masuda will think.' She was even more nervous than Taka was.

As Taka knelt and put the tray on the floor beside her and slid open the door, the conversation stopped. There was silence as she rose to her feet, her mother behind her. The room glowed with a muted light, glimmering through the shoji screens.

She glanced at her brother Eijiro, kneeling in what should have been her father's place. His square face, the very image of her father's, was flushed and puffy and his large dog-like eyes half shut. Hungover again, Taka thought, but at least he had made it back from the pleasure quarters. He fanned himself morosely, head drooping. His robe was hanging open and there was a huge gold timepiece protruding from the breast pocket. He looked positively slovenly compared to the dapper Masuda-*sama*, wriggling one expensively trousered leg, then the other, as if he wasn't used to sitting on the floor.

Taka warmed the tea bowl, measured out powdered green tea, whisked it and slid the bowl across the tatami to Masuda-*sama*'s father, sitting cross-legged in the place of honour, in front of the tokonoma alcove with its elegantly carved shelves, hanging scroll and tall bamboo vase containing a single camellia blossom, perfectly placed. He took the bowl and cradled it in both hands as he drank, taking the requisite three sips followed by a slurp.

'It's been a long time since I tasted green tea. Delicious,' he said with a grunt, licking his lips.

'It's good to see these old arts preserved,' said Madame Masuda. Perhaps she was not as supercilious as she looked. 'I learned tea ceremony myself when I was a girl. We struggle so hard to make ourselves western that we're in danger of throwing away our own culture.' She turned to Fujino. Taka could see she was hesitating as to the proper way to behave towards her, with precisely what degree of respect or familiarity. Her mother was the number two wife of the ex-chief counsellor of the realm, once the most powerful man in the country, though he had now retired; but she was also a geisha, by definition – according to the traditional class system, at least – beneath contempt, the lowest of the low.

'I'm a townswoman myself,' Madame Masuda ventured. 'I hear you've taught your daughter the geisha arts. Tell me, to what school of dancing do you belong?' She gave a bland smile. So she'd decided familiarity was in order. Taka heard the undertone of contempt and bristled. How dare this dry old snob sneer at her mother for being a geisha? She would never have dared mention it if General Kitaoka had been here.

Fujino could take care of herself. She gave a tinkle of laughter. 'We wanted to give our daughter as broad an education as possible,' she said serenely. 'She's studying at Kijibashi High School. Perhaps you haven't heard of it. It's the first high school for girls in this country. We enrolled her as soon as it opened. She was in the very first intake.'

'I know it well,' said Madame Masuda silkily. Drops of sweat stood out on her forehead. Her skin clung to her face like a mask. 'You must find the weather pleasant here after the heat of Kyoto. You're from Gion, I imagine.'

Taka smiled to herself. A mere townswoman could never outdo her mother. Fujino was impervious to barbs.

'I hear you studied in America, Masuda-*sama*,' Fujino trilled. 'Our Taka has learned mathematics and English and history and French. Say something in English, Taka.'

Taka's heart began to pound and she stumbled as she murmured the English phrase, 'You are welcome. Our house very small.' Her face was burning as she stared at the tatami.

Masuda-*sama* drawled, 'Our house *is* very small. Thanks. You speak English well.'

Taka raised her head. She was aware of a pair of brown eyes appraising her. She'd have expected Masuda-*sama* to be nervous too, but he seemed disconcertingly relaxed and confident. He was actually quite handsome and she had to concede that his eyes were kind. But it didn't make any difference. She hated the idea of being forced to marry anyone.

'What did they say?' cooed Fujino. 'It sounded delightful.'

As Taka tidied away the tea things and beat a hasty retreat to the kitchens, she could hear her mother's voice. 'We'll have many years to get to know each other. Taka's an excellent girl and a good housekeeper. As you can see, I've brought her up in the traditional way. Above all, she's obedient, I can promise you that.' That was far from true,

Taka thought, smiling to herself. 'If you're happy to go ahead,' Fujino concluded, 'we'll make plans for the wedding straight away. It'll be a splendid affair.'

Suddenly Taka saw her life stretching in front of her – an eternity of enduring this man's patronizing ways and his mother's sarcasm, always smiling, standing in line with the servants to bow when her strutting, immaculately dressed husband came home and when he left the house. She'd be number one among the household staff. She couldn't imagine anything more lonely. So that was what her expensive education had been for. She bit her lips, blinking back tears.

'You'll get used to it,' Okatsu said gently, taking the tray of tea utensils. 'Everyone does. People always cry when the time comes to marry and leave home. "To catch a tiger cub you have to step inside the tiger's den." Wasn't that what Nobu used to say?' She said his name as though they talked about him every day, glancing questioningly at Taka as she spoke.

Taka smiled, nodding. Nobu, who had appeared so suddenly at the Black Peony, like a breeze blowing in from another world. That was when she had realized that the world was far bigger than she could ever have imagined. An image of a boyish face with sunburnt cheeks and slanted eyes and funny sticking-out ears rose before her eyes.

'He had a better one,' persisted Okatsu. ' "Once fallen, the blossom doesn't return to the branch . . ." '

' "Once broken, the mirror never reflects again." ' Taka finished the proverb. 'Yes, he liked those quaint sayings, didn't he? But that's not it either. It means once something's done it can't be undone. But nothing's decided yet, the knot hasn't been tied. There must be another saying that's more hopeful.'

'What about "Don't put a price on your badger skin before you've caught your badger"? No. "When winter comes, spring can't be far behind." That's the one. Keep thinking of that.'

Taka laughed. 'That Nobu. What a ragamuffin he was, even after Mother gave him clothes. I used to smile whenever I saw him, the way his arms and legs stuck out of his stripy footman's jacket.'

Okatsu's face had softened. 'Do you remember how you helped him study?'

'I gave him books, that's all. He was so proud. He never said a thing about wanting to study until that time I offered to teach him characters. It was really just a way to help myself remember them. Then I caught him peeking at my textbooks. It wouldn't do any harm to give him the ones I'd finished with, I thought. After that, every spare moment he was poring over mathematics or history. He wanted so badly to better himself.'

Okatsu sighed. Taka looked at her. They both had tears in their eyes.

'He was a good lad.'

'He should have been a samurai,' Taka said. 'It was terrible that all he could be was a servant.'

But in the new Japan lots of people were not what they appeared. Even Gonsuké, the rickshaw boy, had once let slip that his life had been quite different before the war. It was as if everyone had been tossed in the air and come down all mixed up. People who had been on top were at the bottom now and people like her family who were of lowly origin had ended up on top. No doubt Nobu would have had a saying for that too.

Once a samurai girl passed ten she was not supposed to mix with boys. But Nobu hadn't been a proud young samurai or a wealthy boy of her own class. He was only a servant, he hadn't really counted as a boy at all. She remembered how he'd cleaned the house and tidied the garden every day and run behind her rickshaw, carrying her books and lacquer lunch box to school and back again. One way or another, she'd often ended up in his company. How she wished he were here now so that she could talk everything through with him, as she used to. But there was no point wishing. He'd long since disappeared.

8

'Here, come over here,' twittered a girlish voice in the sultry lilt of the Yoshiwara pleasure quarter, soft and insistent as if coaxing a cat. 'Yes, you, big brother. What'ya doing hiding in the corner like that?'

Another voice, fruity and ripe with innuendo, rasped, 'There's fun for servants as well as masters here, y'know, son!'

Nobu groaned. *'Trois petites truites cuites, trois petites truites crues,'* he muttered, his jaw aching as he tried to shape his lips around the difficult French syllables. 'Three little cooked trout, three little raw trout.' He still couldn't distinguish 'i' and 'e' or 'ri' and 'ru' or make anything that sounded remotely like a French 'r' but, in these long days of summer, he'd managed to find a corner where the last shaft of light filtered through a hole in the paper screens, though the rest of the room was in near darkness. He knelt, long legs folded under him, his book in the patch of brightness, poring over his French grammar. *'A coeur vaillant rien d'impossible,'* he murmured, repeating one of the endless list of proverbs he was supposed to have learned. 'To the valiant heart nothing is impossible.' The other students were so far ahead, he had no chance of ever catching up, but he had to keep trying.

'If you want to capture a tiger cub, you have to step inside the tiger's den.' He could almost hear his mother's cool voice, admonishing him. She had had a proverb for every occasion. The well-worn syllables reminded him of how she had drilled them into him when he was a little boy in a distant northern town. Trying to learn French was more daunting by far than stepping inside a tiger's den; but it was the only way if he wanted to get anywhere in life. And that was what he had to do. He owed it to his family, if not himself.

It hurt to think of his mother and sisters, his father and brothers, all dead or living in poverty. Time had eased the pain but he still felt a wrench of sadness. He could hardly even picture his mother's face any more.

And Taka . . .

After he'd stumbled away from the gate of the Kitaoka house, it had taken a long time to get back on his feet. Eijiro had done him more damage than he'd realized. He'd ended up at the house of his father's kindly old friend, Nagakura. He'd handed over the contents of the purse Okatsu had given him – he'd found ten yen in it and some clean clothes in the bamboo travelling case – and holed up there like a dog, licking his wounds.

As soon as he could he moved out. Nagakura's house was overflowing with family, students and refugees from up north. He couldn't impose for ever. He found a job as a live-in servant, then as a delivery boy for an eel restaurant, then worked as a bathhouse attendant, carrying shovels of hot coals and scrubbing backs. But even after his wounds had healed and his bruises had faded and he no longer looked like a soldier back from the wars, sometimes when he was on his own he'd come back to the present with a jerk and realize he'd been staring into space, sunk in misery.

The most unexpected things set him back – the way the light fell, the smell of cooking, the sound of a voice. The thought of Taka was a pain just as real as physical pain, as real as Eijiro's beating had been. Sometimes it was a dull ache, sometimes a spasm like a punch in the stomach that stopped him in his tracks and brought tears to his eyes.

Once he was delivering a letter when he glimpsed a slight young girl in a modest kimono, her hair tied back, walking with someone who looked like a chaperone. He'd sped after her and nearly caught up with her when he realized it was not Taka at all. How could he possibly have thought it was her, he asked himself angrily, in the low city dives where he spent most of his time these days?

And once he was sent on an errand that took him through the Ginza. There were rickshaws lined up outside the Black Peony and he found himself looking for Gonsuké and the Kitaoka crest, a feather in a circle. Then some women came out in lavish western gowns and he gawped at them till he was told to move on, but of course Taka was not among them. What a fool he'd been to let his guard down, he told himself, to let himself be seduced into believing that it was possible to be happy, that there was more to life than struggling to survive. And now he had to pay the price.

And then one day something happened that changed everything. He'd dropped in on Nagakura, to see how he was and pick up letters from his brothers. To his surprise the rather grand, slow-moving ex-vice governor of Aomori came racing out to the entryway to meet him. He was usually morose, permanently bemused at the disasters that had befallen them, but that day he was beaming.

'They're having examinations for the Army Cadet School soon,' he said, before Nobu even had his sandals off. 'You're from a samurai family, fighting's in your blood. Why don't you apply? If you pass, you'll be trained to be an army officer. I'll be your guarantor. I don't have much to hold my head up about these days but it's the least I can do for an old friend's son.'

Nobu had dropped the package he was carrying in shock. He was thunderstruck and then, as he thought about it, by turns thrilled, nervous and afraid. He knew that the troops of samurai that had made up the clan armies had been disbanded. There was a national army now, formed only a few years earlier, and even someone like him, from one of the defeated clans, could apply. It was virtually the only job that an Aizu could get. Government positions were monopolized by men from the ruling clans – the Choshu, the Tosa, the Hizen and the hated potato samurai, the Satsuma. He would have somewhere to live in termtime at least and, coming from a poor home, he'd have his costs paid; he'd even get a little pocket money. He'd be able to hold his head up again. He'd have a future – if he managed to get in, that was.

The light was fading. He could hardly see his book any more. He took a pull on his pipe, remembering the wintry day when he had set off for the Bureau of

Military Education to sit the entrance examinations. He had taken his place on his knees on the freezing tatami in a large bare room, along with the other applicants, all lads his own age, shivering as the cold cut through his thin clothes. His fingers had been so stiff it had been hard to manipulate his brush.

When his turn came, he had been asked to read aloud from Rai Sanyo's *Unofficial History of Japan* and had silently offered up thanks to Taka for helping him with his studies. There'd also been arithmetic tests and he'd had to compose and write a letter to a friend in his home town, explaining why he wanted to pursue a military career, and then there'd been an interview and a physical examination.

Then silence. He'd taken one menial job after another, trying to keep a roof over his head and put aside a bit of money, trying not to despair as time passed and no news came. Five months after he had sat the examinations, a letter had arrived. He'd taken it, his hands trembling, not daring to look, then held his breath as he slowly unrolled it. At first he could barely take in what it said. He'd been accepted.

He could hardly believe it. Surely his luck couldn't have changed so radically. He'd read the words again and again until he was sure it really was true, he wasn't mistaken, then shouted and leapt in the air and clapped his heels together for joy and rushed off to send notes to his brothers and father and everyone he knew. He'd scraped together all the money he could to buy a French-style uniform of grey trousers, navy blue jacket with yellow braid and tassels, undergarments, military cap and shiny leather shoes.

When the first day of school came he'd marched up to the Ichigaya section of town, through the great gates, across the grounds, to the intimidating three-storey building on the hilltop – the Military Academy, a vast stone structure with white walls like a storehouse but glass windows and hinged doors like a western build-ing. The echoing rooms and corridors filled him with excitement and dread. He was sure that from this moment on his life would change for ever.

But he soon found that getting into school was just the beginning. He was at the bottom of the lowest class. He was busy morning to night studying, exercising and learning martial arts. All the teachers and military instructors were French, for, as they boasted to the students, the French army was the best in the world and their aim was to make the new Japanese army just as good. The first task was to learn French and all about France – its history, geography, mountains, rivers and cities. Only then could the students start on the manuals of military theory and tactics, all written in French.

Nobu lived like a Frenchman. He slept in a dormitory on a hard bed, not a futon, sat on a chair at a table and ate French meals – soup, bread and meat, with rice and curried meat on Saturdays. It took a bit of time to get used to eating meat but all the same, while the other stu-dents complained about the food, Nobu felt as if he'd been reborn in Amida Buddha's western paradise.

But then the holidays had come. All his schoolfriends had somewhere to go but he had nowhere and once again had to find a job as a servant to tide him over.

* * *

'*A coeur vaillant rien d'impossible*,' he muttered.

There was a giggle and a small hand with grubby fingers and bitten nails slapped down on his page. He started. The sweet-voiced girl leaned her soft body, moist with sweat, against his, enveloping him in the heady scent of sandalwood and aloe. He laughed, acknowledging defeat. The lanterns in the corners cast long shadows and a thick fug of tobacco hung in the air. It wasn't worth trying to read any longer.

'My, but he's the studious one,' the girl trilled. Under the white make-up, thick enough to plaster a storehouse wall, she had an impish face with a pointed chin and questioning eyes. She was young, no more than thirteen. 'But I like them studious,' she said in wheedling tones, looking up at him with big eyes. 'And such a nice-looking boy. Reading, are you? Your master'll be a long time gone, you know. Mori-*sama*, isn't it? It's a big party he's having, he has twenty guests. He won't be asking for you, not for a long while.'

'You know who he's booked tonight?' said the second voice, snickering. 'Our Segawa. Only the best will do for Mori-*sama*, only our Segawa, the most famous courtesan in the whole Yoshiwara – no, the whole country. She's like the cherry blossom, there's none to equal her. She'll keep your Mori-*sama* busy till dawn, I can tell you now! She's a toppler of castles, a ruiner of men, she can bring a nation to its knees with a swish of her skirts, have men tearing at each other's throats.' The old woman gave a chortle. 'Of course, we know you can't afford a castle-toppler yourself. I can't see you bankrupting yourself for anyone, my son, you've nothing to bankrupt yourself with. But you could run to a maidservant or a waitress or a bathhouse girl. We have ladies for all budgets and we can make a special price for a handsome lad like you. We wouldn't want you to end up down some stinking alley with a night hawk or a river duck or a hundred-*mon* woman now, would we? That would be a waste, nice young fellow like you.' The woman cackled and the girl purred with laughter.

There were snorts from the other side of the room, where Bunkichi and Zenkichi, Nobu's fellow attendants, were sharing a flask of sake, long pipes drooping from their lips.

'What sort of talk is that, Auntie?' demanded Bunkichi. His sash was loosely tied and his cotton jacket flapping open, revealing a hollow chest, scrawny arms and stringy thighs. The maids pawed at him admiringly. '"Courtesan", "castle-toppler"? We use more down-to-earth words these days. "Ladies for hire", isn't that what we say? And this establishment of yours – it's a "rental parlour", I believe. And you're "Madam" now, not "Auntie".' He took a hairy green pod from the dish in front of him and squeezed a boiled soy bean into his mouth, then belched.

'Always the sharp one, Bunkichi,' said the woman. She had a withered face and narrow black eyes that took in everything. 'What do they call it – the Cattle Release Act?' She gave a snort of laughter.

'The Prostitute Emancipation Act,' said Zenkichi, thrusting out his chest and enunciating the syllables in comically pompous tones. He was a smooth-faced fellow with the air of a dandy.

'It certainly hasn't done much for business,' said the old

woman dryly. 'Some of the girls in the other houses even took the opportunity to slip away. The gods only know where they went. But the best houses, like ours, haven't had any problems. We've always been kind to our girls.' Her face crinkled into a thin smile. 'But you're quite right, my boy. Nowadays nobody's bought and sold any more and our girls have had their debts forgiven. Though, foolish creatures that they are, they just go on running up new ones. So you see, we still need customers – like our dear Mori-*sama*; and everyone understands the old words better than the new.'

So here he was, back in the Yoshiwara, the city of endless pleasure, where darkness never fell, the lights never went out and the streets heaved with merry-makers. It was years since Nobu had first come here as a child, waiting patiently in the antechamber while his master frittered away the hours upstairs.

As he'd followed Mori-*sama* through the Great Gate and down the Central Boulevard, marching alongside Bunkichi and Zenkichi, the place had seemed grimier, more tawdry than he remembered. Sake vendors and fortune tellers squatted in the dust, teahouse maids dozed in cool corners behind lowered blinds, and a single food stall offered bowls of tepid noodles to servants from the pleasure houses. The sparkle of excitement, the promise of endless possibility had entirely disappeared. The place had lost its glamour. Or maybe it was him that had changed, not the Yoshiwara.

Even the famous Pine Cone House looked distinctly run down. The tatami was worn and shabby, the railings broken, the paper panes roughly patched. The anteroom, where the attendants waited, was dank and airless and reeked of stale food and dirty bedding. From the floor above came girlish shrieks and yells of laughter, the strumming of shamisens and sounds of singing and dancing, growing louder and wilder as the night wore on. Later, he knew, there would be grunts and groans and ecstatic yelps.

'Hey.' The imp-faced girl tried to snatch Nobu's book and, as he grabbed it back, the page tore. Cursing, he thrust it into his bag. '*A coeur vaillant rien d'impossible*,' he repeated to himself. The words were like a mantra. They helped him forget where he was.

'Don't you like having fun?' the girl whined, tugging at his sash.

'You're wasting your time. We've no money,' said Bunkichi. 'Especially our Nobu, all he ever does is read. He might as well be a monk.'

'Maybe he has someone special,' said the girl, tilting her chin and glancing slyly up at Nobu.

'Hey, Nobu. Someone you're soft on, is there?' said Bunkichi with a leer. 'Nothing to be ashamed of. I'm soft on Oshin here, aren't I?' He grabbed at a bony serving girl with a pinched face and protruding lower lip who was running by heading for the kitchens. Giggling, she beat him off with her fists. 'Tell us, who is it?'

Nobu kept his mouth clamped firmly shut. Bunkichi was trying to goad him into speaking so he could make fun of his accent; but he wouldn't succeed.

Zenkichi piped up. 'I don't pay any money, I gets what I wants without paying a *sen*. I have to fight them off, I tell you. I was waiting for the master the other day at a restaurant downtown. Took a stroll round the block and the girls are all calling after me, "Hey, handsome!" One just throws herself at me – not much of a looker, but a good figure. We go to the back of her teahouse and I take her right there.'

'So how was she?' asked Bunkichi, sniggering.

' "A suck like an octopus . . ." '

' ". . . a grip like a trapdoor, tight like a purse",' said Bunkichi, running his tongue around his fleshy lips. He paused and narrowed his eyes to a lascivious squint. 'Reminds me of this teahouse girl I met a few days ago. I'd won at cards and I comes swaggering into the Yoshiwara with a purse full of yen and there she is behind the lattices. Pretty little thing. She sets eyes on me and she's smitten, I could tell straight away. Now that was a suck like an octopus! You fellows stay here and keep an eye on things and I'll slip off and say hello. Just hello, mind.'

'Just hello, Bunkichi?' said Zenkichi. 'Like last time, just hello, is it?'

Nobu laughed. He was used to his fellow attendants' bragging, he'd heard it all before. If he'd had the money he might have spent it that way himself, but he needed to hang on to every *sen* and *mon* he could. In any case he'd rather save it for something better. Even the imp-faced girl was not to his taste. He picked up the bag containing his precious book and turned towards the vestibule.

'Hey, you can't leave. Where you going?'

'Outside,' he grunted. 'Gonna take a look around.'

'What was that?' bawled the attendants, grinning in delight. 'Can't understand a word he says! Whoa, listen to that. You gotta lose that accent. You can talk how you like at home but here in the Yoshiwara you gotta talk sophisticated. You sound like a bumpkin!'

'I understood exactly what he said,' said the maid who'd been lolling against him. 'Anyway, who cares how he talks? He's a lot better-looking than either of you two.'

Nobu squatted morosely outside the door, his thin-stemmed pipe in his mouth, and struck a flint.

Red lanterns glowed along the Central Boulevard, making the street as bright as day. Men dressed for a night on the town jostled elbows, old women with shrivelled walnut faces plucked at passing sleeves.

'The Yamato House, gentlemen, try our wares! Prime young women at knock-down prices!' a voice quavered from one side of the street.

'The Kano House, this way!' came a croak from the other. 'Beautiful young women, moist and tender, waiting to devote themselves to your pleasure. Their skills know no bounds!'

'Prices reduced across the board,' squawked another. 'All fresh new prostitutes. Jug of sake and bowl of soup thrown in for free!'

Fortune tellers and hawkers of food shouted at the tops of their voices while pedlars of woodblock prints designed to enflame desire, depicting clients and prostitutes with unfeasibly large sexual organs entwined in all manner of unlikely positions, held up their wares to the indifferent gaze of the passers-by. When the crowds parted Nobu caught a glimpse of the latticed cage of the brothel across the boulevard and the painted girls in gaudy kimonos crowded inside, staring into the night or plucking listlessly on shamisens.

There were barbarians too, more than ever before – the polite word now, he reminded himself, was 'outsider' – sauntering up and down with their ungainly gait, peering into cages with their big round eyes popping out of their heads. They came in all shapes and sizes, mostly giants but some smaller ones, some fat, some thin, with pinkish, brownish or even black skin, but all uniformly ugly and hairy, with exaggerated features and grotesquely beaky noses.

Aromas of roasting eel, fish-paste cakes and grilling sparrows on skewers swirled enticingly, mingling with dust, sweat and alluring perfumes, with pungent gusts of sewage underlying all.

Nobu inhaled the fragrant tobacco and blew out a long plume of smoke, watching it dissolve into the air. The rough cotton at the back of his neck prickled in the heat. He took a plug of tobacco and rolled it between his fingers, then packed his pipe and took another puff, chewing thoughtfully on the stem. There were so many responsibilities. His brother Kenjiro ill again, for a start. His brothers had come south and managed to find a small house in Tokyo but now he had to pay the rent on it and buy Kenjiro's medicine; and his father and Gosaburo up north needed money too. They all worked as hard as they could but for the time being he was in the best position to earn. Now it was the summer holidays, he had to use this time to make as much money as he could. He'd soon be back in the barracks and then there'd be exams. If he failed he'd be out on his ear and then what? What would become of his family, who depended on him?

Study and earn money. He had to concentrate on that. *A coeur vaillant rien d'impossible.*

Suddenly he caught the sound of a voice, jaunty and teasing, rising above the clatter of clogs and the din of shouts and laughter. 'Hey, Yamakawa, how you doing? Quite a night we had of it, what? That last drinking session about finished me off.' Somewhere in the back of his mind a memory stirred. He knew that self-satisfied drawl but for the life of him he couldn't place it.

He listened intently, but the voice had disappeared. Then he heard it again, floating across the sea of bobbing black heads towards him. It was speaking Edo dialect, but with a hint of a Kyoto twang. 'I'd never have got out of here this morning if it hadn't been for our rickshaw boy waiting at the gate. Suzuki, you're not looking so fresh yourself today, what?' The din of the crowd drowned the answer.

Nobu stared at the crush of bodies, trying to pick out a face he knew. The voice was coming closer.

'And isn't this little Ayame?' It was the tones of a man talking to a child or a woman or a dog. 'Just look how she's grown! She'll be celebrating her first night any time now, won't she? Who's going to share her first night's bedclothes with her?'

Nobu caught the answer.

'You wouldn't believe who the lucky fellow is, Eijiro-*sama*!'

Of course. Eijiro. Taka's brother, Eijiro. Nobu had always known Eijiro was a great patron of the pleasure quarters. It was amazing he hadn't bumped into him before.

As the realization hit home, Nobu started back and shrank into the shadows. He remembered that voice all too well. He could still hear his rough bark: 'Oi, you. Call these boots clean? You should be able to see your ugly face in them. Mother says she caught you reading again. We don't pay you to read.' There had been not the remotest hint of charm when he yelled at Nobu.

'You don't pay me at all,' Nobu had muttered. He flinched, remembering the cuff round the head those words had earned him.

'We feed you, we house you, what more do you want? I know you helped Mother out once, but we can't run a house on charity. Stupid northerners, lazy degenerate sods the lot of you. Don't worry, I'll find a way to get rid of you. You think we'll have trouble finding another servant? You can't take a step without treading on one these days.'

The crowd parted in a flurry of sycophantic bows and Nobu saw a head poking above the rest. He knew the drooping eyes and full mouth. It was a square face, jowly around the cheeks, almost as if some foreign blood had crept in, a little broader, a little fleshier than he remembered, but Eijiro sure enough. He sauntered along in an elegant kimono, nodding to left and right like a daimyo among his subjects. Then, with a lift of his eyebrows, he reached ostentatiously inside his collar and pulled out something that sparkled like gold in the lantern light.

'Eiji-*kun*, is that for me?' a silky voice sang out. 'It's not often you see one of those in here. What do you call it – a timepiece? Won't you give it to me?'

There was a swirl of colour between the black heads

and drab robes. Slinking gracefully beside Eijiro was a dainty figure in shimmering silks with a preposterously huge coiffure studded with glittering hairpins. Nobu glimpsed a porcelain face, camellia lips and slanted fox eyes and heard groans of lust and shouts of 'Tsukasa-*sama*, Tsukasa-*sama*, I'm saving up my yen.' 'Tsukasa-*sama*, wait for me, I'll buy your freedom one day.' So this was the famous Tsukasa – more renowned by far than Segawa of the Pine Cone House, who, people whispered, was beginning to dry up.

'Had a win on the cards, then, Eijiro?' shouted a voice from the crowd.

Eijiro strolled on, lips curled in a supercilious smile. He passed by without looking in Nobu's direction.

Nobu grimaced. That self-satisfied face brought back too many memories. He remembered the gate slamming behind him and found himself thinking of Taka, her wide eyes and innocent girlish face. She'd been kind to him. She'd seen worth in him when no one else had.

It was nearly Tanabata again, the one day of the year when the tragic lovers, the weaver princess and the cowherd, could be together. It would be observed with the greatest fervour here in the Yoshiwara, where love and romance and everything that went with them were celebrated. The thought of Taka made his heart ache and he squared his shoulders. He had a new life; that was all in the past now.

The street was still jostling with people but the mood had changed. The din of voices had turned hostile. A knot of shaggy heads closed in around one burly figure.

'What'ya doing?' It was Eijiro. 'Stop shoving us around.'

Voices growled menacingly in the impenetrable mumble of the Edo underclass. Nobu had lived for years on the rough side of town and could understand well enough what they were saying. 'Hey, you, big man. Daddy send you, did he? Gives you money, does he? Lots of it, too, by the looks of it.'

'Keep my father out of this, you ignorant dog,' Eijiro snarled. It seemed he could understand too.

'Who're you calling a dog? Get your paws off Tsukasa. You bumpkins come here, take our city and our women, strut around like you own the place. Get back to your yam fields where you belong!'

There were yells and thumps and sounds of pushing and scuffling, followed by the screech of ripping fabric and a woman's indignant shout. Nobu hesitated. Eijiro was his sworn enemy, he had every reason to hate him. He'd beaten him, thrown him out on the street, and he was the son of General Kitaoka, the scourge of the north. But he was Taka's brother. He was on his own. Nobu couldn't stand by and see him killed.

He scrambled to his feet and plunged into the crowd of gawping spectators, pushing aside damp silk and sweaty bodies. People staggered back protesting, shouting curses at him.

Eijiro was surrounded by a gang of youths, brandishing sticks and knives. Some were in cotton jackets, others stripped to their loincloths with tattoos rippling across their chests and backs and sinewy thighs gleaming with sweat. Eijiro had squared up to the youths. As far as Nobu could see, he was unarmed. Tsukasa stood beside him, her dainty fingers curled around the hilt of a dagger half drawn from her obi, her scarlet lips pursed in disdain. Eijiro's friends had melted away at the first hint of trouble.

Nobu charged through the gang, shoving them out of the way, trampling over them, sending a couple tumbling like round-bottomed Daruma dolls, and took his stand beside Eijiro.

The youths clenched their fists and crouched, shifting their feet, getting ready to attack. There were ten or twelve of them. If they all jumped on him and Eijiro at once the two of them would be in trouble. But he had a hunch that beneath the aggressive tattoos they were merely shifty-eyed, bandy-legged bullies who'd turn on a soft target like Eijiro but slink away if there was any chance of getting hurt themselves.

Hard black eyes stared back at him and he wondered if this time he'd run out of luck. A fellow with a swarthy complexion and narrow forehead pushed out his scrawny chest like a fighting cock. 'Out of the way, m' boy, or you'll get hurt,' he snarled.

Nobu held his ground. 'Ten o' you and one o' him?' he grunted. He could mumble like a low city gangster with the best of them. 'Bunch o' cowards. You wanna fight, you'll have to fight me too.'

'Northerner, in't you?' growled the man. 'What'ya wanna take sides with this potato-faced bastard for? Don't you know who he is? His dad's the chief of those southern generals who massacred your lot.'

'The war was over a long time ago. Forget north and south. Leave him be.'

The men pressed in closer, brandishing their sticks. Then there were shouts of 'Now then, now then, what's going on here?' Several burly men, sleeves tied back ready for a fight, were pushing their way through – the Yoshiwara police. The troublemakers looked at each other, shuffling their feet. A moment later they'd melted away into the crowd.

Nobu turned on his heel. He needed to get back to his post quickly before Mori-*sama* summoned him and Bunkichi and Zenkichi noticed his absence. If he wasn't careful he'd be out of a job and this job hadn't been easy to find. He was eager to disappear before Eijiro recognized him. He hadn't forgotten the beatings he'd given him.

A large hand landed on his shoulder. 'You certainly took care of those thugs, my man. They scattered as soon as they saw you. I'm in your debt. Let me treat you to dinner and a woman! Well known in these parts, are you?'

Reluctantly Nobu turned. Eijiro was smiling. It was obvious he had no idea who he was. Two years had passed since they had last seen each other. Nobu had been a scrawny sixteen-year-old and a servant, practically invisible, barely human as far as his master was concerned. Now he was a man, tall and firm-muscled. As for Eijiro, he was the same florid, rather flabby fellow that Nobu remembered.

Eijiro's expression changed and his jaw dropped. He snatched his hand from Nobu's shoulder and took a step back. 'It can't be. Not . . . Nobu, is it?'

Nobu cursed himself, wishing he hadn't been so impetuous. The last thing he wanted was for this man to track him down. He didn't want anything to do with him or his family any more. 'Kitaoka-*sama*. At your service, sir.'

'You saved my skin, young Nobu,' said Eijiro, trying to sound bluff. 'It must be your karma, always showing up when you're least expected. Rescuing Kitaokas is your speciality.'

Nobu nodded brusquely, looking for a way to escape. Eijiro was clearly embarrassed. He needed to find a way to save face but Nobu had no intention of helping him out. 'Are they well,' Nobu asked, 'your family, your honourable mother?'

'All well.' Eijiro narrowed his eyes. 'You remember that foolish little sister of mine, Taka? She's to be married soon – an excellent match, to the heir of the Shimada house.'

Nobu froze. He stood stock still for a moment, staring at the rough ground. The trample of feet, the shouts and music and revelry faded. It was the last thing he'd expected to hear. It all came back – the reading and writing lessons, her sweetness, his happy days in the big house in Shinagawa. He'd been so sure he was over all that but nevertheless it was a blow. But there was no point wishing things could have been different, no point regretting or yearning. He swallowed. 'Congratulations,' he said, bowing with what he hoped was a careless smile. The last thing he wanted was to give Eijiro the satisfaction of seeing his dismay. 'Wish her happiness. And give my best to your honourable mother.'

'And you, Nobu. What are you doing here? I didn't know you were a Yoshiwara man.' Eijiro flung out his arms in a sweeping gesture that took in the glowing lanterns, the cages of prostitutes, the crowds pushing back as a procession approached with a preening courtesan parading along on high clogs. He had to raise his voice to make himself heard above the commotion.

'I'm in service,' Nobu said, scowling. 'I'm attending my master.'

Tsukasa tugged at Eijiro's sleeve. 'Eiji-*kun*, it's getting late. Give the footman some money and let's go.'

Nobu heaved a sigh of relief. He was about to flee when a flat, ugly face with protruding lips pushed out of the crowd.

'Nobu! There you are!' Bunkichi was grinning. He stopped short, his face changing as he took in Eijiro's prosperous belly and expensive robes. He visibly shrivelled and bowed his head. 'So sorry, sir,' he mumbled. 'Is this lad bothering you? Nobu, not getting into trouble again, are we?'

'Not at all,' said Eijiro. 'We're old acquaintances. He helped me out.'

Bunkichi tilted his head and gave Nobu a quizzical stare, then made an elaborate bow. 'Bunkichi, unworthy servant in the household of Mori Ichinosuke,' he said, puffing out his chest.

'Mori-*sama*. I know him well,' said Eijiro. 'Is your master here?'

He grinned as Bunkichi's face conveyed the answer that his master was indeed in the Yoshiwara but at present otherwise engaged.

'Young Nobu here is our newest recruit,' said the attendant. 'Glad he's been of service. There's a lot of ruffians hanging around the Yoshiwara,' he added solemnly. 'You'd best watch your step, sir, a wealthy man like yourself.'

As Nobu turned, he felt a prickling between his

shoulder blades. He could feel Eijiro's eyes boring into his back. He hated him as much as ever, it made no difference that he'd rescued him. Nobu would have to make sure their paths never crossed again.

But seeing him had reawakened the memory of his sister, Taka. He told himself firmly not to be a fool. He'd just have to forget her again and as quickly as possible. The best way was by losing himself in the arms of the Yoshiwara girls. Unlike Taka they were for sale, the imp-faced girl most of all.

Morosely he followed Bunkichi back to the Pine Cone House.

9

'I'll be lonely without you, Taka,' Fujino wailed, pushing her needle into the seam of the kimono she was working on. She pulled the thread through, knotted it and cut it off neatly. 'You're all I have left now that Haru's gone. Who will I talk to when you go too?'

Taka pursed her lips and raised her eyebrows. It's your own doing, Mother, she thought. It's nothing to do with me. She kept her mouth firmly shut. There was no point in saying anything.

They were sitting together companionably, finishing off some sewing, while the maids swept and dusted. Light poured in through the paper screens. In the kitchens the servants clattered about, tidying away the breakfast dishes.

'I promise you, you'll thank me in the end,' Fujino said, putting down her sewing, taking out her fan and waving it briskly. 'Don't look so miserable. Why don't we take a couple of rickshaws and go to Ginza, to the Ebisuya dry goods store? We'll surprise Mr Kawakami! He has the most wonderful selection of silks. We can look through his pattern books and order a gorgeous dress for you from that tailor in Yokohama. If you're to be Masuda-*sama*'s wife, you have to know how to run

a house. Madame Masuda will give you a good training, but it will be as well to have a head start. Let me
tell you a secret. Being a rich man's wife won't be all
hard work. You'll be ordering silks, going out to dine,
just as we do now. Speaking of which, I have an idea!'

She dropped her fan and clapped her plump hands.
'We'll go and try the beef stew at Nishikawa. It's just
opened and my dear friend, your aunt Kiharu, tells me
it's the place to be seen. You have to get over your
aversion to beef. All the fashionable people eat it.'

She pushed aside her sewing, slipped her fan back
into her obi, heaved herself to her feet and padded away
across the tatami.

The sounds of the garden floated in – cicadas
droning, birds twittering, the trickle of water, the tock
of the bamboo water pipe. The gardeners crunched
about, chatting to each other, clacking their shears and
scraping their rakes across the gravel.

Her mother was probably right, Taka thought. She
was making a fuss about nothing. Masuda-*sama* had
seemed a perfectly decent man, though she hadn't liked
the patronizing way he'd corrected her English and the
arrogant pout she'd seen when he addressed the
servants. But it wasn't really anything to do with him. It
didn't matter how rich he was. She wanted a chance to
spread her wings, not flit out of one cage straight into
another.

But there was no way out. Fujino was busy drawing
up plans for the wedding, interviewing palanquin
owners, selecting silks for wedding kimonos and
planning an enormous feast, at the end of which Taka
knew she would step into a palanquin even more

luxurious than Haru's and the lacquered door would slide shut and when it opened again she'd be at Masuda-*sama*'s mansion. She'd tried arguing and pleading, but in vain. Her mother kept telling her it was the greatest opportunity she would ever have and that she knew better than Taka what was best for her.

She was probably right. It was not surprising she was worried and afraid when she was marrying a perfect stranger but once she was Masuda-*sama*'s wife no doubt it would all be fine. ' "When winter comes, spring can't be far behind," ' she murmured.

She had picked up her sewing again when she heard something unexpected – raised voices on the other side of the house. The voices stopped abruptly and there was an ominous silence.

Okatsu came pattering through the vast open rooms and dropped to her knees beside her, a worried frown puckering her pretty face. 'Your honourable brother's home.'

'Something must have happened. He never gets back before midday.'

'I think you'd better come.'

Fujino and Eijiro were facing each other across a table, talking in low voices. They were so caught up in their argument they barely noticed Taka as she dismissed Okatsu and knelt beside them.

Fujino was on her knees, her back softly curved. 'My dear son, I really don't think . . .' she began in her wheedling geisha coo. Suddenly her face changed and she leaned forward. 'I will not let you bring this house into disrepute.'

Taka started. She'd never heard her mother speak so fiercely.

Eijiro was sprawled across the mats like a beached whale. He was wearing the rakish silk robes he had put on to go to the pleasure quarters, of finest pongee with an embroidered lining. One expensive sleeve was torn and hung loose at the shoulder.

'You forget, Mother,' he growled, his voice rising. His large square face was dark and his brow creased in a stubborn furrow. Fujino raised her hand, gesturing to him to speak more softly. It wouldn't do to quarrel in front of the servants. 'In my father's absence I am master of this house. I accord you due respect, but you are still a woman. It's your duty to obey my command.'

'Say what you like, my son. We have no money. Your father has been away for years and how often do we hear from him? I'm at my wits' end trying to keep this household together. And now Taka is to marry and we must find a dowry.'

Taka wondered if she was telling the truth. Perhaps that was why she was so eager for her to marry Masuda-*sama* – for his wealth.

'Tsukasa is the most celebrated courtesan in the city, Mother. Even you must have heard of her.' Taka looked at him in surprise. Surely he couldn't be talking about the famous Tsukasa? Many of the girls at school had copies of Kuniteru's woodblock print of her, impossibly elegant and slender, and everyone studied her kimonos and the modern way she wore them. Tsukasa's daring 'eaves' hairstyle, sweeping out over her ears like the eaves of a house, was the latest fashion. Even Fujino sometimes arranged her hair in the Tsukasa style. There were photographs of her too, posed on a chair, as if to show that there was civilization and enlightenment even in the Yoshiwara.

'Everything's arranged. I've negotiated the terms,' said Eijiro impatiently. 'Our family will be disgraced if I don't produce the money. I promise you, Mother, taking Tsukasa as my concubine will bring glory to our house.'

Fujino smacked her fan down hard on the tatami, sending up a shower of dust. 'Fool. It will bring shame, nothing else.' Taka had never seen her so angry. 'You don't even have a wife. How can you take a concubine? We are a secondary house and we're under all the greater an obligation to maintain our respectability. Look at you. You're a wastrel, all you do is drink and whore. You bring shame to your father's good name. And your expensive clothes, all torn. I can't believe a son of mine would let himself be taken in by a whore, and a Yoshiwara whore at that. If your father knew it he would disown you.'

Eijiro sat up, swung on to his knees and brought his fist down on the table. The teacups clattered on their saucers. 'You were nothing but a geisha yourself, Mother, remember? Father bought your freedom. And you refuse me the same privilege?'

'I was a Gion geisha of the very highest class,' snapped Fujino. 'We geishas have style and accomplishments. We're totally different from those so-called courtesans.' She lowered her eyes. 'The glory days of the flower and willow world are long past. These days the Yoshiwara is nothing but a common stew and its courtesans are trumped-up prostitutes. Your Tsukasa has you by the testicles. It's what's between her legs that's snagged you. She's not worthy to be the concubine of the son of General Kitaoka. I wish your brother Ryutaro was still with us. He would never have dreamed of such a thing.'

Eijiro's face blackened and he clenched his big fists till the knuckles were white. He took a breath. 'Your words are harsh, Mother, but I grant you one thing. It's true the Yoshiwara has declined, ever since the Cattle Release Act. There's a lower class of woman now, much lower. That is why I need to buy her freedom. A woman like her deserves a better life.' He leaned forward and looked at Fujino from under his heavy brows, his eyes narrowing. 'Let me tell you something. We were attacked by a street gang, that's why my sleeve is torn.'

'You were attacked?' Fujino turned pale. 'My cherished son, I told you you shouldn't go to those dangerous places. What happened? Are you hurt?'

'There were ten or twelve of them – gamblers, they looked like, or pedlars. They came out of the crowd and blocked our path. Big, tattooed men with knives and clubs. They were after Tsukasa. Everyone envies me, everyone resents the fact she's mine. I didn't even have a sword, but I knew I could take them on with my bare hands. And Tsukasa – you should have seen her, Mother, with her little hand on her dagger. She was magnificent – so cool, so courageous. You would have been proud. She's a woman after your own heart.'

'You mean you fought them off, just you and this whore of yours?' Fujino's lips twitched in disbelief. 'Ten of them, you said, or twelve, with knives and clubs? A fat fellow like you, without even a sword? You're not your father, I know that much.' She burst out laughing as she always did when her wayward son was telling one of his stories, not a tinkly geisha laugh but a loud raucous chuckle.

Taka was staring at Eijiro too. He was frowning, fiddling with the hem of his robe, keeping his eyes averted. She recognized that sheepish look of his. There was something he wasn't telling them.

'Look, Mother, he's not even dirty. He hasn't been in a fight at all. He's making it all up. Or someone helped him.'

Eijiro turned on her. 'Keep out of this, little sister.' He scowled. 'It's true. I was in a fight but we had a bit of help.'

'You had help?'

'If you ask me, he was probably one of them himself. He set it all up beforehand, set the gang on me, everything. He wanted to get me murdered and then at the last moment had second thoughts. It was all a ploy to wriggle his way back into our family's esteem. I'm telling you now, he won't succeed in that.'

'In the name of all the gods, what are you talking about? Who?'

'That boy, that dreadful Aizu fellow who used to work here. Of all people, he was there, in the Yoshiwara. He came bursting out of nowhere. He pushed through the thugs and came and stood beside us. That fellow, you know. That fellow I had to throw out. Nobu.'

Taka raised her head, trying not to smile. She felt herself coming back to life. It was as if a door had opened and a breeze had blown in, carrying scents of somewhere distant and foreign, somewhere she knew nothing about. It was the feeling she had had that first time when Nobu had poked his sun-darkened face around the door at the Black Peony.

She'd done her best to put him out of her mind yet here he was again, emerging from the shadows – from the Yoshiwara, a place of darkness, populated by bad men and courtesans. For a moment a curtain lifted and she caught a glimpse of another world, a forbidden place, irresistibly alluring. It made her want to slip on her sandals and disappear right now.

She took a breath. There were ten thousand questions she wanted to ask – what he'd said, how he was, what he'd been doing there. 'So Nobu came to your rescue.' She didn't bother to conceal the laughter in her voice.

'Little Taka,' Eijiro snapped. 'You think you're so grown up. You should learn not to speak out of turn. A woman should know her place.'

Taka stared at him. 'So tell me.'

He shifted uncomfortably. 'This precious Nobu of yours – he just stood there. He didn't do anything. We took care of ourselves. He improved the odds, that's all.'

'I don't believe a word of it.'

'You know what a weakling he was. You haven't forgotten how I took care of him that time we caught the two of you together.'

Taka chose to ignore that remark. 'And you think he was trying to work himself back into our favour? That can't be true. He was good and honest.'

'Though I'm surprised to hear he was in the Yoshiwara – him, of all people,' Fujino added.

Eijiro gave an arch smile, as if he knew he held the

winning hand. 'He's working for Mori-*sama*, that's why,' he said.

Fujino raised her caterpillar eyebrows. 'Mori Ichinosuke, the Tosa fellow, that miserable jumped-up clerk you're so fond of? Poor Nobu. He was such a serious boy. He must be having a hard time of it. He's the last person I'd expect to hear of in the Yoshiwara.'

Fujino and Eijiro started arguing about Tsukasa again. Taka stared at the tatami, their words washing over her.

Her thoughts drifted back to a sunny day a couple of summers ago. She'd been sitting with Nobu, helping him with his reading, as she always did. He was stumbling his way through a passage about Kusunoki Masashige and his son Masatsura, the loyal warriors who had sacrificed their lives for the emperor in ancient times, when he suddenly stopped and looked up, his eyes shining. 'I know this passage,' he said.

He gazed into the distance and recited it perfectly, his voice rising and falling so beautifully that it brought tears to her eyes. All along she'd thought she was teaching him but now she saw that he was teaching her, too. She asked him where he'd learned that passage and he said, so quietly she could hardly catch the words, 'At my mother's knee.' Her own mother had never recited the classics to her; she doubted if she even knew them. Geisha songs were her great love. Taka had suddenly realized then that she knew nothing about Nobu – who he was, where he came from. He had never said a single word about himself or his past.

After that Taka often begged him to recite for her. But when she asked him about his mother he always said quietly, 'She's far away.' And that was all he would say.

He deserved better than to be a servant, she thought, better than to run around doing someone else's bidding. And now she knew where he was. She smiled. Maybe she'd send him a letter. Nothing unsuitable, nothing embarrassing or personal, something simple, just a note.

'Nobu-*sama*,' she thought, imagining what she might write. It seemed strange to use a respectful term like *sama* to address a servant but in her mind he wasn't a servant. He was a lot more than that. 'Nobu-*sama*. I was glad to have news of you from my older brother. Two years have passed since you left our house. I trust you are keeping well. Taka.' Something like that.

The servants would know where Mori-*sama* lived; they took messages there. Okatsu only had to enquire and Taka could trust her to be discreet. Then Okatsu could deliver it. Between them they would think up a good reason why Okatsu needed to go past Mori-*sama*'s house – on the way to the house of one of her relatives, perhaps, or somewhere she had to go on an errand.

Taka sighed. Okatsu was the maid, she the mistress, yet Okatsu was far freer than she was. Okatsu was always out and about, going here and there, doing errands, but Taka could only go out with a chaperone. And soon she would be married and the prison doors would close for ever. It was totally clear now. She had to find a way to escape – and the key was Nobu.

10

'And there 'e stands, arms akimbo, like the giant Benkei 'imself facin' up to the twenty thousand!' crowed Bunkichi for the third time that day, smirking obsequiously as Mori-*sama* guffawed. 'And these gangsters – if you could a' seen 'em, sir. Big burly fellas with arms the size a' tree trunks, jus' covered in tattoos from head to foot. Takes one look at our Nobu and turns tail, the lot a' them, and flees!'

'Quite the hero, what?' said Mori-*sama*, leering at Nobu out of half-closed eyes. He had a pouchy face and his kimono smelt of tobacco. He was a Tosa, from one of the four outlying clans which had bonded together and marched on Edo less than ten years earlier and taken over the city, the country and the government. He didn't talk like a potato samurai but to Nobu's ears his dialect was just as ugly, full of outlandish words and with the harsh twang of some distant mountain province.

As a southerner and one of the victors, he took particular delight in bullying Nobu and the fact Nobu was at the Military Academy gave him even more ammunition. 'So what does our General Yoshida have to say?' he'd jeer. 'Surely the great general can come up with a solution!' Bunkichi and Zenkichi had quickly caught on that Nobu was fair game and joined in with enthusiasm.

Nobu bowed, trying to shape his mouth into a patient smile. No matter what he thought of Mori-*sama* and everything he stood for, he needed this job; and he knew all too well, as Eijiro had reminded him time and time again, that you hardly had to take a step to tread on a servant.

'You took such excellent care of my good friend Kitaoka yesterday,' said Mori, his voice heavy with irony. 'Perhaps you can do the same for me. Come with me to the bath today.' He took out his timepiece, a big gold mechanism on a chain, and studied it, frowning. These days anyone of any consequence seemed to have one. Nobu had no idea what the marks on the glass face meant. The temple bells still rang out to mark the beginning and end of each working day and that was enough for him and the rest of the servants. He'd worked out that the best strategy was to be ready at all times. 'We'll leave in half an hour,' Mori-*sama* added, tucking the timepiece carefully back in his breast pocket.

In all his previous postings, Nobu had never had to accompany anyone to the bath. Still dressed in his formal hakama skirts and crisp black jacket with the Mori crest on it, he took a basket and a pile of thin cotton towels and waited in the front entrance, smarting from the teasing he had to endure. '*A coeur vaillant rien d'impossible*,' he repeated to himself; but the magic syllables had lost their soothing power. He squatted on his heels, took some tobacco from his pouch and kneaded it into a shiny brown ball, then packed his pipe, struck a flint and heaved a sigh as he drew in a lungful of fragrant smoke.

Mori-*sama* was not particularly rich, certainly not rich enough to have his own bath, though that didn't mean he couldn't afford several servants. Now the fighting was over he'd received a posting as a clerical officer for the Tosa domain and lived in one of the small houses beside what had been the daimyo's mansion, in the shadow of Edo Castle, near Kaji Bridge, which crossed one of the outer moats.

These days the Tosa domain no longer officially existed. The domains had all been replaced by prefectures named after the capital city of each, and the daimyo were no longer warrior princes ruling their own domain, with their own army, but 'governors' doing the bidding of the new regime. The Tosa domain was now Kochi Prefecture and the mansion was being torn down and replaced by cumbersome stone buildings in the modern 'western' style, where government officials were to work. There was hammering and banging morning to night and dust swirling about, prickling everyone's nostrils. The gate and fortifications at Kaji Bridge had already been demolished. Nevertheless, Mori still lived and worked here.

There were footsteps in the hallway and Mori appeared and strutted off down the road. Nobu was sliding the door closed when he glimpsed a woman under the trees at the end of the long street, dressed in an indigo kimono, like a maid. There was something familiar about her. The sight of her sent a prickle down the back of his neck and he wondered if she was a ghost, if his past was coming back to haunt him. It was just his imagination, he told himself impatiently; his eyes were playing tricks on him. When he turned to take another look she had disappeared into the shadows and he had to hurry after Mori-*sama*.

He followed Mori along streets festooned with brilliantly coloured banners and streamers, crowded with promenading holidaymakers. People were singing and dancing, and octopus and squid sizzled on roadside stalls, giving off mouth-watering smells. Nobu felt as if he was the only person in the whole world who had to work.

The bathhouse was a large building beside Kaji Bridge. As they pushed through the curtains into the men's side, steam swirled from the open doors. Men slapped the sides of the tub and voices echoed around the wooden walls. Nobu sniffed the pungent smell of soap powder and heard splashing and singing and raucous laughter, shouts of 'Bucket boy, over 'ere! Cold enough to freeze your balls off. Hot water, quick!' Other voices yelled, 'No, cold water, bring cold water. It's too 'ot!'

Mori's bony backside was disappearing up the steep staircase towards the changing room for the wealthier customers. Nobu hurried after him. There was a large tatami-matted room there, full of men removing their clothes or tying them in place, gossiping and laughing over the latest political developments. A few old fellows sprawled on the tatami, snoring gently, and a couple of youths were engrossed in a game of *go*. Pretty young women with smooth cheeks and glossy black hair scurried around with trays of tea and cakes, ignoring the ogling eyes and fending off hands that grabbed at them as they passed.

Nobu looked them up and down appraisingly. Bathhouse girls were relatively inexpensive, certainly as compared with the proud ladies of the Yoshiwara. Some were scrubbing the backs of customers, some waving large fans, sending gusts of cooling air around the room. There'd be yet others in the bath, scrubbing backs and shampooing. He smiled to himself. A good soak – that would make him feel better.

He had started undoing his obi when there was a snort of laughter.

'Quite the jester, what, General Yoshida!' roared Mori. 'Where d'ya think you're off to? You gotta stay here and watch my clothes. Here, help me off with my obi and make sure you fold it carefully.' Flushing with shame, Nobu tried to ignore the other customers' sniggers as he helped Mori strip off. 'You can rinse out my loincloth while you're waiting. Get it good and clean and make sure you slap all the wrinkles out of it before you hang it up to dry. And none of your heroics while I'm away, mind,' were Mori's parting shots as he set off down the stairs towards the bath.

So there'd be no bath for him that day, Nobu thought gloomily as he picked up Mori's soiled loincloth and looked around for the underwear bucket. Squatting beside the bucket, squeezing out the noxious garment, he closed his ears to the hubbub around him and the image of the woman he had seen in the distance came back to him.

Then he realized who she'd reminded him of: Okatsu, Taka's merry, plump-faced maid. But of course it couldn't have been her. What would Okatsu have been doing here, in Mori's run-down neighbourhood? The

Kitaoka residence was on the other side of the city. He must have thought of her because he'd seen Eijiro the previous day. The Kitaokas were on his mind.

Outside, pedlars hawked their wares. 'Dumplings, sweet dumplings,' sang one.

'Tofu, tofu!' cried another.

'Grilled eel, best eel, freshly grilled, brushed with Kandagawa restaurant's special sauce, following their secret recipe, passed down for generations . . .' Nobu sniffed the succulent smell of grilling eel and remembered how hungry he was.

Much later Mori reappeared, red and glowing like a boiled octopus, steam rising from his head in little puffs. He lounged in the changing room for a while, languidly smoking pipe after pipe of tobacco and bantering with the other customers. The shadows were lengthening by the time he was ready to leave.

Nobu helped him dress and followed him along the street back to the house, trying not to think about how unwashed and sticky he felt. He was startled to see Shige, Mori's mistress, at the door. She was a large, good-natured woman with big teeth, who wafted around in a cloud of face powder and hair oil.

'There you are, young Nobu,' she said, nodding excitedly. 'You'll never guess what happened. You had a visitor! A grand lady, a maid from one of those big government houses. She waited for a while but you didn't come back and now she's gone.'

Nobu stared at her. Who on earth could have come to see him? Surely it couldn't have been Okatsu, with a message from Taka? No good putting a price on your badger skin before you've caught your badger, he told himself sternly.

'I nearly forgot,' said Shige. 'She left something for you.'

She smiled and her teeth, polished to a dull black, turned her mouth into a dark chasm as she held out a small packet. It was a letter, not rolled into a scroll but folded and sealed. Nobu took it in both hands and raised it to his forehead as if it was a precious gift. His name was written on it. His heart missed a beat as he recognized the brushstrokes. It was from Taka. Trying not to show his excitement, he tucked it into his sleeve.

Mori scowled and opened his mouth. Shige swung round. 'Now you stop bullying him,' she snapped. He shut it again. 'Young Nobu, you can have the rest of the day off. Go and read your note. I'd get back to the bath-house if I were you.' She pressed some coins into his hand.

Nobu sauntered outside as slowly as he could and found a quiet corner under a tree, where Bunkichi and Zenkichi would not be able to find him. He took the letter from his sleeve, broke the seal and unfolded it. He read the words slowly, letting his eyes linger on the familiar handwriting, the way the ink flowed from stroke to stroke, broad then tapering to a point, like blades of grass.

Nobu-*sama*. I was glad to have news of you from my older brother Eijiro. I trust that you are keeping well in this hot weather. I often think of you and wonder how you are and what you are doing. It must be two years now since you left our house. It was just at Tanabata, was it not? And now Tanabata has come round again. We must pray for fine weather. Taka.

He smiled. How thoughtful of her to use such a respectful form of address – -*sama* – for him who, as far as she knew, was nothing but a servant. He too would pray for fine weather so that the magpies could form their bridge and the weaver princess and the cowherd could cross the River of Heaven and meet each other that night.

He thought of Taka with her brushes neatly rolled in a bamboo mat and remembered kneeling beside her as she patiently tried to teach him to make his brush-strokes beautiful, like hers. He thought of the sweet scent of her hair, the feel of her small cool fingers wrapped around his as she directed his brush, raising then lowering, helping him form the characters. She had been a stern teacher, not satisfied until every stroke was perfect.

Then had come the dreadful day when Eijiro had stormed in and found them together, writing Tanabata wishes. He remembered his own foolish wish – to stay at the Kitaoka house, near Taka, for ever. Even now the memory made him shudder. That had been the final straw that had given Eijiro the excuse he was waiting for to throw him out. Yet what he had written was true. Even though they were the family of General Kitaoka, even though Eijiro treated him like a dog, he'd been happy. He really could have stayed with them for ever.

He heaved a sigh. Taka was right. It was almost two years since then, though it felt more like a lifetime.

And now, as she said, Tanabata had come round again.

He read the letter once more, folded it and put it in his sleeve. It was touching that Taka had thought of him and bothered to write to him, especially now when, as Eijiro had told him, she'd made this advantageous match. He remembered that the one thing she hadn't wanted was to get married. Her mother must have insisted. He was surprised that Taka had managed to stay unwed for so long.

He picked up his towel and set off for the bathhouse.

Then it struck him. Supposing it wasn't just a kind note? Supposing it was a message? Taka would be going to Sengaku Temple, the temple near her house, to tie her wishes on to a bamboo branch, as she did every year. Perhaps, like the weaver princess and the cowherd, this was their one chance to meet? Perhaps that was what she was telling him.

He told himself not to be foolish. But the idea had entered his mind and he couldn't shake himself free of it. He remembered Taka had said she always went to the temple in the late afternoon when the heat of the day had passed.

He should be careful not to be impetuous, he told himself. It got him into trouble every time. He should just go and relax with the bathhouse girls. She wouldn't even be there. But it was too late. He had to find out.

He turned and headed off through the streets. It was a long walk, he knew. Then he saw a rickshaw and hailed it. He would spend the precious money Shige had given him on getting to Sengaku Temple as quickly as possible.

11

Late in the afternoon, when the heat of the day had died
down, Taka and Okatsu slipped past the gnarled old
guards who stood on each side of the huge gates of the
Kitaoka residence and hurried off down the lane. In
their blue and white cotton yukatas and thonged
wooden-soled geta clogs, whisking their fans and holding parasols over their heads, they could almost have
been sisters.

It was only after wheedling and begging and lengthy
arguments that Taka had persuaded Fujino to let them
go out at all. She had pleaded that Tanabata only came
once a year and sworn that they would go to Sengaku
Temple, nowhere else. Now she pattered between the
high walls that lined the lane, thrilled at the un-
accustomed sense of freedom. Almost anything seemed
possible. As they reached the Eastern Sea Road, a salty
breeze blew up. Seagulls swooped and screamed and,
between the bobbing heads and vivid streamers
and banners of smoke that rose from little stalls along
the road, she caught a glimpse of the sea. Fishing boats
bobbed and masts rocked on the horizon.

She wanted so badly to know what had transpired
when Okatsu had gone out with her precious note that

she had had to struggle not to ask her the moment her maid got back to the house. Taka hadn't dared say a single word there. She'd had the feeling there were listeners everywhere – in the walls, under the tatami, behind the paper screens, in the closets where the futons were stacked, in the creaky wooden chests with their rusty hasps, full of mouldering treasures, in the airless corners behind the staircase – secret listeners waiting to report back to her mother and Eijiro.

She knew that to send a note to a young man, let alone hint at a meeting, was unacceptable at any time. Fujino might once have overlooked it – after all, she herself had led a very unconventional life. But now Taka was to be married and would soon become the property of another family, who would certainly not take such an offence lightly. Okatsu, who was supposed to watch over her, would be severely punished if they were caught. She might be beaten, maybe dismissed. Taka glanced at her as she pattered cheerfully beside her. Okatsu was beaming with excitement. She knew she was taking a risk but that only made it more of an adventure.

'Did you see him, Okatsu?' Taka clasped her hands together and glanced around as if afraid someone might overhear her.

'No, but I met Mori-*sama*'s mistress,' said Okatsu, smiling serenely. 'She seemed kind.'

'You went to the house?' Taka gasped. 'I trusted you to be discreet! What sort of house is it? What sort of area? What's she like?'

Okatsu put her hand over her mouth and laughed merrily at the barrage of questions. 'Nice enough. An ordinary sort of person, not high class. She gave me tea and said Nobu was a very serious boy. I waited a while but he didn't come back. Gone to the public bath or something. In the end I left the note with her.'

'So you think she really gave it to him?' Taka asked doubtfully. 'And even if she did, do you think he understood? I was so careful in case someone else read it. Too careful, perhaps.'

'Best not to price your badger skin . . .'

'Until you've caught your badger.' Taka smiled, remembering how Nobu used to frown when he quoted the old proverb. 'Today is wish-granting day, don't forget that. Perhaps the gods will grant mine.'

Here at Shinagawa the Eastern Sea Road swung along Edo Bay in a half-moon curve. The broad promenade was hung with huge colourful woven balls and lanterns with paper tails that swung and swirled in the breeze, brilliant as the threads on the weaver princess's loom. People crowded beneath the decorations, dancing and singing and shouting.

Higgledy-piggledy along the water's edge were stalls piled with amulets, purses, paper dolls and strings of origami cranes. Long-haired men with black-painted eyes thrust flasks of toad oil – 'guaranteed to heal every ailment' – at passers-by. There were jugglers, comic dancers and hawkers offering boat rides round the bay, and mouth-watering smells issued from stalls where men with scarves knotted rakishly around their heads grilled octopus and squid.

In front of them the great highway turned inland past mansions and temples and streets clogged with tiny houses, heading for Japan Bridge, with its famous fish market, right in the noisy heart of Tokyo. Behind them it wound along the coast and through the mountains, past villages of thatched houses and hills carved into stepped paddy fields, all the way to Kyoto, many days' walk away, where Taka had grown up. She thought of their dark house there with its steep wooden stairs and tiny tatami-matted rooms, and how she used to hang over the balcony in the evenings, watching geishas and maikos clip-clop by, their long sleeves swaying as they walked, and felt an unexpected yearning for those distant childhood days, when her father had been around and life had been simpler.

By the time they got to Sengaku Temple it was almost dusk. They joined the crowds pushing through the shabby outer gate and along the path to the massive two-storeyed main gate with its steep tiled roofs and fierce bronze dragon coiling across the ceiling, then made their way past the great temple building and through the venerable graveyard surrounded by towering cryptomeria trees to the bamboo grove, tucked in a distant corner.

That morning Okatsu had collected dew from the big taro leaves in the garden and Taka had used it to grind ink. She'd written the usual wishes on strips of paper – for her family's health, happiness and prosperity, for her father to come home, for success in her schoolwork – and added an extra secret one. She'd screwed up her eyes and whispered a prayer before she'd brushed it, hoping that if she concentrated hard enough she might make it happen: 'You gods who know the secrets of my heart, protect me from this marriage.' Then she'd folded the paper quickly before anyone could see it.

The bamboo boughs were heavy with coloured strips of paper, paper dolls, purses and chains. Taka pulled down an empty branch, murmuring a prayer as she tied her wishes on to it. When she released it, it sprang back up, decorations flapping madly like blossoms about to fall.

People were dancing slowly and hypnotically, singing the Tanabata song:

sasa no ha sara sara	Bamboo leaves rustle,
nokiba ni yureru	swaying in the eaves,
o hoshi sama kira kira	stars twinkle,
kin gin sunago	gold and silver grains of sand

'I'm glad it's fine tonight,' Taka said, smiling at Okatsu, who was tying her own wishes in place. 'The magpies will have built their bridge.'

As darkness fell, she gazed at the river of stars swirling across the black sky, looking for the two brightest pinpricks of light, the weaver princess and the cowherd, who could only meet that night.

There was a fizzle and a boom and Taka jumped, reminded of the gunshots she used to hear on the streets of Kyoto. A fiery chrysanthemum flowered, filling the sky, showering cascades of petals on to the shadowy temple roofs. Then came another explosion, then another, till the air was fizzing and crackling and the sky was ablaze with colour. At last the fireworks faded, the sky darkened and one by one people began to leave.

So Nobu hadn't come after all. Taka had told herself again and again that he wouldn't – better not to price your badger skin, she reminded herself sternly; but despite everything she couldn't help feeling an ache of disappointment. He had probably never got her message and, even if he had, he hadn't realized what she meant or hadn't been able to get away. Or maybe he just hadn't wanted to, maybe that was the truth of the matter. Two years was a long time. Maybe he'd forgotten her. She had no idea what had happened in his life. He was probably nothing like the boy she remembered. It was for the best that he hadn't come, she told herself firmly.

The seven-day moon was rising, a half-circle glimmering on the horizon, dimming the stars.

'Madam, it's time to go,' said Okatsu firmly. 'Your mother will be waiting.'

Gloomily Taka followed Okatsu back through the grounds to the outer gate. They were on their way out when there was a clatter of wheels and a pounding of feet and a rickshaw pulled up in front of them. They stepped out of the way as a young man jumped down.

Taka caught her breath. The man's face was in shadow but in the pale light of the moon she could make out his features well enough – the firm jaw and slanting cheekbones, the narrow black eyes, the prominent, oddly aristocratic nose, the full mouth and long neck. He was no longer the gawky sixteen-year-old who had left their house two years earlier. He was taller, well built; he'd become a man. But she knew him all the same. She recognized his bearing, the way he held himself, straight and proud when he thought no one was watching him, and remembered how he would stoop and bow his shoulders like an obedient servant when he heard someone coming. He was in hakama trousers and

a jacket, rather formal for such a warm evening, and
carrying a towel as if he was on his way to the bathhouse. She had to smile. Even now he looked as if he
was wearing someone else's clothes.

Then she realized she was staring in a way quite
improper for a well-brought-up young lady, and quickly
dropped her eyes. Now he was here she felt tongue-tied.
She'd quite forgotten why it was she had sent him the
note. She felt as if she had conjured up a spirit from
the past. He couldn't be real.

The clatter of the rickshaw wheels faded into the
distance and the road fell silent. The young man was
tying his purse back on to his sash. He looked up and
saw Okatsu and started as if it was he who had seen a
ghost. Then his eyes lit on Taka. He gasped and for a
moment he hesitated and she realized that she too must
have changed. Then his whole face lit up in a smile. He
took a step towards them then stopped, as if he had
suddenly remembered who they were and who he was.
He bowed deferentially.

'Nobu-*sama*?' said Taka. She was mortified to hear
the quaver in her voice.

'Madam,' he said, keeping his head lowered. She
recognized the slight northern twang though his voice
was deeper now. He was twisting his towel nervously.
His hands had grown big, she noticed. 'I hope I didn't
misunderstand, madam. I received your note. I thought
you meant to summon me. If I'm mistaken, I shall leave
immediately. I don't mean to intrude on you.' His voice
was stern and Taka remembered how cruelly her
brother had treated him. He must feel wary about the
whole family now.

She bowed shyly. 'You're not mistaken, Nobu-*sama*. Today is Tanabata. I wanted to celebrate it with you. It's just two years since you left our house.'

His face softened. 'I'm so happy to see you, madam, and Okatsu too. I never thought I'd see you again.'

Clogs clattered along the road as people left the temple, fluttering their fans. Taka heard the muffled roar of the waves not far away and felt the freshness of sea air on her skin. Clouds scudded overhead. There was a wonderful feeling of space and openness.

'Did you bring a wish?' she asked, smiling at the young man. The moonlight picked out each of his features, carving ghostly hollows under his brow and cheekbones.

'I have one in my heart.'

'Let me show you the bamboo grove.'

Before they'd been children but now he was a man and her consciousness of it made her shy.

Okatsu drew her breath between her teeth. 'It's after dark,' she said. 'Your mother will want me to come with you.' Taka set her shoulders and Okatsu's voice tailed away. She knew very well how stubborn Taka could be. 'We will both be punished if she finds out, I worse than you,' she added, sighing.

'She won't find out,' said Taka firmly. 'We won't be long.'

A few loiterers remained in the temple grounds. Taka and Nobu went through the outer gate and the two-storeyed main gate, under the trees and past the great temple to the graveyard. Taka was walking in front, leading the way. She heard the patter of Nobu's clogs on the flagstones and the sound of his breath in the stillness. The last cicadas had fallen silent. Bats flittered and an owl flapped from the trees, startlingly close. Taka had so much to say; but she didn't want to break the spell.

The moon had risen and shadows chequered the path. They made their way between the tombstones, breathing the scent of incense smoke and fresh-cut pine laid in front of the stones. Water sparkled in the shallow stone basins.

There was a sudden silence. Nobu was standing gazing at a moss-stained tombstone that towered over him, enveloping him in shadow. He reached up and ran his fingers over the worn characters carved on the stone.

'Asa-no,' he read, picking out each hieroglyph. 'Asano Naganori, Lord of Takumi, of the domain of Ako.' Taka was startled to see how his face had changed. He was frowning as if at some painful memory. 'Madam, we should walk with more respect,' he said sharply. 'You must have forgotten. This is Sengaku Temple, the temple of the spring on the hill. These are the tombs of the forty-seven.'

Taka had passed the graves of the famous warriors so many times, placing sprigs of fresh pine on them and putting her hands together in respect, without much thinking about it. She was touched that Nobu knew these difficult characters and recalled how she had loved it when he recited the old chronicles for her.

'Will you tell me their story, Nobu?'

Gravely, he started to speak. 'Asano, Lord of Takumi, on the fourteenth day of the third month of the fourteenth year of Genroku, being goaded beyond endurance by the insults of Lord Kira, Official of

Protocol, drew his short sword and struck him within the precincts of Edo Castle.' Nobu's voice had taken on a northern hue. He spoke softly, in rhythmic cadences, shaping each syllable, his eyes fixed on something in the far distance or the long-forgotten past.

'For that offence he was condemned to die by his own hand. His lands were confiscated and his retainers, now lordless, became ronin.' Ronin – 'wave men', samurai without a master, at the mercy of the wind and the waves. He said the word with fierce emphasis.

'Forty-seven men took a solemn oath that they would do everything they could, even forfeit their very lives, to avenge their lord and take the life of Lord Kira, who had insulted their master and brought about his disgrace and death and the destruction of his domain.'

He walked on slowly from stone to stone, reading the names aloud. At the end of the line of stones was a particularly large, imposing one, set back from the rest, with an offering box in front and scented smoke pouring from the bundle of incense sticks which burnt there. It was freshly scrubbed and flowers filled the stone vases. Nobu read the inscription: 'Oishi Kuranosuke, chief among Lord Asano's retainers.'

The forty-seven knew that Lord Kira would expect them to seek revenge and would fortify his house and surround himself with men at arms. If their mission was to succeed, they would have to find a way to make him lower his guard. To put him off the scent, they went their separate ways as if, now that they were masterless, they had forgotten their allegiance and abandoned their samurai pride. Some became carpenters or craftsmen, others merchants.

Oishi Kuranosuke, their leader, was a famous warrior. He knew that he would be hard put to convince Lord Kira that he was not intending to pursue their vendetta. First he left his home and moved to Kyoto, to the geisha quarters of Gion, and there took to frequenting houses of ill repute and indulging in bouts of drunkenness and debauchery. Passers-by saw him lying drunk on the street and spat on him, appalled at such un-samurai-like behaviour. He even divorced his wife, sent her back to her parents and took a concubine.

He knew very well that Lord Kira would have set spies to watch him. Two years went by, and finally Lord Kira, convinced that the retainers really were cowards who had forgotten their sacred duty of revenge, sent away his guards. The moment had come.

It was midwinter and snow lay thick on the ground when the forty-seven stormed Lord Kira's residence on the east bank of the Sumida river. The cowardly lord hid in the woodshed. Searching for him, the retainers stabbed spears through the walls until one came out with blood on the tip. They had found him. They hauled him out and killed him with the same short sword with which Lord Asano had been ordered to kill himself.

Then they cut off his head, brought it to Sengaku Temple, washed it in the spring on the hill and placed it before the tomb of their dead lord. Their revenge complete, the retainers gave themselves up to the shogun. They had broken the law and, despite his sympathy, the shogun was obliged to sentence all forty-seven to die by their own hands. People crowded the streets to applaud, awed by their dedication and sense of samurai honour, as their bodies were carried to Sengaku Temple to be buried.

'My mother told me their story,' Nobu said quietly. 'She wanted me to be like them. Never to be afraid, to do my duty, to put honour before everything. I may have to work as a servant, but I can still strive to lead my life with honour.'

He seemed like one of the ronin himself, Taka thought, as if he too was Oishi Kuranosuke, pretending to be someone he was not.

'You're not a servant, Nobu-*sama*,' she said. She reached out and took his hand, amazed at her own boldness in doing something so improper. His palm was rather rough and hard and she could feel the heat of it.

He closed his large fingers around her smaller ones. 'I can't believe I'm here with you,' he said. 'It's like a dream. It can't be true.'

A wind blew up, rustling the trees; it seemed to hold the spirits of the forty-seven warriors. Threads of incense smoke rose from before each tomb, filling the air with the solemn smell. They stood for a while in silence.

'I'm sorry my brother was so unkind to you,' Taka said softly. There was so much to be said, so little time to say it.

'He had your honour and your best interests at heart.'

'He said you'd helped him. I was so happy to find out where you were.'

'He didn't need my help. Some ruffians were pushing him around, that's all. I didn't want you to hear I'd been in the Yoshiwara. You must think I'm not a man of honour.'

Clouds scudded across the moon, obscuring it.

As they walked out of the graveyard they saw the glint of water. Beside the path was a small well surrounded by a bamboo fence, with rocks and ferns around it – the 'spring on the hill' where the ronin had washed the villainous Lord Kira's head. Nearby was a stall manned by a shaven-headed priest.

'We should buy incense,' said Taka.

Nobu was looking at the amulets laid out in rows, containing prayers for good health or wealth or protection on the road. 'Sengaku amulets must be particularly powerful,' he said. He picked one out and bought it. Taka felt the touch of his fingers on hers as he put it into her hand. She took it, a small brocade pouch of red silk, with the name of the temple – Sengaku – embroidered in gold and a prayer concealed inside. It was as small and light as a feather. 'All-round good fortune. A keepsake to remember the forty-seven by – and tonight.'

'It only has half a year left,' said the priest apologetically. 'Half a year of good fortune.' Amulets always expired at the end of the year.

'I'll keep it with me always.' Taka tucked it into the sleeve of her yukata as they went to light incense in front of Kuranosuke's grave. She bowed her head, wishing the gods could stop the movement of time.

'Come,' she said, taking his hand again. 'Let's go to the bamboo grove.'

They walked through the bamboos, hearing the whisper of branches sweeping low under the weight of all the paper wishes.

'I want to thank you, madam. I'm in the army now. When I heard I'd been accepted it was the best day of my life. And it was all because of you that I passed the examinations. I'm so grateful for the help you gave me. I've never forgotten how we used to sit together and read. And you, madam . . .' His tone changed. He dropped her hand and moved a little apart from her. 'Your brother told me you are to be married. I should offer my congratulations.'

He bowed stiffly. Taka had wanted so badly to talk about this dreaded marriage with him; that was why she had summoned him, she remembered now. But now he was here she could hardly bear to think about it.

'It's not my doing. I have no choice in the matter,' she said, staring at him wildly.

'My lady your mother is good and kind and cares about you. She wouldn't force you into marrying someone you don't care for.'

She sighed helplessly. Maybe he was right. He was two years older than her, he was an adult, and she'd always been taught that adults had all the answers. 'She's convinced herself it's the best for me and that I'll be happy in the end,' she said miserably.

There was a fizz and a bang and a lone firework exploded in the sky. In the momentary flash, she saw his face clearly lit in the garish light. He looked hungry, haunted.

'So this is the only chance I'll have to see you, my weaver princess,' he said abruptly, in tones of yearning. She started. It was not at all what she had expected him to say. The waves lapping on the shore of the bay made a lonely sound. The hugeness of the sea, the black sky sprinkled with stars, spreading to infinity, made her feel tiny and lost and desolate.

'When are you going back to the barracks?' she asked, her voice shaking. She felt the weight of the amulet in her sleeve. 'Will you come and see me once more?'

A familiar pair of clogs clattered towards them across the graveyard – Okatsu, come to summon her home.

Nobu took her hand in both of his and held it firmly. 'I'll find a way. I promise,' he said.

12

Nobu watched as the two slight figures in their cotton yukatas pattered down the road, looking back again and again to bow. He waited until they merged into darkness, then turned slowly and set off on the long hike back to Mori's house.

Nobu was used to running after his master's horse or behind his rickshaw; for him, walking was no hardship. Striding along the Eastern Sea Road beneath the Tanabata lanterns with their paper tails hanging limp in the humid air, he had time to think. Usually he rushed about incessantly while Bunkichi and Zenkichi kept up a non-stop flow of banter. It was a rare luxury to be on his own.

There was something niggling at him, something that refused to be pushed to the back of his mind. Again and again his thoughts returned to the forty-eight tomb-stones, laid out in tidy rows in their enclosure, lit by pale strands of moonlight. They seemed to loom over him, gazing down in silent reproof, reminding him that he had committed an inexcusable offence: he had neglected his duty.

He had told the thugs who had attacked Eijiro that the war was over, that talk of north and south was irrelevant now, but he had known very well that that was not the case. The Satsuma and their allies had taken all the government positions and all the good jobs while the men of Aizu and the northern clans were reduced to the lives of servants and rickshaw pullers. Truly, the men of the south had harnessed the eel of prosperity while the northerners – his people – had slithered off its tail. Even if he failed to avenge his clan and his family, at the very least he should not be consorting with a daughter of the enemy.

The thought of Taka made him grimace in pain. He could still smell the perfume that scented her glossy hair. His thoughts lingered on the smooth oval of her face, her skin, soft and pale as pear blossom, her large solemn eyes that seemed to have grown darker and more fascinating since he'd seen her last, the graceful way she put her hands over her mouth and looked up shyly when she smiled.

When he'd known her before they'd been children. She'd been a bashful fourteen-year-old, by turns boisterous and confident then blushing with embarrassment, living in a world of wealth and beauty while he, the poor servant, could only watch and admire from a distance. But then this sweet young girl had taken him under her wing, become his stern teacher while he was her gawky pupil. How could he not have become totally devoted to her? At the time he'd hardly understood his own feelings.

Over the years they'd been apart, the devotion she had inspired had lessened to a dull ache. Her memory had lingered like a daydream, comforting him when life became unbearable. Seeing her had reawakened his yearning and turned it into a fever.

There were so many reasons why he should forget her. She was beautiful and wealthy, that in itself put her out of his reach. Worst of all, she was Kitaoka's daughter – Kitaoka, who had marched at the head of the southern armies and wrested Edo Castle out of northern hands by trickery, fooled the gullible northern leaders into handing it over without even a fight. She was not just unattainable; to desire her was to betray everything he believed in and cared for – his family, his clan, his honour. She'd bewitched him, he thought fiercely. He had to free himself.

Suddenly enraged, he shook his head as if trying to shake off the spell she'd cast over him and punched his fist into his palm, shouting 'Fool!' at the top of his voice, oblivious to whoever might hear him. Breaking into a run, he sprinted towards the centre of the city, legs pumping, throat tight, furious at himself for his stupid infatuation and at her for trapping him like this, thinking he might be able to put her out of his mind if he ran fast enough.

Bells boomed from the shadowy temples behind the trees. He pounded across New Bridge and along narrow streets lit with softly glowing lanterns in front of shuttered geisha houses, hearing ghostly singing and laughter and the clinking of sake cups from the pleasure boats that plied the canal. Pausing to catch his breath and wipe off the sweat that dripped into his eyes, he heard the harsh tones of southern brogue and scowled, remembering that the country's overlords whiled away their nights in this part of town. He had been here once before with Mori and sat hugging his knees in the antechamber of one of the teahouses, watching the swaggering yokels grabbing at geishas' skirts.

Across another bridge gas lamps flared, lighting the sky. Even at this hour throngs of people ambled up and down, gawping at the garish brick and stone buildings that lined the Ginza. Nobu passed the sign outside the Black Peony restaurant and swung away abruptly, remembering that fateful day when he had burst in and met Taka and her family. They belonged to this harshly lit new world; but it was closed to him and he wanted no part of it.

By the time he reached Mori's house, he was soaked in sweat. The moon was high in the sky. He'd been away for hours. 'Fool!' he muttered again. Mori would be furious, he might even dismiss him, and Nobu badly needed the money to support his brothers.

As he slid open the door, a wave of rancid air washed out, dank and sweaty. Bunkichi's snores reverberated like a temple bell. Creeping in on tiptoe, Nobu stumbled over a large body. The man grunted and started to his feet.

Even in the dark, Nobu knew him – Jubei, his brother Yasutaro's ex-servant, a bluff giant who had been champion sumo wrestler of his village. Yasutaro had long since dismissed him – these days he couldn't afford even one servant – but Jubei continued to visit and check on him and on Kenjiro.

'*Usss*,' Jubei grunted. Nobu grabbed his sleeve and pulled him into the street. It was good to hear the rough northern greeting but the sight of him filled Nobu with alarm. Something must have happened to one of Nobu's brothers and Jubei had come to fetch him but

Nobu hadn't been here. He'd been too caught up in his foolish adventure with this girl.

'Your brother Kenjiro.' Jubei crinkled his fleshy brow. 'Seems poorly. Master Yasu is away so I came to look for you, sir.'

Nobu grimaced. He would have to beg Mori for more time off. His only hope was that Shige, Mori's mistress, would speak up on his behalf. He brushed a quick note to her, promising to be back by midday.

They snatched a couple of hours' sleep and set off before dawn, following the outer moat of the castle. The ramparts had been torn down, leaving an open expanse dotted with trees and clumps of tumbledown wall. The outer walls of the castle, visible now across the empty land, rose desolate against the sky.

'Every day that passes, there's more gone,' said Jubei, shaking his large head. It was true. The high walls that had lined the lanes, the mansions with their latticed windows where women used to peek out, the guard-houses, the tenements for the samurai guards, had all vanished. The new regime was set on demolishing everything Nobu had ever known or valued or cared for.

Nobu's brothers lived in a run-down district near the gate at Kanda Bridge, in a rented house. At one time it must have been part of a tenement where samurai lived, in the grounds of a daimyo's palace, but the lacquered gates and splendid mansion had been destroyed in the civil war or torn down shortly afterwards. A rank smell of wood ash, sewage and rotting food tickled his nostrils. As they picked their way across the rubble, Nobu spotted the big iron cooking pot he'd bought for them, tucked under the eaves on a mound of rocks and tiles.

Pushing the door back in its grooves, he nearly fell over Kenjiro, huddled on a thin futon in the middle of the room. The sweet musty smell of sickness hung about the place. Yasu was nowhere to be seen.

Nobu crouched down and put his hand on Kenjiro's brow. His brother's eyes were jaundiced and his skin sallow and he was clammy and covered in sweat. He stared up at Nobu, his breath rasping noisily.

'*Usss*,' he croaked. 'Younger Brother is it, and at this hour? You'll be out of a job if you're not careful.' He tried to sit up and fell back, scowling in exasperation. 'I need to get back to work myself.'

'I'll fetch you a drink.' Nobu looked around for a water flask. The small room was neat and tidy, the thin rush mats on the wooden floor well swept. Kenjiro's spectacles lay alongside brushes, ink stone, ink stick and paper on the low table where he did his writing, and there were books piled in heaps on the floor – Chinese classics, neatly bound, works by Saikaku, Bakin and other Japanese authors and even a couple of volumes in western languages. Nobu made out the titles: *On the Origin of Species* and *Das Kapital*. He wondered how Kenjiro had managed to acquire them when he had so little money. He probably saved his last *mon* to spend on books, or perhaps the barbarians he interpreted for had given them to him.

He smiled to himself. Kenjiro was a prime exemplar of the proverb 'Men of talent are prone to sickness and beautiful women destined to die young.' Forever coming down with one ailment or another, he passed the time studying and with the help of a fellow Aizu samurai had learned English well enough to act as an interpreter. He'd been working for a couple of foreign technicians setting up a telegraph system in the provinces and had come down to Tokyo when the assignment ended; but, as they had all discovered, there were very few opportunities of any sort for a northerner, even one as bright as he was.

Nobu poured Kenjiro a cup of water and found him a small rice-husk-filled pillow. Kenjiro sat up and seemed to rally a little. '*Comment vont les études?*' he asked in clumsy French.

Nobu grinned. 'No time for *études* with the fighting dog nipping at my heels.'

Kenjiro chuckled. 'Ah, Mori, the Tosa fighting dog. Well, you'll be back at the Military Academy soon enough.'

Nobu nodded, grimacing. 'Yasu not here?'

'Must have slipped out while I was asleep.' Kenjiro leaned forward, his bony forehead damp with sweat, and gripped Nobu's wrist. 'You know what? It was Tanabata yesterday – the seventh day of the seventh month. I had to count up the days on my fingers. This new calendar's just a ploy to make us forget our festivals, our Chinese learning, everything. The old calendar tied us to our roots; this one pitches us into the future. They tell us we have to discard the past and move forward, but they're wrong. The old ways are part of what we are. Anyway, I've chosen my pen name: Wanderer of the Eastern Seas, like the cowherd crossing the magpie bridge.'

'You'll have to get well before you start wandering,' said Nobu. 'What happened to those clams?'

The last time Nobu had visited he'd gone down to the river behind one of the newly completed brick and stone government buildings and dug up some clams, said to be an excellent remedy for jaundice. He'd boiled them just as his mother used to, with a handful of ash to make the clams separate from their shells, then simmered them in soy sauce and a dash of sweet *mirin* cooking wine. He'd also boiled up batches of beans and wrapped them in bamboo leaves for Kenjiro to eat. There was still some left in a pot under a shelf. He dished up a bowlful and gave it to him.

He was instructing Jubei on how to find and cook the clams when the door creaked open and Yasutaro came in, ducking his head under the lintel.

'*Usss*. You here too, Younger Brother?' he said.

He looked tired and his limp was more pronounced than usual, as if he'd walked a long way. He'd never fully recovered from being shot in the leg in the fighting eight years earlier.

Nobu studied his face. He remembered how grey and drawn he'd looked that day Jubei and some other young soldiers had brought him to their uncle's house on a stretcher. He'd never uttered a sound though Nobu could see that his leg was bent at a strange angle and blood was oozing through the bandages. Nobu had been ten at the time. He'd been out playing and had been so excited to see his brother he'd run around the house shouting that he was back. Yasu hadn't been able to stand. He'd crawled around the tatami using his hands and his good leg.

Nobu remembered the urgent discussions that had gone on. They'd all been worried Yasutaro would be captured if he stayed in the house and had decided to hide him in a ravine in the mountains. Nobu and Jubei had carried him there and made a bed for him out of boards and camouflaged it with a roof of leafy branches. They'd stayed there with him. Jubei had washed Yasu's wound every day with water from a mountain spring and changed the dressings and Nobu had sneaked out after nightfall to fetch food from the house and bury the soiled bandages.

Yasutaro had been ill for a long time. He had been taciturn even before he was wounded and afterwards had turned even more inwards. Nobu had grown expert at noticing the tiniest sign of joy or grief or anger.

Yasu eased himself down on his knees on the floor, grunting as he manipulated his injured leg. Nobu poured him some water.

'What news of the great world?' demanded Kenjiro, his eyes glittering.

Yasu sat for a while, staring at the ground. When he looked up, there was the hint of a twinkle in his eye. 'They say the government's going to abolish samurai stipends.'

'Stipends? What stipends?' said Kenjiro gleefully. 'When we lost the war that was the end of stipends for us. The potato samurai need their stipends, though – without their stipends they'll be in trouble. First they lose their swords, now their incomes. They should have stayed on their sweet potato farms, not come up here throwing their weight around, brandishing their hoes and spades. They'll finally get some idea of how we northerners feel – and about time, too.'

'They'll get jobs easily enough,' said Yasutaro grimly. 'We'll still be at the bottom of the heap.'

'Well, at least we can enjoy our enemies' downfall.'

'Things are getting serious,' said Yasu in measured tones. 'They're forming militias down south. They've got their own military academies there and they're training and carrying out manoeuvres. The word is that the governor of Kagoshima has refused to implement the new mandate. As far as he's concerned, there'll be no abolishing of stipends in Kagoshima or anywhere in the Satsuma lands. There's even talk that Satsuma may rise against the government and declare independence.'

'The government is half Satsuma men. If they rise against the government they rise against themselves. It's as the Chinese sages say. The wise man waits and his enemies tear each other to pieces, like Tosa fighting dogs.'

Nobu was aware of a dryness in his mouth and a queasy sensation in his stomach. There was a thought gnawing at him. He'd been trying to push it away but he couldn't keep it at bay any longer. Taka's father. Everyone knew he'd been one of the leading figures in the government and had stormed out several years ago and gone back to his home base in the south. His name was on everyone's lips – Kitaoka the Great. He must be one of the leaders of this rebellion.

'The Satsuma, you say,' he said. 'So Kitaoka . . .'

'It's politics,' said Kenjiro. 'You're too young to understand.'

Yasutaro looked at Nobu with big sad eyes.

'No one knows what game General Kitaoka's playing. He's biding his time. No one even knows where he is. Everyone's waiting to see what he does. If he gives the word the south will rise, if he doesn't they may still rise. Or they may not.'

'And if they rise . . .'

'They'll send the army to put down the insurrection and we'll all join up. We'll get our own back on the potato samurai.'

13

'Cut off our stipends? Next thing you know they'll be cutting off our balls!'

Eijiro's bellow rattled the paper doors, skimming through the empty rooms to the distant wing where Taka sat on her knees with their mother, Fujino, sewing. Even on the other side of the house she could hear that his words were slurred. His behaviour made her cringe. Drinking with his cronies again. In recent days these drinking parties had become longer and noisier and now went on well into the night.

Taka was stitching together a couple of squares of silk in the flickering light of the oil lamps, attaching the sleeve of one of her wedding kimonos, wiping her hands on a piece of cotton so as not to stain the expensive brocade. She could hardly concentrate for the noise. Transparent moths flitted around the flames. The air was hot and moist. In the darkness outside the circle of light, the doors had been taken out to allow the tiniest breeze to flow through.

A voice growled in Satsuma brogue. 'This government. Every time it's the same. Cut your hair, they say – if you like, that is. Then a couple of years later, we're to chop off our topknots – by law.'

'Come on, Yamakawa,' yelled a dissenter. 'You flaunt your cropped cut as proud as any of us!'

The speaker carried on, his voice heavy with irony. 'No need for swords any more – *if* you like. Then, a couple of years later, they tell us, no swords to be worn by law. And now what do we hear? Trade in your stipends for government bonds *if* you like. Then – you thought you had a stipend, but you don't, not any more. Have some government bonds instead, by law. They're taking everything. By all the gods, what use are government bonds to me? How am I supposed to live without a stipend?'

The chink of sake cups was nearly drowned by the roar of outraged agreement and the thunder of fists on the floor.

Shouts went up. 'For this we fought? For this our brothers died? For a country where samurai can't wear swords or dress as samurai and where they cut off our money? We don't even have jobs, we can't even be soldiers any more. They're rounding up peasants to fight now, as if peasants have the faintest idea what to do with a sword. The very thought of it . . .'

Taka felt a prick and dropped the fabric as a spot of red blossomed on her fingertip. She knew these friends of Eijiro's. Eijiro had grown up in Kyoto but these were hard-drinking, hard-fighting southern lads, Satsuma to the core. Some had minor jobs in the government, others no jobs at all. They were happy enough to swagger around the Yoshiwara in peacetime, acting the playboy, but it was obvious they were champing at the bit, itching for the chance to pick up their swords again.

'They want to turn us into weaklings and women,' shouted the first voice. 'I didn't spend my life notching up honours as a swordsman just to end up wielding a writing brush.'

'You're lucky to be wielding a brush,' responded another. 'Most of us don't have jobs at all. If we can't get our stipends, how are we going to live? And our parents, what are they supposed to do?'

Eijiro's tones soared loud and clear. 'What do they expect us to do – sell our swords and set up shop? Soil our hands with money, like filthy merchants?'

Fujino slapped down her sewing, her plump brow creased into thick furrows of disdain. 'What nonsense. He has money enough to redeem his precious Tsukasa, money enough to show off to his cronies night after night. How much does he need?'

Taka stared in surprise. Usually her mother wouldn't hear a word of criticism of her beloved son.

'They steal our self-respect, everything that makes a man a man, and leave us with nothing. Nothing!' boomed Eijiro. 'The dignity and honour of the samurai class is at stake. We're frittering away our lives in this filthy city. Let's get back to our mountains, our volcanoes, our palm trees, our good Kyushu rice wine! Are you with me, lads? Will you come down to Kagoshima and join my father?'

The men drummed their fists and heels on the floor until the house shook. There was a roar. 'To arms! Kagoshima! Let's go!'

Fujino's eyes flashed dangerously. 'Fool! He's never even been there! How dare he bring your father into it. It's all bluster. They'll do nothing, none of them. Like him.'

Eijiro's voice rose again. 'Okatsu, Gonza, Osan. Useless servants, never around when you need them. Mother, where are you? Sake, now! My guests are waiting!'

Fujino rested a hand on the floor and heaved herself to her feet with surprising speed, her face black. 'They treat this place like a teahouse. What do they take me for? Son or no son, I'm having no more of it. They can take themselves off to the Yoshiwara where these sorts of rowdy gatherings belong.'

She drew herself up, tucked her yukata into place around her large bosom and sailed out.

Sighing, Taka put down her needlework. Even Okatsu had been pressed into serving at the party. Taka pictured her smiling good-naturedly, dodging Eijiro's friends as they grabbed at her skirts. The youths were belting out a Satsuma drinking song. She could hear them stamping and clapping.

Taka went to the veranda and gazed out into the night. Tall bamboos swayed against the sky. She made out the gnarled shapes of pine trees, stone lanterns looming like ghosts and the dark hollow where the path wriggled off around the lake and into the woods.

She chewed her lip. They'd lived in this beautiful house for so long, she'd almost forgotten Kyoto and the dark days of fighting, yet here was Eijiro stirring up trouble again. As long as she could remember, her brother had always been looking for a fight. There'd been too many years of inaction. All these lads were longing for a cause, something to get fired up about, to fight for, die for if necessary.

Eijiro had mentioned their father. It was years since

their beloved father had been in Tokyo, yet everyone still spoke his name in tones of awe. The longer he was away, the more he seemed some god-like being, as if he'd become more than human. He'd come to stand for something greater than himself. Whenever Eijiro or anyone else wanted to criticize the new regime with all the changes it was bringing about, they invoked his name.

Taka had tried asking Eijiro what was going on, but he just said, 'Stick to your sewing, little girl. Don't poke your nose into men's affairs.'

'Your job is to prepare for your wedding and learn how to keep house,' Fujino told her. 'And then to have babies. Leave politics to the menfolk. Remember: a clever woman never lets a man know how clever she is. Never forget that.' And no matter how much Taka had pressed her she wouldn't say more.

Suddenly there was a sound somewhere in the grounds – the rustle of bushes, the pad of running feet. Taka started, her heart pounding, and listened intently, hoping she'd imagined it, praying she'd been mistaken. There was another sound, quite distinct – a twig cracking, as if there was a fox or a badger out there, or an intruder.

It was all too likely in these dangerous times that an assassin would creep in, stealthy as a ninja. There had been rebellions down south; even she knew that. Uncle Shimpei – her father's old colleague Eto Shimpei, who'd been minister of justice when her father was in charge of the government – had been at the head of one a couple of years ago. She'd overheard her mother talking about it with Aunt Kiharu in hushed tones. Apparently it had been put down and he'd been executed. Only the other day a member of the government had been murdered, and Taka knew her father had many enemies who might target his family too. There were guards at the gates, even more at night, and the walls were very high, but someone really determined could still scramble over.

Branches creaked in the darkness and gravel crunched underfoot. Whoever it was, he was very near the house. For a moment there was silence. Not even a mosquito buzzed. Taka held her breath and clenched her fists so tightly her nails dug into her palms. Then she glimpsed a shadowy figure, darting between the trees.

Trembling, she felt for the dagger in her sash and clutched it feverishly. Peering into the blackness she made out a tall lanky body, then a head and a pair of blazing eyes. She let out a gasp as she recognized the intruder: Nobu. He scowled and put a finger to his lips.

Behind her the drinking song echoed through the stillness. The voices fell silent and Taka heard her mother's clipped, angry tones.

Nobu stepped up to the veranda, his features etched in the lamplight. He was panting. There were leaves and bits of twig in his hair and his cheeks were streaked with dirt, but it was the expression on his face that frightened her. He looked hunted, almost crazed. He glanced around, wild-eyed, and Taka realized with a shock of horror that if her brother found him there, he'd cut him down for sure.

She stared at him, aghast.

Five days had passed since they had walked in the grounds of Sengaku Temple. She had counted the hours and days, repeating his words. 'I'll find a way to see you again,' he'd said. 'I promise.' Okatsu had warned her sternly that it would be impossible for him to get a note to her but she'd refused to listen. 'He promised,' she'd said again and again.

But when the silence continued she had finally despaired and told herself that she never wanted to hear from him again. She scolded herself. She'd been too forward. How could she have taken his hand and talked to him about whatever was in her mind? She'd been carried away, but now she'd come to her senses. He was a servant, she the daughter of a famous and important man.

And, though he kept quiet about it, she knew perfectly well he was an Aizu, an enemy. Eijiro always said northerners were traitors, degenerates, poor, backward, uneducated, who lived in hovels and hardly even knew how to use chopsticks. They were barely human, born to be servants, unfit for anything else. Maybe she'd been wrong to be taken in by him. Much though it went against the grain even to think such a thing, maybe Eijiro had been right. After all, her father had fought them in battle and her mother had had to beat them off when they hammered at her door in Kyoto. Surely Taka would be betraying her whole family if she even spoke to such vermin.

But seeing him standing before her, his skinny calves bare, his jacket torn and dirty, her anger entirely drained away. He caught his breath and his face cleared. She no longer noticed his dusty hair and stained clothes, all she was aware of were his full lips and proud nose and the hollows in his cheeks. She hadn't realized how handsome he'd become. It made her feel quite shy.

'You came!' she whispered, glancing over her

shoulder, afraid she might see Fujino's huge shadow approaching. But there was no one. 'How did you get in?'

He grinned. His face changed and for a moment he was the urchin she remembered.

'I climbed in. I know these gardens. It was a bit dark. I tripped over a few times.' He hesitated and glanced around. 'I need to talk to you,' he added sharply. 'Are you alone?' The look in his eyes made her uneasy.

Taka nodded. She picked up her skirts and, with a thrill of excitement at doing something so forbidden, jumped down on to the gravel and slid her feet through the thongs of a pair of geta clogs. She waited for her eyes to get used to the dark then hurried away from the house as quietly as she could. She heard Nobu padding behind her as the blackness swallowed them up.

Sticking to the paths, watching out for stones and snakes and sharp-edged leaves, they skirted the bamboo grove, breathing the rich scents of warm soil and growing plants. It was a beautiful night. Stalks creaked and swayed above them. They cut through the landscaped gardens and around the artificial hill, then crossed a half-moon bridge, leaning over to gaze at the carp that darted below them, silvery backs glinting in the starlight. The sounds of the party faded into the distance as they picked their way through the heavy darkness behind the lake. Bats flittered and swooped and Taka jumped as an owl shrieked.

Deep in the woods, they reached a tiny grove, with branches arching overhead and a fallen tree to sit on. Lights twinkled from the great house below them.

'Our secret place,' Nobu said softly.

They threw themselves down on the dry leaves, catching their breath, leaning their backs against the crumbling tree trunk. Taka smiled as she rested her shoulder against his. They had often sat like that when they were children. He drew a little away from her and took a breath.

'I didn't mean to bother you,' he said, his voice hoarse. 'I should have kept away, but I couldn't stop myself. I was passing your house and saw the rickshaws at the gate and could tell there was a party going on. I guessed everyone would be busy so I climbed in. I thought I might catch a glimpse of you in the room where we used to sit. And there you were, on the veranda.' There was a rustle as he stirred a pile of leaves with his foot. 'I wanted to warn you. There may be trouble.'

Taka felt a jolt of fear.

'Eijiro,' she said, almost to herself. 'He and those friends of his. The war was supposed to be over, but they can't stop fighting, even though it was us that won . . .'

Her voice tailed off and she stopped in mid-sentence, realizing what she'd said. Nobu pulled back as if she'd slapped him. There was a long silence.

'N'da. You got it.' His voice was raw. His Edo accent had fallen away and she heard the fierce northern vowels loud and clear, as if he'd cast off his skin like a snake and revealed something different and chilling underneath. 'You won. My people lost.' She sat hardly daring to breathe. Around them branches rustled and somewhere not far away an animal, a monkey, perhaps, screamed. He gave a long sigh.

'We're not ones for fighting,' he said quietly. 'We've got no heart for fighting any more. We expect nothing, we're grateful for whatever comes our way. But your people – your brother, his friends – they think they deserve the world. They won and now they want their dues.'

His breathing was ragged. She felt for his hand, expecting him to snatch it away. It lay unmoving under hers.

'Not you,' he said softly. 'You're young, you're different.' Insects murmured. The woods were alive around them.

'I don't understand what's happening either,' he went on. 'But I'll try and explain as much as I know. From what I hear, this great government of ours, these fine statesmen who lord it over us, they want to make us all the same – no more samurai or artisans or farmers or merchants, not even outcastes. They want to do away with the caste system, they say. But that means the highest caste has to lose its privileges – and that's the samurai. It makes no difference to us. We northern samurai have nothing to lose, we've lost everything already. No, the winning side, the Tosa clan, the Hizen people, the Choshu men and your lot, the Satsuma, the very same clans who are running the country. That's the strange thing about it. They won, for sure, but now the government wants to take away the spoils of victory, so they feel cheated. That's why they're angry, your brother and his friends.'

Taka was listening hard, trying to make sense of what he was saying. There was something so honest and straightforward about him, she instinctively believed and trusted him.

'You know what we call you Satsuma?' She waited, hardly daring to imagine. 'Potato samurai.' The words made her laugh aloud and she was relieved to hear him chuckle. 'You know what we say about them? Rough tempers and rude tongues.'

'Is that what you think of me?' Taka said uncertainly, stung by the rebuff.

'You're only half Satsuma. The other half is pure Kyoto, like your mother.' There was a long silence. When Nobu spoke again, he sounded hesitant. 'You know your father may be involved?'

Taka frowned. She'd suspected this was coming. 'My father was in the government,' she said, doing her best to keep her voice level and calm.

'He was chief counsellor and commander-in-chief of the army and commander of the Imperial Guard.'

'But he left and we hardly ever hear from him any more. I thought it was because he's with his wife and real family and doesn't think about us.' Her eyes filled with tears and she blinked them away.

A bullfrog honked in the lake below them. Others joined in in a great chorus until it sounded as if all the bells in the city's temples were pealing.

'He'll be back one day,' he said softly. 'You'll marry and have a good life and this talk of trouble will be forgotten. It was selfish and wrong of me to come. Your mother knows what's best for you. You shouldn't waste your time with me.'

He pulled his hand away from hers. Trembling, she grabbed his arm. 'Don't go,' she said, forcing back tears. She tried to steady her voice but her words tailed off into a sob.

Reaching up in the darkness, she found his cheek. She touched her fingers to the hint of bristle on his jaw, then ran them slowly, lightly, over his face, searching out the bump of his nose, the hollows of his eyes, his damp brow, his ears, his Adam's apple and the funny mole on his neck. She felt like a blind person trying to memorize every contour, to fix them in her mind for ever. Her fingers roamed across his mouth, feeling the warmth of his breath and the soft moisture of his lips. She put her arms around him and leaned her head on his shoulder.

She sat for a while, conscious that she was doing something forbidden. But all she could think of was his closeness, his warmth next to hers. Their bodies nested together perfectly, as if they were made for each other. Then she felt his touch, soft and hesitant and shy. He brushed the top of her head, then fumbled with her hair until he managed to loosen it. It swung around her face and spilt in a heavy coil on to her lap. He took up hand-fuls and ran his fingers through it, slowly and wonderingly.

'Like silk,' he said. 'I always wanted to touch it but I never dared.'

He took a breath and then very tentatively, as if he expected her to tell him to stop, he touched the back of her neck. A shiver ran through her, as if something inside her that she didn't know existed was coming alive.

'You're so beautiful, so perfect,' he said. 'I know it's wrong, but this is my only chance. There'll never be another.'

She sat up sharply. 'Why not? Why not?'

'You're young still, you don't understand. I have to go back to the Military Academy, you have to get married, our families are enemies.'

'We'll run away like the lovers in kabuki plays. We'll commit love suicide.'

'Those are stories, this is real life.'

He lifted her chin as if he was trying to see her face in the darkness and she felt his mouth finding her nose and cheek. Then his lips met hers. She shut her eyes and abandoned herself to the moist darkness, letting her body dissolve into his until they were so closely entwined it felt as if nothing could ever come between them.

They heard the creak of rickshaw wheels in the distance and the yells of the runners and realized the party was over. Fujino was shouting, 'Taka, Taka! Where are you?'

Nobu drew back but Taka pressed closer. 'Let her worry,' she said, nuzzling her face into his shoulder. 'She'll think I've gone off somewhere. I often do. The grounds are so huge I could be anywhere.'

He sighed. 'I know what I am and where I belong and who my people are. We have so little left, it binds us together. Yet I can't think of you and your family as the enemy. My brothers would call me a traitor if they heard me say that. But it's true. To me you're more important than anything.'

She knelt on the dry leaves, feeling the stony ground press into her shins, and took his hands.

'If I was a courtesan I'd cut off my little finger and prove my love to you with my blood,' she said solemnly.

'But instead I give you my word. This is my vow. If there's some way we can be together we'll find it. I'll never be with anyone else.'

'There never has been anyone but you,' he said. 'There never will be.'

14

Crashing through the bushes, soaked in sweat, Nobu wondered if he'd gone completely mad. Here he was, in the bowels of the enemy, streaking across the labyrinthine grounds of the Kitaoka estate like a fox with a bear on its tail; yet all he could think of was Taka. The scent of her perfume clung to his clothes, he could almost feel the touch of her lips and warm body. His head swam. He hardly knew where he was or where he was going.

Stopping to catch his breath, he groaned aloud. He had duties and responsibilities and to want a woman, let alone one so far out of his reach, was sheer folly. They could never be together, he knew that perfectly well. Yet every time he had to wrench himself away, he left a part of himself behind.

Stumbling blindly through the trees, he'd reached the edge of the estate. The wall towered in front of him. Hearing a sound behind him, he snapped to his senses, glad of a distraction to block the clamour of thoughts. There were voices and flickering lights – a patrol, he guessed, guarding the estate. If they spotted him, he'd be dead. They wouldn't stop to ask questions.

The moon was rising, casting a watery light. It made it easier to see but also made him more visible. He cupped his hands to his mouth and gave a long, low hoot, like an owl.

Jubei, Yasu's former servant, had given Nobu a leg up on his way in and had said he'd keep a lookout, though Nobu suspected that after such a long time he'd probably have given up or fallen asleep. So he was relieved to hear an answering call.

He stood at the bottom of the wall, looking up. It was as high as a house, of packed earth and stone with a steep tiled roof. He started to clamber up, fumbling for footholds and grabbing at the overhanging eaves, then a tile snapped off in his hands and he tumbled back down with a clatter of pebbles, cursing.

The voices and dancing lights were getting closer. Gritting his teeth, he heaved himself up and poked his head over the roof ridge, keeping low. Jubei was lurking in the shadows a little way away.

Nobu knew he had to get a move on but still he hesitated. There was another owl cry. Jubei was getting impatient. Grimly he turned. Despite everything, he needed to have one last look – at the grounds engulfed in darkness, the shadowy trees and bobbing lanterns and the distant lights of the mansion. He felt the heat that rose in waves from the soil, breathed the scents of the pine trees and the sweet *yugao* flowers, heard the cry of a reed warbler, the trickle of a waterfall and the cool 'tock' of a bamboo pipe striking a stone. It was Amida Buddha's western paradise, a forbidden land where he could never again set foot. That was where Taka belonged, and he was condemned for ever to be outside it.

He frowned. This was no time for foolish thoughts. He turned back and Jubei gave him a hand as he jumped down.

'*Usss*,' Jubei grunted. In the darkness Nobu could see his gap-toothed grin. His sturdy legs were bare and his broad forehead under his knotted handkerchief glistened with sweat. In his blue cotton jacket with a crest on the back he looked like a workman or a porter or the rough gambler he was.

It hadn't taken much to persuade him to come along. Jubei was always up for action, no matter how hare-brained. Nobu had told him that he wanted to look around the Kitaoka estate. Everyone said Kitaoka was behind the trouble brewing on the southern island of Kyushu and he might get wind of a plot if there was one. He'd worked at the Kitaoka mansion, he knew his way around.

They'd strolled past the gates several times already. Then that night when they'd seen rickshaws milling outside Nobu had whispered that this was his chance to sneak in unnoticed. They'd gone round to a side wall of the estate and he'd climbed in, Jubei grinning hugely all the while. If he'd known his real purpose, Nobu thought, he would never have believed it.

When news came that the enemy armies had breached the city walls and the first contingents of warriors were summoned to the defence of the castle, Nobu had been a child. He remembered sitting on his knees in the great hall at home in Aizu, with the kettle bubbling on the brazier and the smoke-blackened beams criss-crossing high above.

There were no classes any more; the school had been

requisitioned as a hospital. His sisters' voices rang out in the morning air, yelling war cries as they sparred with their wooden practice sticks in the garden, preparing for battle with deadly seriousness.

Frowning sternly, Yasu had informed Jubei that he released him from his service forthwith. There was no need for him to give up his life on their family's behalf. Jubei was to go home immediately, Yasu had told him, handing him a purse full of money.

Jubei's broad face had visibly swelled with indignation. 'How can you have such a low opinion of me, sir?' he'd demanded, staring stubbornly at the floor. 'I know I'm a good-for-nothing fellow but my family has served yours for generations. If your city is under attack I'll stay and fight in your defence. I know I'm supposed to obey orders, sir, but I absolutely refuse to leave.'

In the end Yasutaro had relented and thereafter they had fought side by side. Yasu and Kenjiro often laughed about Jubei's recklessness. Whenever he heard enemy troops, he'd head for the door, rifle in hand, and they'd had to grab his sleeve and pull him back. In battle he always made sure he was in the front line. Now, eight years later, he had taken a wife and opened a tofu shop, but he often complained that he could do with a bit of action and he still got into fights.

'Looks like the coast's clear, for the moment at least,' Jubei said, glancing around. 'We'd better get out of here. I tell you, you wouldn't get me scrambling up that wall if you paid me.'

'They were having a meeting,' said Nobu. 'Didn't hear much, but at least we know we can break in if we want to. Could be useful to keep an eye on them.'

He cocked an ear, listening for shouts on the other side of the wall, but there was silence. He seemed to have escaped unnoticed. Then he heard noises coming towards them from the darkness at the end of the road.

'Damn! Rickshaws. Better make ourselves scarce.'

He looked around sharply. They were in a singularly lonely part of town. The road was bordered on both sides with high earthen walls, without a single tree or bush for cover. The only possible hiding place was the moat which ran alongside the wall on the Kitaoka estate side. With no time to think, they dropped to their hands and knees and scrambled into it, praying to the gods that it was dry, and lay on the bottom as still as corpses, the long grass tickling their noses and insects buzzing around their eyes and faces.

The yells of the rickshaw drivers grew louder as the pounding of feet and clatter of wheels turned into a thunder. Then a voice shouted, 'Here, idiot! I said, here! You got no brains at all?'

There was a creaking and thumping as shafts hit the ground, followed by a bang and a squawk of 'Hey! Watch out!' It sounded as if a second rickshaw had had to swerve to avoid running into the one in front. Nobu grimaced as he recognized the accent. Satsuma, for sure, and drunk. Eijiro's friends, no doubt.

There was grunting and panting and a foot scraped on the earthen road.

'What're ya up to, Yamakawa?' the second voice whined. 'We nearly ran into you.'

Yamakawa. Nobu knew that name, one of Eijiro's cronies. Nobu used to see him when he visited the Kitaoka house, a stocky pugnacious youth with a thick neck and jutting jaw who stuck out his chest like a fighting cock. He'd been all deference when Eijiro was around but treated the servants like dogs.

'There was someone over there, by the wall.' Yamakawa's arrogant voice was familiar too, with its rough Satsuma inflections.

'The sake's affected your eyesight, my friend. Hurry up. Get back in your rickshaw or we'll never make it to Daimonji Teahouse. It was one yen we wagered, remember?'

'I tell you, I saw someone – or something.'

'Next you'll be saying it was a fox spirit. There's no one here.'

'Fox spirit? A thief more likely, one of those northern beggars. Kitaoka should keep the place better guarded. Get down and help me look around.'

Nobu held his breath as feet kicked the grass over his head, sending showers of soil on to his face. A small animal scampered along the bottom of the moat. The voices receded up the road. Mosquitoes buzzed and an owl hooted.

Jubei clenched his fists, bringing down another shower of dirt. 'Bastards,' he muttered. 'There's only two and they're blind drunk. Let's give them a scare. It's too long since I bruised my fist on a Satsuma skull.'

He shifted as if he was about to climb out.

'Hold it,' Nobu muttered, slapping a mosquito that had settled on his arm. 'There'll be more on their way.'

Jubei gave a grunt of disbelief. 'Since when did you baulk at a fight? Isn't this the lad that was so eager to climb into the Kitaoka residence?'

'Don't be crazy. You haven't even got a weapon,' said

Nobu, recalling his brothers' stories of what a hothead Jubei was. 'Remember your pride. We can't go round brawling like thugs. Yasu would be furious.'

All the same, Jubei had a point. It made no sense to climb into the Kitaoka residence and then refuse to fight a couple of drunken youths. The problem was that they were Taka's people and somehow that made them Nobu's too. It was hard to share Jubei's blind hatred of them any longer. He shook his head in bewilderment. The spell she had cast over him was taking away his fighting spirit and turning him into a weakling.

There was a belch and a hiccup. The voices were getting louder. The Satsuma men were on their way back.

'What did I tell you? There's no one around.'

'Gi's a moment.'

The footsteps were so close they could smell the sake on the men's breath. Nobu cringed as he heard fumbling and the rustle of starchy clothing. There was a rushing sound like a waterfall and the stench of urine filled the air. He wrinkled his nose as splashes stung his face. At least the bastard hadn't relieved himself right on top of them.

'I tell you it's driving me crazy, cooling my heels around here,' said Yamakawa's voice. 'It's all well and good hanging around the Yoshiwara, like those good-for-nothing northern thugs used to before we got rid of them. But it's not a life for a man.'

'We certainly showed them, though, didn't we! Aizu Castle, remember that? Now that was a battle!'

There was a chortle. 'The flames, yeah. Remember the boom when the gunpowder store blew? Like thunder! Some bonfire, that.'

'That was a brilliant campaign. I didn't put my sword back in its scabbard for a month. Rotting from all the blood, it was.'

'Do you remember those cannons of ours?'

'Fifty. What a noise.'

'And the garrison marching out with their heads shaved, flying their flag of surrender?'

'Pathetic crew, half-starved runts, the lot o' them. Yeah, that was what I call men's work. What I'd give to see action again!'

Nobu was exploding with fury. It was all he could do not to fling himself out and lay into the men. He could hear Jubei spluttering. Before Nobu could stop him, he sprang up, shouting, 'You want action, you murderous bastards, you can have it!'

Nobu leapt out after him.

The two men stumbled back gawping, eyes like plates, mouths hanging open, as if they thought these creatures flying straight out of the ground were tengu demons or corpses rising from their graves. One was Yamakawa, sure enough. Nobu knew that thick neck and fighting dog scowl. They were in western-style jackets and trousers, like dandies, and he noticed straight away that neither had their swords. In the dark, Yamakawa gave no sign of recognizing Nobu. He'd been a scrawny teenager and a mere servant when their paths had last crossed, he hadn't existed as far as Yamakawa was concerned.

The second man was slight with a pointed chin and tufty hair like a fox. He was shaking. 'I've done nothing wrong. Leave me alone,' he quavered.

Yamakawa had already recovered. 'They're peasants,

you fool, not ghosts. It's the riff-raff I saw climbing the wall.'

'Peasant yourself!' Jubei shouted. 'Murderous bastard! Get back to your potato fields, yokel!'

'Show some respect, dog. Bloody northerner, aren't you? Too bad we didn't cut you down sooner. I'll make up for that right away.'

Scowling, Jubei bunched his fists and stepped forward threateningly, looming over the short southerner. He aimed a punch at Yamakawa. The man ducked under his fist and stepped crisply aside, his eyes gleaming. He didn't look drunk at all. His hand flew to his belt.

'Watch out!' The words died on Nobu's lips as Yamakawa raised a fleshy arm. There was a flash like lightning in the moonlight. The southerner had a dagger in his hand. He gave a war cry like a banshee's shriek as he swung it up and before Nobu could move or even shout had driven it straight into Jubei's belly. The big man breathed out hoarsely as if he'd been punched and staggered back, clutching his stomach.

'Insolent peasant! That'll teach you to tangle with your betters!'

As Yamakawa twisted the knife and jerked it out Jubei fell to his knees. Blood oozed black through his fingers and his face slackened and turned grey. The world seemed to stop. Nobu was aware of the moon, three-quarters full, the long grass whispering in the breeze and the wall stretching into the distance. From somewhere inside the grounds came the mournful cry of a fox. Frozen with horror, he saw Jubei's cheeks grow hollow and his eyes sink in his head as his face became a death mask. The stench of butchery, of fresh blood and guts tumbling from the wound, made Nobu's stomach turn. He gagged as if it was he, not Jubei, who had been struck.

Yamakawa was standing over Jubei, a mocking smile on his broad face. 'Too bad,' he said, sneering. 'I wish I had my sword to test it on your neck.'

He raised his arm to strike again, lips pulled back in a snarl.

There was a bellow in the silence. It was Nobu's own voice. Suddenly he was alive again. He leapt into Yamakawa's path and stood over Jubei, legs apart, protecting him. His training took over. As the blade swung down he grabbed Yamakawa's thick wrist and twisted with all his might, using the man's own momentum to steer the dagger towards his chest. Yamakawa was burly and Nobu was slight but rage and grief gave him strength. They grappled for a moment before he felt the blade slide in.

As Yamakawa's grip loosened and he reeled, Nobu wrenched the knife from his hand and hacked at him grimly, feeling the blade cut through bone and gristle and flesh. Blood spurted from the man's face and chest and there was a hiss of air from a punctured lung as the southerner staggered and slumped to the ground, wheezing.

Somewhere behind Nobu there was a strangled scream. The second man was staring, wide-eyed. Footsteps ran towards them as other rickshaws approached.

'Jubei!' shouted Nobu. 'Let's get out of here.'

Jubei had crawled a little way away, then collapsed

on to his side. He was lying in a pool of blood. Nobu slipped his arm under his shoulders and tried to pick him up but he was a dead weight. He tried again but Jubei was too heavy. His eyes were open. Nobu put his hand to his mouth. No breath, nothing.

He looked around frantically. To abandon Jubei now would be to betray him twice over, but he had no choice. If he hesitated he would be dead himself. Gasping convulsively, he turned and ran, his heart racing and his mouth dry. His breath came in great pants. Hardly aware of where he was or where he was going, he ran blindly until he was far away from the road, the featureless wall and the dreadful scene of death. Then he doubled up and fell to his knees, sobbing with horror.

Jubei was dead and it was all his fault. He had hurt, probably killed Yamakawa, but that meant nothing. He could think of nothing but Jubei, Jubei – dead. He took his hands from his face. They were torn and battered. He was soaked to the skin in sweat and blood.

It was the doing of the gods, he thought, those fierce old gods that protected the northern clans. He'd known he was committing an unforgivable crime, consorting with that Satsuma girl, but he'd carried on regardless. And now they'd taken away this good and loyal man, made him their sacrificial victim, to punish him, Nobu, for his treachery.

'Not Jubei. Me! You should have taken me!' he shouted wildly, careless of who might hear. A wind rose like an answer from the gods and shook the trees. He could hear the waves beating on the shores of Edo Bay.

He was outside Sengaku Temple. The outer gate with

its steep tiled roof stood black against the sky. The forty-seven ronin entombed inside seemed to rise from their graves, hovering over him in stern reproof. He'd gone there with Taka only a few days earlier and been with her again this very night, held her, touched her. And now the gods had issued their terrible warning. He had no choice. He would have to give her up for ever. Jubei's death had severed his forbidden passion as cleanly as an executioner's sword.

Jubei, loyal Jubei, who had come unscathed through many battles, only to die in the gutter in a senseless quarrel. He would have to break the news to his brothers. He would tell them they had been on a foolish mission and been attacked by Satsuma. It was near enough the truth. They would go the next morning and retrieve Jubei's body and he would take responsibility for his wife and parents and make sure they were provided for.

No one could ever know the full story. But it would be a lesson to him.

Looking up at the heavens, he made a vow to the gods. He would avenge Jubei. And though it wrenched his heart, he would never, he swore, never see Taka again.

15

Taka woke with a start. Moonlight glimmered through the paper screens, casting a wan light across the piles of rumpled bedding. Fujino's thin cover was pushed back. She looked around sharply. One of the doors was open a crack and yellow light spilled through. Her mother was on her knees there, murmuring in the careful, controlled tones she used when some disaster had occurred.

Taka caught the words, 'How badly hurt?' but she couldn't make out the answer. She sat bolt upright. Her heart skipped a beat and her hands flew to her mouth. With a shock of fear she wondered if it had anything to do with Nobu. The last she had seen of him he had been slipping away under the trees. She screwed her eyes tight shut and prayed with all her might that nothing terrible had happened to him.

Fujino was on her feet now, a large reassuring shadow, the same comforting presence who lay next to her every night, breathing softly, as she had done throughout her entire life. Taka and Haru and their mother had slept together in a row, with the maids curled up nearby; now Haru was married it was just the two of them.

If only she could confide in Fujino like she used to,

Taka thought. Whenever Taka had taken her problems to her, she'd always known exactly what to do. It was only now that complicated matters like marriage had come up that her mother had stopped being her first port of call. You're on your own now, Taka told herself. The thought made her feel horribly lonely.

She could see her mother's shadow disappearing through the darkened rooms, the maids scurrying in front of her, lighting her way. Taka slipped a cotton jacket over her yukata and raced after them. As they neared the great entrance hall she heard agitated male voices, shouting above each other.

Men pushed in, crowding the earthen-floored vestibule. Taka recognized the guards who patrolled the estate in their jackets and baggy trousers, holding rifles, their faces like devil masks in the lantern light. Some of Eijiro's friends were there too. She'd thought they'd gone to the Yoshiwara but they were back, their cheeks sake-flushed but their eyes serious, as if they'd been shocked sober.

They had a look about them that she hadn't seen since the long-gone days in Kyoto, when there were battles in the streets – no longer spoilt rich boys with nothing to do but drink and complain and whore, but men, watchful, on edge, braced for attack. Some joshed with the guards, as if the social niceties had fallen by the wayside.

Lanterns swayed in the courtyard outside the circle of light. Shadowy figures moved and voices hissed, 'Careful. Ease him out gently.' 'Stop. You're jarring him.' There was a sour stomach-turning meaty smell that was oddly familiar. It was a moment before Taka recognized it from those distant Kyoto days – fresh-spilt blood.

She was desperate to know what had happened. Only a few hours had passed since Nobu had climbed in to see her; but she dared not say a word. It was too much of a coincidence.

One of Eijiro's friends stared around, wild-eyed. Taka had never liked him. He was an unappealing fellow who was always pestering Okatsu. Taka started as she saw what a state he was in. His face and hair were plastered with dirt and blood and his smart western waistcoat was torn. He fell to his knees in front of her mother and pressed his head to the ground.

'For-forgive this intrusion at this . . . this hour,' he stuttered. He raised his head. His eyes were bulging out of their sockets like a frightened rabbit's and his face, always pale, was ashen.

'Don't worry, Suzuki,' Taka's mother said briskly. 'Where's Eijiro?'

'On . . . on his way back, I hope. I sent a message urgently. We had a bet,' he added, flapping his hands helplessly. 'We were going different ways to see who got to the Yoshiwara first, but . . .'

There were shouts of 'Clear the way! Get back!' The crowd parted as a group of men pushed through. Hardly daring to breathe, Taka stood on tiptoe, trying to peek between the heads. There was a grating wheeze and a stifled groan. Suzuki yelled, 'Gently. Gently.'

Craning her neck, Taka caught a glimpse of torn clothes thickly caked in blood. The stench turned her stomach. Whoever the men were carrying, he was dreadfully injured. The clothes were of western cut and she made out a broad chest and muscular limbs. She breathed out in relief and uttered a silent prayer of thanks. The injured man was not tall and gangly and dressed in mismatched cottons. It was not Nobu.

The bearers stepped out of their sandals up into the great main room and set the wounded man on the futons which the maids had laid out. There was blood dripping from the makeshift pallet and trailing through the entryway and a pool of blood was already spreading across the futons. Maids brought lamps and set them around him.

Taka glanced at the injured man's face and looked away in horror. It was blackened and pulpy like crushed fruit and smeared with blood, with torn, ragged flesh where his cheek should have been. One eye was so swollen she could hardly see it, the other stared dully. The man's thick hands were locked over his chest as if he was trying to hold himself together. Blood oozed between his fingers.

'Easy, Toshi, easy,' said one of the bearers. Taka gasped in shock. It couldn't be. Surely not Toshi – Toshiaki Yamakawa, Eijiro's closest friend.

Fujino was at his side, exuding calm. The men stepped back to give her room as if, like Taka, they knew everything would be all right now that she was here. Her mother turned to the maids who were hovering anxiously. 'Okatsu, fetch Dr Fujita. Omoto, find Inspector Makihara. Run!'

She knelt beside Yamakawa and laid a soft hand reassuringly on his arm. 'You'll be fine, Toshi,' she said quietly. 'Stay still. We'll fix you up in no time.' The men exchanged glances. No one dared say a word.

Maids ran in with basins of steaming water and warm cloths and knelt around Yamakawa, dabbing at his wounds. Others tried to staunch the flow of blood, ripping cotton sheets into bandages and wrapping them around his injured limbs. Taka tied back her sleeves, wrung out a cloth and knelt beside him, cautiously bathing his sound cheek, wiping back the blood-stiffened hair as she'd done to other wounded men as a child in Kyoto.

All this bloodshed was supposed to have finished but it was starting all over again. Something had gone wrong in their peaceful lives.

Yamakawa groaned and moved his jaw. His breath wheezed in his throat. 'Waste of time,' he muttered, his face contorted as if every word caused him agony. 'Had it. Finished.'

Suzuki pushed in beside him. 'Don't be stupid, Toshi. The doctor's on his way, Dr Fujita, who patched up our men on the battlefield. Don't give up now. You got more fighting to do. We'll settle those northerners once and for all. We'll kill the lot o' them.'

Feet crunched on the road outside, wheels clattered and a rickshaw hurtled through the gates. As the shafts crashed to the ground, a big man leapt out and charged through the crowd, shoving people out of his way, bellowing, 'What's happened? No, not Yamakawa, by all the gods, not Toshi!'

He dropped to his knees beside the bloodied figure on the floor.

'They got me, Eiji. They killed me.' Yamakawa's voice was faint but Taka could hear every word.

Eijiro's face had turned the colour of clay. 'Don't be a

fool. No one would ever manage that. Pull yourself together, man. You've been wounded before, you're a tough son of a bitch. You'll pull through.'

He swung round, his face so racked with anguish that Taka had to look away. 'What happened?' His voice was a sob.

Yamakawa raised his head a fraction. 'Northerners.'

Taka stifled a gasp and tried to still the thumping in her chest. She stared around in panic, feeling as if she was caught up in a nightmare. A dreadful suspicion had gripped her, so terrible she hardly dared frame the thought. Surely Nobu couldn't have had anything to do with whatever had happened to Yamakawa? Surely it couldn't have been him who'd carried out this brutal attack?

She bit her lips in panic. Maybe it was her who'd brought this catastrophe on their house. Maybe she'd made a terrible mistake – meeting him in secret, encouraging him to visit her, to come on to their land, into their house. She'd thought she knew him so well, they'd known each other since they were children, but maybe she'd been wrong to be so open with him, to trust him so completely. She'd closed her eyes to the fact that he was an Aizu, that she and her family were his deadly enemies. He'd always seemed so gentle, but maybe he'd deceived her. She wished she could confide in her mother, ask her if she was behaving like a foolish child, letting herself be driven by her feelings like this. But it was too late for that.

She glanced around, afraid someone might have caught the horror on her face, but everyone was staring transfixed at Yamakawa and Eijiro. No one was paying the slightest attention to her. She was just a girl, of no consequence, invisible, like the maids.

Yamakawa's head fell back on the futon and he gasped for breath, wheezing painfully, his face twisting. 'Suzuki. He'll tell you.'

'No talking,' said Fujino. 'Rest.'

'We'll find them, whoever they are.' Eijiro's threatening tones sent another tremor of fear through Taka. 'You'll have your revenge, I promise.'

Yamakawa was panting with a terrible rattling sound. His eyelids fluttered and he opened and closed his mouth. Eijiro pressed his ear to his lips but there were no words, only a long sigh as Yamakawa's eyes closed. His body sank on the futon, hands still locked on his chest.

There was a dreadful silence. Then Eijiro gave a sobbing howl. 'Toshi!' His big shoulders heaved with sobs. Taka found herself weeping in sympathy.

After a long time Eijiro lifted his head, his eyes bloodshot and puffy. He stared around wildly and his expression changed from anguish to rage. Suzuki was kneeling with his face to the mats as if it was him who had died.

'What happened, Suzuki? Tell me. What happened?'

Suzuki looked up, hollow-eyed. Taka hardly dared hear what he had to say. Her heart was pounding. Supposing it really had been Nobu. Eijiro would kill him straight away, and her too.

'Northerners,' Suzuki groaned. 'Like Toshi said. Northerners.'

'Pull yourself together, Suzuki. You've seen men die before. I want to hear everything, now, before the inspector arrives. Come on, spit it out.'

Suzuki's eyes darted nervously. 'We were driving along beside the estate and they leapt out of the ground.'

'Out of the ground? You think I'm an idiot?' Eijiro mimicked his reedy croak, scowling. Suzuki quailed.

'It was dark. I . . . I thought they were ghosts.'

'Fool!' Eijiro slammed his massive fist on the tatami.

'Huge guys,' Suzuki went on defiantly. 'Three or four at least, maybe five. Northerners, for sure. I could tell by the accent. Northerners with a grudge.'

'What did they say?'

'"Southern bastards," that kind of thing. They jumped us.'

Three or four huge men. Taka had been holding her breath. She let it out sharply and unclenched her fists. So it hadn't been Nobu. She'd been wrong to doubt him. She was so relieved and glad it made her feel weak. But in that case who had committed this terrible crime? Then she remembered what Nobu had told her, about trouble brewing. She hadn't paid much attention at the time, she'd been too happy to see him, but now she was terribly afraid.

Eijiro glared at Suzuki. 'But you got away unscathed. Where are your wounds? Yamakawa's a better soldier than you, far better. He's cut down hundreds. They got him and not you?'

'There were f-f-five of them and t-t-two of us.' Suzuki was stuttering again.

'You didn't help him?'

'I barely escaped with my life. I wounded one and Yamakawa cut one down. We shoved the body into the moat – a monster, as big as a sumo wrestler. I was fighting another one off, battling for my life, when the rest piled on to Yamakawa. He fought back like a demon – you know him – but it was three against one. He didn't stand a chance. The others were just behind us – our friends. They turned up as he fell and the thugs ran off.'

Eijiro's heavy brow was furrowed. 'Why would guys like that run away? Why didn't they lay into all of you?'

Suzuki looked straight at him. 'They went for Yamakawa. They seemed to know who they were after.'

Eijiro thought for a while, then nodded, as if the pieces were falling into place in his mind. 'Huge men, you say, who knew Yamakawa.' He spoke slowly, weighing every word. 'Not northerners with a grudge then, not a random attack. They must have put on northern accents to disguise themselves.' He glared around fiercely. 'No. Killers, professional killers. It could have been me they were after, but they got Yamakawa instead. That's why you didn't get a scratch, Suzuki. They wouldn't waste time on you.'

The men were muttering urgently, nodding in agreement. 'Don't you see?' Eijiro said, his voice rising. 'Father's gathering an army, Satsuma is virtually an independent state. Everyone's already gone, the barracks are half empty, all the Satsuma men have left and gone back to Kyushu. And here we are – fools that we are – holding a meeting right in our own house! It was government agents, it's all too obvious. There are spies in our midst.' He stared around at the assembled men, who shuffled and glared accusingly at each other and made a show of meeting his eye, as if to say, 'Don't look at me. It's not me who's the traitor.'

Taka was trying to follow his argument. She was not sure it made sense but he was probably right. Men were supposed to know about such things.

Eijiro lowered his gaze to the battered body, now hidden under a sheet that was already black with blood. 'I'll miss you, Toshi, old friend. By the gods, I'll miss you. You were the best of us all!'

He buried his face in his hands. When he looked up his expression was determined.

'It's begun,' he said quietly. 'They're picking us off one by one.' His jaw set. 'It's suicide to stay here any longer.' He swung round. 'Mother, tell the servants to pack our bags and book our passage. We leave as soon as we can get a berth – you, Taka, all of us. You can do as you please, lads, but I suggest you join us. My father needs all the men he can find in Kyushu.'

Taka gasped and sank back on her heels. Leave Tokyo, when Nobu had just come back into her life? That very evening they'd pledged themselves to each other. He'd have no idea of where she'd gone or how to find her.

None of them had ever been to Kyushu. Eijiro's friends might be from Satsuma but she and her mother certainly weren't. They were Kyoto women, used to city comforts. They'd be as out of place in that rough frontier country as a couple of dainty butterflies. Taka wasn't even sure her father wanted them there.

But it would be foolish to argue with Eijiro now. They'd do better to wait till morning, when his grief had eased a little and the horrors of the night had faded. He was always making melodramatic statements, like when he'd said that he'd fought off the thugs in the Yoshiwara single-handed. With any luck he would see sense – that there was no need for them to leave, certainly not all of them, not Taka and Fujino. Her mother would talk to him.

Then she realized that if they went to Kyushu, Fujino would have to break off negotiations with Masuda-*sama*. Suddenly a chance to escape this dreaded marriage had been thrust into her hands, like a gift from the gods. It was too cruel a choice – go to Kyushu and lose Nobu or stay here and marry.

In any case the decision was not in her hands. Her mother would never call off the marriage. She couldn't. The loss of face would be unthinkable.

Fujino was on her knees beside Toshi's body, her face an expressionless mask. Taka could tell by the set of her shoulders and the stubborn angle to her mouth that she had not the slightest intention of being dragged away from Tokyo. If General Kitaoka had summoned her she would have gone straight away, but he hadn't, and she was not going to run like a dog with its tail between its legs.

Taka twisted her hands together. Her head hurt from thinking. It seemed the very marriage she'd struggled so hard to escape from would be her salvation; it would enable her to stay in Tokyo. It might be best if she stopped seeming quite so opposed to Masuda-*sama*, but at the same time she would have to put her mind to finding ways to postpone the evil day. There were her studies for a start. She had to finish the academic year. She'd never dared play games with her mother before. Fujino was far too astute. But now she'd have to try.

And as long as she was in Tokyo she'd be able to see Nobu. He'd be in touch soon, climbing over the wall and creeping through the gardens again to surprise her on her veranda, and then they could look for a way to make a life together.

PART III

North and South

16

*Ninth month, year of the rat, the ninth year of the
Meiji era (October 1876)*

'Hai! Hai!'

Hoarse yells announced the approach of a train of
packhorses, snorting and swaying up the hill, snapping
branches and trampling leaves as they lumbered along
the narrow track. Picking his way between hoof holes
overflowing with fetid water, Nobu stubbed his toe on
a stone and cursed. His straw sandal had fallen apart.
His brother Yasutaro's broad back was disappearing up
the path.

'Wait!'

Crouching, he flung the broken sandal to the side of
the road and untied a fresh one from his pack. He'd lost
track of how many he'd worn out.

Yasu leaned against a tree trunk, resting his weight on
his good leg, and rubbed the back of his hand across his
forehead. His face was smeared with mud. 'Can't be
much further,' he muttered. They set off again immediately, stepping off the trail to let the line of steaming
horses with their huge loads push by.

Autumn had come with a vengeance. The fiery heat of summer had been followed by the torrential rains of the typhoon season. Back in Tokyo the trees had just begun to change colour but up here in the north they'd lost nearly all their leaves.

The army had given Nobu and his fellow cadets a few days' holiday in the ninth month to celebrate the Festival of First Fruits. No one quite knew what was going on down south but everyone suspected that they would soon be called up for active duty and it would be a good chance to receive the blessings of their parents before going into battle. But Nobu had an extra reason for making the long journey north. He had a special task to perform, a last responsibility to Jubei, who had been a loyal friend to them all.

He grimaced and thumped his fist into his hand and groaned aloud as the events of the summer came flooding back. Out in the city on his own, away from his classmates, without the discipline and structure of army life, he'd gone completely mad. It was the only way to explain the terrible things he'd done. He'd forgotten himself, let himself be driven by his feelings. If he'd needed a woman that badly he should have gone to a professional, paid for a night's pleasure, then left and forgotten all about it, as other men did, he told himself – as any man with half a grain of sense would have done. But instead he'd let himself be led by the nose like a packhorse by shameful desires entirely unsuited to a samurai and ended up chasing after the sort of girl who could only bring disaster. He'd even climbed into an enemy mansion. It had been pure craziness, asking for trouble. It was a dreadful, humiliating episode in his life and he'd done well to put it behind him.

The lasting result of his reckless behaviour had been Jubei's death. To the end of his days he'd never forget that fearful night. After he'd fled the scene of the fight, he'd pulled himself together and stumbled over to Yasu's. They'd flagged down a rickshaw and rushed back to the silent road alongside the Kitaoka estate, praying that Jubei's body hadn't been ripped to pieces by wild dogs. They'd driven up and down beside the long featureless wall while Nobu tried to remember exactly where the fight had taken place. Then he'd seen the blackened ground and trampled grass.

They'd found Jubei's body, still intact but cold, heavy and stiff, and taken it home and the next day summoned a priest to perform rites and sent letters reporting the death to Jubei's family in the north. To Nobu's relief it hadn't struck his brothers as strange or unlikely that he and Jubei had got into a fight with some Satsuma men; with a couple of hotheads like them, it was not surprising they'd get into trouble. His brothers hadn't asked many questions and he hadn't had to tell many lies.

Yasu had told him sternly, as his elder brother and Jubei's friend and master, that when the opportunity arose he must take a portion of Jubei's ashes to his parents. It was the proper thing to do. Yasu would go with him. It was out of the question to travel alone and he wanted to see their father and pay his respects at the family grave.

The ashes, in a small urn in Nobu's pack, weighed heavy on his shoulders, reminding him with every step of what he'd done.

*   *   *

The brothers had been travelling for seven days now. When they'd left Tokyo, the Great North Road had been a splendid avenue lined with cedars and paved with neatly swept flagstones, broad and smooth enough for rickshaws to rattle by, throwing up dust. By the time they reached the mountains it had shrivelled to a muddy track, winding through woods above plunging ravines with pine trees growing out at crazy angles from the banks. Wealthy travellers jogged on stubborn nags beaten and dragged along by sweating grooms, but everyone, whether on foot or on horseback, had no choice but to move at the same slow pace.

Here in the north they were among friends who sympathized with the northern cause and at night they stayed at roadside inns or took shelter with kindly farmers. That day they'd left at dawn, climbing a narrow mountain path that wound endlessly up through curtains of mist, their breath puffing out like steam in the chilly air. They'd tramped through mulch and fallen leaves, skirting rocks and puddles and keeping an eye out for packhorse trains. Yellowing leaves drifted from the tangle of branches above them.

Sometimes they caught up with lines of travellers or overtook bent old ladies, hobbling side by side, their voices shrill in the mountain air, and now and then a bow-legged courier, naked except for a loincloth, bounded by with a box of letters on his leathery shoulder, leaping from rock to rock, shouting, 'Clear the way, clear the way.' Monkeys squatted on branches over their heads, shrieking, and wild deer sprang away into the woods. The brothers wore bells round their ankles and smacked their staffs against rocks to warn off bears and wild boar when they were on their own.

Even Nobu's army training had not prepared him for walking from dawn to dusk, day after day. He'd given up on his heavy army boots and replaced them with straw sandals, but his feet were still covered in calluses and there was a fresh blister stinging at the side of his little toe. Nevertheless he was happy to be away from the crowded Tokyo streets, out in the fresh air and open country.

His legs ached so much he was seriously beginning to wonder if he'd ever make it to the top when suddenly the trees thinned and he stepped out of the canopy of leaves into bright sunlight. Yasu had thrown down his pack and was sitting on a rock, catching his breath. He jerked his chin towards the distant view. 'Those mountains,' he said, between pants. He shook his head. 'You don't even recognize them. It's Aizu, the mountains of Aizu. Mount Bandai, where the bamboo leaves gleam with gold dust.'

Nobu shaded his eyes with his hand. Far below them was a dry brown plain with cloud shadows moving across it and hummocks like giant molehills, splotched in autumnal shades of yellow, red and orange. In the distance, sparkling against the sky, were rank upon rank of mountains, like the helmets of an advancing army. He'd been ten when they left their homeland. He remembered hobbling through the snow in a long line of refugees in his bare feet, dressed in rags, sucking on a stone to try to dull the hunger in his stomach. He'd seen nothing, paid attention to nothing except keeping close to his father.

Yasu looked up. Nobu hadn't seen him smile since those distant days in Aizu. It made him look younger, handsome. ' "Passing the barrier, we cross the Abukuma river. To the left the towering mountains of Aizu, to the right the districts of Iwaki, Soma and Miharu," ' he declaimed. Nobu picked up the archaic language and cadence. He was quoting some ancient literary work.

The further they got from Tokyo, the lighter of step Yasu became. He still limped, he'd never lose that, but he no longer had that drawn, hungry, desperate look about him. He wore a jacket and patched-up leggings, like a peasant, but he'd shaken off his hangdog stoop and carried himself like the proud samurai he would have been if fate and the gods had not stepped in. He was himself again. He should have been an important man in their domain, Nobu thought, a scholar or a poet or a swordsman. But the gods or whoever it was that ruled men's destinies had had a very different plan for him.

'Matsuo Basho came this way,' said Yasu, his eyes gleaming. 'If you'd grown up in Aizu and had a proper education as you should have, you'd have had his words in your heart. Two hundred years ago, near enough. He was on his way north, like us, with a staff and a bundle and a sedge hat on his back, and as he walked he wrote haiku, on the landscape or some historical event that had happened there, or a flower or a plant or an insect, whatever took his fancy. He even wrote about his thin shanks. He kept a journal of his travels and called it *The Narrow Road to the Deep North*. People came from far away to sit at his feet and make haiku.' He heaved a sigh. 'I used to make haiku myself. I spent afternoons with friends, drinking and talking and composing linked verse. Now I'm just a soldier. No, not even that any more.'

He stared at the stony ground as if he expected to find Basho's words written there, then looked up. The sun cast a fiery glow on the snowy peaks, making them shine like armour. 'That smudge of grey at the end of the valley,' he said, narrowing his eyes to slits. 'It might be Aizu, or maybe it's just my imagination. I've read that men in the desert, desperate for water, imagine that they see lakes and trees. Perhaps that happens in the mountains too.'

Peering into the distance, Nobu thought he caught a glimpse of smoke rising on the far side of the valley. He bit his lips, wondering what sort of home this would be that he was going back to. He closed his eyes and tried to picture the towering keep and sweeping roofs of White Crane Castle soaring over the maze of narrow streets, the squat black warehouses of the merchant district and the samurai homes with their sand-coloured walls.

In his mind he was back at the family house with its many rooms, in his child's hakama with his two swords thrust in his sash, scampering through the tiled and gabled gate and across the courtyard, a servant hurrying behind with his books. He'd run past the front entrance where grandees arrived in palanquins to visit his father and grandfather, then race around to the family quarters and shout, 'I'm back,' as he kicked off his clogs in the entrance. His mother, grandmother and sisters would greet him on their hands and knees, bowing. He'd kneel by the fire, very serious, and tell them everything he'd done at school that day.

He remembered climbing trees, throwing snowballs in winter, playing with his friends on streets walled with snow so high it towered over his head and blanketed gardens and temple grounds and lay in a thick white layer on every roof. Then there'd been the ferment as the town prepared for enemy attack – people rushing about building barricades, lugging water barrels and piling up straw mats to douse and throw over cannon-balls to stop them exploding, men patrolling the streets, people practising in deadly earnest with swords and muskets and at home his mother and sisters busily sewing uniforms.

But that was long ago. There was nothing of that left now, nothing at all.

A spasm of memory knocked the wind out of him like a punch in the stomach and he crumpled, blindly pre-tending to adjust his sandal to hide the tears that sprang to his eyes. He was ten years old again, standing frozen on the hillside, hearing a roar that seemed to come from the belly of some fire-breathing dragon, seeing the sky bathed crimson and black smoke billowing above the city. He'd seen tongues of flame. He'd wanted to run to his mother but his attendant grabbed his sleeve, shout-ing, 'No, young master, no. You can't go down there.'

Until that moment he'd been such a child he'd barely stopped to wonder why his mother had sent him out of town the previous day. 'Be off with you,' she'd said. 'Go and stay with your auntie for a few days and help with the mushroom hunting.' The city was in turmoil, none of his friends came out to play any more and his father and brothers had long since set off for the front. He'd happily agreed.

It was then, seeing the red glow filling the sky, feeling the searing heat, hearing the boom of cannon fire and the incessant rattle of guns like peas popping in a pan, that he'd suddenly realized. She'd sent him away to save him, to make sure at least one of the family survived. But in the end his father and brothers had made it through the fighting. It was the women who had perished. It had been more than a month before the cannon fire had stopped and longer still before the occupying troops allowed people into the shattered streets to look for where their houses had been and search the ashes for bones.

The brothers set off at first light the following day, heading for the smudge of grey at the end of the valley, and soon turned off the highway and took the road to Aizu. Gradually the pile of rocks in the lea of the mountains shaped itself into the outlines of buildings, but no matter how hard Nobu looked he couldn't see White Crane Castle. When he was small he'd always been able to see it, perched above the city. But now there was nothing.

He scuffed at the stones that littered the path. 'That's not Aizu. It can't be. You've made a mistake. We've taken a wrong turn.'

He secretly hoped that they had. The closer they got, the more he dreaded discovering what had happened to his old home.

'Don't be a fool,' said Yasutaro, scowling. 'How could I ever forget? This is the Aizu road. This is the way home.'

Nobu was stumbling along, brooding about his

home, his family, about Jubei and his own stupid infatuation with Taka that had led to Jubei's terrible
death, when he saw something glinting in the undergrowth. It was white and smooth, like a stone. An
animal bone, he thought. Then he saw another and
another. He looked around, startled. There were bones
everywhere, poking out of the ground, tangled in
clumps of plume grass, hidden in maiden flower bushes,
woven around with weeds, scattered in heaps across the
plain. They were walking through a killing ground.

Suddenly Yasu threw his bundle down and plunged
into the tangle of bushes, kicking and trampling the
branches. He dug into the undergrowth and wrenched
out something round, ripping off the stems and leaves
that clung to it and brushing off the dirt. It was a skull,
a human skull, stained black and brown and green but
a human skull all the same. There were others lying
around, weeds growing out of the eye sockets and
shattered crowns. Nobu noticed shards of metal
and shreds of fabric and leather and a piece of helmet
half buried in the ground. The bones had been picked
clean, there were no birds or dogs to be seen. The place
was as still as a graveyard.

Yasu dropped to his knees and started scrabbling
frantically with his fingers in the dirt. He unearthed a
chain and yanked out a metal tag. He breathed on it and
wiped it off on his sleeve, tilting it to the light.

'"Daito-koji. Died in battle, twenty-ninth day of
the eight month, Keio 4,"' he read, spelling out the
characters. He held the small metal square between his
hands and raised them in prayer, head bowed. A bird
shrieked overhead.

'Daito-koji.' His voice was hoarse. 'It's a posthumous name. I don't even know who he was. The priests gave us tags inscribed with posthumous names so whoever found our bodies could give us proper rites. And this is what became of them all.' He brushed his hand across his eyes.

'Eight years?' Nobu gasped. 'They've been here eight years?'

He shuddered with horror. The southerners must have taken away their own dead, buried them some-where or somehow. But these men of Aizu lay where they had died, denied the proper rites to send them safely to the other world, their spirits never laid to rest. The air was thick with the humming and buzzing of ghosts.

'The enemy had laid siege to the city,' said Yasu. 'Four clans, four invading armies. You could see them, camped all around. We didn't have a chance. We battled as hard as we could but they closed in and drove us back into the town, then into the castle. They burnt the city down and sealed the castle gates one by one, then held us there, bottled up. We were running out of food, water, bullets, everything. Every piece of cotton in the castle had been cut up to make bandages. There was no time to bury our dead, they lay around stinking.' His eyes were staring as if he was back in the castle again, surrounded by the corpses of his friends and comrades.

Nobu shut his eyes, wishing he could shut his ears too. As the enemy closed in he'd been on the hillside staring in horror at the burning city or with his aunt, shouting and weeping, demanding to rejoin his family.

But in the end, as his mother had intended, he'd escaped the cataclysm.

'We wanted to face the enemy man to man, not die like bears in a trap,' said Yasu. 'So we sneaked out under cover of darkness and laid about us with our swords and guns. We had nothing in our minds but cutting down as many as we could before we were killed ourselves. Divine retribution, we called it. I was one of the unlucky ones. I made it back. I didn't need my posthumous name.' He spat on the ground. 'I should have died here with the others.'

Flapping at the edge of the path was a wooden sign, split nearly in half, twisting in the wind. It was so weather-beaten it was almost impossible to read. Nobu stared at it, trying to decipher the faded brushstrokes. Yasu spelled out the words: ' "Warning. This ground . . . left untouched . . . penalty of death." So that's what it was. The southerners ordered our men's bodies left unburied.'

Shoulders hunched, he stared at the name tag in his hand. 'At least this one brave soldier,' he said hoarsely, 'at least he'll have proper rites.' There were tears in his eyes. ' "Daito-koji." Was that you, Denshichi, old friend? Or you, Sahei? Or Gen? Brave lads, all of you.' He groaned. 'A whole generation, lost.'

17

'They certainly made a thorough job of it,' Yasutaro muttered, sinking down on a rock and putting his head in his hands.

Nobu shook his head, dazed with disbelief. Where the splendid five-storeyed castle should have been, there was nothing, not a roof or a pillar or an ornamental door, not even a bullet-pocked wall, only an endless expanse of rubble, scattered as far as he could see. Moss, weeds and brambles swarmed over massive blackened beams and clung to shards of twisted metal. Mounds of roof tiles had fused on to slabs of granite as big as houses, scorched rust red. Something huge and metallic caught his eye, glinting in the ruins. It looked dreadfully like the remains of one of the giant bronze dolphins that had tossed their majestic tails at the ends of the roof ridge.

Somehow Nobu had imagined that the city might have been demolished, but not the castle, where their lord had had his seat. Surely even the most brutish of enemies would have respected that, even if they'd left it a broken shadow of what it had been. He turned away. It was unbearable to see.

'I'll tell you something,' said Yasu in a grim undertone. 'It wasn't just the fire that destroyed it. The castle was standing when I left. Those bastards razed it. Now they think they've well and truly clipped our wings, they're kindly letting us move back. I'm glad we stood up to them, at least. We gave them a run for their money, we didn't let them trample us into the dust without a fight. One day, it'll be our turn. One day we'll get our own back – and it won't be long now.'

Nobu grunted assent. If truth be told, it was so long ago, he didn't know if he agreed or not. It seemed a terrible price to have paid. But no matter what, it was his duty to avenge his family and his people. That much he knew.

The roads were still laid out in a grid, like a ghostly memory of what had been, but there were few buildings, only heaps of stones with tumbledown huts of broken planks propped in the ruins. Craters pocked the ground and there were bullet holes in the few remaining walls that had once surrounded samurai mansions. The autumn sky cast a harsh light over the acres of strewn rubble.

Without the castle to orient them, nothing was familiar. Yasu had to ask directions as they went. The streets were full of people, moving like sleepwalkers – old women in hempen robes with babies on their backs, bent-backed men shoving carts or stumbling under panniers hung on each end of bamboo poles, travellers with bundles of belongings. Tradesmen hawked their wares and farmers sat at the edge of the road beside piles of mushrooms and pickled radish, offering them for sale. But there was something missing. It was a city of women, children and the old. The only young men Nobu could see were lame or in uniform.

The brothers glanced warily at the policemen patrolling in peaked caps and boots – Aizu men, by their faces, and not much older than Nobu; the only job any northerner could get in this southern-run world was in the army or the police force. At least they had warm clothes to wear, though their greatcoats were threadbare.

Yet for all the crowds it was eerily quiet. Then Nobu realized what else was missing. There was no bang and clatter of wheels and warning yells from the rickshaw drivers, no rickshaws careering by, sending pedestrians running – just the clop of clogs on stone and the low chatter of voices and occasionally a broken-down nag snorting as it shuffled along in straw horseshoes, bent under an enormous load.

For fifteen years northerners and southerners had confronted each other, first on the streets of Kyoto, where the Aizu were the shogun's police, then on the battlefield, where they'd fought for control of the country. In the end the southerners had toppled the shogun and taken power in the name of the teenage emperor, their figurehead. Not content with that, they'd marched north, to wipe out the last shred of resistance and destroy their old enemy – the Aizu.

Nobu felt anger sparking in his belly. He thought of the Ginza with its gas lamps, its carriages, its rickshaw stands and its restaurants filled with plump, self-satisfied men and women tricked out in fancy western suits and gowns. All that prosperity, and not a grain had made its way up here. The victors lived in luxury, while the defeated had barely enough to eat.

He kicked savagely at a stone, slamming it into a

ditch, and clenched his fists, ready to hack down the southerners who'd brought such ruin on them. Then another memory formed in his mind, of the most luxurious mansion of all, with bevies of servants and rickshaws lined up at the gate, and he saw Taka, with her pale oval face, kneeling in the shadows on the veranda. For a moment he felt a familiar nagging ache, wishing she was here, that he could talk to her, explain to her.

He thumped his fist against his head. All this time he'd managed to keep her out of his mind, to keep his thoughts on his work and his studies, and now, here in this ruined city, destroyed by her people, he was overcome by weakness. She'd bewitched him, made him forget his duty. The thought of her had wormed its way inside him like a maggot in a fruit. Treacherous, foolish, shameful, he thought. And he dared call himself a soldier?

Furious at himself and at her, he looked around. In the past it had been impossible to glimpse the countryside through all the buildings but now he could see right across the valley to the distant mountains. He caught sight of a wooded hill, blazing in autumn reds and yellows, rising above the tumbled city walls.

'Look! Isn't that . . . Heron Hill?'

Heron Hill, where they'd had their country house and where he'd been that fateful day that the enemy attacked, when – foolish, innocent child that he'd been – he'd gone off mushroom hunting, not knowing that he was leaving his family to their deaths. He groaned at the memory.

Pacing out the route from the castle, Yasutaro had

worked out where their house ought to be. There was no name board, just a broken wall covered in brambles and a gaping hole where the gate should have been. Roof tiles lay in heaps, fused into clumps from the heat of the blaze. Nobu stared about him in dismay. There was nothing there that looked remotely like the home he remembered.

They stepped around fallen beams, crunching across gravel, tiles and broken stones, through piles of mouldering leaves. The huge oak and chestnut trees that used to tower over the house had burnt down, though in eight years saplings had begun to grow back, and the landscaped gardens and ornamental lake had disappeared under a mass of moss, vines and ferns. The place was overgrown with bamboo, as tall and dense as a jungle.

Some of the bushes and trees had been hacked down and there were a couple of makeshift huts at the edge of the expanse of blackened earth where the house must have been. Yasu squared his shoulders, his large face pinched and drawn. He seemed to have shrunk into himself. Like Nobu, he was afraid of what they would find. He hesitated, then took a breath and called out.

There was a long silence, then a door creaked open and a man stepped out, blinking. He had the bony frame and pinched, wind-parched face of a peasant and big, work-stained hands. A smile spread across his face.

'Well, if it isn't . . . Father, they're here! Yasutaro and Nobu, here!'

'Gosaburo!' It was Yasu's voice.

Looking at his brother, Nobu felt dismay washing over him again. Gosaburo had been the handsomest of the brothers and a fine swordsman. The third son, he was older than Nobu and younger than Yasu and Kenjiro. But he'd given up any hopes or ambitions he might have had to stay and take care of their father when his three brothers set off for Tokyo.

It was six years since Nobu had seen his father and third brother. The new government – the victorious southerners – had confiscated the Aizu lands and forced the Aizu samurai to live in a new homeland far to the north. But none of them knew when they set out on the long trek to Tonami that it was a fearful place of salt flats and grey volcanic ash where nothing grew, buried deep under snow for half the year.

Nobu had never known cold as bone-chilling as that. With no clogs or straw sandals, he'd had to run around just to stop his bare feet sticking to the icy ground. At night he'd slept huddled close to his father and brothers with only a cotton kimono and straw sacking for warmth. Being samurai, they'd had no idea how to farm, and when their rice allocation ran out they'd ended up grubbing for wild plants and roots. The local people had shied away and muttered 'Aizu caterpillars' when they saw them in the street. Many of the families that had gone north with them starved to death that first winter. Nobu dared not think how many had died since then.

A shadow appeared on the threshold. The old man who stood there was thin as a pole and his hair was nearly white. Instead of the stern warrior Nobu remembered, there was a stoop to his father's shoulders and a querulous frown on his face, but he held himself with pride. Nobu dropped to his knees.

'Yasu. Is that you, my son? And this must be young Nobu. Let me look at you, my boy. My, my, you've turned into a man.'

Nobu bowed, trying to hide his dismay at the changes that time and hardship had wrought in his father. He'd lost his fierce arrogance and intimidating scowl; he seemed to have shrunk like a dog beaten into submission.

He remembered his last meeting with him. He'd been on his knees, head to the ground. The cold stones pressed against his shins and there was a smell of earth under his nose. He'd looked up and spoken the words Yasutaro had taught him, loud and clear: 'Father, I will not come back until I've made something of myself.' And here he was, back again, but he'd made nothing of himself. Yasu had had to intervene with his superior officer and beg extra time off school for him so he could come north on this sad mission.

'Father, we return after long absence.' Yasu uttered the formal words of greeting. 'We are glad to find you in good health.'

A woman had followed their father out, twisting her hands – Yuki, Yasu's wife. She had been a girl when Nobu last saw her, but since then she'd faded and grown bony. She and Yasu had just been married and hardly knew each other when he'd left for Tokyo. Yasu barely acknowledged her, as was to be expected while his father and brothers were present, but Nobu could tell by the way his eyes strayed towards her that he was glad to see her.

'You come with the falling of the leaves,' said Father, his eyes darting back and forth, encased within folds of skin. He had the tremulous voice of an old man. 'I give thanks to the gods and our ancestors that we are alive and here together again, back on our own land.' He smiled ruefully and waved a thin hand towards the overgrown grounds. 'You'll be wanting to go to the family grave. But first you must eat. You've come a long way. Yuki, prepare rice.'

Nobu remembered his father in Tonami, sitting by the river with his fishing rod, staring into the distance. He wanted to hear how his life had been, how the family had got back to Aizu, and to tell him that he, his youngest son, was in the army now. He knew that would gladden his heart. The family had sacrificed so much to send him and Yasu and Kenjiro to Tokyo, he wanted them to know he'd made a success of himself, even if it wasn't entirely true. He dared not tell them that Yasu just did odd jobs and that in the holidays he himself was an errand boy.

'And Kenjiro, your brother, how is he?'

'He's well, he's well,' said Yasu. It was another half-truth. 'Studying, as always. Reading, writing. You know what he's like.'

'No job yet, then?'

'We all get by.'

Nobu was scrambling to his feet when he felt Yasu's eyes on him, reminding him that he had a duty to discharge. The urn weighed heavy on his back.

'Is there any news of . . . Kumazo?' He could hardly bring himself to say the name.

'They took care of our land all the years we were away, he and Otaké,' said Father, his face brightening. 'They take care of us still. They're here.'

There was a footstep behind Nobu and a big man with a few wispy hairs on his head appeared, ducking under the lintel of the second hut.

Kumazo's name meant Bear. When Nobu was a child he'd towered over him like a huge black bear, carrying him on his shoulders or tossing him in the air. Nobu had always been a bit afraid of him with his rough voice and booming laugh. Kumazo had been the chief stable master, adept at taming runaway horses, and his kind wife Otaké had been the head maid. They'd lived with the family as part of the household and it had seemed entirely natural for Jubei, their son, to become Yasu's trusted retainer.

Jubei had told Nobu that when the samurai refugees started pouring out of the burning city, Kumazo ferried them across the river to safety in a leaky boat which threatened to sink under the weight. Jubei's brother had fought in the clan army. He'd been captured and never returned and his sister had disappeared too. The last thing Jubei had heard of his parents was that they'd fled to the countryside.

Otaké, a tiny shadow of a woman, hobbled a few steps behind her husband. Her hips were so bent that her face nearly brushed the ground, but when she looked up she was beaming.

The two knelt painfully before the brothers. 'Welcome back, young masters, welcome back.'

Nobu wanted to abase himself, to bang his head on the ground in penance, but that would have shocked them beyond belief. He took off his pack and fumbled for the urn. It was of lacquerware, not much bigger than a tea caddy. He'd spent all his earnings and bought the best he could afford. He brought out the tiny jar of ash, all that was left of big Jubei with his rambunctious laugh and fierce loyalty, and held it out to them in both hands.

'Jubei . . .' he said, fighting back tears. 'It was my fault, a stupid adventure. Forgive me.'

Yasutaro butted in. 'Your son died a hero, battling the Satsuma. Rest assured, you can be proud of him.'

Nobu placed the urn containing Jubei's ashes in Kumazo's gnarled hands. The old man took it and raised it to his forehead in a gesture of prayer, blinking as if he was just beginning to understand that this last son of his was dead. A tear ran down his furrowed face.

Otaké whispered, 'You don't need our forgiveness, young master. We would never blame you. Jubei was always the wild one. I was sure he'd get himself killed one of these days. We'll always be grateful to you, young master. You took good care of him.'

'It was him that took care of us,' said Yasu fiercely. 'He saved my life many times. He wasn't a servant, he was my friend and I miss him. I always will. Tell them what happened, Nobu.'

Nobu hung his head. 'We were attacked by Satsuma. We were out together in Tokyo,' he muttered. He couldn't bring himself to continue the lie. He shook his head, whispering, 'It should have been me that died.'

18

'So you're a soldier now, young Nobu,' said his father, nodding gravely. A couple of candles lit the hut along with the embers flickering in the hearth, sending shadows dancing on the wooden walls, but at least it was more spacious than their miserable quarters in Tonami had been, Nobu thought. He could hear the clatter of pots and pans outside as Yuki prepared the meal.

'The southern clans are growing restless, Father,' said Yasu. 'Some of them are preparing to take up arms, we hear. The new government hasn't given them what they were hoping for. There've been several uprisings. There was one a couple of years ago.'

'So I heard. Led by one of Kitaoka's henchmen. The news made it all the way to the salt flats of Tonami.'

'There's rumours there may be another soon. If trouble breaks out down south we'll be the first to join up. They'll need all the recruits they can find for the army.'

'And the police force too. I'm glad to hear it.' Father's back had straightened and he looked more like the proud warrior Nobu remembered. There was a gleam in his eye. 'And that treacherous snake Kitaoka. What of him?'

'Stormed off to Kyushu and hasn't been seen since. It seems he's at the heart of the trouble. The Satsuma are massing around him. Not a single Satsuma student went back to school after the holidays. Isn't that right, Nobu?'

Nobu grunted assent. He knew both too much and too little of Kitaoka. He couldn't trust himself to speak.

'We've had news too.' Their father's voice had grown sombre. 'Your uncle Juémon turned up.'

'Uncle Juémon?'

Uncle Juémon had been a legend when Nobu was growing up. Their father's dashing younger brother, he'd been a famous swordsman, and when he was not away at war he used to go outside the city walls at night and pick fights with strangers just to keep in practice, so people said. As a child Nobu used to laugh at the thought of the corpses littering the ground in the morning and dreamed of growing up to be just like him.

Juémon was adept with modern weapons too. He'd fought in many campaigns, then, when the castle was besieged, led a platoon that made daring forays against the enemy positions. When the castle surrendered, the southerners came in search of his head but he'd disappeared. No one knew what had become of him, or if they did, they didn't say. He hadn't been among the prisoners who were marched down to Tokyo and didn't end up in exile in the frozen wastes of Tonami. People said he'd gone into hiding or been killed or was incarcerated somewhere. Then the years passed and no one spoke of him any more.

He'd been Nobu's favourite uncle. He told tall stories, played tricks and taught him how to fight. The last he'd

seen of him had been the day his mother sent him to
Heron Hill to pick mushrooms. Uncle Juémon had just
got back from the front. He'd dropped in and waved
goodbye as Nobu had gone off with his aunt.

His return was thrilling news. Yet Father seemed
strangely downcast. Nobu frowned, trying to see his
face in the gloom.

'So he's alive?'

'What would you expect of a man like that? He went
into hiding in the mountains. When he heard we were
back in Aizu he came down to see us.'

'Into the hornets' nest.'

'He's got a new name now and cut his topknot off
and he's brawnier than he was. You wouldn't know
him.'

'Except for the crazy look in his eye,' said Yasu,
unable to restrain a smile.

'He was on his way to Tokyo. You might see him
there.' Father reached for the poker and stirred the
embers in the hearth till they sparked to life, then leaned
forward, holding his hands to the flames. 'He had something he wanted to tell me,' he added. His voice had
grown so quiet Nobu had to listen hard to catch
his words.

There was silence except for the fire crackling and
candles sputtering. The smell of cooking rice wafted in
from outside. The two sons waited respectfully for their
father to go on.

'About your mother and grandmother and sisters.
What became of them.'

Nobu found himself staring stubbornly into the fire.
He wanted to put his hands over his ears. He knew

enough already about what had happened, he didn't need to know any more.

'We men were all away fighting at the front,' said Father slowly. 'None of us was here when the city was attacked. But we all heard what happened. When the fire bell rang, the samurai families were supposed to take refuge in the castle. But many chose to die.' It was as if the words were being dragged out of him. 'Mother – your dear mother – was a fine warrior. She was fearless and skilled with the halberd. There's no doubt that she'd have joined the women's battalion if she could have, and gone into battle. Or she'd have been in the castle, preparing food for the defenders, bandaging the wounded, throwing wet mats over the cannonballs as they landed to stop them exploding. But she had dependants – my elderly mother, your grandmother, and your two young sisters. She had to think of them.

'Uncle Juémon had gone to warn them that the enemy troops had entered the city when the fire bell started ringing. "Go to the castle, straight away," he told them.'

Their father's quavering voice stopped abruptly and he bowed his head. Yasu reached for the kettle that was hanging over the hearth, filled the teapot and poured him a cup. Father took a mouthful and cleared his throat. When he spoke again his voice faltered so much it was hard to hear.

' "Please don't waste time trying to persuade us," Mother said. She was utterly calm. "You know perfectly well we'd be unable to help at White Crane Castle. We'd only get in the way of the defence and consume precious food and water. We've seen the southern armies outside the city walls. It's all over for us. War is not a tea ceremony. They're bound to take the city and when they do they'll have no mercy. We've heard how they've treated the farmers round about. They'll rape us or kill us or sell us as slaves. We know what we have to do, we've already discussed it, and we're ready." Juémon never forgot her words. I've repeated them exactly as he told me.

'Your grandmother and sisters were also calm, entirely calm and resolved. They were true samurai, all of them. There was no time to dress for death but they all wrote their death poems and entrusted them to Juémon. Mother cut off a lock of her hair and asked him to ensure it was put in the family grave. Then she asked him to administer the last blow and one by one they . . . they cut their throats.' His voice was shaking. He swallowed hard and was silent. Then he spoke again. 'Even little Sato didn't hesitate, though she was only seven. She put the dagger to her throat with great courage and determination. You would both have been proud if you'd been here.

'Your mother was the last, of course. Juémon helped them to die, as they'd requested. He cut off their heads, then set fire to the house.

'So you see, they weren't dishonoured. They weren't killed by the enemy, they didn't burn to death in the flames. They died like samurai by their own hands. They were fine women, all of them, fine brave women. I am proud of them and I miss them.' The last words were more like a sob.

Nobu knew he should be proud they'd died with such dignity. It was what every samurai hoped for, an honourable death. But all he could feel was horror and terrible pain. He'd known they were dead, he'd lived with that knowledge and come to terms with it, but he'd never before had to think about how they'd died. The old wound had been reopened. It was too forceful a reminder of their loss. Groaning, he put his head on his knees and clapped his hands over his ears.

The hut seemed too small. Stifled by the smoke, he leapt to his feet and rushed outside. But as he dropped to his knees, gulping down the cool autumn air in great convulsive breaths, he realized that this was the very spot, this blackened expanse of scorched earth. This was where they'd died. The ground was drenched with their blood.

There was a hand on his shoulder. Yasu had followed him out. 'This is no way to behave. Our mother and grandmother and sisters behaved with courage and we should too.' His voice softened. 'You're young still. When you've seen war, when you've seen your comrades cut down like rice under the scythe, even then is not the time to weep. We have to learn to be dry-eyed, like little Sato. Many Aizu families lost their womenfolk in the same way. We have to help Father. His suffering is the greatest.'

'I wish I'd died myself,' Nobu said. 'It would have been easier to bear.'

It was hard to eat the meal that Yuki had prepared but in the end, sitting with his family around the fire, Nobu began to feel a sort of peace. Father took a mouthful of tea and said, 'Your dear mother must have thought Uncle Juémon would be killed and nothing would be left. After all, who would have guessed any of us would survive – except you, young Nobu; you were meant to survive. Juémon did his best but somewhere along the way the scrolls with our family's death poems were lost. But he gave me this.'

He reached up to the simple altar on the wall of the hut and took down a relic bag. He opened it and tipped something into his hand. Nobu stared at it in the darkness. It was a lock of dark hair. Father held it out to Yasu, who shook his head.

' "If I took it in my hands it would melt",' he murmured.

'Of course. The ninth month,' said Father, swallowing. 'The very same month that Basho returned to his family in Iga.'

' "At the beginning of the ninth month I returned to my native place." Isn't that how it begins, that passage?' said Yasu.

Nobu hung his head, wondering how they could talk of Basho at a time like this. But then he began to get an inkling. Perhaps in some way it made it easier to bear. Perhaps Basho's words helped them come to terms with their pain.

Father nodded and began to recite. ' "At the beginning of the ninth month I returned to my native place. The miscanthus in the north chamber had withered away with the frost and there was nothing left of it. Everything was changed from old times. My brother's hair was white, his brows wrinkled. He said only, 'We are alive.' Without a word he opened his relic bag. 'Do reverence to Mother's white hairs. This is Urashima's magic box. You too have turned into an old man.' " '

He placed the lock of hair in Nobu's open hands. Nobu let it rest there, light as down, feeling the silky softness. His mother's scent lingered. He closed his eyes, feeling the warmth of her lap and her fingers smoothing his hair and her soft voice as she told him the story he'd loved to hear, of Urashima, the handsome young fisherman.

It was long long ago, she always began. Urashima was setting out with his nets one day when he saw some children beating a turtle. He rescued it and put it gently back in the ocean.

The very next day he was out again when he heard a voice calling, 'Urashima! Urashima!' A gigantic turtle was swimming towards the shore, its huge flippers parting the waves. In gravelly tones it told him it was the chief retainer of the dragon king. The turtle Urashima had saved was the dragon king's daughter and she wanted to see him and thank him in person. So Urashima clambered on to the turtle's broad back and held tight to its scaly neck as it dived under the water.

He found himself in the dragon king's palace, where shoals of brilliantly coloured fish swam through labyrinths of rocky caverns, and delicate towers and turrets spiralled towards the surface of the water far above. The turtle he'd rescued turned out to be a princess more beautiful than anyone could ever imagine, with coral cheeks, eyes that tapered like a fish's tail and lustrous rippling tresses.

Three days passed in a dream as he lay in her arms, enjoying singing, dancing and feasting. But then he thought of his aged parents and remembered that he had to go back, to reassure them that he was alive and well. The princess begged him to stay but he had no choice, so she gave him a farewell gift of a jewelled treasure box. He must keep it carefully, she told him, but never open it, no matter what.

The giant turtle took him back to the seashore. But when he got there nothing looked the same. There were new houses in his village and a new bridge across the river and the temple on the hill and the shrine at its base had been rebuilt. He couldn't find his parents' home or anyone he knew. Finally he came across a bent old woman. She thought for a long while. 'Urashima,' she said slowly. 'When I was a little girl people spoke of a boy of that name who disappeared into the sea and never came back. But that was many generations ago, long before I was born.' The dreadful realization dawned on Urashima. He had spent not three days but three hundred years under the waves.

Horrified, he decided he must go back straight away to the dragon king's daughter. Running to the seashore he stood at the edge of the grey roiling sea and called out to the giant turtle, but there was only the crash of the waves. He sat down on the sand and wept. Then he thought of the box the princess had given him. It was the only thing he had left. Perhaps it contained some clue. In desperation, forgetting the princess's warning, he opened it.

A wisp of smoke curled out. His hair turned white and his body grew old and bent, then began to dissolve. In a moment there was nothing left but a heap of dust which swirled around then blew away into the wind. The box had contained the three hundred years.

Nobu raised his head. Perhaps that was who he was

– Urashima. Perhaps they all were. Perhaps they would all have done better to have turned into dust rather than discover what had become of the life they had known. But no. His family was still here, enough of them. They would go together and pray at the family grave. It would be a start towards finding peace.

'Our dear mother was still young,' said Yasu. 'But Basho's mother's hair had turned white as snow.'

His voice quivering, Father murmured the haiku:

'te ni toraba kien	If I took it in my hands it would melt
namida zo atsuki	from the heat of my tears.
aki no shimo	Autumn frost.'

19

Taka peeked from behind the froth of lace around her mother's ample décolletage as they rumbled along the Ginza in their carriage. The maples and cherries that had made the street beautiful had lost most of their leaves and all her hopes had withered along with them.

Everything had got into such a muddle. She couldn't remember a time when she'd felt so confused. She sighed and leaned back against the upholstery, pulling her shawl closer, as the driver shook the reins and the groom sprinted ahead, clearing a way through the rickshaws, carriages and horse-drawn omnibuses that crammed the broad brick-paved mall. Ladies with plaid shawls wrapped around their kimonos, others in gowns with huge bustles and men in Inverness capes and mufflers or bowler hats atop their long huge-sleeved haori jackets and flowing hakama trousers promenaded along the pavements.

'Look at them all, just milling about as if they didn't have a care in the world.' Fujino gripped Taka's wrist, shouting above the hubbub of voices and the clatter of wheels and hooves. The tiered skirts of her elaborate day dress rustled with every bounce of the carriage. 'Life goes on as if nothing at all had happened.'

Taka shook her hand free. She wasn't aware anything had happened. Her mother was behaving strangely today. Her eyes glittered as if she had something on her mind. Taka sighed. She'd find out soon enough.

She sank deeper into her corner as they careered between honey-coloured brick shopfronts adorned with porticoes, arches, balconies and colonnades. The street was changing at an astonishing rate. Everyone agreed there was nothing like it in the whole of Japan, probably not in the world. Even in the short time since they'd last been here, whole new buildings had appeared, springing up like bamboo shoots. Usually, no matter how often Taka visited the Ginza, no matter how bleak life seemed, she couldn't help gasping at such a thrilling sight. But today she felt as if she was seeing it clearly for the first time. The splendour seemed tawdry. The street was rutted, the leafless trees scraggy, the people overdressed and garish and the horses looked like worn-out nags.

They cantered past Komura Bakery and the Tokyo Daily News Building with its portico arch and huge gaslight. A crowd just in from the country stood gawking as if at some famous temple or shrine. To the left, sightseers jammed the balconies of Matsuda restaurant – 'Beef for the masses,' sniffed Fujino, tossing the ribbons on her bonnet. To the right were the new postal offices where modern people took their letters, instead of rolling them into scrolls and sending for the courier with his lacquered box, as those in benighted parts of the country still did.

Fujino had said they were going to the Black Peony. But instead of turning off, they crossed Japan Bridge and rattled straight past the huge Echigoya dry-goods store. Smiling in that infuriating way of hers, she swung round and clamped her plump white hands over Taka's eyes.

'Just wait till you see this!'

When she pulled them away even Taka had to smile.

They'd drawn up in front of a building like a miniature castle. With its gleaming yellow bricks, tiers of red-tiled roofs and balconies with ornate fretted railings, it was a sight to make anyone forget their gloom. It stood five storeys high, like a child's building blocks piled one on top of the other, each of the higher floors a little smaller than the one below. At the very top a golden dolphin, like the ones that adorned the roof ends of warlords' castles, flipped its tail. People strode in and out – Chinese businessmen with long gowns and longer pigtails, ladies in kimonos or gowns with bustles and men in haori and hakama or bowler hats.

'Don't you know where we are?' Fujino asked, beaming and rubbing her hands as if about to let her into a fabulous secret. 'It's the head office of your company, run by your husband – your husband-to-be, that is – Shimada Bank! It's the newest building in the whole of Tokyo. Such a man as you've found! He's a banking genius. He's created a whole banking system for this country of ours – well, the Shimada family has, but everyone knows he's the brains behind it – and this is the Shimadas' private bank. He planned it, he runs it, the clerks who work here work for him – and he's totally bewitched by you!' Her capacious bosom visibly swelled. 'I know it's trying, having to wait so long before you get married and only having seen your betrothed that one time. But don't forget, most girls never meet their husbands even once, not until their wedding day. So you see, there's no need to worry. We'll soon have you happily settled and the mistress of the Shimada empire. You'll be putting on your red silk kimono soon enough, and that lovely white lace western gown too. It'll be the most splendid wedding anyone's ever seen. It'll be the talk of Tokyo.'

Taka nodded, trying her hardest to look excited and cheerful. She was amazed her mother couldn't see straight through her. It never seemed to dawn on her that the last thing Taka wanted was to be reminded of that dreadful day and the three wedding dresses she would don, one after the other.

She stared at her high button boots poking from under her day dress, side by side on the floor of the carriage. She was getting horribly tangled in this web. She was desperately afraid she'd never find a way to escape from it – and the worst of it was, it was all her own doing.

It was an impossible game to play, trying to fool Fujino into thinking she was eager to marry Masuda-*sama* and that the reason for her gloom was simply that she hadn't seen him for so long. She'd been afraid that if she complained too much her mother would say, 'Then let's just go to Kagoshima to join your father.' It was fortunate Fujino was so exuberant. She talked and talked without ever stopping to wonder what Taka herself might want or whether this man, genius or not, really was the right husband for her. The main thing was, Taka thought, she had to be sure Fujino never suspected for a moment that the person who filled her thoughts night and day was actually their ex-servant boy, a gangly young soldier with no money and precious little hope of advancement and, worst of all, an Aizu.

Exactly a hundred days had passed since that night Nobu had suddenly appeared at their house and they had sneaked off together to the woods at the far end of the grounds. Taka could still remember every breath, every word of that meeting, as vividly as if she were there – the bats flitting, the earthy smells, the stars twinkling through the leaves, the heat of his body next to hers in the moist darkness and the feel of his palm on hers as he took her hand.

'There's never been anyone but you,' he'd said. 'There never will be.'

But ever since then she'd heard nothing, only silence.

At first she'd been so sure he'd come again himself or send a message but days had gone by without a word. She tried to imagine what had happened. Maybe he couldn't get a message out from the Military Academy. He was not as free there as he had been at Mori's; it was like being in prison. Or maybe he'd decided there was too much between them, that she was wealthy and he not much more than a servant; maybe that was the truth of it. But poor though he was, he was also proud. She knew that he didn't consider himself one whit inferior to her. She could tell that he came from a distinguished family, even though it might have been cast low by the civil war.

She'd wondered if she could somehow get a note to him, but it was unthinkable to have her maid, pretty round-faced Okatsu, knocking at the gates of the barracks, asking for him. It would make him a laughing stock, he'd never forgive her. She'd just have to wait.

But at least they were still in Tokyo, they hadn't moved to Kagoshima. And while they were here, there was always a chance she'd hear from him.

Her mother prodded her with a plump elbow. 'You're a hundred *ri* away, dreaming about your wedding day. I know you'd like to have a look around the bank. I would myself. But we can't have you bumping into Masuda-*sama* before the great day, can we? Anyway, Aunt Kiharu's waiting.'

20

Aunt Kiharu was perched on a chair in one of the private rooms at the Black Peony, her skirts elegantly draped, her small head rising proudly above the frilled collar of her fitted jacket. Voices and laughter boomed from the main restaurant, shaking the sand-dusted walls and sliding paper doors with their painted chrysanthemums.

Looking around, Taka realized that they were in the very same room where the Satsuma samurai had charged in, waving his sword, three years earlier. Unbidden, an image rose of Nobu's sunburnt young face, scowling with determination as he tackled the assailant, and she blinked hard as tears sprang to her eyes.

While Fujino settled herself with much rustling and creaking over a couple of tiny chairs, waitresses began to file in with plates of dark red meat, cut paper thin and set out in rounds like the finest sashimi, and laid a few slices on the hot iron plate. After all this time Taka still didn't find it any easier to eat meat. She wrinkled her nose and dabbed at her eyes, grateful for the excuse, as smoke began to rise. It smelt like a funeral pyre.

Her mother drew herself up. 'Beef-eating is the mark

of the civilized classes,' she said sternly. 'People like us have to set an example. The emperor himself eats beef. If you're going to be Masuda-*sama*'s bride, you'll have to develop sophisticated tastes. In America, where he lived, they eat beef every day. That's why they're so big and strong. Isn't that right, Kiharu?'

Reluctantly Taka dipped her chopsticks into the raw egg in the bowl in front of her, whisked it up and took a slice of the grey cooked meat, trying not to look at Fujino's unblackened teeth. Every time she spoke Taka could see them gleaming in a most embarrassing way. She wondered what the waitresses made of them, whether they admired her mother for being so up to date or just thought she was odd. Probably the latter, Taka thought. At least Aunt Kiharu kept hers a respectable black.

'Come on, Kiharu, out with it.' Fujino and Aunt Kiharu pressed their heads together and were talking in undertones. Whenever they met they turned back into geishas and gossiped and giggled all evening about kabuki actors they both knew, referring to them by their nicknames. Geishas, of course, were entertainers, and the same low caste as actors, and they were all old friends.

'As for the Third Generation,' her mother would trill, speaking of Kikugoro, the third in his acting dynasty, 'he's incorrigible. You'd think he'd be satisfied with two but he goes and takes another lover – and so young. Really, that boy could be his grandson.' Or, flapping her fan disparagingly, 'That Older Brother', referring to the great Uzaemon, 'he's lost his touch. I saw him perform the other night. He should retire and leave the stage open for someone younger.'

Usually Taka didn't pay much attention to their middle-aged women's chat. But today the conversation seemed to take a different turn.

'You're so cruel, Kiharu,' Fujino was saying to her friend in her most wheedling tones, as if cajoling a customer. She took a sip of warm sake and held it in her mouth for a moment before swallowing it. 'Don't keep me in the dark. That lover of yours, I know he tells you things when you're tucked up in your futons. What was he now? Minister of defence, wasn't it, or the interior? Minister of something, anyway. Come on, be kind. Even my servants know there's something going on. Another uprising, is it?'

Her chair creaked as she adjusted her bustle, shooting a sidelong glance at Taka. Taka played with the stringy grey strands of beef, hoping her mother wouldn't notice she hadn't eaten any.

Aunt Kiharu waved the waitresses away, glancing over her shoulder as if afraid someone might overhear. 'It was in Hagi, in Choshu country, in the south-west. Do you remember Issei Maebara?'

'The Choshu fellow with the horse face and wild hair? Of course. He was imperial counsellor and vice minister of the army. He resigned years ago and we never heard a word from him after that.'

Aunt Kiharu hesitated. 'There's a rumour there was an uprising – only a rumour, mind – and that he was behind it.'

'That makes three uprisings in – what – fifteen days.' Fujino was leaning forward, chopsticks in the air, chewing her under lip, her eyes glittering. 'So what happened?'

'It seems he and his men raided the arsenal and plundered the district treasury and stocked up on weapons and money. Then the government got wind of it and sent in troops. Another of those crazy protests against the government cutting off samurais' stipends – that's how my *danna* sees it, anyway.' She flashed her black eyes at Taka's mother. Whatever Aunt Kiharu's *danna* – her patron and lover – said was not to be questioned.

'It's all very well for him,' Fujino snapped, bunching her caterpillar eyebrows. 'He has a job. What are these men supposed to do without their stipends? They can't wear swords any more, they've had to cut their hair, there are no wars to fight. They have to make a living somehow.'

'My *danna* says there's been rioting in the countryside too. The farmers are up in arms.'

Taka stared wildly at one then the other. An uprising, and they'd sent troops to put it down? Perhaps Nobu had been called upon to fight. Perhaps that was why she hadn't heard from him. But no, she told herself. They wouldn't use students to put down a rebellion.

Aunt Kiharu was fiddling with her fan.

'And what about Maebara-*sama*?' Fujino demanded, her voice hoarse. She was panting, her large bosom rising and falling. 'What happened to him?'

There was a long silence. 'He went on the run.' Aunt Kiharu hesitated and dropped her eyes and drew her breath through her teeth.

For a moment Fujino's air of regal self-possession crumbled, as if a curtain had been lifted, and Taka caught a glimpse of someone very different, someone she didn't recognize at all. The colour drained from her mother's cheeks, her shoulders slumped and her round face hollowed and grew haggard. She stared blank-eyed into the distance.

Taka turned away. She couldn't bear to see her proud, strong mother suddenly defenceless and afraid. She had a dreadful feeling that whatever was happening was going to change all their lives, though she couldn't yet imagine how.

There was a long silence. Fujino dabbed at her eyes, her hand shaking. 'So he's been executed.'

'Not yet, but he will be. After a proper trial, of course.'

'Poor Maebara.'

'You knew him?' Taka was desperate to know why her mother was so shaken by the news. 'Was it in Gion? Did I meet him?'

But the façade was firmly back in place. Her mother smiled ruefully. 'It was before your time, my dear. A bit serious for my taste, but he liked his drink as well as the next man. And to hear him sing! To see him dance! He could do Sukeroku's grand entrance as well as the greatest kabuki actor. And utterly committed to the southern cause.' She heaved a sigh. 'Yet he ends up with his head cut off – and by his own comrades.'

They sat in silence while meat hissed and sizzled on the iron plate. Shouts and laughter and the banging of plates echoed from the main restaurant. Fujino and Aunt Kiharu seemed caught up in their thoughts. At least there'd been no mention of Masuda-*sama*. Taka was not sure how long she could carry on the pretence that she missed him and was eager to be married.

Aunt Kiharu put down her chopsticks. 'What a bunch of hotheads they were!' Her eyes were shining. 'But how we loved them! I don't remember Gion ever being so exciting, before or since.'

Taka's mother chewed silently, the lightest of frowns creasing the smooth pale flesh of her forehead. She shook her head. 'Poor Maebara-*sama*!' she said again.

'When did they first turn up in Kyoto, those southern lads with their ponytails and their sleeves tied back, itching for a fight?' Aunt Kiharu persisted. 'I can't have been thirteen, I hadn't even come out yet. I still had my hair in the *ware shinobu* style and painted my face and wobbled around on those absurdly high clogs and had long flapping sleeves like the little virgin that I was. Let me think. I didn't meet them in a teahouse.'

'I should think not. They didn't have any money, unlike the usual customers,' said Taka's mother. She took a folded tea-ceremony paper from her bag and blotted her lips, leaving a scarlet imprint.

'And unlike the usual customers they were young and handsome. Do you remember those awful merchants we used to entertain with their wrinkly jowls and bellies hanging over their sashes? Sometimes, when I was snuggling up to one, telling him how handsome he was and how much I loved him, I had to bite my cheeks to stop myself laughing. You're lucky you don't have to play those silly games, Taka. They were forever throwing money around, showing off the flashy silk linings to their coats, doing business deals over dinner and getting disgustingly drunk. It was all fun, though – until those young men appeared. They were a breath of fresh air.'

Taka opened her mouth to protest. Her mother too had been swept off her feet by these romantic young warriors when she was Taka's age. How could she possibly imagine that Taka could want to marry a banker? But if she refused to marry Masuda-*sama*, she and her mother would be on their way to Kyushu in no time, she reminded herself. She really had got herself into a fix.

'They must have stayed in cheap inns to begin with or slept under a bridge, until they found us geishas. We really did fall in love with them, it wasn't play-acting when it came to them.'

'So much we didn't even care that they had no money.' Fujino's skirts ballooned as she rocked back on her chair. She patted them down with a plump hand, fluttering her lashes as if she were once again surrounded by handsome young warriors.

'And then the fighting began. If truth be told it was those young men wreaking havoc.' Aunt Kiharu glanced at Taka. 'You were just a little girl then, Taka. You don't remember.'

'I do,' Taka protested, but her mother and her friend were too caught up in their memories to pay the slightest attention.

'I used to run in and out with flasks of sake when they were having their secret meetings. They'd be on their feet, arguing, or heads together, plotting. "Revere the emperor, expel the barbarians", that was their slogan. You know what they wanted, Taka? It was to drive out the foreigners. It's hard to imagine that now, isn't it? And to throw out the shogun, who ruled the country in those days, and kill the northern clansmen.'

The two women looked at each other and smiled and shook their heads.

'They were ronin,' said Taka's mother. 'Young people today don't even know what that means. They'd left their clans so their lords wouldn't have to take responsibility for them. That meant they were free, they could do anything they liked. Of course they all had principles, but the trouble was, one clan's principles were the opposite of another's.'

'And then the whole place went mad – battles in the streets, swordsmen breaking into the mansions of the shogun's advisers and cutting off their heads. I remember walking across Fourth Bridge, trying not to look at the heads stuck on bamboo stakes all along the riverside.'

Fujino flung Taka a worried look. 'That's enough, Kiharu,' she said sharply.

'I was there too, Mother,' Taka protested. 'I saw the heads. There was always fighting when I was little.'

'And the next thing you know, the shogun's police come knocking on our door and I'm standing right there, blocking their way, while they shake their swords at me.' Aunt Kiharu grabbed the sake flask and filled Fujino's cup, then held out her own for Fujino to fill. 'Cool as you like, swearing blind there was no one there, when all the while my lover's under the house, not daring to breathe.'

'And which lover was that, my dear?'

'There were more than enough in those days! Do you remember Hiro? He always had a twinkle in his eye, that one. What was that song he used to sing?' Aunt Kiharu cocked her head and sang in her geisha warble:

'*Drunk, my head pillowed in a beauty's lap;*
Awake and sober, grasping power to govern the nation.

'Dear Hiro always said they had to hold him back to stop him cutting down everyone in sight with his sword. Yes, they were certainly firebrands, those young men. Until Masa came along and calmed everyone down.'

Taka had been toying with her meat. She sat up with a start. It was her father Aunt Kiharu was talking about. All this had something to do with him. That was why her mother was so agitated.

Fujino had lowered her eyes and was staring at the table, her plump cheeks flushed, trying to compose her face, tearing her tea-ceremony paper into shreds.

'Now that was a man!' said Aunt Kiharu blithely. Nothing could stop her when she was in full flow. 'Those broad shoulders of his and that bull neck. He towered over everyone. And those eyes. You felt as if he could see straight through you. The other lads would be talking and shouting, whipping out their swords at the first opportunity, but he . . . You'd say something and he'd think for a long time, then answer very slowly and carefully in that Satsuma accent of his. I couldn't understand a word until I got used to it. And once he'd decided something, nothing would budge him. All that pent-up energy waiting to burst out. He was like a volcano.'

Taka's mother laughed, not a high-pitched geisha tinkle but a throaty chuckle. 'He was hefty, that one, as big as a horse. In fact, you couldn't find a horse strong enough to carry him. Good thing you don't take after him, Taka. Good thing you don't take after either of us.'

She sighed. 'Not surprising he and I got together, I suppose. He could certainly put away his rice – you've never seen such an appetite.'

'An appetite for other things too, I imagine,' said Aunt Kiharu, glancing slyly at Fujino out of the corner of her eye.

'An appetite for life. I remember when he first turned up at the teahouse. I'd always been rather a specialized taste in Kyoto. Men didn't usually go in for large women.' She dimpled. 'They didn't call me Princess Pig for nothing. I was no smaller then than I am now.'

'No need for modesty, my dear,' said Aunt Kiharu. 'You ended up with the best man of all.'

'Well, I could sing and dance as well as anyone, I made sure of that.'

'You were witty, too, you had them all in fits of laughter. And you knew how to make a man feel good.'

'Then one day this hulking fellow turns up. One of the Satsuma leaders brought him, if I remember rightly. I was a geisha, of course – can't sink lower than that – and he was a low-ranking samurai; we both came from unassuming backgrounds. And neither of us was small. He looked at me and I looked at him and that was it.'

'And a few years later, when a troop of Choshu lads tried to kidnap the emperor and got right to the imperial palace gates—'

'There was our Masa, at the head of the Satsuma troops, defending it.'

'Half the city went up in flames. You were a little girl by then, Taka, such a pretty little girl.'

'I ran out into the road and saw flames filling the sky,

like a wall of fire,' said Taka, joining in. 'And heard the crackling and the roar.'

'And in the end they won. Who would ever have imagined that? The Choshu and the Satsuma joined forces and won and the next thing you know, our lovers have taken over the realm. They put on western clothes and cut their hair and grew up and became statesmen.'

'Some of them even married the geishas who'd taken such good care of them. Ikumatsu, for one. She's the lucky one.'

'She deserved it. Do you remember how she used to charm all the northerners who went to her teahouse to drink? She'd winkle secrets out of them, then pass them on to Kogoro. And when he ran away from the shogun's police and hid under Fourth Bridge disguised as a beggar, she saved rice balls and took them out to him every night.'

'And now Kogoro Katsura is one of the most powerful men in the land . . .'

'. . . and she's the honourable Madame Katsura. I meet her at parties sometimes. She still plays the shamisen and dances very nicely.'

The two women looked at each other and smiled ruefully.

'Some did better, some did worse. My *danna*'s kind enough to me but there was never any talk of marriage,' said Aunt Kiharu.

'Don't be silly. He already had a wife. As for my Masa, perhaps he had another wife he never told me about or perhaps he just didn't want to marry me. Perhaps he wanted to keep me as his geisha, not his wife. Geishas are geishas, wives are wives. Some men want both. Most do, in fact. I must say, I miss that man. He'd scold me if he knew what kind of a life we lead here. He doesn't believe in spending money or living in luxury.'

'They joined forces and won the war and did exactly what dear Hiro used to sing about – they grasped power to govern the nation. And now – would you believe it? – they're falling out with each other. Maebara-*sama* was the vice minister of the army, no less. And now . . .'

'Well, well.' Fujino helped herself to another piece of beef.

Aunt Kiharu narrowed her eyes and gave her a long hard look. With her pointed chin it made her look even more like a little bird. 'So far these uprisings have been barely tremors.' She raised her chopsticks, little finger extended, and dunked a piece of beef into her bowlful of raw egg. 'Take Masa, now,' she said, measuring her words. 'If he were to rise with that Satsuma army of his, that would really be something. That would turn this country on its head. That would be a real earthquake.'

A shiver ran down Taka's spine. Ever since Eijiro left, her mother hadn't said a word about her father or what was going on in Kyushu. Despite what Nobu had told her, despite Eijiro's dramatic departure, she'd been praying they'd all been wrong, that nothing would happen.

Fujino slapped down her chopsticks and stood up so sharply her chair fell over. 'Be careful what you say. He's not a fool.'

'Of course not, my dear. But those men of his – keeping them reined in must be like trying to hold together a rotten water barrel with a frayed old piece of rope. That's what my *danna* says.' Aunt Kiharu unfurled her fan and gave it a flap. 'But what do I know? I'm just a silly woman.'

'He leads a quiet life down there,' Fujino retorted a little too sharply. 'He hunts, he fishes, he farms, he goes for walks with his dogs. That's all, nothing else. There is no army.'

A waitress picked up her chair and she settled herself down again, her face once more placid and aloof. Taka stared at her. She wondered if her mother really had any idea what her father was doing. Perhaps he wrote to her; after all, they had always been devoted to each other. Perhaps she knew exactly what was happening; but she was certainly not going to reveal a word of it to anyone.

'Well, well.' Aunt Kiharu pursed her lips. 'He's certainly got the government rattled. If I were you I'd be gone. I'm taking a risk just being seen with you.'

'I'm just his geisha, not his wife. They don't bother with little fish like us,' said Taka's mother. In that case, Taka thought, why had she told the servants to paint over the family crest on the rickshaws and carriages?

'To be honest with you, Kiharu, I'm hanging on here by a thread. If it wasn't for Taka I'd be down there with Masa. He's as stubborn as an ox. Once he starts something he'll see it through to the end. But I want to wait till Taka's taken care of. She'll be free of the Kitaoka name soon, she won't have to carry that stigma any more. She'll be home and dry, she'll be a Masuda. The government needs money and the Shimadas hold the purse strings. You know the new Shimada Bank? Our Masuda-*sama* is virtually running it.' She smiled. 'I'm trying to educate her on what he does so when they're married she can take an interest. I want to make sure she satisfies him in every possible way so he won't be going to visit geishas or taking concubines.'

'Well, I hope you've given her pillow books and instructions on the night-time side of things,' said Aunt Kiharu in her bird-like trill. Taka cringed, wishing she could disappear under the table. 'You'd better make sure she knows all the tricks – how to give a man pleasure, how to sing out in the night. You know about that better than anyone. She needs to be the perfect wife and the perfect geisha, both. That's the best way to make sure a man never strays. Though to be honest, a man that didn't stray would be a real skinflint!' She turned to Taka. 'Tuck in, child. This beef is delicious, it simply dissolves in the mouth. It's really no different at all from eel, you know. Think of it as mountain eel, it'll go down easier.'

Strands of smoke mingled above the grilling meat. Aunt Kiharu took a scrap, dipped it into the raw egg and popped it in her mouth, smacking her lips. Taka reached for a strand of the stringy meat and pulled it apart with her chopsticks. It was not like eel at all but, if she tried hard enough, she could pretend it was.

21

The next morning when the servant brought in the *Tokyo Daily News* for her mother, Taka ran after him and snatched it from his hands. It was brimful of news about Maebara and his failed rebellion. She was so engrossed in the paper that it was late when she started for school. As she climbed into the rickshaw all she could think about was the conversation she'd overheard the previous day. She wondered what effect this new turn of events would have on their lives.

Her school, Kijibashi, had opened three years earlier, around the time that Taka's father stormed off to Kyushu. The other girls all came from wealthy, powerful families, with fathers broad-minded enough to be willing to pay for their daughters' education. Some were the languid offspring of Kyoto aristocrats, others of daimyo warlords now reappointed as provincial governors. But most, like Taka, were the daughters of the new elite, the southern samurai who had fought and won the civil war and pushed their way up from humble origins to grasp power.

Taka was undoing her boots at the door of the sprawling temple complex where the school was held when she heard voices piercing the thin wooden walls.

'That rebellion in Hagi.' She started and looked up, listening hard, as she caught what they were saying. 'You'll never guess who the leader was.'

'Counsellor Maebara. Imagine that! He used to visit our house.'

She recognized the voices. It was not the Kyoto girls; they were far too grand to take the slightest interest in politics. It was the southerners' daughters, her closest allies and friends, who listened in on intense political discussions at home and whose statesmen fathers knew what was happening long before anyone else did. But usually the girls discussed their schoolwork or gossiped about the teachers or each other. It was unheard of for anyone to talk politics at school.

A second voice piped up. 'Father says there's going to be another war soon and everyone knows who'll be behind it. General Kitaoka, that's who. He's a traitor, that's what everyone's saying.' Taka gasped with horror. She knew the earthy vowels – Okimi, with her cropped hair and rolled-up sleeves, who thought herself bolder and more unconventional than anyone else. Her father was a leading figure in the new regime and he and Taka's father had been close. Okimi had been Taka's most devoted friend until their fathers fell out.

'He wants to destroy everything we've achieved and take us back to the feudal age!' It was willowy Ofumi, the bespectacled daughter of a government minister, who always behaved as if she was a cut above everyone else.

Voices sparked one after another until the buzz echoed through the halls and classrooms, drumming in Taka's ears. 'Kitaoka's a traitor, a hateful traitor.'

Taka knelt for a moment, her face blazing, her heart thundering in her chest. She couldn't believe her erstwhile friends could turn against her so treacherously. Furious, she kicked off her shoes and slid open the door to the classroom with a bang. A sea of accusing eyes turned towards her and quickly looked away.

'My father's not a traitor,' she shouted, on the verge of tears. 'He has principles. He left the government because he disapproved of everything they were doing. You call my father a traitor – yours are crooks.' The words came rushing from her mouth before she could stop herself. She remembered everything she'd heard her father say. 'They're in the pay of the banks and the finance corporations. They've forgotten their ideals, all they're interested in is lining their own pockets, and they don't care if they destroy the entire samurai class while they're at it. Yes, your father, Okimi, and yours, Ofumi.' Her words dropped into the silence like stones into a lake. She knew she'd gone too far, but she was too angry to care. 'My father's at home in Kyushu, where half your families come from too! He's got nothing to do with Maebara or his insurrection. How dare you speak of him with disrespect!'

She sat back, panting. She was expecting her classmates to argue but no one said a word. They stared grimly at their desks. Even the Kyoto girls were silent; not one of them wanted to be associated with her, as if she was infected with some dreadful disease. It was a relief when the teacher came in and made them open their books.

Throughout the rest of the day, as Taka went from class to class, she heard voices rising and falling.

Conversations tailed off as she approached, then started again as she walked away.

She kept her head high. That was what her father would have wanted. But in the rickshaw on the way home, she held her sleeves to her face and sobbed aloud.

They were racing along the broad avenues of the samurai district, between high walls lined with moats, when she noticed a face bobbing alongside. It was a man with veined cheeks and a cloth knotted around his head like a labourer. 'Hey, you! Kitaoka girl!' he panted, trying to grab at her skirts. She started in horror. He'd recognized the rickshaw even though the family crest was painted over. 'Tell your father we're with him! The men of Edo are ready to rise. We'll get rid of those southern embezzlers.'

Others joined him, sprinting alongside. The driver was running so fast the rickshaw swerved violently and Taka was thrown across the seat, clinging to the rim until her knuckles were white.

Suddenly a stone ricocheted off the back. A different accent shouted, 'Kitaoka! Traitor!' and she jumped so violently the rickshaw tilted and nearly turned over. She caught a glimpse of someone running off and remembered the samurai who had burst into the Black Peony. This time there was no Nobu nearby to save her.

Usually Taka went round to the family door but today she just wanted to get inside as quickly as she could. As they rattled through the gates, she shouted to the rickshaw boy to stop and climbed down shakily. She ran to the great main door, stumbled in and leaned against it, breathing hard.

'I hate that place. I'm never going back.' Her words echoed round the empty hallway.

The vestibule smelt dank and cold. The front door was reserved for formal callers and the family seldom came here. Taka dried her eyes on her sleeve, bent down and fumbled with the buttons of her boots, wishing she was wearing sandals that she could slip out of more easily. Western clothes just weren't made for Japanese houses, she thought, struggling with the hard leather.

She was prising the first boot off when she noticed a couple of pairs of men's shoes lined up in the vestibule, smelling of leather and polish. When Eijiro had been around there'd always been visitors but since he'd left, the house had become very quiet. No one came to visit any more.

The inner doors slid open and a round, pretty face appeared.

'Otaka-*sama*!' It was Okatsu, rosy-cheeked and panting. She must have been waiting at the family door and had come in search of her. She glanced behind her, raising her eyebrows. 'Visitors, just leaving.'

Taka kicked off the second boot and had scrambled to her knees when two men appeared, bony hands poking from the cuffs of their western suits. They looked like the shopkeepers who brought silks to the house, pale and stooped, as if they spent their time lurking in sunless rooms, fingering abacuses.

Fujino glided behind them like a great ship in full sail. She was wearing a kimono today, a particularly lavish one, with an elaborate design of chrysanthemums and pine branches on a white background and a richly embroidered olive-green obi, the sort of garment a top-class geisha would wear, not the modest, self-effacing consort of a great statesman. Taka had last seen her in it when her father hosted a party for his colleagues, some time before his sudden departure. She must have known there were visitors coming and dressed for the occasion.

She held herself tall and had her geisha face firmly in place, serene and impassive, but her eyes flashed dangerously. Taka hoped the men had not brought bad news. Perhaps something had happened to her father or Eijiro; or perhaps there'd been another insurrection.

'*Ara*. Taka, you're back.' Taka bowed to the floor and pressed her face to her hands. 'Gentlemen, my worthless daughter, Taka. Taka, these gentlemen are from the Shimada company. Mr Hashimoto was kind enough to . . .'

Taka looked up. The older man was bowing nervously, like a nodding Daruma doll. He had a sagging, lugubrious face with pouches like money bags under his eyes and a wispy grey moustache flaring out on each side of his mouth. So this was Mr Hashimoto, the go-between. He'd probably come to make some final arrangements for the marriage. The net was tightening.

The men bowed again, stumbling into each other as they backed towards the door.

'So kind of you to grace our humble abode,' Fujino said in bell-like tones. Taka looked at her in surprise. The note of sarcasm was unmistakable.

'A privilege to have met you,' said Hashimoto, bobbing his head. 'I've heard so much about your famous Kyoto hospitality.'

Fujino raised an ironic eyebrow. 'Too kind.' She

smiled sadly. 'If you get the chance you should go to Kyoto, gentlemen, and see the places where the famous battles were fought. But these days Gion is not what it was. We're all in such a rush to be modern, we've lost those old-fashioned ideals that our men fought for – honour and loyalty and pride. But don't let me keep you, gentlemen.'

'Please pass on our respects to his lordship. We'll be in touch when all this – er – business is over.'

The two men clambered to their feet, bowing and apologizing, and backed out of the door. They climbed into their rickshaws. There was a volley of shouts from the rickshaw boys and a creak of wheels and they disappeared in a flurry of dust.

Taka was desperate to find out what news the men had brought but she knew better than to rush her mother. Moving at a stately pace, Fujino led the way back to the family quarters and settled on her knees beside the brazier in the great main chamber. She pressed two fingers to her forehead and gently smoothed out the creases and sighed, shaking her head. 'What a lesson. We should never have had anything to do with merchants. They've no idea how to behave. Shocking ill manners. It's really too bad, my dear – and just as you'd become so enthusiastic, too. Okatsu, tea!'

Taka dropped to her knees beside her. She was beginning to guess why the men had come. Her mother reached out a plump white hand and laid it on hers.

'You mean Masuda-*sama* . . . ?' asked Taka.

Okatsu lifted the steaming kettle from its hook over the brazier, filled the teapot, poured out two cups of tea, put them on a tray and held it out to Taka and her mother.

Fujino's large bosom rose and fell and she sighed again. 'I thought if I could push the deal through quickly enough, you wouldn't have to endure the life I used to lead. I wanted so much to find you a husband. It's a shame, but it can't be helped. You can't play games with the Shimadas. They're a wily lot.' She hesitated and looked questioningly at Taka. 'Mr Hashimoto brought a letter.'

She held out a document, not rolled into a scroll in the traditional way but neatly folded. The paper was some modern weave and the script was crabbed and tight, the writing of a man who spent his days counting money, not the grand unreadable flourishes of a swordsman or a calligrapher:

Greetings. We hope this autumn season finds Madame Kitaoka in the very best of health and we offer our sincere gratitude for all the kindnesses Madame has deigned to shower upon us. We offer profound apologies for our recent silence regarding the marriage of Madame's honourable and virtuous daughter to the unworthy young master of our house. We are informed that Master Eijiro has returned to Kyushu to join Lord Kitaoka and fully understand that Madame will wish to postpone all marriage plans until his safe return. We would not like to put Madame to any inconvenience, nor do we wish to embarrass Madame, and therefore happily agree to put all plans in abeyance until Master Eijiro's safe return. We will not stand in the way should the honourable House of Kitaoka choose to look elsewhere. Signed this thirteenth day of the tenth month, Hiroyuki Hashimoto, chief clerk at the House of Shimada, Banking and Trading Corporation.

Taka had to read the words several times before she could grasp the meaning. The letter must have taken a long time to compose, she thought. It was carefully phrased to make sure no one lost face, but also that there was no mistaking the intention. So Masuda-*sama* was withdrawing his offer. Now that her father was spoken of in the same breath as outlaws and rebels, the last thing the Shimadas wanted was an alliance with his family. Far from being a highly desirable match, she'd become a pariah. The only surprise was that the letter hadn't come earlier.

She breathed out hard. It was a stinging rebuff but also a reprieve. Her plan – to pretend she was eager to marry so that she could stay on in Tokyo – had been completely misconceived, she could see that now. If Masuda-*sama* hadn't pulled out she would have ended up marrying him. She had had a lucky escape.

But instead of relief, a shock of fear swept over her, as if she'd been pushing against a great rock which had suddenly given way, leaving her teetering at the edge of an abyss. She put her face in her hands, trembling, aghast at the looming emptiness before her. She'd been so busy praying to be saved from this marriage, she hadn't stopped to think what she would do if her prayers were answered. Now they had been – and she had not the faintest idea what would become of her.

'Every stream has its depths and shallows,' she reminded herself, trying to find reassurance in one of the proverbs Nobu used to quote in that touchingly old-fashioned way of his. It still hurt to think of him. After their two romantic meetings, she'd waited day after day for him to come back, daydreamed about how they might run away together, like people did in the old stories. But he'd simply disappeared, as he had before, into thin air. He hadn't even sent a message. She couldn't believe he could be so cruel. A terrible thought came to her – that he'd been sent to the front, perhaps killed. Even that was better than thinking he'd stopped caring about her.

Perhaps she shouldn't have tried so hard to postpone the marriage. Masuda had been a decent enough man. She pressed her hands to her face and gave a long shuddering sigh. At least marriage would have been a familiar fate. But now instead she saw her life stretching out ahead of her, an empty road, long and bleak, with no marriage and no Nobu.

At least she didn't need to hide her feelings. Her mother would just assume she was distressed by the abrupt end of all her marriage hopes.

'Come, come, my dear,' said Fujino, gently patting her thigh. 'You're better off out of it. Between you and me, I never liked Madame Masuda. Jumped-up townswoman with those snobbish airs of hers. They're an arrogant lot, the Shimadas, they don't care what anyone thinks of them. No sense of honour, no idea how decent people behave.

'I know you're sixteen, nearly seventeen, but don't worry. There's still time. We'll find someone for you. One man's much like another. Your father would have hated you to marry a banker, anyway. What you need is a dashing soldier, like the men I adored when I was your age. One of your father's lieutenants, for example. Do you remember the imperial guards who were always around the house? Wasn't there one you used to look at with big eyes? I'm your mother, dear. Mothers notice such things.'

Taka glared at her. She wanted to tell her never to interfere in her life again. But despite everything she found herself picturing the young men in their splendid uniforms and the tall, serious one with the pale face and intense eyes who'd been her father's right-hand man.

Okatsu took a poker and shook the glowing embers in the brazier until they crackled and spat and burst into flame. She was avoiding Taka's gaze. In front of Taka's mother she couldn't say anything.

Fujino sat back, took a sip of tea, smoothed her skirts and tucked them neatly under her knees. It was what she always did when she had something momentous to say. Taka waited, eyes narrowed. Her mother took a breath. 'I've been too selfish, dear. We'll go to Kagoshima, to your father. The imperial guards are there with him. Perhaps we can—'

'Kagoshima?' Taka's mouth fell open. She'd had a feeling this was what her mother was leading up to but it was a shock all the same. Okatsu had stopped poking the fire and was staring at Fujino in consternation, her eyes huge.

'Kagoshima?' Taka said again. 'You mean . . . leave Tokyo? Leave our house?'

'Don't pucker your forehead like that. It's very unbecoming. You'll give yourself wrinkles. Gonsuké will book the passage. It'll be an adventure. Your father needs us. He'll be pleased to see us.' Taka stared at her. She was not sure about that at all.

'But . . . but what about Haru?'

'Your sister belongs to another house now.'

'But she still visits from time to time and it's comforting to be close. It will be lonely for her if we disappear off to the ends of the earth.' Taka took a breath. 'Mother, it's a foreign country down there. We'll be like exiles. We won't understand what people say. Are there four seasons, like in Tokyo? Do they have cherry blossom? We don't know anything about it.' She was shouting now. 'And you don't want to go there any more than I do.'

Fujino slammed her teacup down on the edge of the hearth. 'We're going to Kyushu whether we like it or not.' Her voice was shaking. 'We're out of choices. I hadn't realized how dangerous our situation had become till that letter arrived. Now that your father's being branded a traitor we have to go quickly, tomorrow if we can. We may already have left it too late.'

To Taka's horror her mother's eyes filled with tears. She suddenly saw that it was far worse for her. She and Taka's father had been apart for three years and Fujino had no idea what had happened in that time. He hadn't summoned her, he probably wouldn't even want to see her.

He had a wife, if not two or three, and probably some geisha mistresses. After all, he was a man, and that was the way men were. How would he feel when they suddenly arrived? Her brother Eijiro could fight alongside him in battle but Taka and her mother were useless women. Why should he be glad to see his old mistress,

no matter how much he'd loved her in the past? Far
from his being glad to see them, they might even have
to make their own living arrangements. They would
probably just be in the way.

No news had come from Kyushu for months. No one
knew what was going on down there.

All this time Taka had fought against leaving behind
everything she knew and loved in order to go to
Kagoshima. It was the fate she'd feared most. And now
it was happening. It was a step into the void.

'Can I . . . Can Okatsu come too?' she whispered,
aghast at the immensity of it all.

'Of course. The maids will come.'

Taka gazed around at the spacious room with its pale
tatami smelling of rice straw, at the upholstered western
sofa that no one ever sat on at one end of the room, the
ancient chests, the brazier with the kettle hanging over
it, the low table and oil lamps and cushions, the
polished wooden staircase leading to the upper floor,
the smells of cooking from the kitchen. It had been
home for more than half her life. She barely remembered the war-torn streets of Kyoto or the long journey
from Kyoto to Tokyo. And now they were to leave, to
make another journey, far longer and harder, to a place
which none of them knew at all.

And Nobu. Here in their house she'd been
surrounded by memories of him. At least while she was
here there'd always been a chance he might get in touch.
Once they left it would be impossible to find him or for
him to find her.

Perhaps, she thought, she could send him a message.
She would write a letter and Okatsu could take it to the

postal office. It would be like setting a lantern on the water at the Obon festival to light the spirits of the ancestors on their way. It might reach him or it might not, but it was the only thing left for her to do. But where would she send it? The only place where he might be was the Military Academy.

But her father was an enemy of the state, virtually an outlaw. People denounced him as a traitor.

It was not north versus south any longer, she saw that now. The old days her mother loved to reminisce about so fondly had long since disappeared. It was her father's own erstwhile colleagues who were against him. They'd all risen in rebellion and fought a war together but they'd had different aims. And once the government set to work on its reforms, her father had become more and more convinced that what they were doing went against everything he stood for – the samurai code, the old values. His colleagues were determined to throw away the past and move into the future and line their pockets while they were at it, or so her father said, but as far as he was concerned they were moving too fast and in the wrong direction.

When she'd met Nobu in the garden that summer's night, he had warned her, 'Your family and mine are enemies.' When he'd worked at their house, her family had been the wealthy rulers, his the impoverished defeated, struggling to survive. But now it was her father who was the rebel. And the bitterest irony of all was that Nobu, who'd been the underdog, had joined the army, whose task it would be to put down any rebellion. Everything had turned upside down but one thing had not changed. No matter what happened, they were still on opposite sides, doomed to be apart for ever.

The servants were starting to pack up around her. Taka rested her elbows on her knees and buried her face in her hands. She had never felt so lonely in her life.

PART IV

No Turning Back

22

'Yeeaah!'

A high-pitched yell rang out, so ear-shatteringly ferocious that Eijiro stumbled and nearly dropped his practice sword. Before he had time to recover, the drill instructor's sword smashed down on his and the smack of wood on wood echoed off the hills. Eijiro's knees buckled and he staggered, blowing out hard. He towered over the small, slender instructor, but that gave him not the slightest advantage.

The two hilts rammed together and the instructor drove Eijiro back relentlessly step by step until he slipped and fell. Cursing, he scrambled to his feet. The sword master was waiting quietly, glossy ponytail swinging. He didn't have a hair out of place.

He raised his stick again and there was another nerve-rattling shriek as he swung it through the sky straight towards Eijiro's head. Eijiro's arms were giving way but he braced himself and managed to raise his own practice sword to parry. Stick cracked on stick but this time he fought back and managed to land a few blows of his own until the instructor drove him back against the wall again. He bowed, heaving a sigh of relief as the barrage stopped. Legs quivering, he stumbled to the nearest tree, leaned his sword against it and bent over, panting hard. His breath was like smoke in the icy air.

He straightened up and rubbed his sleeve across his face. The rough hempen cloth snagged on his unshaven cheeks. The earth was hard and cold under his feet and a stiff wind stirred the trees and shook the wooden walls of the converted stables where the students lived and classes were held. There'd been a sprinkling of snow that day though generally winter was a lot warmer here than it had been in Tokyo; but apart from that, this place had precious little to recommend it. The worst thing was having to kowtow to this whipper-snapper – he, Eijiro Kitaoka, universally acclaimed one of the best swordsmen in Tokyo. Here he'd had to learn that perfect form was not all there was to it. These fellows sparred as if they were fighting for their lives.

If pushed, he'd have to acknowledge that in Tokyo he'd let himself go just a little. He was a lot leaner and trimmer now than he'd ever been back then and his arms were like iron from hours of daily sword practice. It was good to exercise, to feel the blood rushing through his veins, to know he'd be good and ready when the time came. Though privately he doubted if it ever would; and if it did, he was far from sure that any amount of swordsmanship was going to win out over soldiers with guns.

'You've worked hard. Well done.' The instructor

clicked his heels and bowed politely, sinewy calves gleaming beneath his hiked-up kimono skirts.

'Thanks.' Eijiro knelt on the icy ground and made a perfunctory bow, then stood up, brushing black volcanic dust off his knees. 'I'm off. I'm on dock duty today.'

The snow was coming down hard as Eijiro headed through the streets of Kagoshima. It dusted the broad leaves of the palm trees and settled in the fibrous crevices of the trunks, etched the tiles on the castle roofs, frosted the *tori* gates in front of the shrines and lay thick in the curving eaves of the temples. It crusted the stone foxes and small Jizo images along the road and collected in tiny pyramids on the offerings of Satsuma oranges and bottles of shochu in front of them. The hills that rose behind the city, where the training camps were, glistened white. Cocks crowed and woodsmoke drifted from thousands of houses as women lit breakfast fires.

Eijiro hurried along, head bowed and shivering, pulling his coat closer around him and rubbing his hands up and down his arms. He hadn't realized it could snow in this tropical place. He thought back to his handsome western clothes and grimaced. He'd had to leave behind his smart woollen-worsted topcoat and expensive waistcoats, shirts, cravats and trousers. These days all he had to wear was a cheap cotton kimono with leggings, an overcoat and wooden geta clogs. He could feel the snow crunching under his toes.

Life in Kyushu had come as a terrible shock. He hadn't expected it to be so primitive and tough, apart from which he couldn't understand a word anyone said;

but now, four months on, he felt like an old hand. In the end most of his pals had come along with him, even that little bastard Suzuki who'd let Yamakawa down so badly. For all their Tokyo airs, they were Satsuma lads after all. Like it or not, they were from Satsuma families, they had Satsuma blood in their veins, and with the government sending hired killers after them they'd had precious little choice but to clear out fast.

It had taken almost a month to get here – a miserable trek down to Yokohama, then a much more miserable ten days on board ship. None of them had ever been on a long journey by ship before and they had spent most of the time in their cabins, throwing up. It was a relief to see palm trees swaying along the seafront in Kagoshima and the spectacular hulk of Mount Sakurajima – Cherry Island – squatting over the bay, spewing out ash and smoke. Now and then there'd be a rumble and black ash would shower down on the city, so much that people put up umbrellas.

They'd arrived in September, the eighth month by the old calendar, just in time for the typhoon season, and been separated straight away, sent off to different schools around the city or in the countryside. He hardly saw any of his Tokyo chums any more. But it was only little by little that he had begun to grasp what was really going on.

As far as the people here were concerned, Satsuma was an independent country. Orders came from Tokyo – 'Disarm the samurai! Take away their stipends!' – but the governor, a fierce warrior called Tsunayoshi Oyama, paid not the slightest attention. After all, they had their own army and a damn strong one at that, well armed and well trained. There was no need to take orders from anyone, particularly not a bunch of corrupt bewhiskered bureaucrats in some distant city who were completely opposed to everything they stood for.

Down at the port, a group of men stood gazing out to sea. Eijiro greeted them and pulled out his timepiece, the one thing of all his possessions he'd managed to salvage. The thick gold chain and big round face marked with foreign characters sparked a rush of memories and for a moment he was back in Tokyo, in the Yoshiwara pleasure quarters, sinking into the lavish bedding of Tsukasa's magnificent chambers. Tsukasa, the most desired courtesan in the whole country. He could smell her scented hair, feel her soft flesh . . . Of all that distant, almost unimaginable life, it was her he missed the most. She sent him letters every now and then, on paper drenched in perfume, going on about tears and eternal love. But he was no fool, he knew what courtesans got up to. No doubt she already had plenty of lovers to console her. He could barely restrain a groan.

He came back to the present with a start. Hoving round the headland was a small triangular speck. It grew larger and larger until Eijiro could see sails, white on the horizon. Steam poured from the funnels, echoing the huge plume of smoke that lay ominously above the volcano. The men peered through their telescopes. They always kept a watch out to make sure the approaching vessel was not a warship loaded with troops.

Eijiro was on the reception committee who vetted new arrivals. There'd been a big influx a few months after he arrived, after the summer break, when the army cadets were due to go back to the Military Academy in Tokyo. As one, the Satsuma lads had upped sticks and headed for home instead.

They all had to be interviewed to find out their allegiance, their reasons for coming, what their skills were and to check their height, health and strength. Once everyone was satisfied there were no bad eggs in their midst, they were packed off to one of the military schools and training camps in the area. There were over a hundred schools and several thousand men, all fighting fit and ready for action.

Since then refugees had continued to arrive. Eijiro had been on duty when his mother and sister had turned up a month ago. He'd had to put up with a lot of ribbing from his colleagues as they'd climbed out of the launch in their fancy clothes, with a bevy of servants with suitcases on their heads straggling behind them. He'd scolded them. 'What are you doing here? This is no place for women,' he'd said. But in fact he'd been mortifyingly pleased to see his mother's plump face and reassuring bulk and hear her voice and be reminded of home. He'd had to wipe his nose on his sleeve and blink back tears as he'd bowed.

The committee had packed them off to the farming village at Yoshino, which his father had founded. The people there were supposed to live a simple, pure life according to samurai ideals, working the land, growing rice, millet and yams, studying Confucian texts and practising martial arts. Quite how his pampered mother and sister were going to get on in a place like that he didn't know.

*　*　*

The ship that was approaching was the regular mail steamer from Yokohama. Eijiro watched as a group of men climbed into the launches and headed for the quay. The committee counted them in. Besides the crew and shoremen there were some fifty others, including a few police officers and cadets, straight-backed in their western-style uniforms, knee-high boots, greatcoats and caps. As everyone knew, half the Tokyo police force was Satsuma men. The policy was to use men from distant clans so no one would be put in the position of having to arrest their own clansmen. Quite a few police deserters had already shown up.

They shepherded the new arrivals into a holding area they'd set up in an empty warehouse and the men lined up, shivering, in front of the officers' desks. Eijiro and his colleagues deliberately made the process as harsh and long-drawn-out as possible so as to weed out from the very beginning anyone who was less than whole-heartedly committed to the cause.

Eijiro enjoyed interviewing new recruits. It was a pleasure to meet men fresh from Tokyo, hear their Tokyo accents and catch up on the news. All too soon they'd become stiff and self-righteous like everyone else round here.

The last man to end up in front of Eijiro's desk was Corporal Hisao Nakahara of the Tokyo Police Department. He seemed a pleasant enough fellow. He had hair cropped in the fashionable *jangiri* cut and a pointed beard which made him look a bit like a fox. He bowed deferentially. Eijiro responded with a haughty jerk of the chin. In normal times a corporal would never be able to come anywhere near the son of General Kitaoka.

Nakahara was a Satsuma man, though he'd been in Tokyo so long he seemed more comfortable speaking Tokyo dialect. Eijiro interrogated him about his origins and work and how he'd ended up in Tokyo, then quizzed him about what people were saying there and what the government was up to. Satisfied, he closed his ledger.

'Welcome. Glad to have you with us.' He glanced over his shoulder and checked that his fellow committee members were all busy barking questions and out of earshot, then leaned forward and lowered his voice. 'So . . . What other news?'

'Let me see now.' Nakahara stared at the ground respectfully. 'Kitaoka-*sama* no doubt heard about the revolts in Hagi and Kumamoto? Maybe you heard that Maebara and the others were executed? Terrible business.' He frowned and shook his head. 'The government is cracking down on the samurai and anyone else who dares stand up to them. We've been ordered to round up anyone breaking the new laws. I could see they'd be sending us down here next to kill our own people. That's when I decided it was time to come home.'

'Yes, yes,' said Eijiro impatiently. The fellow didn't have to keep proving he was on the right side. 'What about real news? How's Umegatani getting on? When I was there he hadn't lost a bout.'

One of the things Eijiro missed most about Tokyo was the regular sumo wrestling tournaments at Eko-in Temple, in the East End. Umegatani was a phenomenon, a hulking fellow yet light on his feet. He easily toppled giants a lot heavier than he was. He ranked low still but anyone could see he had the makings of a grand champion.

Nakahara grinned. 'Still unbeaten. He took on Makuuchi the other day. It was over before you could count to ten.'

'Makuuchi, huh? He wouldn't have a chance; anyone could tell you that. Umegatani's much the better man for weight and skill. No one put any money on that one, I shouldn't think.'

Nakahara started plying him with bouts, scores and form, but Eijiro had something else on his mind. 'What about the Yoshiwara? How're things there? You're a policeman, you must get around a bit.'

'Got called to take in a foreign sailor a few days ago. He'd found his way over there, got a bellyful of sake, barged into the Matsubaya and demanded a woman. The Matsubaya, imagine that!' Eijiro nodded knowledgeably. The Matsubaya was one of the grandest houses in the Yoshiwara and never accepted foreigners. Nakahara waved his hand in contempt. 'You know what happened? The madam showed him the door and he stabbed her – right in the face. Not a pretty sight. Blood all over the place. We took him off to Kodenmacho and locked him up. These foreigners think they own the world.'

'He'll get tried in one of those foreigners' courts and they'll dismiss the case, fine him a yen or two and that'll be the last we hear of it.'

'And there's the government cosying up to foreigners. So tell me, what's going on down here?'

'You'll find out soon enough.' Eijiro had taken a liking to the man. 'I'll have a word with the captain at our school. I'm sure there's a spare tatami mat for a fellow like you.'

'I'm a bit old for school,' said Nakahara. He had an open, easy smile.

'We call them schools but they're more like private military academies, training camps,' said Eijiro. 'But you'll recognize the sleeping arrangements from your schooldays – one man, one mat.'

23

In fact the men had less than half a mat each. With upwards of eight hundred students, the school was hard pressed to fit them all into the rickety old stable buildings and they spent the nights squashed together or curled up on the wooden floors of the corridors. But comfort was the last thing they were worried about. Some were youngsters, others battle-hardened veterans who'd proved themselves in the campaigns to bring down the shogun and smash the resistance up north. Young or old, they loathed the corrupt bureaucrats up in Tokyo who were out to destroy the entire samurai class. They couldn't wait to take up arms and teach them a lesson.

Nakahara settled in quickly enough. He shaved off his beard and started growing his hair, though it would be months before it was long enough to tie back in a samurai ponytail, and took to wearing a rough cotton kimono and leggings like everyone else. Handy with a sword, staff or rifle, he chipped in cheerily with kitchen and cleaning duties and was soon a popular figure around the school. He was a good-humoured fellow, always ready with a joke.

He frequently joined Eijiro for a quick pipe. Like

Eijiro, he was not afraid to express doubts about what they were doing – in private, of course, where no one could overhear them. It was a long time since Eijiro had had a real friend and very soon he felt as if he'd known him since he was a boy.

One morning, about a month after Nakahara had arrived, the wake-up call sounded as usual, well before dawn. Eijiro had been dreaming of the pleasure quarters; he could almost smell Tsukasa's perfume. It was a shock to find himself back in the freezing hall, surrounded by sweaty male bodies. As the men climbed over each other in the darkness, groping for their over-kimonos and hakama, he groaned and pulled his quilts over his head. He was the last to roll up his futons and stumble out to the practice ground.

Outside, the drill sergeants were already lined up, standing smartly to attention, as the first streaks of light coloured the sky. The hillside rose steeply behind, a tangle of bamboos and skeletal trees etched in frost, eerily silent. After roll call, men picked up rifles or heavy packs and headed off around Mount Shiroyama at a good clip; some sprinted down to the ocean for a bracing winter dip. Eijiro volunteered for kitchen duty. The others probably took a dim view of such skiving but he was the son of Kitaoka, he told himself. He could do as he pleased.

After breakfast there were classes in the Confucian classics and foreign languages, English, French or German. In the breaks most of the men were out in the practice ground, sparring, and in the afternoon they headed to the firing range for musket training. The infantry had Snider-Enfield rifles, carbines and pistols and there were two artillery units equipped with field guns and mortars. At the end of the day local Kagoshima lads arrived from the city to join the students for more study and military drill and in the evening there was to be a debate. War hung over the city like a dark cloud and everyone wanted to be sure that when it came they'd be good and ready.

Late in the afternoon, Eijiro and Nakahara wrapped themselves in padded haori jackets and sneaked off into the woods behind the school. They'd found a place in the lea of the hill, protected from the fierce winds. At least the cold kept the vipers at bay. They settled themselves side by side against an old tree trunk, brought out flagons of shochu, the fiery local brew, and lit their pipes. Sharp yells and the smack of wood on wood echoed from the practice ground on the other side of the stables.

Eijiro drew in a lungful of smoke, savouring the fragrance, then let it out bit by bit, watching it dissolve into the mountain air. This was his favourite time of the day, smelling earth and moss and mouldering leaves, feeling the twigs crack under his feet and hearing startled birds squawk and flap away through the trees.

Nakahara was staring into the distance, twirling his pipe in his fingers. He put his flagon to his lips, took a swig and shook his head, frowning. 'Doesn't look good,' he grunted. Eijiro took another puff on his pipe. He glanced at him and raised an eyebrow. Usually they exchanged ribald stories about geishas and courtesans they'd known, before getting down to the serious stuff – what they really thought about what was going on. But today Nakahara seemed to want to plunge straight in. 'There've been manoeuvres in Tokyo, in Hibiya Parade Ground – a big show of strength. To reassure the populace, they say.'

That was easy to counter. 'Nothing to worry about. They're commoners, an army of commoners!' Eijiro spat out the word. 'My granddad used to test his swords on their necks; that's all they're good for. Do you think commoners know how to swing a sword or fire a rifle straight? They don't even want to be in the army in the first place. Blood tax, they call it. There's some new-fangled word for it – "conscription". They're "conscripts". I've never heard anything like it! Forbidding samurai to wear swords and handing out weapons to commoners! The world's turned upside down. If those commoners think there's a rat's chance of getting hurt, they'll run. It'd be a massacre to send them down here against our boys.'

Nakahara tapped out his pipe and took a plug of tobacco from his tobacco box. 'Yeah, but look at the numbers. There are six garrisons, you know: Tokyo, Sendai, Nagoya, Osaka, Hiroshima, Kumamoto.' He counted them off on his fingers. 'Six garrisons, say thirty thousand in each. That makes nearly two hundred thousand men. That's a lot more than us. And Kumamoto's – what? – a couple of days' march away at most. They could have troops down here in no time to sort us out.'

'Cowards and weaklings, the lot of them. Look at it this way. Our boys are samurai born and bred, the toughest men in the country. Most have seen action and they've all taken an oath to die for our cause and our leader. One of ours is worth ten of theirs!'

There was a pause. Deep in the woods an owl hooted, long and low. The last slanting rays of sunlight penetrated the trees.

'They've got arsenals too – four right here in Kagoshima, for a start,' said Nakahara, his voice low and grim. 'Our weapons are outmoded and we've not got much ammo, don't forget that. They'll slaughter us, I tell you. Things have changed. We should come to terms with the Tokyo government and hope they go easy on us. They're not as bad as you think. They'll make concessions. You're Kitaoka's son. The men respect you, Eiji; they'll listen to you. Hammer some sense into them. Tell them not to be foolhardy. There's no point going to our deaths for nothing.'

Eijiro couldn't believe what he was hearing. The blood thundered in his ears and he clenched his fists so hard he nearly snapped the stem of his pipe. Nakahara's cynicism had been amusing to begin with, but this was going too far. He was beginning to sound like a coward – or a traitor.

'Not as bad as you think?' he spluttered, exploding with rage. 'They sent hired killers after me. They had my best friend killed. And you call yourself a samurai? Have you lost your nerve or what? Whose side are you on, anyway?'

Nakahara took another mouthful of shochu. 'I'm a Kagoshima man, same as you. You've got to be realistic.'

Eijiro took a breath. Nakahara really was a Kagoshima man whereas, as Eijiro knew very well, he wasn't. He didn't fit in at all. He was more at home in the fleshpots of Tokyo. But he was his father's son and that was that. He scowled.

'Anyway, we never even see the great leader, that famous father of yours,' said Nakahara. So he was back to Eijiro's father again. He was always asking about his father. 'He ought to be around more to fire us up. I haven't set eyes on him once myself. I doubt if he even exists.'

In truth, Eijiro hadn't seen his father himself for more than three years. He'd been out of town in his country place in Hinatayama when Eijiro arrived and then had gone on a hunting expedition. Eijiro wasn't even sure he'd be glad to see this dissolute bastard son of his.

'It's not your business what my father does.'

'So where is he, Eiji? When's he coming back?'

Eijiro sighed. It was good that the fellow recognized his superior status. Nakahara talked too much and he asked too many questions. But he was a policeman and policemen were always poking their noses into other people's affairs; that was their job. And for all his outrageous opinions, he was his friend. This time at least he'd go easy on him. 'He's hunting,' he said. 'You can meet him when he gets back. I'll introduce you.'

He took a long last draw on his pipe. 'Better get moving before someone notices we've gone. It's nearly dark.'

Eijiro stood up, stretched and knocked out his pipe on a tree, sending sparks showering into the darkness. The moon was rising, a sliver of light in the black sky.

Bats flittered and a monkey shrieked. A branch snapped, then another – deer, probably; there couldn't be any bears in this part of the country. But surely, Eijiro thought, there shouldn't be any animals around at all at this time of year, even in the warm south. Then he noticed something glittering in the trees. Eyes. He started. There were people there, lurking. They'd crept up without him even noticing.

He jerked to attention, cursing. Then there was a rush and a trampling of branches. Shadowy figures leapt from the darkness and charged across the frozen ground, brandishing sticks.

'Over here,' shouted a voice. 'We got them.'

'Don't move!'

A heavy body landed on him and he crashed to the ground, his face smashing up against a pile of stones. He tasted blood and earth in his mouth. He twisted his head, struggling fiercely. A knee rammed into his back and his arms were wrenched behind him.

'Bastard!' A foot slammed into his side. He thanked the gods his attacker was wearing straw sandals. If it had been a hard leather boot it would have broken his ribs.

'Traitors, bloody traitors!' Another foot hit him.

Traitors? Gasping with shock, he realized that he recognized the voices. These were their own men, some from their school. Dazed, he tried to pull his thoughts together. He needed to work out what was going on and how he was going to get out of this – and quickly.

Footsteps crunched and lights flickered. More men had arrived.

'Got a couple here, sir. Can't see if it's him or not.'

Rough hands dragged Eijiro to his knees. His shock was rapidly being replaced by fury.

'Don't you know who I am?' he spluttered. There was a beam of light and a smell of tallow as a lantern swung in front of his face. He jerked his head away and blinked, dazzled. The men sucked their breath through their teeth.

'Kitaoka-*dono*,' said one, using the title of greatest respect, reserved for those of the highest rank. 'Ah. Sorry, sorry.'

His captors relaxed their hold but continued to restrain him, firmly but gently, as if he was a valuable wild animal they'd captured.

'How dare you treat me like this! Just for sneaking off for a smoke. You got nothing better to do than spy on your fellow students?'

No one was paying the slightest attention to him. Nakahara was a little way away, on his knees, men pinioning his arms. Shadows moved as lanterns swayed close to his face. Eyes glared accusingly in the yellow light.

'It's him, for sure.'

'You wormed your way in, you bastard,' shouted one of the men, leaning close to Nakahara and yelling in his ear. 'You lied to us. You thought you could fool us.'

'Confess, you bastard. Who are you working for? What are you up to?'

'Yes, what are you up to?'

Then they were all shouting at once, their Kagoshima dialect so thick that Eijiro had to listen hard to make out what they were saying. He took a breath and shouted above the uproar. 'What's going on? Wait till my father hears about this! You'll pay, I tell you. You'll pay!'

There was a sudden silence. 'That's right,' jeered a lone voice. 'Just wait till your father hears!'

Eijiro struggled to free himself as the men laid into Nakahara, kicking and punching him and beating him with their sticks. 'Confess, confess. What are you up to? Why are you so keen on Kitaoka-*dono*?'

Nakahara grimaced but made not a sound. Eijiro smiled to himself. At least his friend knew how a samurai ought to behave, unlike these bullies.

A scrawny fifteen-year-old whom Eijiro worked with in the kitchens drew his fist back, eyes narrowed and mouth twisted with venom, and punched Nakahara full in the ear. The blow knocked him sideways. The men pulled him back to his knees. Eijiro gasped as he caught a glimpse of his friend's face in the lantern light. His nose and mouth were bloody and one of his teeth was missing. He spat out a mouthful of blood and shook himself, scowling defiantly. He straightened his back.

'Find someone else to bully, I've done nothing wrong,' he growled.

'Tough guy, huh?' A man was standing in the shadows, brawny arms folded. Eijiro recognized his broad shoulders and rugged face – Chief Inspector Makihara, the police chief. He turned cold. They were really in trouble, though he still couldn't for the life of him work out what it was all about. 'You're coming with us, Nakahara,' said the inspector. 'You can tell us what you're up to or we can make you talk. It's up to you.'

'He's not done anything wrong.' Eijiro had decided it was time to speak up. 'He's a loyal soldier. I can vouch for him.'

'With respect, Kitaoka-*dono*, this man has been deceiving you. He's a traitor. He's a government agent. We have to find out exactly what he's been up to.'

'You're making a mistake,' muttered Nakahara, gritting his teeth as another foot hit him in the ribs. 'I got nothing to hide.'

'Is that so? What have you got to say, Taniguchi?'

A man stepped into the circle of light. Eijiro had seen him round town, a surly-looking fellow with the flattened nose and leathery skin of a countryman. Nakahara started when he saw him and his cheeks turned the colour of tallow but his face was fiercely impassive. You had to admire the man's guts, Eijiro thought.

Taniguchi stared at the ground, then at the police inspector as the other men gathered round. His eyes shifted; he was trying to avoid Nakahara's gaze. Then he looked straight at him.

'That's him, all right, sir,' he grunted. 'Told me everything, he did. Everything. "Come on, Taniguchi," he says. "You're a country samurai, same as me. You know these nose-in-the-air city samurai despise us rustic types. What're you licking their arses for? Look around you. They got no equipment, no ammo. They don't have a chance. It's crazy to stand up against the government. It's suicide, that's what. Tell you what – do some good for yourself. Work for your country. What do you want to fight against the emperor for? Join me, help me persuade these idiots to give up. You'll do well out of it." "You're kidding," I says. "I'm no traitor." "You can trust me. We're old mates," he says. "I got friends in high places. You'll be well rewarded, I'll see to that."'

Eijiro had a sick feeling in his stomach. 'No

equipment, no ammo.' It was exactly what Nakahara had been saying to him. But something else bothered him even more. Why had Nakahara taken such an interest in his father? Why had he been so keen to meet him? What plan had he been cooking up?

'I don't know this man,' Nakahara protested. For all his bravado there was an edge to his voice. 'He's a troublemaker. Why believe him and not me?'

He glanced at Eijiro, as if pleading with him to intercede. Suddenly Eijiro was overcome with such fury he hardly knew where he was.

'Bastard!' he yelled. 'You made a fool of me.'

He jumped to his feet, shaking off the restraining hands, lunged towards Nakahara and hit him with all his might. Blood sprayed out and soaked his fist and arm as the man's nose crumpled under the blow. He raised his hand to hit him again, then let it fall.

'Do your job, Inspector.' He could hear his voice cracking.

No one tried to stop him as he turned away, his face burning, and stumbled blindly towards the school buildings huddled at the foot of the hill. He clenched his fists and cursed aloud. He'd brought shame on himself but worse, much worse, he'd brought shame on his family and his father. He'd been tested and found wanting. The only thing left now was to cut open his own belly – or find some other way to redeem himself.

24

Eijiro pushed his way through the woods. The last place he wanted to show his face was the school. But all too soon the branches thinned and he clambered down into the practice ground, rage and shame buzzing so loud in his ears he couldn't think of anything else.

The ground was full of men, pressed together so close Eijiro could hardly make out the shadowy walls of the buildings around them. They were dressed like warriors preparing for battle, sleeves tied back, hakama hitched up and headbands knotted in place. Lantern light glittered off pistols, rifles, axes and crowbars; voices muttered, low and intense. As always, Eijiro stood a good head above the rest. He glanced around the faces, wondering if the gathering had anything to do with Nakahara and his treachery. At least it wasn't the men on the hill. They were still up there with Nakahara. No one here knew of his disgrace – not yet.

A head poked out of the crowd and launched into an impassioned rant. Eijiro was still too full of his own humiliation to pay attention to what the man was saying or even notice whether he knew the voice. There were shouts of anger and yells of agreement, then someone bawled, 'To Iso! To the factories, to the docks!' Fists and rifles waved in the air as the men took up the chant: 'The factories! The docks!'

They surged forward, hundreds of straw sandals crunching over the icy ground. Swept up in the crush, Eijiro stumbled along with them.

'Here.' Someone thrust a rifle into his hand and a pair of sharp eyes peered at him in the lantern light. It was Ito, a wiry young fellow with hair sticking up in tufts above his white headband. 'Oh. It's you, Kitaoka-*sama*. Got better things to do, I'm sure, than muck in with us rank and file.'

Eijiro felt the blood hot in his cheeks. He knew he had a reputation for keeping clear of the action but tonight he wanted to make sure everyone knew he was as committed as the rest of them.

'I'm with you.' He gripped the rifle as the men quenched the lanterns, marched out of the grounds and headed through the sleeping city. Feet crunched and breath rose in the cold air as they broke into a run and swept like a divine wind out of the samurai district and into one of the townsmen's quarters, darting along narrow alleys, between houses and shuttered shops, past shrines and temples, thickets and trees. They pounded across a bridge and up and down a rocky hillside covered in a tangle of trees. Eijiro cursed as he stumbled on a stone, sending it clattering into the darkness. It was good to have nothing more to think about than keeping quiet.

At the seafront they broke into twos and threes and darted from wall to wall, moving like cats, keeping to the shadows. Water rippled, black and oily, and ships bobbed gently at anchor. The great volcano filled the sky, its plume of ash blotting out the stars.

Abruptly the men stopped. Voices hissed, 'There. Over there.'

A shadow loomed in the lea of the volcano. As they watched there was a sparkle of white and a faint splash as something hit the water beside it. Eijiro stared into the gloom, puzzled. Whatever this vessel was, it didn't have the shape of a warship. There were no gun ports, it wasn't a sleek low-lying ironclad. It looked more like a solidly built merchant craft. But in that case why was it docking so late? Even stranger, there were no whistles or bells or gongs. It was docking in silence. Whoever the newcomers were, they didn't want to be seen.

'That's it. Quickly, let's go.'

As the men pounded along the quayside, Eijiro ran with them, taking in lungfuls of salty air. He was beginning to wonder what the hell was going on.

At the far end of the wharf was a cluster of massive stone buildings with pointed roofs and hefty wooden doors. Eijiro grabbed Ito's arm as the others jostled past.

'What are you doing? That's the naval arsenal.' Ito tried to shake him off but Eijiro kept his huge hand closed around the man's bony wrist. 'That's government property. We can't be planning . . .'

Everyone knew the government had taken over every arsenal in the country, ready for use if there was even the hint of unrest. The biggest stockpiles of all were in the most troublesome province, Satsuma. The Satsuma had the most sophisticated weapons factories and produced more weapons and powder than any other clan. Iso, right beside the Satsuma lords' summer villa where they could oversee proceedings, was an industrial complex the old lord had established more than thirty years earlier, with blast and reverberatory furnaces, a cannon-manufacturing plant and armaments factories. It also produced chemicals, medicines, glassware and textiles.

To demonstrate his loyalty to the new government which he had helped set up, the present lord of Satsuma had handed control of the entire complex to the Army Department, who had stationed a small contingent of the navy here to guard the weapons stocks. But now, to the weapons-starved rebels, the arsenals were glittering treasure boxes crying out to be seized.

But no one had yet suggested actually breaking in. That would be outright rebellion and Eijiro knew his father, for one, had no intention of pushing things that far.

'Do as you please, Brother,' Ito spat. 'No one's forcing you to join us. Let go of me.'

'Just tell me. What's going on?'

Ito tried to wrench his arm free but Eijiro was bigger and stronger.

'You saw the ship,' Ito growled. 'They're sneaking in by night, sending launches. Those police spies . . .' Eijiro's blood ran cold at the mention of spies. 'Took some beating, but confessed in the end. Sending messages to Tokyo, they were, telling them what we were up to; government ship on the way, they said, come to load up with arms and take them away. A merchant ship, so as not to look suspicious.' So that explained why the supposedly innocent merchant vessel had been lowering a launch in such a surreptitious way. 'We'll beat them to it. This is war. It's us or them.'

Foam crested the waves as a dark shape, long and narrow, cut across the water towards them. Eijiro made out the splash of the oars and two rows of pale faces, getting closer and closer.

'This is war . . .' he repeated to himself. Something was niggling at him, a memory. Then he remembered.

It had been when he was a little boy, on one of those rare occasions when General Kitaoka had come to visit. They'd taken out wooden practice swords and sparred together. He could hear the crack of blade on blade and see motes of dust whirling in the sunlight as he'd backed cautiously down the narrow street, between dark wooden geisha houses, his father with his barrel stomach towering above him, as huge and terrifying as a mountain-dwelling giant.

Several times the general had let him beat him back as Eijiro flayed about with his little sword. But then he bore down on him and forced him to his knees. Eijiro had wriggled away and tried to run, then pouted and stamped his feet and started to wail. His father had crouched and taken him on his massive thigh.

'Listen to me, little Eiji,' he'd said, his expression stern. 'You're a samurai, a Kitaoka and a samurai. Sometimes you'll win, sometimes you'll lose, but you must never run away. A townsman is allowed to run away but a samurai never. Do you understand?'

'Yes, sir,' Eijiro had said, sitting up very straight, proud that his father thought him worthy to be spoken to in such a serious way.

His father put his jowly face close to Eijiro's. 'A samurai never worries about losing his life. He worries about losing his honour. Being shamed is far worse than losing your life. A samurai is always ready to die – for his lord, for his honour. That's the samurai way.'

Eijiro scowled as ferociously as he could, knitting his brow in the way his older brother Ryutaro did. '*Hai*. I understand.'

'Now, Ryutaro.'

Ryutaro was waiting in the shadow of the geisha houses. He'd just shaved his pate and bound his hair into his first topknot whereas Eijiro, four years younger, had a tuft of hair tied in a forelock, as little boys did. Ryutaro was grave and serious. He worked hard at his studies and found playmates to practise his swordplay with, while Eijiro was heavy like his father and always getting into trouble – beating up the other boys who roamed around the geisha district, cutting through their strings when they flew kites together, stealing coins from his mother's purse.

The general picked up his stick. Ryutaro faced him, his stick in his hands, balancing his weight. This time there were no concessions. In a single blow their father had Ryutaro on the ground and raised his stick for what would have been the death blow. Ryutaro didn't flinch.

The general patted him on the shoulder as he scrambled to his feet and bowed. 'Good lad.'

He broke into a grin, turned to Eijiro and chucked him under the chin with his big hand. 'I wish I could stay and train you too in the samurai way.' He sighed. 'But I have to go away again. Ryutaro is coming with me and one day I'll send for you too. For now you're the man of the house. Take care of your mother and little sisters.'

Eijiro ran his chubby hand across his father's bristly cheek. 'Will you come back soon?' he asked.

'As soon as I can.' But in fact he never sent for him and years would go by before Eijiro saw him again. Later he heard that his father had been in exile, then in prison, and then that he was a great general, at the head of an army. In the last great battle of the civil war the Satsuma and their allies had been victorious but then news had come that Ryutaro had been killed. For the family it was a bittersweet victory. By then Eijiro already knew that his father had another family and other sons – sons he acknowledged, not sons, like Ryutaro and Eijiro, that he kept secret.

It had been a strange childhood, growing up in the geisha district surrounded by women, with his father far away. Perhaps that was why he had ended up whiling away so many of his days in the pleasure quarters. It was just as people warned: hanging around with women sapped your strength and made you weak, like a woman, too. In the end he'd completely forgotten what his father had told him.

But now he remembered. He was a samurai, of warrior stock. Despite the lazy, profligate ways he'd fallen into, he bore the Kitaoka name, the Kitaoka blood ran in his veins. With Ryutaro dead, the responsibility for upholding the honour of the Kitaoka name lay in his hands. And here was he, a Kitaoka, holding back, letting others charge before him into the fray. He felt as if he'd suddenly woken up. His whole life so far had been nothing but a dream.

He released Ito's arm. 'Let's go!'

As they pounded across the quay towards the mob

baying outside the arsenal, he let out a war cry that felt more like a whoop of elation.

The naval officers charged with guarding the arsenal had backed up against the doors. There was just a small contingent, ten or fifteen of them, burly fellows with cropped heads and scowling faces, staring around at the crowd of attackers, fingering their weapons. One tried to cock his rifle but five or six of the rebels sprang forward and wrestled it away from him.

A voice rang out above the shouting and arguing and scuffling of feet. 'Stand clear! We're seizing this arsenal in the name of Masaharu Kitaoka!'

A shiver ran along Eijiro's spine and the hair on the back of his neck prickled. His father was a long way away. He had no knowledge of this adventure and hadn't sanctioned it. But it was too late to turn back now, way too late.

'We got reinforcements on the way,' yelled a guard. 'You'll suffer for this.'

There was a flash and a bang. One of the guards had let off a shot that screamed harmlessly into the air.

There was a sudden silence. The stand-off had been breached. Ito looked at Eijiro and one by one other faces turned towards him. They were waiting for him to make the next move.

He took a breath, then thrust his arm in the air, rifle in hand. 'The arsenal!' he shouted.

There was a moment's pause, then the youths piled on to the guards and beat them out of the way in a mass of flailing fists.

Eijiro stared up at the hefty wooden doors. They were held in place with thick wooden bolts and huge rusty padlocks. The others stepped back and he gripped his rifle by the barrel and brought the butt down hard on one of the locks. His hands were ripped and bleeding but the lock didn't budge. He took a breath, raised his rifle again and whacked it down.

'Wait,' said Ito. He grabbed a hammer and with three or four others smashed at the lock till it gave way. Eijiro beat at the second until it too fell apart.

As the men pushed back the bolts and shoved the door open, a smell of dust and oil puffed out. They pressed into the clammy darkness. The place was far larger than it looked from outside. Someone lit a lantern on a tall pole and held it up. Peering around in the wavering light, Eijiro saw stacks of wooden crates, some big, some small, some square-sided, some oblong, piled to the ceiling, row upon row of them, disappearing into the cavernous depths of the warehouse.

There were a couple of crates at floor level, pushed up against a wall. Some of the men tugged at them but they didn't budge. Eijiro squatted behind one and shoved it out into the middle of the room. The contents rattled as it scraped across the floor. He thrust a crowbar under the lid and leaned hard. There was a creak as the bolts gave, the nails tore loose and the lid sprang open. The crate was full to the brim with bullets.

Scowling with the effort, stopping to wipe their brows and grunt, the men started shoving boxes against the stacks, clambering up and lifting down the crates. It took four men to shift each one. Besides crate upon crate of bullets and wooden boxes full of gunpowder, there were crates of rifles, boxes of pistols, breech- and muzzle-loading guns and even cannons and Gatlings.

Among them were models Eijiro had never even seen before, more deadly by far than any of the old-fashioned ordnance they had. Ito took out a revolver and spun the barrel and cocked it. He straightened his back and turned to grin at Eijiro. It was a treasure trove.

There was a warning shout from outside where the men were standing guard at the dock. Eijiro grabbed his rifle and sprinted out. The launch sat unmoving like a sinister black fish, bobbing up and down a little way from shore. Waves sparkled in the moonlight as the rowers put up their oars. A faint red glow lit the clouds, marking the top of the volcano.

Silence fell. Each side was waiting for the other to make a move.

Eijiro strode to the dockside. 'This is Satsuma territory,' he shouted. 'We can't allow you to land. Go back to your ship.'

A voice yelled back across the water. 'That's government property and you're trespassing on it. Surrender your arms and it'll go easier on you.'

'If you come any closer we'll shoot.'

The men aboard put their heads together.

'We're unarmed. We're on government business. Stand back. We don't want trouble.'

'This arsenal belongs to the people of Satsuma. It's been seized in the name of Masaharu Kitaoka. Go tell your bosses that.'

The rowers picked up their oars again. They were so close now that Eijiro could see their faces and the buttons on their uniforms glinting in the moonlight. As the launch edged closer to shore there was a crack. One of the Satsuma lads had fired off a warning shot.

Eijiro looked around, grimacing. It was too late now. The men were raring for a fight.

More shots rang out, sending up explosions of spray around the boat. The Satsuma men readied themselves, waiting for a return of fire, but none came. Expecting treachery, they grabbed poles and grappling irons. Some picked up rocks and bricks and started lobbing them towards the approaching boat. Most splashed into the water, pocking the sea with white. There was a yell from the launch as one made a direct hit.

Some sixth sense made Eijiro swing round. Where the quay disappeared into the shadows, other launches were scudding towards shore. One had already reached the dock and sailors were securing it with ropes while others climbed out.

'This way, lads!'

Eijiro slung his rifle on his back and pounded along the wharf, Ito close behind him. Several of the sailors were already racing in his direction towards the arsenal. He charged at the first and caught a glimpse of the man's shocked face and wide-open eyes as he slammed straight into him, sending him flying. There was a thud and a splash as Eijiro swung round and bore down on another. He let out a yell so piercing that the man stumbled, then picked him up bodily and hurled him into the icy water.

Another sailor was nearly on top of him, sword at the ready, so close that Eijiro barely had time to draw his own. As it slid from the scabbard he swung it in a half-circle, catching the man across the throat. Blood fountained into the air and the sailor's head flopped back while his body stumbled on, then tottered and collapsed.

Drawing breath, Eijiro swung his rifle into place against his shoulder. A fourth sailor was approaching, a skinny youth with close-cropped hair and the pale undernourished face of a northerner. He took one look at Eijiro's rifle, pointed straight towards him. For a moment he seemed to freeze, then turned tail and ran.

Ito had brought down a couple more of the enemy. Eijiro wiped his brow and grinned. All that training hadn't been in vain. It was too long since he'd had a chance to wield a sword in earnest.

Feet pounded along the quay as other Satsuma men came up to join them. There were yells of derision as the sailors fled back to their launches and started rowing madly, throwing up sheets of spray. The rebels watched, rifles at the ready, until the last launch had disappeared into the darkness and the ship raised anchor, turned and steamed out of the bay.

25

The sun was rising behind the volcano, casting it into deep shadow, as the men loaded the last crates of weapons. Convoys of men had been coming and going all night, taking away cartloads. They'd found pack-horses to pull the carts and commandeered rickshaws and piled crates on to them. Some of the students loaded up boats and took away their captured arms to hide them in the huge Somuta arsenal deep in a valley behind the city.

Eijiro straightened up, wiped a grubby arm across his face and looked across the bay to the jagged black silhouette of the volcano, a plume of ash hanging lazily above it. His muscles ached, he was black from head to foot with dust and gunpowder, and volcanic grit had shredded his straw sandals, but he'd never been so happy in his life.

The students had sneaked along back alleys to get to the dock but they took the main road back, waving their captured rifles in the air and wheeling their carts of pilfered ammo. As they passed through the city, people came out of houses and shops, bundled against the bitter wind in padded jackets. They stared at the mob prancing by and began to laugh and cheer. More and more appeared, shouting encouragement, pressing back into the trees, peering out of the houses and shopfronts.

As the youths marched they joined up with bands of men from other schools. They too were laden with rifles and ammo and some wheeled cannons lifted from other government arms dumps. The numbers swelled until they filled the whole town, marching shoulder to shoulder.

Eijiro was in the middle of the crowd, mingling sweat with his comrades, yelling at the top of his voice, intoxicated with pride and glee. Then he felt a twinge of dread. He fell silent. In all the excitement he'd entirely forgotten. His father knew nothing of all this and would be far from pleased when he found out.

He punched his fist in the air and let out a yell, but the spring had gone out of his step. The thought would not go away. They'd loosed a monster. They'd set something in train that could not be undone.

Back at the stables the students had turned one of the buildings into an arsenal. They added their arms to the stack of weapons there. One of the men took an inventory: twenty-eight 5.28 mm powder mountain guns, two 15.84 mm powder field guns, thirty assorted mortars and 60,000 rounds of ammo. And that was only their arsenal. There were plenty of others. Each school had its own. It was enough for them to defend themselves for a long while.

Eijiro was ravenous and looking forward to breakfast. He was setting off across the practice ground when he glimpsed a group of men coming through the gates. He stopped dead. His fellow students dropped to their knees and pressed their noses to the grit. The same thought was in every mind.

He kept his head down as heavy footsteps approached. When he looked up he saw a pair of fierce black eyes staring down at him. He gulped. 'Father.'

'Earthquake, thunder, fire and Father – the most frightening things in the world; and the most frightening of all is Father.' He remembered the saying and trembled as he looked down to avoid his father's gaze. He had forgotten how huge he was. He dwarfed even Eijiro with his broad shoulders and vast bulk.

General Kitaoka didn't bother to address Eijiro or even acknowledge him. He folded his arms and looked around at the cowering youths, then said very softly, almost to himself, '*Shimatta!*' Eijiro wondered what he meant. Was it a simple exclamation, 'Damn! That's it!' Or did it have the full force of the word: 'We've well and truly had it!'

His father was with some of the Satsuma elders. He was wearing coarse leggings and several thick cotton robes under a padded haori jacket. Small wiry dogs, twelve or thirteen of them, ran around at his feet, tails wagging. He must have returned that same morning from his hunting trip and couldn't have helped but hear the commotion as the youths marched through the city. Some of the imperial guards were behind him, forming a bodyguard. When Eijiro had seen them around the Tokyo mansion they'd always seemed a bit zealous for his taste, but now he'd spent time in Kagoshima he had a grudging respect for these dedicated soldiers.

There was someone else with the general too, tall,

slender and handsome with a clear open face, the very embodiment of upright samurai youth. Eijiro gritted his teeth. He could guess who this was – his younger half-brother, Kazuo, his father's son by his wife. He didn't have to have met him to know that he thoroughly hated him.

The general's voice was ominously quiet. 'This has been a busy night. What a monstrous affair!' Then his face blackened. 'Fools!'

Eijiro nearly fell over. He'd never heard such a shout. It was louder than the most fearsome war cry, louder than the loudest belly shout his sword instructor could make. It shook the air and made his stomach churn. The other youths started, scuttling backwards like crabs. Someone would have to pay for the night's work.

Eijiro straightened his back and frowned. As Kitaoka's son he should take responsibility for their terrible deed. If need be he would commit ritual suicide to atone for their crime. He raised his head. 'It was me, Father. It was my stupid idea. I take responsibility.'

Other youths shouted out. 'No, sir, it was me.' 'No, me. I claim responsibility.'

'I know we acted without orders, Father,' Eijiro persisted. 'I'm sorry.' He bowed to the ground. 'I will atone for my fault immediately by cutting my belly.'

There was silence. His father stared at him, then threw back his head and let out a roar of laughter. 'There's no need for that, dear boy. You're a pleasure-loving fellow. I can assure you, there'd be no pleasure in that at all. In fact I'm afraid you'd find it rather painful.'

Eijiro scowled. He was about to protest that he was a samurai through and through when there was a shout.

'Kitaoka-*don*.' '-*don*' was the affectionate abbreviation of the respectful title '-*dono*' that everyone used to address their beloved general.

A group of uniformed men was hurrying into the grounds. At the head was the burly figure of Chief Inspector Makihara. For a moment his sharp brown eyes met Eijiro's.

Eijiro's heart sank. As the inspector bowed to his father, he studied his shaven pate and gleaming topknot, wondering nervously what he was going to say.

'Grave news, sir. We captured the leader of the government agents. A man called Nakahara.' Eijiro's cheeks blazed. He'd almost forgotten the events of the previous night in the excitement of storming the arsenal. Perhaps the inspector would reveal his shame to his father in front of everyone. But he was a decent man; it would do him no good to make Eijiro lose face. He listened in an agony of suspense as the chief inspector continued. 'He was a hard man to break, sir. It took all night to make him talk but we got a confession out of him in the end.'

'He won't be walking again for quite a while,' said one of the other men, baring a mouthful of crooked teeth in a grin. 'You can be sure of that.'

Eijiro breathed a sigh of relief. So they weren't going to talk about how and where they had found Nakahara.

'A lot of the new police recruits have turned out to be spies,' said the chief inspector in clipped official tones. 'They've infiltrated half the schools. We were suspicious of them from the start, then my men apprehended them sending messages. They were reporting on what we were doing here and receiving instructions back from

Tokyo. One confessed that there was a government transport due to arrive this very night, camouflaged as a commercial vessel with a civilian crew. Their mission was to remove arms from the government arsenals. Luckily our men got there first.'

The general nodded. The chief inspector waited, head bowed respectfully, for him to speak.

'And this Nakahara, what did he tell you?'

'He made a written confession, sir. They were sent by the government to destroy our movement by any means possible. His orders were to assassinate you, sir, if that was what it took.'

Eijiro shuddered with horror. So that was why Nakahara had been so eager to befriend him, that was why he had taken such an interest in his father and where he was. He'd planned to use Eijiro to get close to him – close enough to stab a sword into him or shoot him. And Eijiro had been about to introduce him. He breathed out hard. He would kill Nakahara with his bare hands, given half a chance.

The young men had leapt to their feet, gripping their swords. They gazed at Eijiro's father as if he was a god. Eijiro could see that any of them would happily die for him.

'I'm not so attached to this body of mine,' said General Kitaoka. 'They can kill me if they want.' He grimaced as he studied the document the inspector had handed him. 'My old friend, Okubo,' he said. 'We grew up together, we fought side by side – and now he signs my death warrant.'

Eijiro noticed that he looked older, more careworn, than he had three years earlier when he saw him last.

His jowls sagged a little and there were streaks of grey in his oiled hair.

'We'll execute these men forthwith, sir. We're just waiting for your authorization.'

'Execute policemen? They were just doing their jobs. Lock them up and leave them be. We have bigger things to think about. The real criminals are the politicians in Tokyo who are out to destroy us and our way of life and everything we stand for.' He looked around at the youths. For a moment there was a slightly bemused look on his face. Then he frowned as if he'd reached a decision. 'I built these schools, I encouraged you to train as warriors. And I will lead you now. The die is cast. There's no turning back.'

26

The ancient steps creaked as Taka picked up her skirts and raced up the steep staircase two at a time. She darted across the upper-floor room, sending dust smelling of rice straw puffing from the ancient tatami mats, pushed back the screens and leaned out over the rickety balcony.

Below her, geishas swished along the lamp-lit alley in elaborate festive kimonos, long sleeves swinging, trailing musky perfume and *bintsuke* oil, the pomade they slathered their hair with to keep it in place. They looked up and bowed and smiled, calling out greetings in bird-like coos, every bit as glamorous as the Kyoto geishas she'd known. Taka's new geisha friend, sixteen-year-old Toshimi, with her perfect oval face and wide-eyed air of innocence, dipped her head as she passed, tossing the frilled skirts of her western gown. Boys pushed by balancing stacks of lacquered food boxes, their breath puffing out like steam in the icy air.

From behind closed doors and shuttered windows came the plucking of shamisens and women's thin voices, plaintively singing. Smoke wafted out, heavy with the tang of grilling eel, roasting beef and stewing pork, and Taka thought of her father and how he used to enjoy tucking into his meat.

The chatter grew louder as the first customers started to arrive, handsome young samurai with swords thrust in their belts and ponytails or hair cropped short. There were shouts of welcome as they strutted through the crowds and disappeared into the teahouses. The geishas loved these gallant young men. The only ones who could afford the geishas' fees were the merchants and money brokers and businessmen, and being down-to-earth working girls they made their living entertaining them. But they all took impoverished young samurai as their lovers. And now, with their men setting off for war the very next day, they wanted to be sure they had the best possible time before they left.

It was the third night of celebrations. The first battalions had marched out of town two days earlier, the second the following day and many of the men had spent the night in the geisha quarter before they left. The last would bring up the rear tomorrow.

Even Taka felt her heart quicken at the sight of these fine youths. Before she'd come to Kagoshima she hadn't thought of any man other than Nobu. Back in Tokyo everything had reminded her of him – the polished veranda where they'd sat when she used to help him with his reading, the glade where he'd taken her hand that last fateful night. But time and his long silence had dulled the pain.

Besides, in this exciting new city it was impossible to stay miserable for long. She was seventeen now. Most girls of her age were married and had had their first children, or had settled into careers as geishas, depending on which world they moved in. It was high time she put Nobu and the foolish events of the previous summer out of her mind.

She and her mother had certainly come down in the world since the days when they'd had their own rickshaws and rumbled grandly along the Ginza. Taka had forbidden herself to think of the great mansion with its servants and rooms full of beautiful things and landscaped gardens and woods. Their small house in the Kagoshima geisha district was home now.

She had been here two months and had almost forgotten the horror she'd felt at the thought of being banished to this distant barbarous land. Now, strange though it seemed, she felt as if she'd never lived anywhere else. As they'd steamed round the headland and had their first sight of the great volcano with its plume of black smoke, she'd suddenly noticed how intensely blue the sky was, how green the woods, even in winter, and how steep and craggy the hills, like mountains in an ink painting. Steam spurted out of the ground here and there, smelling of sulphur, staining the rocks yellow, and there were mineral-rich hot springs right at the foot of the volcano, where they went to bathe. Even the people seemed more alive as they shouted and laughed in their rough impenetrable dialect.

Her brother Eijiro had been at the dock to meet them. He'd grown thinner and browner and his face was less puffy and dissipated. Sticking his chest out importantly, he'd told them they were to live in a farming village in the countryside, somewhere way out of town. That was where new arrivals always went.

Taka had smiled to herself. Eijiro of all people should

have known their mother wouldn't put up with any such nonsense. Fujino had waited till he was safely gone, then turned to the young men who stood around bowing deferentially and said very firmly in her most fluting tones, 'We've already made our own arrangements, thank you very much.'

In fact they'd had not the slightest idea where to go. In the end her mother's geisha instincts had come to the fore. She'd commandeered rickshaws to take them to the townsmen's district and found a room at the best inn there, the Tawaraya. A few days later they'd moved into a house in Daimonguchi, one of the city's two pleasure quarters.

At first Fujino and her old friend Aunt Kiharu, who'd come along with them, had grumbled incessantly about the precipitous fall in their living conditions. But after a few days they'd discovered that most of the courtesans and geishas were from Kyoto or Osaka, shipped in by the clan lords who were eager to populate the quarters of their distant southern city with high-class women. They'd even bumped into a couple of old friends and very soon felt completely at home. The pair of them relished being back in the flower and willow world, as the geisha community called themselves. Among the geishas, even the fifteen-year-olds were experts at flirting and teasing and scrutinizing the ways of men. Fujino and Aunt Kiharu were soon joining in the endless gossip about other geishas and parties they'd been to and men they knew.

Staring up and down the street, Taka still couldn't see the face she was looking for. She sighed. She'd been so sure he'd come – that her beloved father would come, tonight of all nights, when he was setting off for war first thing tomorrow. She felt utterly dispirited.

She noticed a man peeking shyly up at her. It was a young samurai who often lingered outside their house. She'd grown used to these fellows gazing at her with big puppy eyes whenever she went out, though this one was more persistent than most.

It was obvious, by the closed doors and the fact there was no lantern outside, that theirs was a private residence, not a geisha house, added to which, even though they'd never mentioned their link to General Kitaoka, everyone seemed to have worked it out; news travelled quickly. The fact Taka was the general's daughter made her all the more desirable but it also put her entirely out of reach.

Nevertheless today she found herself looking more kindly at the lad who stood gazing up at her. For a moment their eyes met and she flushed and drew back quickly behind the screens.

When she looked down again there was a group of men coming out of the shadows at the far end of the street, walking purposefully towards the house. Most were armed; she could see their rifles and swords. A pack of hunting dogs padded at their heels. Right in the middle was a giant of a man, towering over the rest. People stood aside respectfully as he passed or stepped forward to bow and greet him. Taka made out a square head with short-cropped hair, a bull-like neck and powerful shoulders and recognized the way he ambled along, chin lowered, as if deep in thought.

She shouted with joy so loudly that she set the flimsy walls of the house quivering. The next moment she was charging downstairs, tripping over her feet in her haste. She raced to the back of the house, calling, 'He's coming! He's coming!'

'Already? He can't be!'

Her mother was on her knees, large and buxom in her long under-kimono – not white, like a virtuous samurai wife would wear, but a voluptuous shade of scarlet. Okatsu, Taka's maid, was holding a bowl of iron-infused tea and gallnut powder – the usual mixture – while Fujino topped up the black polish on her teeth. Taka wrinkled her nose. The smell took her back to her childhood. It was unnerving the way they'd stepped back in time since they'd left Tokyo. Fujino had reverted completely to the mother she remembered from Kyoto days. She'd even started shaving her eyebrows again.

She had been trying on western gowns, which lay heaped around the room in mounds of lace, silk and satin where she'd tossed them aside. Splendid kimonos hung on kimono stands.

'Quickly, Taka, come and help. What do you think of this one?' she cried, her large bosom heaving as she let out a noisy sigh.

Okatsu lifted down a lavish green creation covered in swirling patterns of clouds and birds. Fujino threw it on, turning this way and that in front of the mirror. 'It won't do. Too gaudy, it makes me look huge. No, no, we need something more plain and tasteful.' Her plump hands were shaking.

It frightened Taka to see her so agitated. She was usually so calm and competent; no matter what happened, she always made everything all right. With her there Taka always felt safe. But whenever General

Kitaoka's name was mentioned, her mother started behaving like a dizzy young girl.

The general, so they'd heard, had led a simple life since he'd moved back to Kagoshima. He spent most of his time in the countryside, fishing, hunting with his beloved dogs and relaxing in mineral hot springs. He had a wife here too, a woman of impeccable samurai stock, a Kagoshima native, like him, chosen by his family and friends. Taka tried to imagine what sort of person she must be – an unsmiling samurai wife, perhaps, who dressed in severe homespun kimonos.

But tonight it didn't matter who or what she was. On his last night in the city before he went to war, he'd decided not to stay at home with his wife but to visit his old love, his geisha. He'd written to Fujino to tell her so. It was more than three years since they'd seen each other. Taka shuddered. Supposing he changed his mind? Supposing he walked straight past and went to another house? She put the thought aside.

'He knows you're not his wife, Mother. That's why he wants to see you. Put on the red kimono, the one you used to wear in Kyoto. He liked that one.'

'Don't be silly. Red is for young girls. I'd be embarrassed.' Fujino heaved another sigh, then took down a simple lavender kimono with a delicate pattern of plum blossoms and held out her arms for Okatsu to help her into it.

Okatsu had barely finished tying the last cord around Fujino's obi and smoothing her hair when there were voices outside. The outer door slid open, letting in a blast of cold air that sent the candle flames flickering so violently they nearly went out. Taka caught a glimpse of burly figures as a powerfully built middle-aged man ducked his head under the lintel. The door shut behind him.

Taka and her mother were on their knees to greet him.

'So sorry to bring you to this poor, humble place,' Fujino babbled, as if desperate to fill the silence. 'Come in, come in. Where have you been, neglecting us all this time? We've been here two months and you wait till now to visit us? I should send you straight home again.' She gave a high-pitched peal of laughter.

Taka raised her head. She didn't care how poor their house was or how reduced their circumstances. She just wanted to see this long-lost father of hers.

He stood awkwardly, almost filling the narrow vestibule. He was in a thick homespun jacket over several indigo-blue kimonos and wore dark blue leggings like he used to wear in Kyoto. She studied his big eyes and bushy eyebrows, his jowly face and stubbly chin. There were threads of grey in his thick black hair, but he was still her father, as huge, dependable and all-knowing as ever. She recognized that expression of his, thoughtful, calm, yet fiercely stubborn. He'd grown larger, she noticed; it was all the Castella cake he liked to eat.

'Father!' she said.

He was gazing at Fujino. A smile spread across his large face.

'You,' he said softly. Taka thrilled at the sound of the well-loved deep tones.

'Father!' she cried impatiently. 'I wanted to see you so

badly. I've so much to tell you! We've had such adventures.'

But he didn't seem to hear her. He was looking at her mother still. He shook his head as if he could hardly believe he was awake and said again, 'You.'

Fujino was still on her knees, her hands on the ground. She dabbed her eyes with her sleeve. 'Come in,' she whispered. 'I've sent out for a meal for you.'

Taka had gone to fetch a flask of shochu, the local beverage, brewed from sweet potatoes. She knew it was her father's favourite drink. As she came in she heard his booming laugh.

He'd taken off his jacket and was sitting cross-legged beside the firebox in a small downstairs room at the back of the house, warming his hands. Her mother, large and curvaceous, was on her knees next to him, keeping his cup filled. A couple of lanterns lit the dark corners of the shabby room.

'Are you really leaving tomorrow?' Fujino said softly, leaning towards him. 'You . . .' – she barely breathed the word. 'Always the stubborn one. No one could tell you a thing.'

She tried to top up his cup again but he held a large hand over it. He never had drunk much.

There were so many things to talk about – everything that had happened in the three years they'd been apart; why he hadn't been in touch, why he hadn't come to visit even after Fujino had written to tell him they'd arrived in Kagoshima, why he had to go to war. But they probably wouldn't discuss any of that. He came here to forget. The two of them would laugh and chat and talk nonsense as if they'd seen each other only yesterday.

'Why don't I come with you?' Fujino said, smacking him teasingly on the thigh. 'It's not only samurai women who can fight, you know. I can ride a horse with the best of them!'

The general threw back his head and laughed till tears ran down his face. 'That would have to be quite a horse! No, you belong here. I want to know you'll be here, waiting for me, when I get back.'

Taka knelt beside him. She had so much to tell him and there was only this one night.

'We had such a journey, Father,' she said. 'We had to leave everything behind – well, nearly everything. Ten days on the ship and Mother was seasick all the way! Do you know, I've been learning English. I can read and write it now too.' She paused to take a breath, remembering that her English lessons had come to an end when they'd left Tokyo. So much had happened that she didn't fully understand.

'Little Taka,' General Kitaoka said, chuckling. 'You've grown into a beautiful young lady. And such a slender little creature too.'

'It's just as well she doesn't take after either of us!' said Fujino. 'Haru is married now, you know. I arranged a marriage for Taka too but it . . . it didn't work out.'

'To whom? Who were you plotting to give my precious little girl to?'

'There's a young man called Hachibei Masuda, a very clever fellow. He's a merchant, the heir to the House of Shimada . . .' She glanced at him timidly; he was bound to disapprove of such a person.

'A merchant? The Shimada heir?' He scowled. 'Those merchants certainly know how to make money. Those one-time colleagues of mine – Inoue and the rest – are all in their pockets. They hold the puppet strings, they make the politicians dance to their tune.' He leaned forward and looked at Taka, his big eyes gentle. 'Taka-*chan*. Did you want to marry this Masuda?'

'Not in the slightest,' Taka said. 'He was a dreadful, pompous, preening man. He sent a horrible letter saying he'd changed his mind and didn't want to marry me after all. I was so glad his letter came.' She glanced nervously at her mother, afraid she'd be shocked at such an abrupt change of heart; she simply couldn't keep up the pretence any longer.

Fujino gaped at her, then clapped her plump hands and laughed. 'Well, I never. And there I was thinking you were heartbroken. So you just wanted to please me!' She sighed. 'I don't know what we'll do with you, Taka. We have to find a husband for you or you'll be too old and then what will happen?'

' "Pompous, preening . . ." ' That's not right for my girl,' said the general. 'You need a strapping young samurai like those brave lads of mine, keeping guard outside the door. When we get back we'll find the perfect husband for you.'

They fell silent. Taka guessed that her mother was wondering, as she was, if he ever would come back. The general picked up his long-stemmed pipe from the tobacco box on the floor, took a puff and blew out a long plume of fragrant smoke.

'I wish you would introduce me to your wife,' Fujino said in her most matter-of-fact tones. 'You know I could be of service to her – help with the children, help around the house, do whatever I can, now you're going away.'

Taka shook her head. Help around the house? In theory, of course, that was what geishas did. Many of her schoolfriends' mothers had been samurai women and there had often been geishas at their houses, helping out.

But Fujino had been a grand lady herself, in charge of a house full of servants. Despite her down-to-earth tone, her sadness was palpable; it filled the room. Taka wondered why her father hadn't ever married her. She knew that in the old days samurai men had always had arranged marriages with women of good samurai families; but her father's generation had been different. They'd been revolutionaries, they'd rejected the old ways and they'd thrown aside that convention too. Many of the colleagues who'd fought beside him in the streets of Kyoto had married their geisha lovers. Only he had not.

But those were the same colleagues he had gone on to despise, who he felt had betrayed the revolution and used their new-found power to line their own pockets, the ones who were destroying the samurai class and its ethos.

Maybe that was why he'd chosen to take the traditional path instead. Maybe he'd felt that, as a Kagoshima samurai, he should take a Kagoshima wife. All the time he'd been in Kyoto he'd been with Fujino. He'd only married later, when he'd gone back to Kagoshima, and he'd never once brought his new wife to Tokyo. She'd always stayed in this tropical southern city. It had been Taka and her mother and siblings he'd lived with in the grand Tokyo mansion during his days as counsellor and commander-in-chief.

Taka looked at him. She wanted to ask, 'Why? Why didn't you marry her?' But she didn't dare.

The general was gazing at Fujino. Taka wondered if he was asking himself the same question. 'You were there when we were fighting in Kyoto,' he said softly. 'It was always you, only you.'

'That was long ago.'

It was sweet and touching to see these two plump, middle-aged people together. Taka had always thought that only people her own age felt passion. Fujino was always so calm, so collected, Taka had imagined she would never understand her feelings for Nobu, that she could never have been swept away by feelings as intense and overpowering as those.

But she saw now she'd been wrong. She'd only ever seen the two of them as her parents. She'd never thought of them as people like her, with feelings like hers. But now she saw that they cared for each other as deeply as she did for Nobu, maybe even more.

She'd been so excited at seeing her father she'd been chattering away, taking up precious time, when this was their only chance to be together. Quickly she murmured an excuse and backed towards the door. As she slid it open she saw her father reach out and take her mother's hand. Fujino wiped away a tear.

27

Standing in the darkness of the vestibule, Taka put on a thick jacket and wrapped a scarf around her head and face. Her father's straw sandals were neatly arranged side by side where he'd left them, and she remembered with a pang how he used to sit quietly weaving them himself, specially large for his large feet. She wished she could have kept him there for ever. There'd been a gaping hole in their lives ever since he'd left for Kagoshima.

She slipped her feet through the rope thongs of a pair of wooden geta clogs. She needed to leave the house but had no idea where she would go – perhaps to the tea-house where her friend Toshimi was entertaining that night. There'd be a party going on but she could sit in the kitchen with the maids and keep warm. She wished Okatsu could come with her, but she had to stay in the house in case Fujino needed her.

Outside it was as noisy as a festival day or New Year's Eve, with everyone chattering and laughing. Despite herself, Taka brightened up at the prospect of mingling with the crowds. It was the first time she'd ever been out on her own; usually Okatsu or one of the maids was always with her. Even though the geishas wandered the streets as they pleased, her mother liked to keep an eye on her. She had a reputation to uphold, she was the great general's daughter. But all the rules had fallen by the wayside now the men were leaving town the next day.

She was about to open the door when she heard shuffling and stamping and people blowing on their hands.

'It's no good, I tell you,' grumbled a voice in a thick Kagoshima brogue. The words were muffled as if the man was speaking through a scarf. 'He should've let us search the place before he went in. Especially after those men we found the other night. There could be killers under the floor. They could easily have crept in and be hiding down there and cut through the tatami with their swords once he's asleep.'

Taka started, listening in alarm as she made out what the man was saying. It sounded like one of the guards her father had posted outside. It was typical of her father to be so careless of his own safety. He hadn't said a word about the risks he was taking or the danger he was in.

'What, you mean some would-be assassin crawls under there and waits, day after day, just in case 'e 'appens to come by? They'll have frozen to death by now if they haven't starved,' came the answer, followed by a snort.

'Anyone could work out he'd come here his last night in town.' It was a stern older voice. 'It'd be easy for an assassin to slip in with all these mobs. We mustn't lower our guard. We haven't flushed out all the plotters yet by any means.'

'And 'im so visible, too. It's a good thing we posted

men round the back of the house. He should have let some of us in there with 'im. I told 'im so but there's no arguing with 'im.'

'You'd have men inside with you, would you, if you were spending the night with your geisha?'

'If only I was, not out 'ere freezing my balls off!'

There were chuckles.

'He must really want to see 'er to take such a risk.'

'Princess Pig, they called her,' said the older voice softly. 'Lovely lady. I remember her well. We all do, all of us who fought in Kyoto.'

Taka slid the door open abruptly. She didn't want to overhear impertinent remarks about her mother.

There were fifteen or twenty fearsome-looking fellows outside, standing around in bulky jackets, thick kimono skirts and leggings with nothing of their faces visible except for watchful eyes, glittering behind the folds of their dark scarves. A couple were tall, some short, some slight, some burly. It was impossible to tell which were the ones Taka had heard. Long swords poked from their hems and they held rifles in gloved hands. They straightened up as she appeared and bowed, backing respectfully out of her way.

Taka bowed in return and hurried off along the narrow street. Despite the cold it was crowded with people, watching for geishas as they emerged from one teahouse and flitted off to the next, their painted faces glowing white in the lantern light, surrounded by groups of rowdy young men.

Taka was slipping through the crowds, pulling her jacket closer round her, when she heard footsteps behind her. A hand snatched at her sleeve.

She started. She hadn't told anyone she was leaving or where she was going.

'Sorry, lady. You can't walk alone. It's not safe.'

It was the voice she'd heard a moment earlier, speaking with a Kagoshima accent, the one who'd been so concerned for her father's safety. She turned with a sigh of relief. 'I often walk at night.' This man had no need to know she'd never been out alone before.

The guard had pushed his scarf away from his face to speak. She looked at him, puzzled. She had a feeling she'd seen him somewhere before. There was something familiar about the angular face, narrow eyes and hair tugged back into a tiny topknot.

'Things have changed. There've been threats against the general's life. You can't trust anyone any more. Someone might kidnap you or take you hostage.'

Taka had regained her composure. She laughed. 'Everyone knows me round here. I have nothing to fear.' She walked on but the guard fell into place behind her.

'At least let me accompany you, madam.'

She sighed. 'Well, if you insist. What is your name?'

'Kuninosuké Toyoda, ma'am, first lieutenant in the general's personal bodyguard.'

Kuninosuké Toyoda . . . The name was not familiar; but people often changed their names when they started a new phase of life.

'Shouldn't you be back there with the others, guarding him?'

He jerked his chin dismissively. 'There are plenty of guards there already.'

* * *

Towards the end of the road the houses were darker and there were fewer people about. Taka heard the crunch of the guard's straw sandals on the frozen ground and saw his large shadow stretching behind hers. It was unexpectedly reassuring to know he was there.

They'd reached the crossroads at the centre of the Daimonguchi pleasure quarter and the red-painted Inari shrine, with its glowing lanterns and stone foxes, where the geishas always stopped to pray for prosperity and good luck. It was a haven of quiet in the noise and revelry of the geisha district. Taka clapped her hands and tossed a coin into the box. The guard stepped up beside her, put his hands together and bowed too.

She pushed her scarf away from her face. In the distance figures bundled in thick clothing hurried to and fro and lanterns blazed. All over the quarter people were dancing. Laughter and singing, the shuffle of feet and the plaintive twang of shamisens echoed from tea-houses where men were abandoning themselves to drink and pleasure, putting aside their responsibilities, duties and ranks for this one night. Tomorrow they would wake up and be soldiers again, marching to war.

But this stubborn protector of hers was missing all the festivities. It was his last night too. She wondered what he was praying for – success in battle or just to come back alive?

He raised his head. His brow was furrowed as if he was already on the battlefield, ready to cut down any enemy that dared get in his way.

'It's sad that you have to work tonight,' Taka said shyly.

He lifted an eyebrow as if startled that she was

addressing him and bowed stiffly. 'Not at all. It's my good fortune. The general chose me for his bodyguard. It's a great honour. I wouldn't have it any other way.'

'But you're leaving so soon,' she persisted. 'Just a few hours now. Aren't you afraid?' Her own life had changed, and for the worse, but this man was marching off into the unknown, heading for the mountains in the middle of winter, not knowing where he would spend the night, maybe into battle. She couldn't imagine how it must feel to be setting off for war the very next day.

'Afraid?' He stared at her then threw back his head and laughed. His whole face had changed. He looked like a boy. 'I can't wait! I've been kicking my heels here much too long. I want to feel my sword in my hand again. This is what we've been training for all these years. We're going to clean up this country. We'll march on Tokyo, toss out those corrupt officials and put in a government of honest men. It'll be a second revolution, a glorious revolution.' His eyes were shining.

In his excitement he'd lost his Kagoshima burr. Hearing him speak like a Tokyoite, Taka remembered where she'd seen him before. He'd been a junior officer in the Imperial Guard and used to come to their house in Tokyo when her father was a member of the council of state and commander of the guard. She'd been a child back then but she'd loved to watch these dashing young men with their fine uniforms who strode around the grounds arguing about how to run the country. They were so totally different from Eijiro and his dissolute friends. Most of them had resigned when her father did and left for Kyushu with him, as many of the Satsuma had. This young man must have been among them.

There'd been one in particular she'd found intriguing. He was tall and rather aloof and seemed to keep apart from the others. She could see he was her father's right-hand man. He was always at his side and when her father wanted something done he summoned him.

In those days his hair had been cropped short like a westerner's and he'd worn a crisp uniform with gold braid and shiny buttons and a red stripe down the trouser legs. She looked at the man in front of her in his thick jacket and leggings with his sword poking menacingly from his skirts. In the dim light that glowed from the stone lanterns in front of the shrine she recognized the clean jaw and sharp cheekbones and realized it was the same face she'd admired from a distance.

He looked younger than she'd thought, more ordinary, not as manly and dignified and splendidly tall, but it was him all the same. Her heart skipped a beat. She felt a curious mixture of disappointment and excitement tinged with relief that he didn't know what was going on in her mind or that she'd ever noticed him before.

His eyes lingered on her face. His expression softened and he gave a clipped military bow. He'd recognized her too, though she must have been a chubby thirteen-year-old when he'd seen her last.

'I was with the Imperial Guard in Tokyo, madam. We're all devoted to your father. Those jackals in Tokyo are out to destroy him and everything he stands for. All that power has gone to their heads. We have to get rid of them for the good of the country.'

He scuffed the ground with his foot. He was wearing rope sandals, as all the men did. A seagull shrieked and waves crashed in the bay a couple of streets away.

Above the rooftops an angry red glow lit the clouds above the volcano. The guard's eyes glittered in the darkness. 'Forgive my impertinence, madam. May I ask – is your mother in good health?'

'My mother?' It seemed an extraordinary question. Taka bowed. 'Thank you, yes.'

'I saw her dance in Kyoto.' He spoke softly, hesitantly. 'She was beautiful, so beautiful. Her face was luminous. I was just a young lad then but I never forgot that.' A group of men passed by, heading for the geisha houses on the other side of the crossroads. They paid no attention to the two figures swathed in thick jackets and scarves in front of the shrine. 'I remember you too, madam, and your sister, two little girls serving drinks, very solemn. I saw you in your big house in Tokyo too and thought, those must be the general's daughters. Excuse my rough soldier's manners, madam,' he added hurriedly. 'I mean no disrespect. I'm not used to the company of fine ladies like you.'

Taka laughed. He was far from a rough soldier. At another time she might have complained he was excessively familiar but not tonight. His friends were drinking, forgetting their cares in the arms of the Kagoshima geishas. He deserved a little kindness too.

She knew she should walk on but she was enjoying the forbidden pleasure of being alone with a man – not just any man but this man she'd admired when she was a child. She remembered that her father had said she should look for a husband among his samurai, and her mother too had spoken of the Imperial Guard. Perhaps she'd do better to forget about marriage and follow her heart, as her mother had done.

She wanted to stretch out the moment a little longer. 'You've served with my father for many years.'

'Since I was a boy. I grew up not far from here. My parents lived near your father, we were neighbours. I learned to fight at his side and went with him to Kyoto.'

'You must have known my brother,' Taka said softly. By the looks of him he was about the same age as Ryutaro would have been if he'd lived.

'Ryutaro was my best friend. We sparred together when we were boys, after he moved down here to live with your father. He was fearless, he'd always put himself in danger to help out a comrade, but he was modest too. The perfect samurai. We were fighting side by side when he was killed, at the battle of Toba Fushimi. I'll never forget that day.' He heaved a sigh.

The moon had risen, flooding the dark street and the small red-painted shrine with its two stone foxes with light. Taka could see the guard's breath, like smoke in the cold air.

'Life is strange,' he said. 'You never know where it will take you. When I left Kagoshima I thought I'd never come back and here I am again. My life has come full circle. And now here you are in Kagoshima too.'

He fell silent. She felt a tremor run through her. He had extraordinary eyes, pale and piercing. Then he reached out and, to her shock, snatched up her hand. She felt the touch of his fingers on hers as he held it for a moment then raised it and pressed it to his lips.

He dropped it as abruptly and rubbed his hand across his forehead. 'I never expected to be with you of all people, tonight of all nights,' he murmured.

In the streets around them the lights were going out,

the music dying down and the crowds beginning to disperse as the geishas walked off into the night with their lovers. There was excitement in the air.

The guard ran his fingers across her cheek. 'I don't even know your name.'

'Taka,' she said, so softly he had to bend his head to hear.

'Otaka-*sama*,' he murmured, using the polite form. 'Do you remember mine?'

'Kuninosuké-*sama*.' She felt as if she was in a trance. It was a long time since she'd been so close to a man. She could smell his sweat, feel his breath hot on her face.

He took her hand in both of his. 'I'm a humble soldier. I know I could never be worthy of you, but when I'm in the mountains I wish I could believe you might think of me from time to time.'

Taka looked at him, trembling. He was leaving the next day and they would probably never meet again. Whatever happened tonight would leave no trace, no karmic trail. There was only the present.

His hand was on her shoulder. She knew she should resist but she had lost all will. She let him pull her towards him. Then she was in his arms, her face smothered against his jacket. She felt the hard muscles of his chest and the pounding of his heart through the thick cotton.

'Otaka-*sama*. You're like a bird,' he whispered.

He pressed his mouth to her head and ears and face. Her knees were quivering. She felt his fingers run through her hair and find the tender skin at the back of her neck, stroking and soothing as if she really was a little bird. She leaned against him and felt her body fit into the curves of his. Cocooned in his arms, she felt herself coming alive again.

She felt a pang of sadness and anger. It should be Nobu, she thought, Nobu she should be pressing close to, not this man, not Kuninosuké. For a moment she wondered where he was and what he was doing and yearned for that slim body and soft voice. He was never coming back, she told herself. She would never see him again, she might as well accept that. It was a lost cause. In any case she was not betraying him, not doing anything wrong. Kuninosuké was leaving the next day, going to an unknown future, maybe to his death. It was only right that she should leave him with good memories to look back on, send him on his way with kindness.

She drew back slowly from Kuninosuké's enfolding arms and looked up at him and smiled. 'I will think of you,' she said. 'I'll pray for your safety.'

'I'll never forget this face,' he whispered. 'I'll carry it in my mind as long as I live.'

Across the road the lights were going off in the house where her geisha friend Toshimi was entertaining.

'I'll go now,' Taka whispered.

She crossed the road. When she stopped and looked round, Kuninosuké was watching her, a tall figure, silhouetted against the darkness.

28

The next morning she woke with a start. There was something she had to do, something urgent. It was well before cock crow still, but there was an unearthly light filtering between the wooden rain doors and paper screens. Muffled footsteps padded by, soft as a cat's.

She pushed back the musty bedding, slid open a shutter, and looked out. Snow – falling in huge flakes, crusting the roofs and eaves and windowsills of the houses across the way, more snow than she'd ever imagined possible in this southern tropical city. The lanterns outside the geisha houses had long since been extinguished but the snow made everything bright. It lifted her spirits too. Perhaps her father wouldn't leave that day after all.

She had spent the night in one of the unused upstairs rooms so as not to disturb her parents. Shivering, she examined the miserable furnishings – a dusty trunk, a tall cabinet that contained her mother's precious kimonos, neatly folded and wrapped in tissue paper, a vase of dried branches and a frayed painting in the alcove. She peeked inside the wall cupboards where the bedding was stored, opened the tiny drawers in the ornamental shelves in the alcove and heaved up the lid of the trunk.

She pulled out dolls, ceramics, incense containers and

tea-ceremony ware, all neatly labelled in boxes, which they'd shipped from the house in Tokyo and would probably never look at again. Tucked underneath were some plain winter kimonos of thick cotton. She took out a couple and bundled herself up in them as quickly as she could, pulling them on over the gown she'd slept in and tying a sash around each to keep it in place. There was no time to dress as carefully as she normally would. She smoothed her hair back, knotted it into a coil and tip-toed down the polished stairs, stepping lightly so they wouldn't creak.

The wooden floor of the vestibule was icy cold under her feet. She fumbled around in the darkness and ran her hand across the sandals and clogs in the shoe cupboard. Her father's huge straw sandals had gone. She sat back on her heels with a dreadful sense of emptiness and swallowed a sob. She'd just been reunited with him, only to lose him again. Everything was coming to an end and she hadn't even had a chance to say goodbye.

She took a thick jacket and an oiled paper umbrella, slipped her feet into geta clogs and stepped outside into the luminous white landscape. The snow was criss-crossed with the slatted prints of clogs and the woven markings of straw sandals. Usually at this hour geishas would be going to bed after a long night but today women who never saw the dawn were already out, heading for the castle. They hurried along, bundled in kimonos with straw capes tied over the top like farmers, bobbing like moving haystacks.

Taka tried to keep close to the buildings where the drifts were shallower but even there her feet sank into the snow with every step. The long straight street with its dark wooden houses seemed endless. She was panting hard by the time she reached the turn that marked the end of the geisha quarter. She hurried through the merchants' section of the city, past lumberyards and storehouses and the high walls of rice warehouses, skirting men brushing snow into mounds, sweeping again as more fell. At least the streets were clearer here. People huddled around braziers, warming their hands over the glowing charcoal. The sky was lightening, turning an ominous shade of mauve, like a bruise, and as the clouds lifted Taka glimpsed the volcano behind the warehouses, magically white, a ribbon of ash streaming like a banner from the crater.

Slipping and sliding, trying not to lose her footing, she reached the samurai district with its broad avenues lined with stone or stucco walls and hurried past the city granary and the governor's offices. Not far off voices shouted, drums throbbed and shamisens played. Ahead of her a mass of people, more than she'd ever seen, spilled out of the parade ground, filling the streets, balancing on walls and stones and gateposts. Every stone of the massive granite walls and battlements of the castle behind them was etched in white, and behind that Shiroyama – Castle Mount – rose like a cliff, shrouded in a snow-covered tangle of foliage.

Taka searched for a gap in the mob and tried to worm her way in. People were pressed so tight she was swept along in the throng, driven one way, then another. She fought her way deeper, watching out for her unprotected feet in their thonged geta clogs among the leather boots and heavy straw sandals. All she could see was huge backs covered with padded jackets or straw capes.

For the space of a breath the bodies parted and she caught a glimpse of the parade ground. It was full of men milling about, most in dark blue jackets and striped hakama trousers, like a uniform, with white headbands and swords tucked into their sashes. Many carried rifles too. Some wore white armbands and some were in military uniform, like soldiers of the Imperial Army.

In the middle of them, surrounded by troops, was her father. While most of his men were in traditional samurai garb, he was splendidly dressed in his general's uniform, black with gold braiding and buttons and a red sash, his gold sword at his side. Taka's heart burst with pride, mingled with dreadful sadness. She knew that uniform so well. He'd worn it for ceremonial events in Tokyo, when he was field marshal of the Imperial Army and leader of the government.

She pushed forward, trying to reach him before she lost sight of him again. Towering above his troops, he strode with his dogs at his heels, stopping and speaking to each man in turn, smiling and joking, exchanging words here and there. He seemed to know all their names and he had encouraging words for each. The men laughed or nodded seriously as he spoke to them and each held his head higher after he'd gone. Among his men the general looked entirely at home, more himself than she'd ever seen him.

Then she noticed the young samurai walking beside him. He was swarthy as if he was of southern stock, with a clean-cut, rather noble face. Taka stared at him. She'd heard General Kitaoka had had a son by his wife, a son he'd publicly recognized and acknowledged as his heir. Perhaps this was him. Seeing him made her wonder how her father would receive her, whether he'd be pleased or embarrassed to have the offspring of a geisha greeting him in front of his troops.

There were heavyset men close by, keeping a watchful eye on the crowd. Taka wondered if these were her father's guards and if Kuninosuké was among them. She was hoping she might see him. They'd both let themselves get a bit carried away the previous night and behaved in unseemly ways. She'd thought about it afterwards, wondered whether she'd betrayed Nobu or misled Kuninosuké, whether she'd done anything to shame her family, and decided, no, it was just an innocent hug, offering support to their brave men, saying farewell to a soldier going to the front. After all, it had been his last night in the city. All the same, it had created a bond between them. It wouldn't do any harm to exchange a few words. And she was curious to see his face in daylight, this shadowy figure who'd held her so close.

Bugles blared and the men stepped back to clear a space for the general, her father. He stood, legs apart, his great chest pushed out, hands clasped behind his back, huge and solid like a mountain. Every eye was fixed on him.

'It's snowing.' His voice boomed out, echoing off the buildings that surrounded the square. There was silence as if the men had been expecting something more momentous, followed by a roar of laughter that shook the air. He waited for the laughter to stop. His face was serious.

'It snowed on the day the forty-seven ronin carried out their vendetta, and it's snowing today too. It's a sign that our hearts are pure and our cause is just. The gods are on our side.'

Listening, Taka remembered Nobu telling her the story

of the forty-seven lordless samurai and how they'd waited years until the time was ripe to carry out their bloody revenge. She could almost hear his young voice and see his large earnest eyes as he spoke. He was still there in her heart, she realized, no matter what had happened with Kuninosuké. They belonged to each other.

There had been a snowstorm on the day of the ronins' vendetta too, as if the gods had wanted to mark the purity of the loyal warriors' deed by cloaking the city in white. Everyone knew the story and the symbolism and how, having done their duty, they'd been sentenced to die by ritual suicide and had gone to their deaths as to a lover's embrace.

In the silence horses snorted and pawed the ground. Snow lay in a thick layer, its unearthly glow reflected in every face. Taka looked around. Many of the men were as young as she, some younger, all gazing at their leader with eyes afire, impatient to set off, as ready to fight and die as the ronin had been. She shuddered, wondering if she would ever see any of them again.

'Today we march for Tokyo.' The general was speaking again. 'Unscrupulous men have taken over the government of our country and we must wrest it from their hands. We will confront these traitors, ask why they send assassins to attack us and destroy our way of life. We will demand the restoration of the pure ways of old. And if our demands are not met we will fight in the name of the emperor.'

Taka gazed at him, full of pride. His eyes were blazing.

'We are the samurai of Satsuma, the nation's finest.' There was a cheer, followed by thuds as clumps of snow crashed from the branches of the tall trees in the castle grounds. 'We have trained day and night. We have fought many battles and won . . .' – another huge cheer drowned his words – '. . . and we will win this time too. Two divisions have already left and are marching north. There are fifteen thousand of us – seven battalions of infantry plus artillery and support troops. And thousands more will join us on our march to Tokyo. Our packhorse drivers are all volunteers. Even our women and children beg to come along.

'Our cause is righteous and our force is overwhelming. And if we die our deaths will be glorious. Better to die with honour than live with shame!'

The men shouted and cheered and stamped their feet and rifle butts on the ground. The roar was deafening. Tears pricked Taka's eyes and she shouted too, thrilled to be part of such a glorious throng, proud to be the daughter of such a leader.

As the clamour died down Taka stepped forward. Women were making their way through the ranks, pushing hand-kerchiefs and amulets into the men's hands, wishing them luck. The guards had gathered protectively round General Kitaoka. Black eyes glinted from behind their scarves as they looked her up and down.

'Father!'

He was standing by his horse, running his fingers through its thick black mane. To Taka it looked a monstrous beast, huge and powerful with muscles rippling under its glossy coat. It tossed its head and snorted impatiently, puffing out a cloud of white steam. He whispered a word to it and turned.

Taka had been afraid he might be angry that she'd

come, unannounced and uninvited, to interrupt him at such an important time. But he laughed when he saw her and folded her in his arms. She breathed out in relief. She always forgot that he was not like other fathers, not cold and stern. Standing in his shadow she felt protected from everything. Even the cold wind no longer chilled her.

'My little girl.' She looked around for the young samurai, his son, and was relieved to see he was not there. One of the dogs licked her hand with its raspy tongue.

'I wanted to see you so badly one last time,' she began, her words tailing off. He looked so splendid in his uniform she was tongue-tied. 'Is Eijiro here? Is he . . . ?' She didn't want to voice her doubts about her brother.

Her father smiled as he read her mind. 'He's doing well, very well. I'm proud to call him my son. He left two days ago. He's with the advance guard, in the first infantry division.'

'I wish you didn't have to go.' She drew herself up and tried to speak with dignity as befitted the daughter of General Kitaoka. 'Do your best. Be careful.' She swallowed hard and added in a whisper, 'Mother misses you. We all miss you so much. Come back soon. Please come back soon.'

There was a silence. She ran her eyes across his jowly face, his bushy eyebrows and piercing eyes, shiny like black diamonds. She had a dreadful premonition that this was the last time she'd see him. He looked at her gently, his forehead creased. There was a bemused expression on his face, as if he had set something in train that he didn't fully understand and could no longer control, as if events had taken on a momentum of their own and he couldn't stop them.

'In the end all we can do is hold on to what we think is right,' he said softly. 'We have to follow our ideals, otherwise we're no better than our enemies. As for our fate, that is in the hands of the gods and our ancestors.' He smiled at her. 'You look so like your mother. I see her in you. Take care of her for me.'

She felt tears running down her face and turned away quickly.

When she turned back the general was heaving himself on to his horse. He settled in the saddle, thrust his shoulders back and looked down at her, all trace of doubt gone. On his face was the proud steadfast scowl of a warrior about to lead his army on a glorious crusade.

'You're a Kitaoka too,' he said. 'Never forget that.'

She dabbed her eyes with her sleeve and bowed.

It was then that she saw Kuninosuké, standing among the bodyguards, laughing and talking. He must have noticed her with the general and had turned away but his scarf had slipped. As she recognized him he pushed it back further, as if wondering if the general's daughter would acknowledge him, a mere foot soldier.

In daylight he looked younger, more vulnerable than she'd imagined, not intimidating or even particularly good-looking, rather ordinary, in fact. After all that had happened the previous night she wanted at least to wish him good luck. She took a breath and stepped towards him.

He drew himself up. 'Madam. You are here to say goodbye to your father.'

'And to you.'

He smiled. He had crooked teeth and his face was gaunt

but he had the same pale unfathomable eyes. 'Like your father said, we're the forty-seven ronin – except there's more of us, a lot more!' He laughed, a careless, boyish laugh. 'With the gods on our side, we can't lose. We'll crush our enemies and be back before you've even noticed we've gone. This isn't the last you'll see of me!' His face softened. 'I should beg your forgiveness for my behaviour last night but I'm not sure I'm sorry.'

'I'll think of you,' she said. 'I won't forget you. Please take care of yourself and come back safely.'

'Does my life matter so much to you?'

She didn't know herself what she felt. She didn't want to give him an answer that wasn't true. She blushed and lowered her eyes and fumbled in her sleeve. 'I'd like to give you something . . .'

Usually she carried all manner of things in her capacious sleeves – a fan, a purse, a handkerchief, a tobacco pouch. But today she'd rushed out with nothing. All she had was the amulet Nobu had bought for her at Sengaku Temple, a small brocade pouch, red embroidered with gold, containing a prayer for good fortune. It was old now and had lost its potency; amulets always lost their power at the end of the year. But she carried it still in memory of him.

She couldn't bear to give away something so precious. But then she thought of Sengaku Temple where the forty-seven ronin were buried. She pictured their graves, in four neat rows, with incense burning in front of each. Kuninosuké was a man in their mould. He was about to risk his life for the Satsuma cause. How could she begrudge him anything? It was only right that she should give him the amulet.

She took it from her sleeve. 'This is from Sengaku Temple. It's a bit old, I'm afraid, but it might still have a little power to protect you.' As she pressed it into his hand she felt the touch of his fingers. He knotted it carefully on to his sash. Their eyes met. His were like dark hollows through which for a moment she thought she could see into his soul.

'I'll keep it with me always and think of you.'

'I'll think of you too – all of you. I'll offer prayers and incense for your success.' She stepped back, bowing, conscious of the other guards watching.

'Good luck,' she added formally. 'Be careful.'

Drums were beating and people cheering and in one of the neighbouring houses shamisens played. General Kitaoka put on his plumed hat and set off on his horse, surrounded by his bodyguards, at the head of his troops. The men marched in formation, battalion after battalion, filling the broad avenue. Snow glistened on the dark blue jackets, on the weapons, on the horses' backs. Banners flapped noisily in the wind as the straw sandals tramped inexorably away.

Snow was falling again, more and more heavily.

Taka watched until the huge figure dwindled to a black dot against the glistening hillside, then disappeared. She watched the line of men marching proudly into the mist and snow, into the high mountains, into the unknown, until the last soldier was gone, followed by the packhorses laden with ammunition and the baggage train and finally the women, straggling along behind. It was impossible to imagine that any army could resist such a mighty force.

She watched and watched till her feet were like ice and

the last figures in the distance had faded and dissolved into the blizzard. She almost wished she could have gone too.

She turned to go home. The city was frighteningly empty. There was no one left – only women and children, the old and infirm. Even the geishas had gone. Under the make-up and perfume and exquisite kimonos, they were tough working girls, and many had bundled themselves up in thick jackets to follow their men. It was going to be lonely.

PART V

Across a Magpie Bridge

29

*Third month, year of the ox, the tenth year
of the Meiji era (April 1877)*

'Oi, Yoshida. Nose in your book again?' The taunt rang
out above the din of engines, the creak of the paddle
wheel and the sailors' shouts. Bells clanged amidships
and footsteps pounded across the metal deck above
Nobu's head.

Sweat trickled down the back of his neck and his
clothes stuck to his damp skin. He heaved a sigh and
hugged his manual of French infantry tactics to his
chest. He knew that sarcastic twang – Sakurai, a
thuggish third-year man from one of the minor clans
who delighted in tormenting the junior cadets. He and
his classmates had been eager to beat Nobu down to
size when he joined up and had discovered to their
surprise that, studious though he was, he was well able
to take care of himself. They had treated him with
grudging respect ever since.

Nobu was sitting with his knees pressed to his chin in
the four-man cabin he shared with ten other officer

cadets, holding his book under the shaft of light that shone through the porthole. His fellow cadets were squashed in around him in their shirtsleeves, some sleeping, some reading, wearily fanning themselves. Caps and overcoats hung on hooks on the wall and there were clothes draped anywhere they could find a place for them. It was as hot and moist as a bathhouse.

But at least he was in the officers' quarters. He'd been sent on an errand to the bowels of the ship once and plunged down the narrow steps to the dungeon-like hold where the conscripts were billeted. He felt the heat and smelt the coal fumes and the stench of sweat and vomit before he even got there. The hold was right above the engine room and he could hear the roar of the furnace and feel the floor judder as the pistons drove the mighty ship. There were men everywhere, the lucky ones in hammocks strung one above the other, the rest side by side on the floor, never seeing daylight, eating where they slept while their fellow soldiers threw up around them. He'd picked his way through them, steering clear of the overflowing latrines, thanking his lucky stars he wasn't down there with them.

It had been two months earlier, in late February, that rumours had begun to spread that the Satsuma had risen. The principal had called the college together and told the assembled men that the Satsuma had invaded the neighbouring prefecture, Kumamoto, and that imperial orders had been issued to put them down.

The First Infantry Regiment of the Imperial Guard had left for the south straight away, followed by several contingents of soldiers. Everyone knew that the Satsuma were battle-hardened veterans, some of the finest soldiers in the land. But there were other fine soldiers too, who had excellent reasons to hate the Satsuma, and soon unemployed ex-samurai from the northern clans were queuing up to go to the front.

Nobu knew that for his fellow northerners, the details of what they were fighting for or why were irrelevant. In the new Japan, all the good jobs had been monopolized by men of the winning clans – the Choshu, Satsuma, Hizen and Tosa. A few northerners, like Nobu, had been lucky enough to get into the army. For a man of warrior stock, a samurai, it was a chance – virtually the only chance – to keep his head up, maintain his pride and make a decent life by working his way up through the ranks. Above all it was a job, one of the few jobs available to a northerner. It was not a matter of ideology but survival.

But most northern samurai, like Nobu's brothers, were living in poverty, reduced to scraping around to survive. And now it had been thrust into their laps – the chance to take revenge on their old enemy, the cause of all their misfortunes. They wouldn't have to break any laws or be punished, all they had to do was join the army or police force to kill Satsuma – legitimately. They'd even get paid for it. Their positions had been reversed. It had been the Aizu who had been ground under the heel of the other clans, and now it was the turn of the Satsuma. It was a gift from the gods. They'd finally given the Aizu their chance to make the enemy pay – to avenge themselves on the Satsuma for the terrible suffering and humiliation they had meted out to them.

Nobu should have been overjoyed. It was the best news

any Aizu man could ever have imagined, the government declaring war on the potato samurai. But his joy was soured by the fact that the enemy they were fighting was Taka's people, led by her father, General Kitaoka. He dreaded coming face to face on the battlefield with his old nemesis, her brother, Eijiro, or being ordered to attack her beloved father; and worst of all he was full of fear that she herself might be in danger. He couldn't celebrate whole-heartedly as a loyal Aizu man should, as his brothers and clansmen were doing.

At the Military Academy everyone was far too keyed up to study. Nobu was promoted to officer cadet and issued with a Snider and spent his days at the firing range, learning to manipulate the heavy rifle until he was on target every time. There were regular manoeuvres, grand heart-stirring events when the soldiers lined up in their thousands and presented arms, marching and wheeling in perfect unison to the sound of the French drill masters' barked orders:

'*Attention! En avant – marche!*'

'*Sur le pied droit, halte. Repos!*'

They'd paraded through the city in their splendid uniforms, rifles gleaming, while crowds lined the streets to watch.

With the chafe of rough wool on his neck, hearing the shouts and the stamp of boots, Nobu felt home and dry. At the barracks, every moment was accounted for – reveille at dawn, roll call, uniform inspection, drill, breakfast, and so on through the day. He didn't have to worry about money or where he would live or how he would find the next meal; and there was not a single spare moment when he had a chance to stop and reflect, to brood about Taka and Jubei's death and the terrible events of the summer. He obeyed orders and that was all. It was best that way, best to lose himself in the daily routine of army life. Thinking only brought pain and confusion.

Then on 11 April came the call Nobu had been waiting for. Along with his classmates he packed his kitbag, tied a jaunty red blanket on top and an extra pair of shoes, one on each side, put on his uniform, overcoat and cap, strapped on his sword and picked up his rifle, and boarded the train for Yokohama, carrying himself tall and proud. There he lined up at the jetty along with thousands of others to be ferried out to the towering Mitsubishi troopship.

Along with everyone else Nobu had spent his first days on board laid out on his pallet, groaning and retching with every pitch and lurch of the ship. But as soon as he found his sea legs he was back at work. While most of the others spent the voyage drinking, gambling and grumbling, he cleaned his rifle every day and occasionally fired a few shots to make sure it stayed in good working order. For the rest of the time he pored over his textbooks, boning up on French military tactics. All his training was soon to be put to the test and he wanted to be sure he was good and ready.

'These coves say they know you.' Sakurai loomed over him, casting a huge shadow, as he propelled a short, bow-legged fellow into the cabin. Grumbling, Nobu's fellow cadets cleared a way as the man stumbled in, tripping over their kitbags and bedrolls. 'Conscripts,' Sakurai added, wrinkling his nose. 'The gods know when this one last had a wash.' One of Sakurai's side-kicks, Sato, hovered in the doorway, holding a second man by the scruff of the neck.

The conscripts had the stunted, undernourished look of townsmen or peasants. They were wearing ill-fitting, crumpled uniforms with sleeves that dangled below their wrists, and they shifted awkwardly from foot to foot as if they weren't used to leather boots.

All the officer cadets thought of conscripts as a lower order, almost another species. Nobu had heard very little good and a lot of bad about them. He knew the army was desperate for manpower in the face of the southern threat and was using the new conscription law to round up thousands of raw recruits; but, as the officers knew all too well, the new men were virtually useless. They were there under duress, they were untrained, but above all they were not samurai; they lacked fighting spirit, they were not ready to die, as samurai were. By all accounts they'd proved no match for Kitaoka's veterans. Most ended up getting cut down straight away. He'd heard that in the heat of battle many were so nervous that they shoved two bullets into their rifle instead of one and the rifle blew up in their hands when they pulled the trigger.

'Conscripts? I'm not acquainted with any conscripts,' Nobu grunted. Sakurai was needling him again. The only course was to humour him until he lost interest and went away.

Sakurai's prisoner gave a strangled squawk. 'No . . .'

'Shut your mouth. Who told you to speak?' Sakurai whacked the man around the head. 'Caught them snooping around outside, looking for something to nick, most like. I was about to give them a thrashing when this worm starts mouthing off. Looking for Nobu, he says, Nobuyuki Yoshida. Old friends, he says. Likely story, I thought, but you never know, what with our Yoshida's dubious origins. What do you say we give them a good beating, teach them some respect?'

The bow-legged man was struggling, flapping his arms, trying to break free of Sakurai's unyielding grip. 'No . . . Nobu, it's us, your old mates.'

Nobu stared at him, startled. He knew that cocky Edo chirrup. 'Bunkichi! Zenkichi!'

He threw down his book and sprang to his feet in delight. The last time he'd seen them had been back at Mori's, at the end of the summer holidays. They'd been apprentices then, with shiny shaven pates and oiled topknots, in cotton jackets and leggings. Now their hair had grown in on top and been chopped off into a ragged fringe, making their faces broad and square instead of egg-shaped; but he recognized those ugly mugs all the same. He remembered trailing along the main boulevard of the Yoshiwara pleasure quarters with them while Mori-*sama* swaggered on ahead, and sleeping squashed together in the servants' quarters at Mori's meagre house.

'Bunkichi and Zenkichi, grooms at Mori-*sama*'s. We worked together. Leave them be!'

'You certainly have odd friends, Yoshida,' drawled Sakurai, looking down his crumpled nose with a sneer.

'Not grooms no more, we ain't, nor coves neither.' Bunkichi thrust out his scrawny chest as Sakurai released him. 'Privates, if you don't mind. Private Kuroda and Private Toyoda, fifth division, second battalion, Fifth Infantry Regiment, at your service.'

'Kuroda? Toyoda? Since when did you have sur-
names?' said Nobu, laughing.

'Always 'ave 'ad. Trouble with you, young Nobu, is
you never gives us the respect we deserves. Thought
you'd seen the last of us, didn't you? We're not so easy
to get rid of. Isn't that right, Zenkichi?' He scowled at
Sakurai. 'Bloody samurai, think you're so high and
mighty. We can handle a rifle good as anyone. I'll show
you one of these days.'

'Townsmen? With rifles? You wouldn't even know
which end to hold,' snarled Sakurai. 'I'd watch it,
Yoshida, wasting time with conscripts. It won't look
good on your report. Shouldn't you be on mess duty?'
He strode off, Sato at his heels.

Nobu glanced around the airless cabin at his fellow
cadets, squashed shoulder to shoulder, staring blank-
eyed at the new arrivals with a mixture of curiosity and
contempt. He could smell their bodies and feel their
collective misery.

'Let's go on deck,' he said. 'I could do with some fresh
air.'

'Are we allowed up there?' Bunkichi asked nervously.

'With me you are.'

The officers lounging around the corridors and the
grand staircase looked at them curiously as they
brushed past.

Nobu leaned over the railing, hearing the roar and rush
of water and the creak and clatter of the paddle wheel as
the ship cut through the waves. There was a gentle swell,
no more. Above them the furled sails flapped and banged
in the wind. Steam poured from the funnel.

He took a breath, enjoying the smell of sea air and the feel of wind on his cheeks. The water was iridescent and the sky bluer than he'd ever seen. Even the light was different, sharp and clear. The crags lining the coast were a tangle of green, with the purple and blue cones of volcanoes shimmering mistily behind. Seagulls swooped and shrieked.

'Give me dry land any day,' shouted Bunkichi. He and Zenkichi were keeping well away from the railing, eyes screwed up, big work-roughened hands shading their eyes. They looked distinctly uncomfortable, like creatures of the shadows who belonged in small smoky rooms in the narrow alleys of the townsmen's district, as if all their dark secrets would be revealed in the glaring sunlight.

Nobu grinned. 'So how's Mori coping without me?'

'That Mori. "Not taking no more students," says he after you left. "Eat my food, never do any work, come and go as they please any time of day or night . . ." He found a new servant soon enough, though. You know what they say. "Can't take a step without . . ."'

'". . . treading on a servant."' Nobu was back in the wooden house near Kaji Bridge, remembering Mori's pouchy face and kimonos stinking of tobacco, the trips to the bathhouse, washing out his loincloth, the regular humiliations . . . No matter. The job had served its purpose, it had tided him over the summer and he'd been able to give money to his brothers too.

Other memories bobbed up, memories he'd done his best to erase – the meetings with Taka, Jubei's dreadful death. He'd thought he'd buried those memories for ever but here they were rising to the surface again. He grimaced and shook his head.

'So there I was, thinking I was going to be with that bastard till I was old and bent.' Bunkichi seemed to have regained his confidence. His large mouth cracked open in an expansive grin and he leaned forward with a conspiratorial air. 'Then what do you know, there's a knock at the door and it's some official, all dressed up in western togs – jacket, trousers, the lot.' He pushed his chin out and screwed his face into an officious scowl. ' "From the Ministry of War, I am," says 'e. "Lookin' for one Kuroda." "Kuroda?" says I. "No such person 'ere." I'm rackin' my brains, trying to think what I've done wrong; or maybe it's young Nobu, I think, in trouble again, maybe he wants us to bail 'im out.

'Seems they've been making a record of every fellow in the country and Mori told them we worked for him. They asked 'ow old we were and he told them, "Twenty." Don't know where he got that figure from; you'd have to dig up my old ma and ask her, she's the only one knows for sure. "I'm not twenty," I says. "Not me. Eighteen if I'm a day." This official, 'e says, "Look near enough twenty to me. You gotta pay blood tax." "Blood tax?" says I. "It's my blood you wants, is it?" '

'You know perfectly well what blood tax is,' said Nobu, grinning. 'It means you've been called up, my friend, you've got to join the army. No one wants your blood.'

'You should hear what they're saying down the bath-houses – they're draining conscripts' blood to make wine for those blood-guzzling foreigners. Don't worry, we don't believe that stuff, we're not simple-minded.

Anyway, Zenkichi tries to do a runner, heads over the wall at the back but they've stationed policemen there with those long hooks of theirs.'

Zenkichi elbowed Bunkichi out of the way. 'They hooks me right through the obi. It was an expensive obi, too. They drags us over to the barracks, gets our clothes off, gives us a physical, then it's off with our topknots and on with these uniforms. All we have to do is march up and down, they says, and we gets our pay and our meals. Didn't sound bad – not at first, anyway. And guess what?' He cocked his head, narrowed his eyes to slits and gave a knowing smile. 'Turns out the girls will do anything – anything – for a fellow in uniform. On Sundays we takes ourselves down the Yoshiwara. No need to risk a dose of the clap at some cheap joint any more. Anything you like, no charge, says the girls.'

Bells rang and whistles sounded. The ship was veering around the headland, tacking closer to the coast.

'Then just as we're thinking life can't get any better, suddenly it gets worse, much worse. We've barely settled in there when they puts rifles in our hands and packs on our backs and shoves us on to the train. Next thing we know we're down the docks. And here we are, off to teach the Satsuma a lesson. That's what they tells us, anyway.' Bunkichi's bony shoulders drooped and his scrawny chest deflated. His cockiness had completely evaporated. 'Can't say I'm looking forward to being at the sharp end of a Satsuma sword. I've no quarrel with the Satsuma. Why should I die for something I don't know anything about?'

Nobu slapped him on the shoulder. 'And there I was thinking you were the tough one. I thought you liked a bit of a brawl. In the army we don't ask questions, we just do as we're told.'

'We're not samurai,' wailed Bunkichi. 'We're towns-men. We're not made for fighting.'

'The Satsuma are the enemy,' Nobu said, dutifully reciting the official line. 'They want to overthrow the government. If they get their way the whole country will be a battlefield again.'

He pictured the burnt-out ruins of Aizu Castle and the graves of his mother, his sisters, his grandmother, lined up on a bleak windswept hillside. He could never forget that sight, it was seared in his memory for ever. 'The Satsuma have done terrible things,' he added with conviction. He knew from his own experience it was true. 'They need punishing. Though from what I hear, sadly there won't be much fighting where we're going.'

'We don't even know where that is. They don't tell conscripts nothing.'

'You'll find out soon enough.' Nobu hesitated. The three of them went back a long way. There was no harm in them knowing. 'Kagoshima. We're going to Kagoshima.'

Across the water the hills undulated, a great curtain of green, wild and rugged, an impassable mass of foliage. Nobu wondered uneasily how their northern troops would fare in such an alien land.

Bunkichi gulped and his pockmarked face turned the colour of rice porridge. He opened and closed his mouth like a frog. 'Not . . . the Satsuma capital? But that's . . . We're putting our heads in the hornets' nest!'

Nobu smiled wryly. 'No such luck. From what I hear it's undefended. There's just women and children and townsmen there, hardly a samurai left. We'll be an occupation force, that's all. We've fairly well finished off the Satsuma. They were hunkered down around Kumamoto Castle but we broke that siege and they're on the run now. All that's left is to mop up the stragglers and track down the leaders. I was looking forward to cutting down a few Satsuma myself. Shouldn't think I'll have much chance.'

He didn't add that they had good intelligence that the Satsuma were racing to get back to the city before the army did. There was no need to fill these raw recruits with terror. They'd find out soon enough.

Bunkichi looked puzzled for a moment as if he was trying to take all this in. He scratched his head, then a grin spread across his face. 'Well, that's a relief.' He was his cocky self again. He looked at Zenkichi. 'Kagoshima. Wasn't there something . . .'

'Yes, to do with . . .' said Zenkichi.

Bunkichi scratched his toe on the deck then looked at Nobu with big frog eyes. 'That lady came,' he said.

Nobu stared at him, wondering what he was talking about. One of Oshige's friends, he guessed; what had that got to do with him? Bunkichi glanced at him knowingly.

'The maid from the big house,' he added.

Okatsu! Taka's maid. Nobu started. He felt a surge of hope and excitement that set his heart racing. Shocked and angry at himself, he tried to rein in his joy. This wasn't what he was supposed to feel. He'd put all that behind him. Guiltily he wondered how much Bunkichi knew about his meetings with Taka. It was hard to keep secrets in Tokyo, least of all in Mori's house; he should have remembered that. At this point consorting with the enemy could almost be seen as treason.

'Remember Oshige?' said Bunkichi.

Nobu nodded, picturing Mori's thick-lipped, good-natured mistress and her cloud of powder.

'The lady had brought a letter for you. She wanted Oshige to pass it on.'

Nobu swallowed. The last thing he'd expected when he saw Bunkichi and Zenkichi was news of Taka. It was all he could do to keep up a pretence of indifference.

'Oshige didn't know where you were,' said Zenkichi. 'I don't think she wanted to get involved.' The two grooms exchanged glances.

'So what happened to the letter?' Nobu tried to speak casually, as if he didn't care, but he couldn't iron out the tremor of excitement in his voice.

'Oshige wouldn't take it.'

'You mean there was no message, nothing?' He'd let his hopes rise too high. Now they came crashing back to earth. Bunkichi looked at Zenkichi.

'It was the tenth month she came, a long time ago, and we only heard about it from Oshige. I think she said they were leaving Tokyo. Had to go rather suddenly. When you mentioned Kagoshima, I remembered. It seemed a strange place to be going but now we're all going there. Kagoshima. That was where they were going. Kagoshima.'

Bunkichi and Zenkichi went back below decks and Nobu returned to his cabin. It seemed smaller and more cramped than ever; if anything the temperature had risen even higher. His fellow cadets were sprawled around, fanning themselves. He could smell the sweat in the air. He climbed over them, reached for his kitbag and dug around in it. There were books, changes of clothing, a jumble of underwear, pens, towels. His fingers closed around a folded sheet of paper – the letter his brother Kenjiro had sent him.

He went up to the deck and found a corner where he'd be left undisturbed. He needed to sort out his thoughts, get some perspective. He unfolded the letter and gazed at the beautifully brushed characters. He'd read it so many times he knew it off by heart.

It was dated 25 March by the new calendar.

Greetings. The wanderer of the eastern seas is on his feet again. I have recovered my health and am no longer pressing my nose into books. An end to indolence! Sword in hand I am departing Tokyo with all haste to join the government forces in Kyushu. Our time has come and we must seize this chance to take revenge on the Satsuma, or how can we face the spirits of those who lie beneath the soil in Aizu? We will meet on the battlefield or on the day of victory or in whatever place we find ourselves after we depart this life. Your brother, Kenjiro.

Nobu could barely see the words through the tears that filled his eyes. The last time he'd seen Kenjiro, he'd been on his sickbed, yellow with jaundice, feebly trying to raise himself on one elbow. Time and time again he'd been ill but he was not a man to let poor health stop him fighting alongside his clansmen. In fact he seemed to need war to restore him to health. Nobu remembered how he'd pulled himself to his feet in their home in Aizu and stumbled out of the door to take part in the defence of the castle nearly nine years earlier.

Still he didn't know how his delicate brother would cope with the hardship. Hopefully he was alive and healthy, on the front line somewhere in Kyushu with a rifle in his hand, probably sleeping out on hillsides in rain and wind. Nobu's eldest brother, Yasu, had also gone south at the first opportunity despite his injured leg, while Gosaburo, the third, had left their father in Aizu and joined the police force so he could go too.

The government was well aware of the hatred of the northerners for the Satsuma and soon after hostilities began had set about recruiting northern samurai to fight. Soldiers returning from the front were full of tales of the extraordinary courage of the Aizu warriors. Men who'd seen them in action spoke with awe of the savagery with which they fought with rifles, swords, whatever came to hand, battling at closer quarters than anyone else dared, hacking their way through the Satsuma ranks, cutting down rebel after rebel until they were killed themselves.

They were shining examples of the old adage that Nobu had learned as a child growing up in Aizu: 'In battle there's no samurai code and no mercy. If you lose your sword, grab a rock. If you have no rock, use your hands. Lose your life but make the enemy pay.'

For the men of Aizu, their time had come at last.

30

Taka took a breath, let out a piercing yell straight from the belly then lunged forward and swung her staff down with all her strength towards the demure young woman opposite her. Yuko, her opponent, didn't flinch. She kept her eyes firmly fixed on Taka's. She had a solemn round face like a child's but her staff spun like the wind. In less than a heartbeat she'd parried Taka's blow then twisted round, skirts whirling, and brought her practice stick slicing straight towards Taka's head. Taka leapt aside, tried to dodge the blow, stumbled and nearly fell and with a gargantuan effort thrust her own stick up just in time to deflect it.

The white oak staffs were light but long and, for Taka at least, fearsomely unwieldy. Moving with crisp steps like a dancer, yelling at the top of her voice, Yuko struck again and again. Taka's knees quivered and she staggered under the impact, parrying blow after blow. Wood cracked down on wood as they circled, walls, trees and bushes revolving in a blur behind them.

Taka was dressed for war, her sleeves tied back with cords, the hem of her kimono tucked into her obi to free her legs and a white headband round her hair. The trampled grass felt soft and moist under her bare feet and the air smelt of earth and flowers. The last of the cherry blossom had fallen and pink and purple azalea and rhododendron bushes filled the grounds. Around her, women sparred with steely concentration, their yells punctuated by the hoarse cawing of crows.

It was a perfect morning. Fluffy clouds floated across a dazzling blue sky, stained with the ever-present veil of black ash that drifted from Sakurajima's mouth. To the east the volcano's dark hulk rose above the compound walls, a fresh ball of ash already ballooning out. It had turned hot far earlier in the year than it ever did in Tokyo. It was going to be a scorching summer.

Yuko gave a shout and charged, whirling the blade so fast Taka could hardly see it. As it sliced through the air, she made a feint, swung round and dropped to one knee, her staff pointing straight at Taka's throat. Had they been using real blades, it would have been the death blow.

Taka bowed in submission. She was panting hard and her arms and wrists and shoulders felt like lead. Yuko hadn't even broken sweat.

'Let's practise with real blades.' She handed Taka one of the halberds which were resting on a stand. It was a beautiful weapon with an elegant lacquered shaft, as long as the wooden practice staffs but heavier by far and much more difficult to handle. Holding it with care, Taka slid off the sheath. The curved blade had an edge sharp enough to cut a man in half and a channel along the blunt side to drain away the blood and there was a spade-shaped butt at the other end which was almost as lethal. Among samurai the halberd was the women's weapon, lighter than a sword and much longer. A skilled fighter could keep a man at bay and slice open his shins or wrists, where he least expected attack, before he could get anywhere near her with his sword.

'Watch. This is the returning wave attack,' said Yuko, lifting out another halberd.

She took her stance, legs apart and knees bent. With her implacable glare and the white headband wrapped around her glossy hair, she looked like a warrior woman in one of the old sagas. She let out a war cry so loud it made Taka jump and leapt forward, then drew back and in the same breath swept the blade upwards, slicing open the chest of her imaginary foe. She twirled on her toes, whirled the shaft and slammed the butt towards the enemy's face, jabbing his eyes, scything his legs and aiming a slashing blow at his shins.

She swung the heavy weapon as easily as if it were a dainty fan. Taka watched in awe. She couldn't imagine ever being able to wield it with such ease and confidence. She wished she'd learned to fight when she was a child, but only samurai women were trained to fight. She'd grown up in the geisha district, then, in Tokyo, she'd lived the life of a modern young woman, worn a fashionable gown and shoes, driven in a carriage along streets of brick houses and taken not the slightest interest in the warrior arts.

It had been more than two months since Taka's father had marched out of the city at the head of his army, more than two long months since she'd watched the last figures dwindle into ant-like specks until they were swallowed up in the vast white expanses of the hillside.

The city had become a husk from which all life had

fled. As she'd made her way home along the broad avenues of the samurai district, between the shops and warehouses of the merchants' section of town and into the narrow streets of the geisha quarter, her father's last words to her had echoed in her mind. 'You're a Kitaoka too,' he had told her in his deep voice. 'Never forget that.' She could still see him on his horse, in his uniform, with his broad shoulders, gleaming eyes and thick black eyebrows.

It was so obvious it should hardly have needed saying, yet she'd never thought about it before. She was not just a geisha's daughter. She was a samurai's daughter, the daughter of the greatest samurai of all. But what did that mean? What was she supposed to do? She'd have to work it out.

As the dreary days went by, her mother, Aunt Kiharu and Okatsu tried to keep up the pretence that nothing had changed. They dusted, polished, sewed, chatted, cooked and visited the few geishas who had not left town with the army. Everyone started eating less to save supplies for their men. The townsfolk filled storehouses with barrels of shochu, the fiery local liquor, and huge sacks of rice, preserved vegetables and millet, to be sent on packhorses through the mountains when messengers arrived requesting supplies. They kept nothing for themselves but sweet potatoes.

Whenever they asked what was happening, the messengers told them, 'We're winning! We're winning!' At first they were overjoyed but after a while they began to wish they had a few more hard facts.

To begin with there was plenty of news. The tramp through the snow around the bay and up into the forests and mountains had been tough but the men had made it and been greeted like conquering heroes. For the first few days in every town people had lined the streets, cheering and drumming and strumming shamisens. It had taken seven days of hard marching to reach the great city of Kumamoto. Along the way the rearguard had met up with the other battalions that had left earlier, and the whole great army advanced together on Kumamoto's formidable castle.

General Kitaoka had written to the general in command of the castle requesting free passage. The soldiers there were Kyushu men and their general was a personal friend of General Kitaoka, so they would most likely welcome them and join them on their long march to Tokyo. Even if they chose to side with the government, most were mere peasant conscripts, raw recruits who wouldn't have a chance against the well-trained battle-hardened Satsuma.

But strangely – or so it seemed to the women waiting anxiously at home – the general did not grant free passage and General Kitaoka and his massive army settled in to besiege the castle. It was obvious the garrison there couldn't hold out for long. Then news began to dry up. There were rumours that the Satsuma had taken the castle and were on their way again, but then the following day there'd be another rumour that no, they were still outside the castle. Soon all the messengers would do was grunt, 'Don't worry! We're winning!'

One worrying thing had happened right at home in Kagoshima. Some twenty days after General Kitaoka and his men left, three sinister grey warships had appeared in the harbour. With all the samurai gone, the city was defenceless. For a few days black-uniformed government soldiers patrolled the streets then, equally suddenly, they left. The townsfolk gathered at the waterside to watch them steam away. Then news had spread that they had arrested the governor of the city, Governor Oyama, General Kitaoka's loyal ally who had refused to abolish samurai stipends, and taken him with them. They had also emptied the arsenals, taken all the powder and arms and spiked the guns.

There was nothing left to do but pray.

Every day Taka and her mother, Aunt Kiharu and Okatsu burnt incense at the family shrine for Taka's father and Eijiro, camped out in front of the great castle. And every day Taka silently added a prayer for Nobu, wherever he might be, that he might be safe too.

She seldom thought of Kuninosuké. She'd always known he could never take Nobu's place in her heart. Too much bound them together. Kuninosuké was a good man, she knew that, but with him it had been no more than a hug, a warm goodbye to a soldier going to the front. And then the next day she'd given him her amulet. Now she almost wished she hadn't. It was the only thing she'd had to remind her of Nobu and now she had nothing.

But as the days and months passed she was more and more sure she'd never see either of them again.

So many things made her think of Nobu. One day after the snow had melted she went to the local temple to see the plum blossom. Looking at the tiny aubergine-coloured petals sprouting on the gnarled branches, smelling the delicate scent, she remembered the time in early spring when they'd walked in the woods in the grounds of the Tokyo mansion together. He'd been a lanky sixteen-year-old, she a gawky fourteen. She was the mistress, he the servant, but out in the woods he was the one who knew his way around.

He was scuffing through the grass when his face had lit up. He'd bent down and picked a strange little weed, a pale beige shoot no bigger than a newborn baby's finger, and held it out to her as if it was the most precious thing he could possibly give her.

'A horsetail shoot,' he'd said, bursting with excitement. 'I never knew they grew here.' His black eyes were shining. 'We eat them up north.' He'd laughed as she sniffed the flimsy stem and screwed up her face. It had a peculiar mossy smell. 'We eat everything up there – bee grubs, locusts, bear meat, the lot.'

She'd held her breath, hoping he'd tell her more. He hardly ever spoke about himself. But then his face had clouded as if he was angry at himself for saying too much and she'd sensed some painful memory that made him hunch his shoulders and clasp and unclasp his fingers and scuff his feet and kick at the stones. Anyone would have thought he was just a surly servant but she knew better.

As they went into the house he'd looked around with a haunted expression as if he was still in the grip of memory. Then he'd said, 'There's not even a halberd here.' He was gazing at the lintel. There were two large hooks hidden in the shadows there, covered in dust and cobwebs.

'Halberd hooks,' he said. 'There were always halberds at home. All the women knew how to use a halberd. You've got to be ready for anything, that's what my father used to say.' He'd looked at her as if he'd woken from a dream and his face softened. 'But it's different for you. You have such a rich, peaceful life. You'll never have to defend this place. You don't need to be ready for anything.'

Things had changed since then. Now Taka too needed to be ready for anything. She needed to be a warrior.

There and then she'd set off for the samurai section of town. She'd ended up in front of the formidable tiled gate of one of the mansions along the broad avenue facing the castle. She was plucking up courage to speak to the gatekeeper when a young woman came out.

Yuko and her elder sister Masako were the daughters of one of the senior commanders of the Satsuma army, a close colleague of Taka's father. Their brothers, uncles and cousins had all gone to war and only the women and children were left. Like Taka and her mother, they were fiercely proud of their men and also desperately anxious for them though they kept a brave face.

The samurai women reminded Taka of the girls she'd known at school – wide-eyed and innocent yet also brave and fierce. She admired their spirit and felt strangely at home among them. Perhaps because it was wartime, perhaps because she was General Kitaoka's daughter, they welcomed her. It didn't seem to worry them that her mother was a geisha. They were happy to have any and all additions to their ranks. They needed every hand they could get. Everyone knew that they had to be on guard, ready to defend their town.

They were more than happy to teach her the halberd.

She ended every day with bruises and aching muscles and soon realized it would be a long hard struggle. They teased her for being a soft city girl, but she was determined to prove she could fight every bit as well as they did. And little by little she started to get the hang of it, as if she was transforming herself into a warrior woman such as Nobu, such as her father, might approve of.

31

The morning sun warmed Taka's bare arms as she balanced her practice stick, feeling the weight of it in her hands. She heard the rushing of the stream as it flowed through the grounds and splashed into a pond of fat orange carp.

She'd been learning the halberd for a month now, joining the samurai women every day to practise morning to night. A month was not long; they'd all been training since they were children. But when her arms ached so badly she could hardly bear it, when she felt dispirited and thought she'd never improve, she'd think of her father and Nobu. She had to succeed, for them. And little by little she began to feel that the heavy halberd was part of her, an extension of her body.

Imagining a thickset samurai warrior charging towards her, she closed her eyes and reminded herself of the four targets – head, shin, neck and forearm. She took a breath, braced herself and prepared to lunge.

Suddenly there was a shout from somewhere outside the estate. It rang out above the crack of wood on wood, the women's yells and the caws of the crows.

The sound broke Taka's concentration. She hesitated

and glanced at Yuko. But Yuko no longer had her eyes fixed on her.

There was another shout, then another. Footsteps pounded through the quiet streets. The women lowered their halberds, eyes and mouths wide. It was news of some sort – but what?

Then a white-haired servant came rushing through the trees and hobbled across the grass, stumbling and nearly tripping.

'Ships, a whole fleet of them,' he wheezed. 'Coming this way.'

The colour drained from the women's faces. The harbour was full of ships. Merchants transported goods to and from the city in ships and barges and people shuttled around the bay in flotillas of boats. The whole traffic of the city was maritime. But a fleet . . . That could only mean one thing: warships. That was a very different matter.

There was a long silence. Then someone uttered the dread syllables: 'The army.' The women nodded, whispering in tones of horror, 'The army, the army's coming.'

'It can't be,' Taka said. 'Why would they send the army here?'

A moment later a bell clanged, then another, confirming the servant's words, first fire bells, high and tinny, then temple bells, a deep sonorous boom, until every bell in the city was ringing in a wild clamour that sounded inside Taka's head, setting her heart pounding with fear. Crows rose with a great flapping of wings and seagulls swooped low, their shrieks drowned in the din.

Yuko's sister Masako, tall and fearless in pleated

hakama trousers, like a man, glared down at the quailing servant. 'How many?' she demanded above the noise of the bells. 'How far away? Who saw them?'

'A . . . a messenger came,' the old man stuttered. 'Lookouts sent . . . messages. Four ships, maybe five, on the other side of the peninsula, coming towards the headland. Maybe half a day away . . .'

Taka's stomach knotted in panic. With the menfolk gone, there was no one here to defend them. Hemmed in on a narrow strip of land with the mountains on one side and the sea on the other, the city was hopelessly vulnerable. Even the castle had no defences, just a wall and a moat and a bridge which led straight into the grounds. The house she was in now, with its gardens and stream and carp pond, was just a few steps from the harbour.

Last time the army had come they'd looked the place over and gone away again. But this time no one could doubt their intentions. This time they'd come to make the city theirs.

'But why?' she croaked, her voice a tremulous squeak. 'There's no one here, just women and children and townsfolk. We're no threat.'

Masako drew herself up. 'What do you expect of those crooks in the government? They wait till our men are gone then send the army to attack us instead. They're cowards, that's what they are, cowards.'

Taka stared grimly at the ground. Masako was far too clever to really believe her own words. She was just trying to boost their spirits. It was far more likely that the army hugely outnumbered their brave Satsuma warriors. There were probably enough of them to have units in the mountains fighting her father, others on their way here and still others swarming across the island. Or perhaps their men had been defeated. Perhaps that was why the government had sent the army to take the city. She could see the same fear on every face, but nobody dared voice the thought; they were all afraid that if they put it into words it would make it real.

Yuko's large eyes blazed. She for one didn't need her spirits boosted. 'We'll form a women's corps. There's enough of us left. We'll fight to the death.'

'All we have is halberds. We can't fight soldiers with guns, it would be suicide,' snorted Fuchi, a big-boned woman from a neighbouring estate who swung her halberd rhythmically as if scything a rice field. Her husband and brothers too had left for the mountains, to fight alongside Taka's father.

'We must gather our belongings and run,' gasped a thin-cheeked younger woman, her voice shaking.

The bells clanged loud and insistent, making it hard to think. The servants came running out to summon the women into the house. Taka took a breath. 'You call yourselves samurai and you refuse to risk your lives? How can you talk of running away?'

The women stared back, anger in their eyes. She could see that they blamed her father, they thought he'd let them down. Perhaps he'd assumed the army would never attack Kagoshima, or never even considered it. It was too late now. As his daughter, the least she could do was stay and fight for this stricken city.

'You're a child,' snapped the younger woman, her lips pale. 'You don't know what war is. Armies do dreadful things. It would be madness to be here when they arrive.'

'We have a boat,' said Fuchi. 'We'll take you all with us, as many as can fit in.'

Masako gripped her halberd. 'Never. I'm staying.'

'Me too,' said Yuko.

The women were hurrying towards the house in a rustle of silk. Taka was about to pass her halberd to a servant but Yuko thrust it back into her hands. 'Take it. We have plenty.'

Taka picked up her skirts and raced across the grounds and out through the gates. She needed to get to her mother. She'd soon left the samurai mansions with their stone and stucco walls and was back in the dust and noise and stench of the townsmen's district. The narrow streets were jammed with people laden with bundles and clothes, so many she could hardly see where she was going. Once she missed her street and realized to her panic that she was running in the wrong direction. Boys elbowed through, yelling at the top of their voices, bent nearly double under rickshaws piled high with bedding, chests, cushions and tables, even doors and tatami mats. Above the hubbub the bells clanged wildly.

Taka was trying to see a way through the crowd, keeping her halberd upright, when a florid towns-woman with a bouffant knot of hair gripped her elbow. 'Hurry! Hurry!' she shrilled. 'The army's coming. They're going to rape us and kill us and burn the city down.'

It was Matsu, the wife of a wealthy merchant. She was wearing five or six silk kimonos, one on top of the other, and panting heavily. Gold linings glinted at cuff and collar. Her powdered cheeks were blotched with sweat.

'Omatsu-*sama*, what's happening? Where's everyone going?'

'The harbour. Someone saw a boat with the lord's family crest on it, heading for Sakurajima. Even he's fleeing. Where's your mother? Quick! Run and fetch her.'

Matsu's eyes fell on the halberd with its lacquered shaft and her mouth dropped open, revealing her blackened teeth. The crowd swept her on and she turned, gesturing frantically towards the harbour. The surly bathhouse-keeper, the ferret-faced barber and the tatami-maker's bevy of hefty apprentices heaved into view, foreheads gleaming as they beat a path through the mob. Their eyes popped as they saw thc halberd and they shouted to Taka to hurry up and leave.

The geisha quarter was ominously quiet. The shamisens had fallen silent and the leaves on the willow trees drooped forlornly. A couple of women staggered along under bundles so huge they could barely see over the top. They were heading in the opposite direction, away from the harbour.

'We've got relatives in the mountains,' they shouted. 'Come with us.'

Taka wanted to ask them about her friend Toshimi but they'd hurried on before she had a chance.

She was panting by the time she reached the only house in the district that did not have a lantern outside to show whether it was open for business. As she slid open the door she heard her mother's tones, ominously low. 'I don't care what you say. I know my duty.'

'But you don't even know where she lives.' There was an edge of hysteria to Aunt Kiharu's voice.

Taka caught her breath. She had a dreadful suspicion she knew what Fujino was talking about, though it was hard to believe even she could be so misguided.

She rushed inside. The shutters were pushed back and pale light filtered through the yellowing shoji screens. Aunt Kiharu was tying a wrapping cloth, her mouth pursed and her thin fingers shaking, while Okatsu sorted kimonos in their paper wrappers, her pretty round face composed in an expression of silent resignation. She glanced up at Taka, swivelled her eyes towards the two older women and raised an eyebrow a fraction.

Fujino was on her knees. Even in a kimono rather than a bulky western gown she filled the room. She smoothed her skirts. 'Thank the gods you're here, my girl. We have to leave immediately.'

Taka propped the halberd against the wall. Her father's words echoed through her mind. 'Take care of your mother,' he'd said. She remembered how brave and stubborn her mother had been in Kyoto, blocking the door with her enormous bulk when enemy troops came looking for him. She was not just fearless, she was downright reckless.

Fujino gestured towards the halberd. 'You're not planning to defend yourself with that, are you? You and those samurai friends of yours. We've been wondering where on earth you were.'

'I'm sorry, Mother. There's no time to pack. Let's just

take what we can and go. We may have to wait for a boat.'

'We're not taking any boat,' said Fujino. 'We're going to the Kitaoka house.'

'The Kitaoka house?' Taka stared at her in exasperation. She felt as if she was the grown-up one and Fujino the child. 'The enemy are nearly here, Mother. We have to leave. Everyone's heading for the harbour or the mountains.'

Fujino's eyes flashed. Taka recognized the stubborn set to her shoulders. She was scowling like a sulky child. 'I should have gone when your father left. I failed in my duty then but I'll make up for it now. I must introduce myself to Madame, your father's wife. Wherever she's going, we'll go there too. It's the only thing to do.'

Taka couldn't imagine how Madame Kitaoka would feel if a large middle-aged woman arrived claiming to be her husband's concubine. She knew she shouldn't contradict her mother but this was no time for deference. 'You're wrong, Mother. Madame Kitaoka doesn't know anything about you. Why should she believe you are who you say you are?'

Aunt Kiharu nodded emphatically, her head bobbing like a Daruma doll. 'She's right, Fujino. Listen to her.'

'Masa told her about me. I'm sure he did.' There was a shrill, argumentative edge to her voice. She straightened her back and took a breath. 'I don't care what you say, Taka, I don't care what any of you say. My mind's made up. It's what your father would want.'

Taka looked away, tears filling her eyes. It wasn't at all what he would want, she was sure of that. Her mother's sadness wrenched her heart. She missed him so desperately, yet the only course open to her was to throw herself on the mercy of this wife of his, who knew nothing about her and cared even less. She might be a paragon of virtue, this wife, this interloper who'd come into their lives, but Taka hated her with a passion. The last thing she wanted was to see her.

She shook her head. 'I'm not coming with you.'

Footsteps pattered by along the road outside. Fujino stared at her. 'Of course you are. You can't stay here. I order you to come.'

'I don't want to see that woman. I'm seventeen, I'm an adult. The samurai girls in the big house are staying. I'll stay too and take care of our house. We don't even know for sure the army's coming, and if they do they'll take over the samurai houses. They won't be interested in townsfolk like us. We're not even townsfolk, we're geishas. They certainly won't bother with us.'

'Townsfolk, geishas,' her mother snorted. 'That's as it may be. We're the family of General Kitaoka too, don't forget that. If the army knows we're here, they'll be looking for us everywhere.'

'The last place they'd expect to find us is in the geisha quarter.'

'And you expect me to go to the harbour when there are enemy ships on their way? We Kitaokas need to stick together. Madame may need our help. I'm your mother. How dare you disobey me?'

Taka groaned. Her mother knew she was wrong but she just wouldn't listen. 'You don't even know where her house is.'

'Everyone knows your father, everyone loves him.

Everyone will know the house. We just have to ask. We're family. It's right for us to join her.'

'And if she's left already?'

'All the more reason to hurry,' her mother said. 'There'll be a watchman to tell us where she's gone. This is the last time I'm saying it, Taka. You can't stay here on your own.'

The two glared at each other. Taka's mother lowered her eyes. There was a last clang and the bells stopped ringing as if even the bell-ringers had left their posts and fled. In the silence a bird chirruped and Taka heard the rush of the wind and the distant roar of the sea.

Her mother was flushed and there were beads of sweat on her forehead. She was breathing heavily. She put her hand on the mats and heaved herself to her feet. 'Very well, stay if you must. Okatsu will stay with you.'

'Take Okatsu too. My father would want you to be properly attended.'

'I can't argue with you any longer, my girl. You're even more stubborn than me.'

Taka watched the three small figures set off along the road, tears filling her eyes. Everything had fallen apart and they were reduced to this, just three lone women walking away together.

When they'd disappeared from view she hurried towards the harbour. A few gatekeepers and servants peeked nervously from the gates of some of the merchant houses. Most were closed up and sealed with the rain doors pulled across, turning them into fortresses. The massive whitewashed storehouses where the merchants kept their valuables were locked and bolted. Not a shop was open and the market stalls were deserted. Pieces of paper and scraps of cloth littered the ground and blew around in the gutters. It looked as if people had taken more than they could carry and had dropped things in their haste. Oranges and sweet potatoes rolled about. It was a city of ghosts, an empty husk, a shadow of the bustling place it had been just an hour before.

There were people at the waterside still, anxiously waiting to see which would come first – a boat to take them away or the dreaded warships. They were poor, to judge by their clothes. Some had bundles, others carts loaded with furniture. The bay was full of boats, heading for the volcano or south towards the islands.

Taka was watching the boats shuttling south when she saw a tiny puff of smoke where the dazzling sea met the paler blue of the sky. As she gazed, mesmerized, there was another puff, then another, as a sinister grey hull slid into view around the headland. She counted five ships still far in the distance, sails hoisted, growing larger by the moment. The crowds at the dock shouted in panic and piled into the last remaining boats, throwing in bundles and furniture until the boats looked ready to sink.

As Taka fled back through the merchant district she heard shouts and crashes and pounding feet. She rounded a corner. Gangs of loinclothed youths were smashing doors and shutters, breaking into homes and storehouses, running off with sacks bulging with belongings. They were too busy looting to pay any attention to Taka. She raced home and bolted the door, trembling.

She'd made a mistake, she realized now. She should have gone with her mother. She wished they hadn't parted on such bad terms. In fact, her life had been a catalogue of mistakes. Perhaps she should have married Masuda-*sama* before all this blew up. He hadn't been so bad and she'd be in Tokyo still. But it was too late for regrets. She'd just have to wait for the right moment before the army arrived to go and join Yuko and the others.

It was eerie alone in the house with its faded tatami and creaking stairs. Now she'd seen the warships, the halberd leaning against the wall in the entryway looked as puny as a child's plaything. She thought of her father and his fifteen thousand warriors. No matter how brave and well trained and determined they were, even if they were the best soldiers in the world, they couldn't possibly stand up against such might.

As she always did, she thought of Nobu. Was he in Tokyo still, at the Military Academy? Or had he been called up to fight? Perhaps he was in the mountains, fighting her father, or on one of those ships, steaming towards Kagoshima. It would be a strange and bitter twist of fate if he were on that fleet, coming here to her city to kill her people – and her.

32

'We'll teach those damned Satsuma a lesson they won't forget. Right, Sato?' Sakurai's growl rose above the rumble of engines, the creak and flap of the sails and the roar as the great ship surged through the water. The railing rang as he smashed his fleshy fist down, his ruddy cheeks mottled and his cropped hair bristling.

'Right.' His loyal sidekick, Sato, grunted laconically.

Nobu groaned. It just wasn't that simple. A lot of soldiers, including some of the men on this ship, were Satsuma, the brothers or sons or cousins of rebels who'd gone to fight in the mountains. He knew they were secretly relieved there were no samurai left in this city, so they wouldn't have to fight their own kin. There were many of Nobu's and Sato's and Sakurai's comrades among the rebels too, men who'd left the Military Academy last autumn to return to Satsuma. The three of them would be shooting down their fellow students – or being shot by them – if they ever came face to face. But Sakurai wasn't one to worry about such details. He just wanted to make sure everyone knew he was raring for a fight.

'Even Lieutenant Yoshida, even our Yoshida with his head stuffed full of French verbs and French history, even he might get a shot in – if he can aim his rifle straight.' Sakurai guffawed.

Nobu ignored him. The rugged cliffs and hills of the coastline veered towards them, mantled in foliage as thick as the wax on an ancient candle. Smells of leaves and blossom and shoots wafted on the breeze. Even on the balmiest spring day it was never this green in Aizu or Tokyo, never this warm and sultry. Insects buzzed, seagulls screamed and dipped and a cormorant flapped by, stretching its black wings. Boats laden with people and furniture sculled low in the water, keeping well away from the massive grey warships.

Nobu tipped his head back until his starchy collar dug into the back of his neck, screwed up his eyes against the glare of the mid-morning sun and stared up at the volcano filling the sky above them. A fist of ash and smoke punched out of the jagged mouth, writhing and curling like a dragon's head. He smelt sulphur, saw steam seeping from clefts in the rocks.

The cluster of houses huddled into the hillside grew larger and he reached for a telescope.

Kagoshima, the famous Satsuma stronghold. He made out the castle, a line of fortifications along the hillside. Buildings sprawled around, larger squares surrounded with green near the castle, cramped streets of small houses further away, and along the bay a dockyard with imposing grey structures that might house the Satsuma armaments factories.

He wondered if the city really was undefended. He half expected cannon fire suddenly to blaze out. The place looked unnervingly empty. There was no smoke rising from the houses, no figures moving about on the docks or streets, no signs of life at all. He wondered what was going on behind that blank façade, what scheme the inhabitants had dreamed up to fool the approaching army.

'Looks like it was hit by the plague,' grunted Sato.

'They're there, all right. Just keeping their heads down, readying their rifles to welcome us. We'll show them, like we showed them at Kumamoto, won't we, Yoshida?'

Nobu barely heard him through the storm of thoughts that battered in his head. The moment was at hand – the moment of victory, of sweet revenge. He had the enemy in his sights, the bastion of the Satsuma, those killers who had burnt his city and trampled through his house and caused the deaths of his mother, his sisters and his grandmother, reduced his clan to penury and continued to oppress them to this day. Yet instead of hatred and joy and bloodlust, all he could think of was Taka.

The boat smacked against the sea wall and rocked violently. It was a big flat-bottomed lighter, crammed with soldiers sitting crushed together, hanging on to anything they could find. Nobu stood up, found his balance, waited for the wave to crest and jumped. Hands pulled as he scrambled up the stones. He took a few breaths, enjoying the feel of dry land under his feet, then looked around and his jaw dropped.

The great brick warehouses that lined the wharf had been smashed open, rusty iron doors hung loose on their hinges and rice, sugar and yellow safflower spilled across the paving stones. Slabs of lumber and bolts of silk lay scattered around as if the looters had dropped half their booty as they fled. The Satsuma hadn't waited for the army to come, they'd sacked their city themselves.

Boats shuttled back and forth and soldiers climbed ashore, filling the quay with black caps and bristling rifles. The sun blazed down. Standing to attention in his greatcoat with his pack on his back and his sword at his side, Nobu heard the creak of new leather boots behind him and sent up a fervent prayer to the gods that there really would be no one here to fight. If there was, these men of his would have a real job to prove themselves. For all their splendid uniforms, half were raw recruits, conscripts sent south without even knowing how to load a rifle. The rest were former samurai – and, as everyone knew, samurai took orders from no one. As for Nobu, he was an unseasoned lieutenant with a head full of French verbs, as Sakurai had said, and a theoretical knowledge of tactics, but no practical experience at all.

As the first units marched smartly away, boots thundering on the stony ground, there was a shot, echoing from the mountains and ringing out across the water. The conscripts shouted in panic, broke ranks and charged into the warehouses. Nobu looked around, his heart thundering. Snipers, an ambush. He raced over to a water barrel and crouched behind it, rifle raised.

Cautiously scouring the empty quay, he noticed a lone conscript standing nervously, a hollow-cheeked youngster with the big hands of a peasant, his greatcoat hanging on him like a tent. Smoke curled from the barrel of his rifle. The other soldiers stumbled back into the sunlight, laughing sheepishly. Nobu broke into a grin.

'I . . . I thought I saw a movement,' the youth muttered, cheeks blazing. Cats peered nervously out of the shadows as the men resumed their march.

Battalions of soldiers filled the narrow streets, sweeping towards the castle which spread along the foot of the hill, bristling with battlements, turrets and watchtowers. Nobu kept a wary eye open for snipers but if there were any they were keeping well out of sight.

He'd been expecting a thriving town with shops and supplies but the place was entirely empty, except for scraps of paper and shreds of fabric and rotten fruit filling the gutters. He glanced around, convinced it must be a trap. There had to be people hidden inside the buildings, preparing to loose a hail of bullets on the intruders.

But they marched on without incident. Battalion after battalion assembled in the parade ground in front of the castle while the advance units stormed across the moat into the grounds of the castle itself. Nobu listened for the roar of cannons and rattle of gunfire, but there was only the thunder of boots on baked earth.

Then a uniformed figure appeared at the head of the bridge, waving his arms and shouting. There was no defending army, not even any occupants. The castle was deserted. There was even a barracks in the old stables which would house at least part of the occupying force. The soldiers raised a cheer.

With the castle and barracks secured, the lieutenants ditched their greatcoats and packs and prepared to check every street and house in the town for snipers and nests of rebels.

But Nobu had a mission of his own and nothing would stop him carrying it out. Tomorrow, once they were sure the town was theirs, they'd be busy from morning to night building defences, preparing for the attack that was bound to come when the rebels tried to retake their stronghold. But today, while they were prowling the city, nosing into every house and every back alley, he had a chance – his only chance – to find Taka. He had to find her quickly, before some brute like Sakurai did. He hadn't forgotten what the Satsuma had done to the women of Aizu. The Imperial Army prided themselves on being more disciplined but every army contained thugs and Taka's pale-skinned beauty, added to the fact she was Kitaoka's daughter, made her an irresistible prize. The only problem was that he had a whole huge city to scour and no idea where to start.

'Hey, Yoshida.' There was a powerful stench of damp wool, gun oil and boot polish. It was Sakurai, massive and sweaty in his uniform, sporting a pistol as well as his rifle and sword. Sato tacked along behind him like a little launch behind a huge warship. 'What do you say we scout out this godforsaken place together? Safety in numbers and all that.'

'I'm fine on my own, thanks,' Nobu said, quietly but firmly. The last thing he wanted was Sakurai on his tail.

'So Yoshida wants to play the hero, flash his sword about like a samurai,' said Sakurai. 'Let's see how you do without us, my man. We'll come and rescue you if you don't come back. Bet we root out more rebels than you do.'

Nobu looked up and down the road. He knew how Sakurai's mind worked.

In front of the castle was a broad avenue. To the right, tall trees swayed above stone and stucco walls. It reminded Nobu of the area where Taka used to live in Tokyo, with high walls hiding palatial mansions inside.

He made a big display of studying the area to the left, grunting and nodding, taking his time, making sure Sakurai didn't suspect he was desperate to get on the move. 'Nothing much down there but I suppose someone has to take a look. Why don't I head over? You two can see what's behind those big walls over there. Safety in numbers and all that.' He jerked his chin towards the prosperous-looking road to the right.

Sakurai stared at him, eyes narrowed. Nobu could almost hear the wheels in his brain grinding as he tried to work out what Nobu was plotting.

'Safety in numbers?' he snorted. Nobu smiled to himself and heaved a sigh of relief. He'd taken the bait. 'You think we're fools? You're not having all the adventures to yourself. Come on, Sato, let's flush out a few rebels.'

They pounded off down the road to the left, dodging behind a tree, cautiously peering out, then racing to the next. Nobu heard a crash and the splinter of wood as Sakurai slammed his rifle butt into a gate. He waited, drumming his heel, till they'd disappeared inside the grounds, then turned and sprinted for the street that reminded him of Taka's.

The first gate he came to had been smashed in. Shards of wood hung from the frame and lay scattered across the ground. Looters had been at work in this part of town too. Nobu paused in his stride, his heart sinking, half wishing he'd taken up Sakurai's offer. It was sheer stupidity to be wandering alone through enemy territory. The entire populace was probably lying in wait, preparing to loose a barrage of shots at the first enemy soldier they saw.

He looked around, the back of his neck tingling, imagining eyes peering out through every crack in the walls, then pulled himself together and forced himself to concentrate. The first step was to locate the Kitaoka mansion. He looked for a nameplate and groaned in disappointment: 'Nakamura'.

There was an endless expanse of stone and stucco walls to race past before he came to another gate. The nameplate there was not 'Kitaoka' either, nor the one after, nor the one after that. Crows cawed and seagulls screeched and a sudden wind that smelt of the sea shook the branches of the trees that rose behind the walls. The place was eerily empty.

He cursed and thumped his fist into his palm. The day was half over already and he'd found nothing. He wished there were someone around, anyone. It put his nerves on edge to be alone in this deserted place.

He'd been running from street to street more and more desperately, checking nameplate after nameplate, no closer to finding anyone, let alone Taka, when he came to a particularly large, splendid gateway set deep in a wall, with a steep tiled roof and the latticed windows of a guardhouse alongside. It looked like the entrance to the residence of a powerful man, perhaps the sort who would know General Kitaoka. The place warranted further investigation.

Like the others, the gate had been staved in. Above the squawks of crows and honks of bullfrogs, Nobu heard a crack, like someone cocking a gun. It seemed to come from the guardhouse. He took a breath, fingered the trigger of his rifle, then pushed aside the splintered wood and stepped through.

There was a crash. The door to the guardhouse burst open and a weaselly fellow lurched out, clutching a hefty staff. So the place wasn't deserted after all. Nobu glared at the man but before he could even raise his rifle the gatekeeper dropped his staff and threw up his hands, his cheeks quivering, his eyes darting from side to side like a rabbit's.

Nobu stifled a grin. He'd never inspired fear in anyone in his life. It was the uniform and the rifle, not him, he knew that perfectly well. Far from being a skinny nineteen-year-old, in this fellow's eyes he was a hulking representative of His Imperial Majesty's Army, armed to the teeth.

Nobu drew himself up with what he hoped was a ferocious scowl. 'Imperial Army, 7th division, requisitioning this house,' he growled.

The gatekeeper backed away slowly, then turned and scuttled off through the grounds. Nobu allowed himself a triumphant grin. The tables had turned. The Aizu held their heads high again.

Inside the walls the grounds were planted with cherry and pine trees, pink azalea bushes and purple rhododendrons. He crossed a stream and passed a waterfall, a carp pond and a lawn big enough for sparring. The house itself was large and sprawling, surrounded by verandas and raked gravel pathways,

grander by far than the samurai houses of Aizu.
He left his boots on so that he could trail dirt across
the tatami, as the Satsuma had done in Aizu, and
marched straight in through the grand main entrance.
The house was full of servants packing up. The air
shimmered with dust and there were doors and upended
tatami mats propped against the pillars. The servants
staggered back, dropping armfuls of kimonos, staring at
Nobu wide-eyed, mouths gaping, faces pale as tofu. He
felt another surge of triumph and reminded himself he
needed to keep his wits about him. Once they realized
there were no more soldiers outside waiting to swarm
in, he'd be in trouble.

He flung open doors and poked into futon cupboards
with his sword, then ordered a sullen-faced servant to
open the storehouse. The man hesitated but Nobu
raised his rifle and he nodded and scurried to the back
of the house.

The storehouse was huge, the most lavish Nobu had
ever seen. The servant pulled open the door to reveal
scrolls, vases and boxes of pottery piled in heaps,
higgledy-piggledy, as if thrown in in a hurry. Nobu dug
through the mountain of goods, throwing things aside,
but it was just the usual samurai furnishings, nothing
marked with Fujino's flamboyant geisha taste. He'd
cleaned and polished Taka's house for half a year, he
knew every dish, every hanging, every scroll. If anything
of hers was stored here, he'd have known it straight
away. But there was nothing.

He was wasting time, he realized. There was nothing
here; but before he left, at least he'd make a few
enquiries. He frowned, wondering what he could ask

that could possibly produce the information he needed.

'Where are your masters and mistresses?' he barked. The servants glowered at him. 'Don't try anything stupid,' he added, playing for time. 'My men are on their way. They'll be here any moment.'

They gawped at him, mouths hanging open. He could see they were beginning to guess he didn't have any back-up. They were testing him, playing stupid. Or perhaps they couldn't understand his dialect. He repeated the question slowly and clearly with a good Tokyo accent but they still stared stubbornly at the ground. As he swung round, a burly youth with a heavy brow and jutting lower jaw twisted his mouth into an insolent leer. Nobu grabbed him by the collar. 'Come on, lad, you've got a tongue.'

The youth's face contorted into a grimace of hatred and he raised his fist and lashed out. Nobu saw the blow coming, stepped back, clamped his hand around his assailant's wrist and twisted hard, pulling the fellow off balance, using the force of the man's own movement to send him crashing to the floor. There were no tatami mats to cushion his fall and he hit the ground hard.

A couple of other brawny young fellows had slunk forward. Nobu glimpsed a flash out of the corner of his eye as one snatched up a poker and lunged at his head. He dodged, swung his rifle round and drove the barrel hard into the man's stomach. The poker clattered to the ground and the fellow exhaled like a punctured balloon and crumpled, clutching his stomach and wheezing painfully, gasping for breath. The third man drew back nervously. The burly youth was scrambling to his knees.

Nobu cocked his rifle and levelled it at the men. 'Anyone else want to take on His Imperial Majesty's Army?' he demanded. 'Wait till my boys arrive. You'll be wishing it was only me you had to deal with. Just give me an answer.'

An old man with a darkly tanned shaven pate and white hair oiled into a topknot limped forward. 'They can't understand you.' He had a thick Satsuma accent. 'And even if they could they wouldn't know. We're just servants. We don't know anything.'

'I don't believe you. Your masters and mistresses, where did they go?'

'They just cleared out. Wish we could have gone too before you bastards arrived. We've had half the town rabble in here, rampaging through the place, scaring the wits out of us, taking everything they could lay their hands on. Look around if you like. You won't find anything.' The man threw up his hands.

The other servants had pulled the attackers to their feet and they lined up against the wall, scowling. Nobu needed to be out of there quickly.

He groaned. He wasn't getting anywhere. Then out of the corner of his eye he noticed that something looked wrong. There was something out of place. The lintel. The halberd hooks were freshly polished but the halberd was missing. He thought back to the lawn he'd crossed. It had been flattened as if people had been sparring there so recently that the grass hadn't had time to spring back. The weapons racks in the entryway were empty too. The men would have taken the swords and rifles when they went off to the mountains, but that didn't explain why the halberds were gone.

'Your ladies aren't planning to attack us, are they?' he demanded. 'That would be very foolish.'

The old man shuffled. 'Ladies have their hobbies,' he mumbled. 'Needlework, tea ceremony, flower arrangement, halberds – you know what ladies are like.'

Halberds. Unbidden, a memory surged up of Nobu's sisters practising with their halberds in Aizu. He could almost hear their sharp young voices and the crack of wood on wood and remembered the sun slanting through the trees in the crisp morning air. Tears sprang to his eyes and he blinked fiercely. That had been no hobby, they'd been preparing for war. He wondered if Taka had taken up the halberd too. It would be like her to fight if her city was threatened.

He'd had enough of beating round the bush. There was nothing to lose by asking as directly as he dared.

'We're looking for . . . for a family.' He didn't mention the name. No one would give away anything about the great Kitaoka or anyone related to him. 'We intend them no harm. We heard they moved down here from Tokyo.'

The old man studied him, eyes narrowed.

'You won't find them here, whoever they are,' he said cautiously. 'It's all old families in this part of town. People from Tokyo don't settle here. By the time they get here they're in reduced circumstances, they've left everything behind. Once they get here they lead modest lives.'

Nobu nodded. The old man was right. General Kitaoka himself might not have lived in a splendid house in the samurai quarter such as the family had had in Tokyo. He might have lived somewhere small, without space for Taka and her mother. Or perhaps he hadn't even acknowledged them, hadn't wanted them to live with him. Perhaps he'd simply left them to their own devices.

Fujino was a geisha. Arriving in an unknown city, surely she would have looked for a place to live in an area where she felt at home – such as the geisha district.

'Keep the volcano on your left,' the old man had told him, looking at him quizzically from under straggly white eyebrows when he asked for directions. 'You'll find the geisha district on the edge of town, as it should be, well away from where decent folk live. Look for salt fields and a salt kiln and a sand mountain and a huge graveyard, largest in all Satsuma, and you'll be there. Salt fields and graves and prostitutes go together, that's what we say round these parts.'

Salt fields, graves and prostitutes . . . As Nobu left the samurai district for the seedier parts of town, he knew he was putting distance between himself and the army, camped out at the castle and the barracks. He was further from safety but also further from prying eyes. He came across scouting parties and some of his fellow lieutenants patrolling alone or in pairs. There were quite a few like him, it seemed, who preferred to be out on their own.

By the time he crossed the line of pine trees that marked the beginning of the merchant district he'd been searching for most of the day. He was tired and hungry, his legs ached and his feet, encased in hard leather boots, were chafed and raw.

The looters had been hard at work. The wealthy

houses of the merchant district looked as if they'd been hit by an earthquake. They were right on the road, not hidden behind high walls, which made them that much easier to break into. Nearly all the rain doors were splintered or torn down and there were broken chests and upturned drawers, rolls of paper and bolts of silk littering the road. The shops were barred and shuttered but most of those had been broken into too. A dead rat lay in the gutter alongside piles of rotting vegetables and mangy dogs tore at bloodied pieces of meat, snarling and baring their fangs at Nobu as he hurried by, keeping a wide berth.

He still hadn't seen any salt flats or a sand mountain and certainly no huge graveyard when he came to a narrow street lined with small wooden houses jammed together side by side. Smells of hair oil and perfume mingled with the dust and sewage. Without people the road was desolate, the houses faded and shabby in the afternoon light. Outside nearly every house was a lantern and he sensed people behind the closed doors. The stubborn old battleaxes who ran the place wouldn't be so easily separated from their livelihoods.

He checked the nameplates but none read 'Kitaoka'. Of course, Kitaoka was far too grand a name to splash across the door of a geisha house. If Fujino was here, she probably went under her professional name, but he didn't know what that was. Once again he was banging his head against a stone wall.

He stared at the little plants pushing up through the black volcanic silt that dusted the ground. A cat sidled up to him, purring, and wrapped itself around his legs and he bent down to pat it. It was hopeless. She probably wasn't even here. He should just give up and go back to his fellow soldiers and forget this absurd quest.

Then a bird swooped across the tiled roofs with a flash of white and landed on a willow tree, setting the leaves rustling. Nobu recognized the long iridescent tail, like a folded fan, and the white breast and black and blue plumage. A magpie, a bird of good omen.

It spread its wings, revealing its white underbelly and wing tips, and swooped down and hopped along the street. He thought of the kind-hearted magpies in the Tanabata story who put their wings together once a year to form a bridge across the River of Heaven so that the weaver princess and the cowherd could meet, and wondered idly if it had come to lead him to his own weaver princess.

The magpie paused outside a house with no lantern and no nameplate. The rain doors were bolted shut, like a blind eye in the street. It cocked its head, looked at him with a beady eye and let out a caw. Nobu had run straight past the house. Now he looked again. No lantern: so it was not a geisha house, not open for business. It was a private residence. He gasped. The scales seemed to drop from his eyes and he wondered, with a lurch of the heart, if this could be the place.

He'd stretched out his hand to knock when the magpie flapped its wings and flew away. The movement shook him awake, as if from a dream. He started and looked around and saw, as if for the first time, where he was and what he was doing and shuddered with horror. Here he was, in the uniform of His Imperial Majesty's

Army, in the geisha district of all places, about to rap on the door of a house of ill repute.

Voices clamoured in his head. He remembered how excited and proud he'd been when he left Tokyo, determined to bring their sworn enemies to heel, how he'd taken the train to Yokohama and boarded the ship shoulder to shoulder with thousands of his fellow-soldiers, all with the same mission, fired with the same zeal. The time had come for revenge – and by an extraordinary stroke of luck, the revenge of the Aizu clan coincided with the welfare of their country. It was their patriotic duty to attack their enemies.

He thought of his father, living like a peasant, grubbing around just to stay alive, when he should have been enjoying a prosperous old age, and of his brothers, in the mountains fighting, maybe wounded or dead. He thought of his mother and his sisters and his grand-mother, of his city reduced to rubble and his people living in destitution. He owed it to all of them to destroy the enemy who'd ruined his family and his clan.

Whatever wild impulse had brought him here, it was against all his better judgement. He'd had a moment of madness but now, thank the gods, he'd come to his senses. There was work to be done. It was time to go – get back to his unit, get on with unearthing the last nests of rebels.

But he couldn't bear to leave. He stood rooted to the spot, squeezed his hands into fists and screwed his eyes tight shut. He knew what was right, he knew what he had to do but it wrenched his soul to do it.

He took a breath, summoned up all his willpower and turned to go. But then the wind rattled the door and he caught a whiff of aloe and musk, of *kyara* and myrrh. In a heartbeat he was back in Tokyo, kneeling on a veranda, reading aloud while a small white hand pointed out the words, character by character. He was walking with a slender girl in the woods of her estate, collecting horsetail shoots; in a garden on a sultry summer evening with a soft sweet-smelling body nestling against his, feeling her hair brush his cheek.

Before he could stop himself he'd knocked. He held his breath and listened, half hoping there'd be no one there. He would just go, he told himself, he'd leave in peace. But there was someone there, he heard a faint noise.

He knocked again more loudly. There was silence now but he was beyond caring. The door was old and wobbly, it stuck in its grooves, but he wiggled it impatiently and it opened a crack. That scent wafted out.

33

Crouching on the stairs in the darkness, Taka held her breath, her heart thundering, staring mesmerized at the thread of light framing the door as it wavered and broke, then flickered into view again. A pebble clattered somewhere nearby. There was someone there. There was definitely someone outside.

Normally there'd have been women gossiping, geishas chatting in bird-like coos, men shuffling around in clogs, talking and laughing at the top of their voices. But now there was just the cawing of crows, the wind rustling in the trees, the murmur of the ocean and, far away, like distant thunder, the rumble and roar of the advancing army. Dogs barked and a fox let out an unearthly wail.

She'd been rummaging through the trunk in the upstairs room, pulling out musty books, perfumed hair ornaments sticky with oil, faded letters from her father, things her mother wouldn't want to leave behind. She'd hoped against hope she might find something there to remind her of Nobu but the only thing she'd had was the amulet and she'd given that to Kuninosuké. She hoped at least it was keeping him safe, keeping all of them safe.

Then she'd heard footsteps in the silence. She sat back on her heels and listened, wondering who could be abroad in this city of ghosts. It was not the crunch of straw sandals or the patter of clogs but boots, pounding along the street. She'd crept to the balcony and peeked out just long enough to see a figure all in black, with a rifle slung on his shoulder, coming towards the house. She could tell by the clothes and the cap it was not a looter. It was something much more frightening – an enemy soldier.

The boots passed by and she let out a sigh of relief, then her heart began to thump again as the footsteps turned and came back and stopped right outside her door.

Suddenly she remembered with a shock of horror that the door wasn't locked. She'd thought she'd be safe from looters or soldiers in this run-down neighbourhood. Not that a lock would be much use against soldiers' boots. They probably wouldn't even stop to check if it was locked or not. She sat silent as a mouse, expecting to hear a deafening crash and the splinter of wood. There was a long silence, then a knock that sent a shudder of fear along her spine.

She summoned up her courage. Her mother had stood up to the soldiers when they broke into their house in Kyoto. She had to be as strong as her. Her halberd was downstairs, not far from the door. If she could get to it, she'd show him what a Satsuma woman was worth. She stood up, edged to the stairs and crept down step by step.

The intruder hammered again, then began to shake the door. Panting in terror, hardly daring to breathe, she huddled in the shadows, wondering why, of all the houses on the street, he'd chosen this one. How could he have known there was anyone here? She watched, frozen, as the pale thread grew wider and daylight flooded in, speckled with dust and flies. A tall figure stepped inside edged with a fuzz of brightness, like a demon in a halo of flames, smelling of starch and boot polish and gun metal.

She stared transfixed at the dark silhouette, wondering if she could make it back up the stairs. There were iron kettles and heavy vases up there she could throw at him or she could try to upend the trunk and heave it. But she was shaking so much her limbs simply refused to move.

Then she made out features emerging from the shadows – a chiselled cheek, a fine, rather aristocratic nose, the curve of a full mouth – and realized with a shock it was not a demon at all. She knew that face. She'd seen it so often in her dreams.

He'd come, her beloved Nobu, after all this time. Or was she seeing things? Could it possibly be him? Rooted to the spot, she clasped her hands and peered eagerly into the darkness.

She was about to jump up, race down the stairs, fling herself into his arms and shout, 'You! It's you!' But then she saw an army uniform, a pair of white spats, the glint of buttons and the unmistakable shape of a rifle.

Trembling, she fell back against the wall and clenched her fists, her head spinning. The young man she had prayed would come back to her had been a dreamer whose leggings and baggy cotton jackets never quite seemed to fit him. This was an enemy soldier. It wasn't him at all. The gods had granted her prayer but they'd put a terrible sting in the tail.

The intruder shut the door and darkness fell again like the sudden coming of night.

'Taka.' That voice, the beloved voice with its northern burr, the voice she'd so longed to hear. But it didn't matter who he was, he was the enemy.

She stumbled to her feet, leaning against the wall to steady herself, and felt for the dagger tucked in her obi. She would kill him and herself too. It was the only thing left to do.

She opened her mouth but no sound came. She licked her lips. 'Don't come near me,' she whispered.

He was bending, fumbling with his spats. 'Taka, Taka, I can't believe it. Is it really you?' His voice was shaking. She could hear his breathing, fast and shallow, loud in the silence. He was as shocked as she was.

'Get out.' Her voice was a croak. 'You don't belong here. We're enemies. Get out.'

She'd never felt such despair. She closed her hand around the silken binding of the hilt, slid the dagger from its scabbard and almost fell as she took a step towards him. She raised her arm. She would strike him and that would be the end of it.

He looked at her steadily.

'I never thought I'd find you.' In the darkness his eyes were blazing. 'I thank the gods you're safe.'

She lowered her arm and thrust the dagger back into her obi. Her knees gave way and she sank down on the stairs. Tears spilled down her cheeks and she tasted salt as she wiped them away with her hands. 'I waited for you, I prayed you'd come and you never sent a word, not a word,' she wailed. 'And now you come, now when we're at war, when you're fighting my father and my brother. It's too late, can't you see that? Too late.'

With the door shut it was hot and airless. She felt grimy and clammy with sweat.

'Our clans may be enemies but we're not, not you and me. We belong together. You're only half Satsuma, remember that. Your mother is pure Kyoto.' He'd said that once before, when he'd crept into their garden and they'd sat together under the stars. It was the last time she could remember feeling happy. 'Forgive me, I didn't mean to shock you, but we have to leave quickly. There may be fighting. The army's going to burn down the city to build fortifications. You're like a fox in a trap here. Let me take you somewhere safe.'

'Burn down my city?' she gasped. 'Take me somewhere safe?'

He put down his rifle and dropped to his knees. 'What are you doing here all alone? Where are your mother and Okatsu?'

Taka peered at him in the darkness, more alarmed than ever. He could take her captive, hold her hostage if he wanted, but she would never betray her mother. If she let slip even a hint of where she was, she might betray Madame Kitaoka too. That was unthinkable.

She tried to see his face, scrutinizing it for treachery. Maybe he was a fox spirit who had taken on human form – it was him who was the fox, not her. Or perhaps he was a demon, with Nobu's features but the body of an enemy, conjured up by her own loneliness and yearning. Surely he couldn't have come all this way just to deceive her?

She put her hands over her face and gave a long shuddering groan.

'It doesn't matter.' His tone was gentle. 'We have to go. Soldiers will be searching the neighbourhood soon. There are good men in the army but bad ones too, who will want to take you as a prize. You don't have to believe me but please see that.'

'I'm not a fool,' she said through her fingers. 'I'm General Kitaoka's daughter. I know how valuable I could be. How do I know you haven't been sent here to capture me because you think I'll trust you?'

'No one's sent me, no one knows I'm here. I'm on my own. I heard you were in Kagoshima, I had to find you. I can't prove anything to you, I can't prove I'm telling the truth except . . . except . . . what I owe your family, your mother's kindness and . . . and my feelings towards you. How can you not know that?'

'When I heard nothing from you for so long?'

He looked at her, wild-eyed. 'I can explain everything but later, later. Please trust me. I swear to you by everything I hold dear, I swear on my mother's grave, I'd never do you harm.'

She backed away, trembling. His voice, his words cast a spell over her, lulling her fears, making her forget her suspicions, drawing her towards him with a force so powerful it frightened her. She wanted more than anything to run to him and let him take her in his arms. But even if she trusted and believed him, even if his intentions were sincere, it made no difference. It was too late. She could never be with him now.

*   *   *

Suddenly a commotion broke into her thoughts. There was a crash that sounded like a door being kicked in and the sound of feet running up and down outside. She had been so caught up in Nobu and their talk, she hadn't even noticed. Soldiers, in their neighbourhood already. Nobu had found her just in time. If he was really going to help her escape, he'd have to lie to his own men, maybe fight them. He might end up being court-martialled, even executed for her. He was taking a terrible risk.

He frowned and gripped his rifle.

Her halberd was propped against the wall in the inner room. She jumped down the last steps and tried to slip past him but he grabbed her sleeve, pinioned her arms and clamped his hand over her mouth. She struggled, aware of the warmth of his body, his hard muscles holding her, feeling her resistance ebb away.

'Let me deal with them,' he hissed.

He pushed her up the stairs, putting his finger to his lips, and she backed into the shadows of the upper room, stumbling over the clothing and books and papers strewn across the floor, and crouched behind the open trunk, dagger in hand.

The ancient door rattled in its grooves and light flooded the lower floor as Nobu stepped outside.

'Yoshida, 7th division,' he barked. 'On house-to-house search.' His voice was sharp and fierce and he spoke in a rough Edo accent. Taka listened, her heart pounding. There was a note of authority she'd never heard before. She hardly knew him any more and it made her wonder if she ever had. An unfamiliar sensation, a knot of excitement, stirred in her belly, hearing him transformed into this stern warrior.

Shadows moved and boots crunched. 'Sorry, sir. Didn't know you were here.' It was the voice of a young lad, barely old enough to be a man.

'Bloody lieutenants, running around like ronin, making up their own rules,' drawled an older voice. 'Found a woman, have you? We all know what goes on round here.'

'He's keeping her well hidden!' From the laughter Taka guessed there must be five or six of them. She held her breath.

'Wish I was, my friend.' Nobu's commanding tone brooked no contradiction. 'Private mission, General Nakamura's orders. Checked half the houses on this street. Found a few old ladies but apart from that the place is a graveyard.'

'General Nakamura, huh?' She could almost see the men scraping and bowing.

'Confidential. Found anything yourselves?'

'Beggars, old women. Not a rebel in sight.' There were a few more pleasantries, then Taka heaved a sigh of relief as the older man said, 'We'll leave you to it.'

Feet shuffled, heels clicked and there was a rustle of starch as the men saluted. The footsteps faded away and Nobu shut the door and slid the bolt into place.

A moment later he was at the top of the stairs. 'That's given us a bit more time.'

His face was lit by the late afternoon sun, filtering through the screens across the balcony. It was so open and guileless, she felt ashamed for ever having doubted him. She remembered the skinny boy who'd burst into their lives at the Black Peony, the mysterious youth she'd taught to read and who had shown her a new way of looking at the world, the young man she'd waited for and despaired of ever seeing or hearing from again. And now he was here, in this room smelling of mildewed tatami, with its faded walls and open trunk.

There was dark fuzz on his chin and cheeks and he was sunburnt and leaner, but that only made him handsomer. He'd taken his cap off and his hair was cut short. His presence filled the room. She took a deep breath, clenched her fists and stared fiercely at the tatami, at his thick foreign socks and her bare feet. But despite her resolve, despite everything, she couldn't help herself. She raised her eyes to his.

'I missed you so much.' Tears welled up again. She stretched out her hand and suddenly, hardly knowing how she got there, she was in his arms. She closed her eyes and buried her face in his chest and clung to him as if she was drowning, smelling his familiar scent mingled with the starch of his uniform, feeling the beating of his heart, his slim young body against hers.

He bent his head and pressed his face to her hair. 'I found you, my weaver princess,' he murmured.

It felt right and safe to be with him, nestled like a little bird. She wanted more than anything to stay with him for ever, but she knew she couldn't. It would be the purest treachery. It went against everything that mattered – especially now, with the army, his army, occupying their city. He'd come back to her after all this time, yet she had to send him away.

'I wanted you so much, I waited so long, but I can't

be with you,' she groaned. 'I can't . . . I can't betray my father.' She felt as if the words were being forced out of her against her will. She tried to push him away but he gripped her hand. She knew the feel of his palm, cool against hers. The last time they'd been together had been in her garden in Tokyo. Then she had been the mistress, he the servant; she had been rich, he poor. But now he held the power. He could do anything he wanted. She shuddered, realizing her own helplessness.

'This is all the time we have,' he said hoarsely. 'Only this one day.'

She raised her face and before she knew what was happening he put his lips to hers, not a boy's timid kiss but the firm kiss of a man, claiming what was his.

She tried to turn her head away but then didn't want to resist any longer. She was filled with fury at the cruelty of fate. Just this one time she wanted to forget her scruples, taste the happiness she'd dreamed of and which she would have to toss away all too soon. It was the first time and it would also be the last.

She dropped to her knees, feeling the touch of his lips bringing her senses to life. Then everything disappeared – the war, the house, her family, all her fears and duties and regrets – and there were only the two of them in that small dusty room with the sun glimmering through the screens and flies buzzing.

He lifted her hair and brushed his fingers across her neck. His touch sent a shiver through her and she gasped for breath. She reached up and stroked his neck, his hair, the stubble on his chin, trying to imprint the feel of him on her fingers so she would never forget it.

The familiar scent of him, dense and dark, drew her back to happier childhood days.

He fumbled under her kimono collar and felt for the soft skin of her shoulder, then drew back and looked at her as if asking permission, his dark eyes glowing.

'You,' he said as he kissed her throat.

She let her head fall back. Hesitantly he eased open the collar of her kimono and she felt the touch of his lips and tongue on the soft flesh between her breasts. Somehow her hair had come loose. She sank back on the tatami, fumbling at the cord of her obi. The stiff brocade loosened and her kimono fell open.

Somewhere in the distance there was a shout. It seemed to bring her to her senses. This was madness. She had to remember her duty, remember what was right. Gasping, she scrambled to her knees and pushed him away.

He drew back uncertainly but he was holding her hand still, so tightly she couldn't escape. 'This little hand, I pictured it so often. This soft skin, your hair.' He gazed at her almost timidly. 'We're not enemies, you and I.'

'How can you say that? You, in your uniform. And me, I'm my father's daughter. Nothing can change that.'

The heat of the afternoon closed in around them. Flies buzzed, a cockroach scuttled along the skirting board, and a couple of cats yowled and chased each other along the alleyway outside. A flowerpot crashed over. Smells wafted in, old perfume mingled with dust and sewage.

Taka pulled her clothes together, her cheeks hot, and twisted her hair into a knot and knelt primly, facing him. She would be strong, she could face anything, she told herself. Despair washed over her like a wave, engulfing her. She swallowed hard, her lips trembling. Samurai don't cry, she told herself fiercely, nor do geishas. She put her hands over her face. She would not cry now – and later, when the time came to part, she would not cry then either. Her shoulders bowed in pain. She tried to speak but couldn't. She took a shuddering breath, then another.

'I thought I'd never see you again.' The words tumbled out. 'I can't bear it that you're leaving, that we have to be apart and my city is to be burnt and there'll be war.'

She felt Nobu's arms around her.

'You have to be brave. You are brave.' His face was very serious. 'Our fates are out of our hands. We just have to do the best we can.' In the time they'd been apart he'd grown up. She gazed into his eyes, looking for hope, but she couldn't see any.

'I wish we could run away together, somewhere where no one could find us,' she groaned.

'We'd have to spend the rest of our lives in hiding.' His voice was gentle. 'The war will be over soon, and then we won't be enemies any more. But before that there'll be fighting.'

'In this city?'

He nodded and held her tight. Then he said, 'But why is it so empty? Where has everyone gone?'

'They were afraid when they saw the warships. They said the army would kill everyone and burn the town down.'

'Like the Satsuma did to the people of Aizu – my

people.' A shadow crossed his face and his eyes became dark hollows. She shuddered, wondering what terrible things he had seen that she would never be able even to imagine and hoped she would never have to see for herself. He looked at her sternly. 'But His Imperial Majesty's Army is different. We have to build fortifications to defend this place, we can't let your father take it back, but we'll behave with honour. We pride ourselves on that.'

'You told me you feared for my safety.'

'There are bad men too. It's a big army and they conscript men who are not samurai, whom we know nothing about.'

She bowed her head. She had to trust him, to do whatever he wanted. 'Everyone left, everyone except me. Some went to Sakurajima, some to the mountains.'

'To Sakurajima? You mean the volcano?'

'They grow oranges on the lower slopes, farmers live there. But my mother's so stubborn. She wanted to find Madame Kitaoka.'

'So that's why . . .'

She nodded. 'I refused to go. She went with Okatsu and her friend, Kiharu. They were going to find the Kitaoka house.'

'Let me take you there now, to your mother.'

She laughed ruefully. 'I was going to join the samurai women, we were going to form a halberd corps and fight, but when I went to find them they'd gone.'

'I searched the samurai district for you. There are no samurai women there. You're the only one that stayed. You're the bravest of all.'

'Or the most foolish.' At least she would let him take her to her mother. It would give them another precious hour or two together. What else could she do? She had nowhere else to go.

34

Readying his rifle, Nobu glanced up and down the narrow street. Faces drew back into the shadows behind the slatted bamboo blinds that shaded the upper floors. He wondered how many hidden watchers had noticed a soldier go into the house with no lantern outside, and a traditionally robed man come out.

He'd put on one of Eijiro's gowns over his uniform, trying to make himself look unobtrusive. Luckily there was nothing strange these days about a man wearing boots under a belted robe and carrying a rifle.

A breeze rattled the blinds, sending them banging and flapping, and a bugle sounded in the distance. Nobu heard a faint rumble of marching boots, horses and cannons and shook his head in bewilderment, wondering what magic had him in its spell. He should get away from here before anyone suspected he'd been up to anything illicit, not risk everything on some crazy mission.

But then Taka stepped into the sunshine and his heart gave a lurch. He remembered her in her western dresses with their billowing skirts that rustled as she walked. How much more beautiful she was now in a plain kimono with the hem tucked up, baring her slender white calves, and a conical hat over her glossy black hair. It was hard to take his eyes off her.

She'd left behind even the few precious things she'd brought from Tokyo. All she had was her halberd and a wrapping cloth bulging with oranges and sweet potatoes. No one would ever have guessed that she'd once lived in a household full of servants and ridden about in a horse-drawn carriage.

She drew herself up and gripped her halberd, frowning. 'Go back to your regiment. I can find my way by myself. There's no need to put yourself at risk.'

He knew she was proud but he was equally stubborn. 'I searched for you all this time. I'm not letting you go alone. I'll see you to the Kitaoka house. We'd better get a move on.'

Taka hesitated, then bowed in acquiescence and set off. Nobu followed, covering his cropped army haircut with a travelling hat deep enough to hide his face and hitching up his robe so it didn't tangle round his legs. Anyone watching would see his spats and the red stripe down his trouser leg but he hoped they would think it was the latest fashion.

It felt strange to be walking behind her; usually women kept a modest three paces behind a man. But perhaps it was for the best. People would think she was a samurai lady on her travels and he was her servant and bodyguard.

He watched her as she pattered ahead with little steps, her head gracefully bowed. He could hardly believe he'd found her. She was everything she'd ever been and, most extraordinary of all, she cared for him. He was in danger of forgetting the peril they were in, the need for speed and the chance he was taking just by being there. None of it mattered while he could walk behind her, see her smile and her dark long-lidded eyes, hear her soft, grave voice. He knew it was madness and that he would have to pull himself together soon enough but he wanted to treasure every moment, knowing how soon they must part.

At the small red-painted Inari shrine at the centre of the geisha district, she turned inland, away from the sparkling water of the bay and the great volcano spewing ash.

They were walking through the kind of neighbourhood where outcastes lived, people who did the jobs that members of the higher classes were prohibited from doing for fear of ritual pollution, like carrying out executions or working with dead animals. They were people so lowly they were outside the caste system altogether, considered to be untouchable and less than human.

There was a meaty, rancid smell, a sign that leatherwork and tanning and butchery took place here. Salt kilns like monstrous beehives rose out of the barren salt-covered fields, but instead of roaring flames and billowing smoke they were grey and silent. Seagulls wheeled and screamed. Nobu sensed people lurking behind closed doors, but there was nobody to be seen. They cut through a graveyard, Nobu walking cautiously, feeling horribly exposed among the tiers of black granite blocks. There was no incense smoke and no fresh flowers, no people clapping their hands and praying and cleaning the stones, only the dead.

They'd reached a maze of streets with pine and cherry

and plum trees hanging over bamboo fences surrounding neat thatched houses. Footsteps hurried down alleys and robes disappeared through garden gates. Nobu felt his rifle on his shoulder and his knife in his belt and remembered that this was enemy territory.

He breathed a sigh of relief when they came to a broad river with a wooden bridge across it and willow trees alongside. Taka scrambled down the grassy bank.

'The Kotsuki,' she said breathlessly, kneeling and dipping her fingers. 'No one can see us here. Can we rest for a moment?' She was panting. Red and orange fish darted in the clear water. She looked up at him, cheeks flushed and eyes sparkling. 'My father was born round here. His family were poor samurai, so they lived a long way from the castle. As far as I know his house is on the other side of the river somewhere, a little way north, across Nishida Bridge.'

Nobu smiled at her. 'I thought he lived in a samurai mansion,' he said. 'I looked for you there.'

She put her hat on the grass and sat down, curling her legs under her. He crouched beside her, ready to spring to his feet if need be, and laid his hand on hers, enjoying the feel of her soft cool skin. The sun would be setting soon and he knew they had to hurry but he wanted to stretch out the time they had together while he could. Bees hovered around the tangle of yellow, blue and purple wildflowers.

'He's not that sort of person,' she said, plucking at a primrose. 'If you met him, you'd understand. He's modest, he's not interested in riches or luxury or fancy living. He used to scold my mother for being extravagant and she'd get cross because he refused to spend money on household things or clothes. He has a thatched house at the top of the bay. He spends most of his time there – he did until he went to war, that is. He likes to write and study and go rabbit-hunting with his dogs and fish and bathe in hot springs. He likes being with students. He hates the smug politicians in Tokyo who are only interested in money. He says men of power should be men of principle too. I don't care what you think. He's a wonderful man.'

She had tears in her eyes. He pulled his hand away, picked up a stone and hurled it into the water. He wanted to say, 'There's more to it than that, more to it than corrupt politicians. We can't have a country split into princedoms. We need to bind together and be strong.' He took a breath. The words were on the tip of his tongue, threatening to spill out. *He's leading an armed insurrection against the government. He can't just take the law into his own hands. And he's the general of the army that destroyed my city and my clan and my life and my family.* The unvoiced thoughts sent a stab of pain through his chest. He clenched and unclenched his fists.

But he said nothing. Some day he would tell her about Aizu Castle, about his mother and sisters and grandmother; but if he put that bitterness into words, it would drive a wedge between them. Better to stay silent. She'd been right. They were not individuals, they belonged to their clans, they could never escape them. With such a history of hatred behind them, how could they ever be together? And yet whatever it was that bound them seemed to transcend everything, even that.

'The war will soon be over.' The words were

inadequate but what else could he say? Besides, he knew the war could only end with her clan's defeat and then she would hate him.

'Either you'll win or we will,' she said, her eyes flashing. 'When our scouts come back for supplies, they tell us victory is close, our men will be on their way to Tokyo soon.'

He frowned. *How can you be so blind?* he wanted to say. *Look at your city. Everyone's run away. Isn't it obvious who's winning?* But seeing her so wide-eyed and innocent, he couldn't bear to dash her hopes. All the same, he felt needled by the talk of General Kitaoka. She knew her clan had defeated his but she never stopped to think how he must feel.

'What do they say about Kumamoto Castle, these scouts of yours?' The words were out before he could stop them.

'My father said that when the garrison saw his army they'd surrender and join him and they'd march on Tokyo together.' She looked at him then and he wondered if she was thinking that her father had already led one army to victory – against his people.

'That's what he said before he left,' he said. 'Do you want to know what really happened?' She'd turned pale as if she'd already guessed. She twisted her hands, clenching her fists till the knuckles were white. He took a breath. He would tell her, he thought, just a little of what havoc her beloved father had brought to the country. 'Your father and his men laid siege to Kumamoto Castle for almost two months. The garrison were terrified when they realized they had the great Kitaoka at their gates, but they didn't surrender. Even when your father's men attached messages to arrows, telling them they had no chance and urging them to join him, and fired them over the walls, they still held firm. Then we sent our armies to dislodge him. Day after day there were battles. Thousands have died on both sides and many more have been wounded. But in the end we lifted the siege and your father and his men fled into the mountains.'

She'd put her hands to her mouth and shut her eyes as if she wanted to block out his words. 'Is he alive?' she whispered, her voice shaking. He put his arm round her small shoulders, immediately remorseful. It was wrong to spoil their last hours together. She'd learn the truth soon enough.

'If he were dead, the war would be over and we'd all be going home,' he said quietly. 'There are other things you should know too . . .' He rested his head on hers and closed his eyes, smelling her sweet perfume. There'd be another time to tell her about Aizu Castle and all that had happened there.

Above the murmur of water and the cries of birds, Nobu heard a distant thrum. Boots, marching, slow and cautious, stopping, then marching on again. He sat up sharply. The last thing he wanted was to encounter his own men. His disguise was far too successful. They'd take one look at him and see a local, a Satsuma man humping a rifle, out and about in this deserted city, up to no good. If they found out who he was and what he was doing – which they would if he was killed – his family would be dishonoured for ever. But to shoot his own men was treason. He was in an impossible position. He smashed his fist into the ground, sending up a shower of earth. There was nothing for it but to run or hide.

Taka had jumped up in alarm. He snatched up her hat and pushed her down the bank and into the shadows under the bridge, out of sight. There was a towpath there, fetid with urine and excrement and rotting food, and some reeking piles of rags on the grass. The rags stirred and he realized they were beggars, sleeping.

The footsteps stopped right above them and he heard thumps as the men threw down their rifles and settled themselves on the grass. Three or four at most by the sounds of it. Taka crouched behind him. He could feel her heartbeat.

'Talk about disappointed. You'd have thought there'd be life in the geisha district, at least.' The man had the rapid-fire patter of a downtown Edo man, a Tokyoite born and bred. Conscripts. 'I was looking forward to a pork cutlet. The pork's famous down here.'

'Or a dish of grilled eel!'

'It was a woman I was hoping for . . .'

'Too bad we scared everyone off.'

There were chortles and grunts followed by a splash. They were throwing stones into the water.

There was a rustle as someone lurched down the bank. One of the piles of rags stirred and snorted and Nobu froze, hoping the soldier didn't come over to investigate or, even worse, to relieve himself. Taka's hand was on her halberd. If Nobu didn't defend them, she would.

He glanced around. There was a boat banging lazily in the reeds a little way away. If the conscripts came any closer, he and Taka could make a break for it and head for the opposite bank.

'Found a flat one.' The voice boomed out just above him. A stone skimmed the surface of the water, jumping a few times, kicking up spray.

'Better get back to base or we'll be in trouble.' It was an older voice.

'Where're we spending the night?'

'On shipboard, with luck. Anyone on land is asking for it. The place may look dead but I tell you, there'll be rebels swarming out of the hills as soon as we turn our backs.'

'We should count ourselves lucky. If we get sent to the mountains we'll be sleeping under the stars.'

'And marching through the rain.'

Nobu crouched under the bridge till the voices had faded away, then jerked his chin towards the boat.

'We'd do better to wait till dark but we don't have time. We'll have to take our chances.'

Water cascaded off the rope, soaking his sleeves, as he hauled the boat to shore. The wood was bleached and slimy with moss but it was sound enough, with a couple of plank seats and oars and a pole inside. Waves slapped the sides and the boat rocked as he gave Taka a helping hand, gesturing to her to stay low, then sculled towards the far bank.

Three men were sauntering along, dark against the afternoon sky. A voice drifted across the water. 'Hey, over there. Who's that? Rebels, looks like. Satsuma bastards.' It sounded like the fellow who'd been looking forward to a pork cutlet. One of the silhouettes lifted a rifle.

ACROSS A MAGPIE BRIDGE

'They're peasants. Leave them be.' It was the older man. 'One's a woman, look. We're not supposed to rile the locals.'

'A woman?' the first voice sang out. The lecherous tone was unmistakable. The warble changed to a bark. 'You, get over here and be quick about it. Government officers, on inspection duty.'

Nobu scowled. They were far from officers, that much he knew. It was a good distance to the next bridge and the soldiers were on foot. As long as he and Taka stayed in the boat they were out of reach.

There was a click as the man cocked his rifle, followed by a bang like the crack of a whip. Birds squawked and rose in great flocks out of the trees. Taka gasped and the boat rocked as she ducked, clapping her hands to her mouth. The bullet screeched through the air and splashed into the water a good distance away. Nobu thanked his lucky stars the men were raw recruits and poor marksmen.

'Don't be a fool.' The older man's voice floated across the water. 'Let's get out of here before we bring a swarm of the bastards down on our heads.'

By the time Nobu and Taka reached the granite arches of Nishida Bridge they'd left the conscripts far behind. They tied the boat up under the bridge and climbed the bank to the road. Steep-roofed houses with morning glories rambling across the thick yellow thatch peeked from behind tall hedgerows dense with camellias, globe flowers and pear blossom. They were getting close to the hills.

The volcano was still behind them, black ash curling

from the lip. Turning to check for soldiers, Nobu saw a couple of men heading for the bridge. One was tall and heavyset, the other short and skinny. They carried themselves straight and tall like officers.

As he looked, they broke into a sprint, waving their rifles and shouting, 'Halt. Who goes there? Stop or we fire!'

'Run!'

Taka gripped her halberd, hitched her skirts and they raced for the nearest corner. A loud bang split the air. The men were a long way behind and the bullet slammed into the bridge, sending shards of granite flying.

Nobu wondered who these fellows could be, so far from base – lieutenants, probably, hoping for glory, on the lookout for rebels. And they'd spotted one, armed and dangerous, ripe for shooting. He – their comrade, Nobu – was undoubtedly the first rebel these men had seen all day. It would almost have been funny if it hadn't been so desperate. And here they were, looking forward to a fight, though they wouldn't win much glory from one lone rebel. The trouble was that, unlike conscripts, these fellows knew how to handle a gun.

They sprinted around the corner, out of the line of fire. There was another bang and a bullet slammed into the road behind them. He glanced around. They were in a narrow, winding lane lined with hedges so high it was impossible to see over. The place was a maze. The boots were getting closer.

They raced from lane to lane, trying to shake off their pursuers, then stopped, hearing the pad of feet and the panting of the soldiers like a wolf pack on their tail.

There were not just two sets of boots any more. The conscripts must have joined them.

Nobu realized they were running in circles. No matter which way they turned, they couldn't escape. Suddenly they came out on a broad avenue. He stared around in horror. They were totally exposed. The street was lined with houses, boarded up and shuttered like blind eyes, deep inside gardens surrounded with high walls or hedges, gates firmly shut. Dogs skulked and a cat dived under a hedge. It would have been a peaceful country scene except that there was not a person in sight.

The footsteps were closing in on them. Soldiers burst from the bushes at the far end of the road and a bullet kicked up dust.

Desperately Nobu and Taka turned and dived back into the maze of lanes. Taka stumbled. She was flushed and panting. Nobu raced up the lane past a couple of gates then shoved one open, grabbed her arm and tugged her inside, slammed it shut and bolted it. They crouched behind it. The leaves rustled and he put his finger to his lips. He hoped Taka wouldn't notice that he was sweating and his hands were shaking. He took a couple of deep breaths and looked around sharply. There were cracks in the boards of the gate and a gap between the dense leaves and branches of the hedgerow just big enough for a rifle.

The men were charging down the lane, beating at the hedges and kicking open gates like bloodhounds on the scent. A moment later they'd reached Nobu's and Taka's hiding place.

'Where's he gone, that bastard?' snarled a voice.

Nobu's heart was pounding so hard he was sure the man would hear. 'Come out, we won't harm you.' He started. He knew the ruse. Surely it couldn't be . . . Peering cautiously through the leaves he made out a heavy brow and burly shoulders. Just his luck. Sakurai. He dared not move a muscle for fear of shaking the hedge but he grimaced, imagining punching his fist into his palm. The other one must be Sato, and those were the conscripts behind them.

The soldiers swung their rifle butts into the hedge, sending leaves and dust showering down. A moment more and the fugitives would be discovered. There was nothing for it but to shoot. Nobu's hands were clammy. He'd only ever used his rifle for target practice before, never in earnest, let alone against his own classmates. Feverishly he fumbled under his gown for his ammunition pouch, felt for a bullet, cocked the hammer of the rifle and slipped the bullet into the breech. Frowning, trying to remember everything he'd learned, he took aim. There was a flash and a deafening bang close to his ear as he sent the bullet screeching over Sakurai's head. Panting, he reloaded.

Now Sakurai knew where he was. A bullet smashed through the hedge and slammed into the ground right by Taka's foot, so close it sprayed her with earth and twigs and dust. She jumped back. Nobu shuddered in horror. A fraction closer and it would have crippled her. A pall of smoke filled the air with the acrid smell of gunpowder. His first experience of battle, and it was his own comrades; but he couldn't see any way out.

There was no time to think. He scowled and readied his rifle. The last thing he wanted was to shoot Sakurai but he might have to put him out of action if he was to protect Taka. At least none of their assailants were members of the Aizu clan.

Taka had sprung to her feet and darted away from the gate. There was a clunk on the other side of the road that sounded like someone kicking a stone. Nobu looked up, wondering if they'd got an ally. Then he realized it was Taka. She'd picked up a stone and lobbed it high into the air. She must have practised at the annual New Year's shuttlecock game, Nobu thought, or learned to throw at that modern school of hers. She tossed another and it rattled against the wall of the house opposite.

The men started and their heads jerked towards the sounds. Nobu grinned to himself. Trust Sakurai to fall for that old trick.

Taka was smiling triumphantly. He'd never seen her so beautiful. It occurred to him how extraordinary it was to be together not in Tokyo but Satsuma, of all places, and in wartime. The gentle young woman he'd thought he knew so well turned out to have a core of iron.

'We need reinforcements,' Sato shouted. His voice was shaking. 'It's a whole nest of them.'

'Nah, it's only one, plus a woman,' Sakurai yelled back, but he sounded uncertain.

'We're sticking our heads in a hornets' nest. They'll be all over us.'

Suddenly a stone flew out of nowhere and hit Sakurai on the shoulder, then bounced off and rattled across the ground. The big man yelped and jumped back. Nobu stared around in bewilderment. Another stone hit Sato's shoulder and a third smashed into Sakurai's leg. He hopped about, cursing. The soldiers raised their rifles and shot wildly, peppering hedges and trees, sending flocks of birds darkening the sky, pocking the walls of the houses and bringing down clumps of thatch, but they hadn't made the smallest headway against their invisible assailants. There were stones flying from every direction.

Nobu was loading and firing as fast as he could, sending bullets screaming past the men's faces. Taka had her hands over her ears. The noise was deafening.

Then there was a bang from the house opposite Nobu's hiding place and a bullet tore past the soldiers and lodged in a tree trunk. They leapt back and stared around, gawping in confusion. One of the conscripts pulled a white handkerchief from his pocket and waved it. 'We give up,' he bawled. The three turned and fled, churning up clouds of dust behind them.

Nobu grinned from ear to ear. It was locals who'd been in hiding. They'd come out of their lairs to defend their fellow Satsuma – him and Taka. Unless Sakurai and Sato were lucky they'd be wounded, maybe killed. It flashed through his mind that he ought to help them; but they'd never been friends to him and in any case, if he did help them, he'd be dead himself. The main thing was, he wasn't going to desert Taka, no matter what.

Another stone hit Sato on the leg. He was limping now. He stared around, as pale and hollow-eyed as a ghost, then he and Sakurai turned and stumbled off.

Nobu's heart was pounding hard still and his ears were ringing. Everything had happened so fast, there'd been no time to think. He'd protected Taka, he hadn't done anything he need be ashamed of; nobody had even been hurt. But he knew this was just a first taste of war. Soon he'd be swept up in the real thing and there'd be no quarter for him or anyone.

'If they'd come any closer I would have hacked them down with my halberd,' Taka said quietly, brushing twigs from his hair. He nodded. Women had no need to know about war. It made his heart ache to see her, her face flushed with excitement, her eyes shining. Her hair had come loose and was hanging round her face in glossy strands. All too soon their time together would be over and he'd be back in the harsh world of the army.

People crowded out, filling the narrow lane, lobbing rocks after the fleeing figures. 'Call yourselves soldiers? Go tell your generals to leave the Satsuma alone.' An old man holding a rifle took a pot shot, making the retreating soldiers skip and jump.

Nobu unhitched his robe and pulled it down to hide his spats and he and Taka shook the dirt and leaves from their clothes and pushed open the gate.

The people outside were small and thin with nut-brown faces, dressed in traditional style, as if modern Tokyo didn't exist. There were thin-cheeked women in baggy trousers and indigo work jackets, snotty-nosed barefoot children, gnarled war veterans with missing arms or legs and an old man with a couple of holes in his face instead of a nose. They had all been unable to go with the army or even flee. But although they were farmers and country dwellers, they were not afraid. They were a clan of warriors, ready to take on the enemy if need be.

They were all brothers-in-arms now, no one was

suspicious of him and Taka. Nevertheless Nobu kept his mouth shut. It was best to play dumb. He didn't want anyone to pick up on his Aizu accent. Taka was obviously well spoken and well bred and Nobu, as he knew, was dirty and dishevelled with his sleeves stinking of river water and his uniform bulging through Eijiro's crumpled cotton gown. These people would probably think that she was the samurai mistress and he her servant.

Taka stepped forward, bowing and smiling. She stood a head above most of these country dwellers. 'Thank you, thank you,' she said. 'You saved us.'

A child with the front of his hair tied in an old-fashioned forelock twisted his mouth into a ferocious scowl. 'We showed them what the Satsuma are made of,' he piped in the local brogue.

'Too bad we didn't hit one, we could have kept him as a hostage,' said the old man, leaning on his rifle.

'That'll show them,' mumbled the man with no nose. 'Think they can march into our city and just take over, go anywhere they like.'

'That's right, Granddad,' answered a chorus of voices.

Men, women and children gathered eagerly around Taka, bombarding her with questions. 'Have you come from the city? What's the news? So it wasn't just a rumour, the army really has come. Headed for the mountains, are you?'

'We're on our way to the Kitaoka house.' The people looked at each other and beamed, bowing low at the name.

A woman hobbled forward, her back so bent her face

was nearly on the ground. She reached out an arthritic hand and stroked Taka's sleeve, rubbing the fabric between twisted old fingers, and gave an appreciative rumble from deep in her throat. 'Family, are you?' she croaked.

Taka nodded shyly.

'There was a lady passed this way just yesterday, isn't that right?' Other women with crumpled, faded faces pushed forward, nodding solemnly. The birds had settled back in the trees and were twittering again, more loudly than ever.

'A lady?' Nobu heard the hesitation in Taka's voice. 'Just one?'

'No, three. Grand ladies, Tokyo types. Geishas, if you ask me. Don't see ladies like that down this way very often, not ever, in fact.'

Taka looked for Nobu and their eyes met. Her mother. So they were on the right path. He could feel her reluctance now they were so close. She hadn't wanted to go to Madame Kitaoka's in the first place, she didn't know what she would find there or even whether she would be welcome, and she didn't want to say goodbye to him.

But he had a war to fight. There could never be any other woman, that went without saying. She was everything he'd ever wanted. But there was also work to be done. He needed to deliver her to safety and be on his way.

'We'll take you, if you like,' the women volunteered.

'We can't ask you to do that. Just tell us where to go.'

'Masa of Bamboo Village, we call him. He's a farmer, our Masa, he likes ploughing, digging, carrying nightsoil. Go back to the main road and look for the second lane on your right. Masa's house is towards the hills. There's no one there now, mind. Well, there might be a watchman still, you can ask him where they've gone.'

35

'Kitaoka. Bamboo House'. The nameplate was so small they almost walked straight past it.

Taka had stopped to admire a black pine that stretched gnarled branches above the road, so perfectly shaped it could have been in an ink painting. Pale knobbly pine blossoms were scattered across the ground. She stood on tiptoe, pulled down a branch and rubbed the spiky needles between her fingers. Whenever she smelt that sharp fresh scent she would remember this day, she thought.

They were nearly in the hills. Houses hidden behind hedgerows looked out over a patchwork of rice, vegetable and millet plantations, smelling of rising sap and fresh leaves and newly turned earth, with the volcano misty in the distance. Rice shoots poked like brilliant green spears from the dazzling water that flooded the fields, but there were no people working there. Bullfrogs croaked and a heron flapped its white wings and settled on a bank between the fields.

They walked hand in hand, stopping at each gate to check the nameplate.

Taka's heart was still pounding. She'd never imagined

that if she was attacked she'd fight, not flee. She'd never felt so alive. But now it was all over she was shaking. She heard explosions in her ears, felt bullets screaming past her face, saw smoke, smelt gunpowder. Now it was over, now she felt afraid – not for herself but for Nobu and her father, who must somehow survive day after day of dreadful battles far worse than this.

She clenched her fists, her hands clammy with fear. She wished there was more she could do than just hope and pray they would come back alive.

'This is it,' said Nobu. She read the tiny characters on the nameplate and her eyes filled with tears.

She'd almost forgotten where they were going. Now she was horribly aware of how uncertain it all was. She had no idea whether Madame Kitaoka or her mother would be there, or how Madame Kitaoka would receive her. Once inside this gate, she'd be in another world, which Nobu was not – could not be – a part of. It was more than she could bear.

'Maybe there's no one here . . .' Maybe they'd run away together after all. They could disappear into the hills and no one would ever find them. The thought was like a ray of sunshine. Their eyes met and she wondered if Nobu was thinking the same. But it could never be. Like birds that flocked, like bees that swarmed, they were part of their clans. They couldn't exist without them.

Nobu drew himself up. 'I'm a soldier of the Imperial Army and this is General Kitaoka's house. I'll wait at the gate till you're settled.' She could see him stiffening, growing more reserved, now that the time to part was near.

'Please come with me. If there's a watchman, he'll just think you're my servant.'

He'd pulled his obi tighter but the uniform under-neath still made Eijiro's once-smart kimono look crumpled and baggy; and he'd taken off his straw hat, revealing his military crop.

The gate of her father's house was faded and rickety with a sun-bleached straw roof. It creaked in its grooves but slid straight open. Inside was a hedge-lined path with bamboo groves and vegetable gardens behind. But there was no one ploughing or digging the vegetables. A hoe and some bamboo baskets lay discarded to one side, along with a hod still reeking of nightsoil – human excrement used as fertilizer.

They made their way along the path past thickets of swaying bamboo to a cluster of steep-roofed houses with earthen walls and irises growing from the thatch. So this was where her father lived. Like him, the build-ings were solid, unpretentious, down-to-earth. There were strings of bright orange persimmons and fat white radishes hanging from the eaves and trays of mulberry leaves drying on the ground.

There was no grand front entrance, just verandas running around the buildings. It was a modest place, a retreat, very different from the Tokyo mansion where Taka had lived.

They passed a well with a tiled roof, a whitewashed rice storehouse and a building that looked like a kitchen. There was a man squatting on his haunches there, skinny brown arms resting on his knees.

Taka approached him timidly. 'Excuse me . . .'

He took a long draw of his pipe, puffed out a cloud of smoke and looked up.

'First people I've seen all day.' He had a broad leathery face and more gaps than teeth in his mouth. 'Heard a lot of noise a while ago. Can't be fireworks, thinks I, not at this time of year. Must be the army in town. Madame's gone, they've all gone. Left as soon as we heard the soldiers were coming. Not that anyone would do Madame any harm but it's better to be safe. What have you got there?'

Taka took off her hat, laid her bundle on the veranda and untied it. The pile of oranges and sweet potatoes glowed like gold in the afternoon sun. The watchman helped himself to an orange.

'You must be the master's daughter,' he said, peeling it neatly so the skin opened out into petals. 'You've got something of him in your face. Lucky you didn't inherit his girth, or your mother's either.'

Taka laughed. 'So my mother came?'

The watchman eased the segments apart, lifted one out and put it in his mouth. 'She went with Madame. She said you'd turn up in the end. Told me to take you up there. It's not that far, one *ri* or so, through the valley beside the river, then up a mountain track. There's a bit of a climb. We can take horses most of the way.' He narrowed his eyes and glanced at Nobu, squatting silently beside the veranda.

'That's my servant. He's going back. What's the best way for him to get a message to me?'

'Deaf mute, huh? Always safest if you've secrets to keep. He can come find me here. Even if soldiers over-run the place, I'll stay. If he can't find me, he can look for Madame in her cottage in the hills. Write the name down for him: West Beppu. Though if things get really bad there won't be anyone here at all. We'll all be dead.'

Taka walked Nobu back along the path beside the hedge to the gate, thankful that the watchman couldn't see them there. They didn't hold hands, it was too late for that. She scuffed her feet in a haze of sadness. There was nothing to say, no plans or promises to make. She daren't even beg him to come back to her or promise to be here when he did.

'I hope you find your way,' she said helplessly. The bamboo stirred and rustled and tiny birds flittered about. Insects swarmed and buzzed.

'I'll head for the volcano.' She saw it rising over the fields in front of them.

He gestured at Eijiro's robe, tangling up around his legs as he walked. 'Do you mind if I keep this till I'm back in army-controlled territory? I'll try and get it back to you.'

She laughed sadly. 'Just throw it away.' Their city was to be burnt, Eijiro was gone, everything would be destroyed. Who cared about the garment? It had done its job.

They stood together at the gate. She bowed and said very formally, 'Thank you for taking care of me.'

She looked up at his intense brown eyes, his prominent nose, his sculpted face and full mouth and remembered the feel of his lips on hers. She wanted to run her fingers across his cheek for the last time but she felt shy. Something had changed in his face. In his mind he was already back in the army, preparing for battle. He was a samurai through and through, she saw that now. That was why he'd always seemed mysterious, why he'd made such an unlikely servant.

And she too, she remembered, was a samurai, the daughter of the greatest samurai of them all.

He took her hands and pressed them to his lips. 'I shall never forget you. If the gods spare me, if I am alive when the war is over, I'll come and find you. I promise you that.'

She swallowed and stared at the black ash-strewn ground, blinking hard. She wanted to leave him with the memory of a smiling face.

'I beg you, please take care of yourself and come back safely,' she whispered.

'It's in the hands of the gods.'

'So this is goodbye . . .' If they'd been on the same side she could have wished him good luck and success; but success for him would mean disaster for her father, and she couldn't wish him that. She looked at him, hoping he would understand.

But there was something that could still be said. Suddenly she had the conviction that if she voiced the wish strongly enough, the words would take on magic power, like a spell, and weave a protective armour to keep him safe. They'd been parted before and each time they'd found each other and each time it had been different. They could find each other again.

'Come back to me,' she said, as firmly and as strongly as she could. 'I'll wait for you.'

He nodded and smiled. Then he took her in his arms and she squeezed her eyes shut and pressed against him, feeling their bodies mould together, the warmth of him, his firm chest, the beating of his heart, trying to fix it all in her memory. She prayed that time would stop and they could stay there forever while the earth revolved around them and the sun moved.

He released her and she felt his cheek brush hers and his fingers touch her hair. 'My weaver princess,' he whispered.

Then the gate opened and he was gone.

PART VI

The Last Samurai

36

*Eighth month, year of the ox, the tenth year of
the Meiji era (September 1877)*

A twig cracked and a chill ran down Nobu's spine. The
hairs on the back of his neck tingled. Thorns and
brambles scratched his skin, bees buzzed around his face
and ants swarmed up his arms but he moved not a
muscle, praying to the gods he'd not been spotted.

He was crouching in a thicket halfway up the hillside,
his grey cotton uniform torn and sodden with sweat.
He'd been climbing since dawn, fighting his way
through pines, cedars, camellia trees swathed in vines
and groves of creaking bamboo. Buzzards soared overhead, looking for carrion, and volcanic ash drifted on
the breeze.

The faint noise might have been a deer or a boar or a
fox or a rabbit but most likely it was Satsuma, moving
as soft as creatures of the forest. He cursed silently. He
hadn't even heard them approach. They were familiar
with the terrain and he wasn't, and they were used to
the sweltering heat while he, from the cooler north, was

exhausted and panting, even though he'd been down here for months. His only relief was that he was allowed to wear straw sandals now instead of the hard leather boots that tore his feet to shreds.

An ominous sound confirmed his suspicions – the scrape of a sword sliding from its scabbard. The Satsuma didn't bother with sparring; they brought the blade down in a single lunge that killed the enemy before he'd had a chance to take a breath. 'If you need a second strike you're already dead,' was their motto.

Once a sword was out it could not be returned without tasting blood.

A field lark trilled in the silence, a breeze rustled the long grasses, crickets chirruped. The air was heavy with moisture.

If he was to die, he would face it stoically, like a samurai. His life was of no consequence. He'd always known sooner or later it would end.

In the last five months he'd seen people shot or cut to pieces right next to him, heard the screams as limbs were blown off and guts spewed out and jaws shattered. He'd fought ferocious Satsuma warriors who'd ambushed him and his fellow soldiers, sent limbs flying himself until the ground was slippery with blood and he was trampling over corpses. In the Kagoshima hospitals there was an epidemic of illness. Men lay wasted and hollow-eyed, dying of typhoid and dysentery without even having seen the enemy. The mortuaries were overflowing.

Yet somehow he'd not been killed, not even wounded. He'd always thought the gods were indifferent to men's fates, but for some reason they'd given him a reprieve.

Until now, that was. Today it seemed his time had come.

A poem Yasutaro, his brother, liked to recite revolved in his mind:

tsui ni yuku	Though I had heard before
michi to wa kanete	there is a road
kikishikado	which some day all must travel –
kino kyo to wa	I never thought for me
omowazarishi o	that day would be today.

Yasu had told him it was the death poem of a famous warrior, lover and poet of ancient times. Nobu remembered how, when he was a child in Aizu, samurai had composed poems before they went into battle. In this era of rifles and cannons, death sneaked up on you and took you by surprise. There was no leisure for poems.

He could almost hear the swish as the sword swept down. He shuddered, imagining it biting between his shoulder blades, tasting the oblivion that would surely follow. Taka's face swam before him, as she'd been at the moment of parting. 'Come back to me,' she'd said, in her soft, sweet voice. 'I'll wait for you.' He thought of her slender body and silken hair and the days and months they'd spent together in Tokyo. At least he'd found her again, they'd found each other. There was nothing left undone. That was some consolation. Like a warrior he would go calmly to join his mother and sisters and grandmother, and perhaps his brothers too; perhaps they too had already crossed to that other place.

But to fail in his mission now, when he was so close. That was truly bitter.

He could feel the letter inside his jacket, pressing next to his heart. He didn't know what was in it but he knew it was of vital importance. It was his duty, his responsibility to place it in the hands of General Kitaoka, no one else. Along with Sakurai and Sato he'd been honoured with this task, entrusted by General Yamagata himself, the commander-in-chief of all the government forces.

But with the sword descending on his neck there was no chance of that. He was going to die and that would be an end of his mission. The disgrace was unbearable. A samurai didn't fail.

Suddenly a voice barked, 'Stop!' The lark paused in its song and even the air seemed to stand still. Instead of the death blow, a foot kicked him hard in the back, slamming his face into the rocky soil.

'We need him alive,' snapped the voice. 'We'll take him back to our master. He could have information.'

Nobu recognized the accent. He knew how ruthless the Satsuma were, all the more so now they had their backs to the wall, like beasts at bay. At least these men were not master swordsmen, he thought. If the blade had been in Aizu hands, his head would have been rolling down the hill by now. He was thankful too that they wore straw sandals. A boot would have done far more damage.

He tried to get to his knees but another kick knocked the breath out of him. He tasted earth and blood and wondered if he'd lost any teeth. Rough hands snatched the rifle from his shoulder and held him down while others seized his sword and dagger and rummaged through his pockets. Four or five of them, he guessed.

'Bullets! We could do with those.'

'Rice balls. And what's this? Water. Fellow's well equipped.'

'We'll take some back.'

'There's not enough to share.' Nobu heard lips smacking and grunts of appreciation as the men wolfed down his supplies. At least they hadn't found the letter. He knew they'd destroy any missive from the head of the enemy command.

A sandal slammed into his ribs and a voice shouted, 'On your feet, hands in the air or you're dead.'

The sun beat down on Nobu's head. His sandals were in tatters and his feet were torn and bruised. He had no idea how long they'd been walking. He needed to keep his wits about him, to work out a way to get the letter into Kitaoka's hands, but all he could think of was his bruised ribs and the pain in his legs and the rifle barrel slamming into his back whenever he stumbled or stopped for breath.

He heard panting behind him and wondered if Sakurai and Sato were there, if they'd been caught too.

He'd been climbing for what felt like hours over rocks, around trees and bushes and through bamboo groves until he came to an enormous stockade stretching right across the hillside. His captors shoved him through an opening and he found himself in a stone-paved trench with woven bamboo walls topped with mud pats bound with straw, thick enough to stop bullets.

He was stumbling along in a daze when a shove in the back sent him staggering forward. He tripped over something, lost his balance and fell.

When he raised his head, he was in a broad open space with crags all around, bristling with trees and bamboo. To one side was a vertical cliff, forming a natural fortress. The place was packed with men, bearded like brigands, toting rifles or swords. They closed in around him, black eyes glittering out of dirt-stained faces. Even to an unwashed soldier like Nobu the stench of sweat and grime was enough to make him retch.

So this was the dragon's lair. He'd been searching for the rebels and he'd found them – the rump of them, that was, those who hadn't died or given themselves up. There were fifty or a hundred, maybe more, some with bloodstained bandages around their heads, others with the stump of an arm or leg swathed in dirty rags. They looked half starved and half crazed.

There were veterans of the civil war, grizzled and beefy with thick beards and square jaws, who must have taken part in the assault on Aizu nine years earlier. But under the dirt and stubble a lot looked like youngsters. Some were in tattered broad-sleeved jackets and striped trousers, like peasants, with thick rags around their feet and rope sandals, others in army uniforms, faded, torn and filthy.

They stared at him with hostility, contempt or blank indifference. Voices boomed around the rock walls.

'Went hunting for rabbits and look what we caught. Spies!'

'Why drag them here? You should have chopped off

their heads.' One skeletal fellow licked sunburnt lips. His skin was leathery but Nobu could tell by his voice he was young.

Another stepped forward with a swagger. He'd lost an eye and had a scar across one cheek. 'We certainly fooled you, didn't we? Last thing you were expecting was for us to turn up back on Castle Hill! You may have the numbers but we have the strategy, we have the brains, we have the ideals! You just do your job. We fight for our cause and our master.'

Nobu tried to get to his feet but hands shoved him back on his knees. He stared at the earthen floor. He wondered if he should tell them that he was a messenger with an important letter for their revered general. But when messengers had been sent to the Satsuma besieging Kumamoto Castle, they'd ended up with their heads tossed back over the castle walls. He couldn't expect any more mercy himself. He was a dead man.

It had been a long and bloody five months.

Most of Kagoshima's grand samurai mansions, the merchant quarter, the shops and markets, even the rows of dilapidated houses in the geisha district had disappeared. A lot had been burnt or torn down by the army to make way for ditches, bamboo fences, piles of sandbags and rifle pits big enough to hold fifty men. The rest had been destroyed in the fighting.

Troops of rebels had swarmed over the mountains and attacked again and again and eventually pushed the army back to their ships and thrown up earthworks of their own. It had been another month before the army had managed to drive them out and retake the city – or what was left of it.

But the war was far from over. The enemy broke up into guerrilla bands and vanished into the hills. As summer began, Nobu had been dispatched from one battlefront to another. When he wasn't on the road, he was firing his rifle or wielding his sword, deafened by gunfire and the roar of cannons, his eyes and nostrils burnt and blackened from the smoke of battle, so dense it was like fighting in a fog. At night he slept out on stony hillsides or under rocks with ants and lice nipping at him relentlessly. Then the rains had come, so heavy it was impossible to see anything at all, turning streams into rivers and paths to mud. Men began to fall ill from disease. For a while the army had almost given up trying to break the enemy.

Bands of rebels wore the soldiers down with sneak attacks. Once, plodding through the hills, Nobu heard the men in front of him shout a warning. The track had been planted with bamboo spikes under a layer of earth. As the soldiers scrambled to leave the path, sharpshooters in the undergrowth picked them off. Nobu barely escaped with his life that time and many other times too. Sometimes he wondered if the gods were watching over him but he doubted it. He suspected they didn't care.

Then summer set in in earnest. Nobu had never known it so scorching. Men fainted from the heat.

One day Nobu's unit met up with a contingent of police, sent to swell the ranks. Nobu was overjoyed to find his brothers among them. They'd all three joined up when the government put out a call for ex-samurai –

the only men who could withstand the mighty Satsuma swords.

They'd spent the night drinking and exchanging stories. Sickly Kenjiro, his glasses miraculously intact, now had colour in his cheeks. Yasu, with his limp, was full of stories of the Satsuma he'd cut down, each one a blow for their womenfolk and for Jubei, he'd said. And Gosaburo had come all the way from Aizu to join the fighting.

No matter how many soldiers fell, there were always thousands more. Shiploads of conscripts arrived from Tokyo and the government armaments factories worked day and night, churning out bullets and gunpowder, cannons and rifles.

As for the rebels, local men swelled their ranks and the peasants, who were on their side, kept them informed of where the army was. But by now they were running out of ammunition and food and places to hide, as well as men. One by one they began to surrender. The army flushed them out again and again, beat them back by sheer weight of numbers till they were sure they had them cornered. Then they'd disappeared completely. For a few days no one knew where they were. And suddenly they'd popped up again, not in the north of the island, as the army generals had expected and planned for, but where they'd started – Kagoshima. They'd come home to die.

After pursuing them round the island, Nobu too was back where he'd started. He even had a mattress to sleep on in the Kagoshima barracks. And he knew Taka was close, up in the hills somewhere. He wished there was some way he could be sure she was safe.

He bowed his head to the ground and groaned. To think of her filled him with pain. Just as the war was nearly at an end, just as he could see a future ahead of him, just as he might finally have the chance to get back to her, to lose his life now – it was too unfair, too cruel.

37

A short man in broken glasses prodded him in the ribs with a foot wrapped in vile-smelling rags. 'You. What were you up to, sneaking around down there?' The reedy voice echoed off the rock wall. The man might have been a schoolteacher before the war.

More and more unwashed, unshaven men had gathered round Nobu and were glaring down at him. He wondered if they knew they were hemmed in like foxes in a trap. The army had thrown up defences right around the hill – bamboo fences as high as a man, then boards studded with nails, then a wide, deep ditch, then bamboo boards raised above the ground so if a man trod on them his feet would go through and his legs would be cut to shreds by the splinters, then a second ditch filled with branches, then a barricade of earth and sandbags, and behind that lot a line of soldiers, armed with muskets. Every bolt-hole was sealed. This time they had not a worm's chance of escape.

There was a thickset figure on his knees not far away. Sakurai. His head looked bloodied. But there was no sign of Sato. Dead, most likely, thought Nobu, as he and Sakurai would be too, very soon.

He heard Sakurai's nasal whine, pleading for mercy. When they'd come back from that first reconnoitre, five months earlier, Sakurai had boasted about how he and Sato had unearthed a nest of rebels and beaten them off single-handed. They had the bruises to prove it. In the telling Nobu and Taka and the villagers had turned into a whole army, of whom Sakurai and Sato had supposedly left a good ten or twenty dead. Nobu was the only one who knew the true story and he wasn't saying anything.

The two braggarts soon realized they'd made a bad mistake but by then it was too late. They'd been promoted and dispatched to the front lines and whenever there was a particularly dangerous task they were chosen. Somehow they'd managed to stay alive. Nobu too had been promoted and now, after not having seen each other for months, all three had been sent on this mission.

Some of the rebels had already lost interest in the captives and shuffled away. Nobu heard voices and sounds of singing and music and recognized the tones of a *biwa*, a lyre. Someone was playing a Satsuma folk song. The place was as hot and close as a furnace. There were fires crackling but instead of food he smelt metal. He'd heard that the rebels were so desperate they'd started melting down cooking pots and spent bullets to make ammunition. It seemed the rumours were true.

He scowled. These bullies were rank and file. It wouldn't work to tell them his mission. They'd just destroy the letter. Somehow he needed to get into the presence of General Kitaoka. For the time being it was best to keep his mouth shut. His Aizu accent would only make things worse. Sakurai was silent too.

Nobu heard the smack as the bespectacled man hit Sakurai round the head with the palm of his hand. 'What were you up to?'

Sakurai flinched. 'We've got a . . .'

A surly-looking fellow put his face close to Sakurai's. 'You know what we do to spies?'

'Show him, Taniguchi.'

The man bunched his fists and scowled at Nobu, then at Sakurai, as if trying to decide who to hit first. Nobu braced himself.

'What's going on?' The crowd fell back and a pale man in an army uniform stepped through. He carried himself with an air of authority. Nobu made out a faded red stripe along the side of his ragged trousers. He'd once been an officer of the Imperial Guard, or perhaps he'd just stolen the uniform.

'We caught them on the hillside, sir.'

The officer stared down at Nobu. 'What were you doing there?' He had a stern impelling voice and spoke in a tone that required a reply.

'I have a message for General Kitaoka, from General Yamagata.'

The officer had an amulet dangling from his belt with a carved wooden toggle to keep it in place. It seemed an odd affectation. Usually people tucked them into a sleeve or a pocket.

'So you're an Aizu lad. You say you're a messenger, so why not take the path? Why creep around like a thief?' Nobu scowled and stared at the ground. The man knew as well as he did that he'd have been shot down before he'd managed more than a couple of steps. 'What's your message?'

It was best not to mention the letter. 'My orders are to speak directly to General Kitaoka.'

'You think you can just walk into our master's presence? How do I know you're not an assassin?'

'Hey, Kuni-*don*! Kuninosuké! What have we here?' The crowd parted again and a swarthy man with his hair tied in a bushy tail pushed through.

Nobu started. He knew that voice. Behind the dirt and thick beard he made out drooping eyes and a sensual, full-lipped mouth. Taka's brother, Eijiro. He was suntanned, fitter and leaner, but it was him all the same. Nobu's heart sank. Now he was really done for.

He bent his back and lowered his head. With luck Eijiro wouldn't recognize him. He remembered the last time they'd met, in the Yoshiwara, more than a year ago. He'd helped Eijiro out that time but it hadn't done him any good at all. They'd been enemies from the start and they were enemies still. Eijiro wouldn't hesitate to kill him, especially now that the rebels were at the end of their tether, and here was Nobu, tossed into their midst like a sacrificial offering. Eijiro must know he was going to die himself and it would no doubt give him the greatest pleasure to take Nobu along with him.

'Prisoners!' A pair of feet wrapped in filthy rags and encased in rope sandals planted themselves in front of Nobu. A hand grabbed his hair and wrenched his head back and Nobu found himself looking up at coarse black hairs sprouting from large nostrils. Eijiro drew back, spat on his hand and smeared the spittle across Nobu's face. His eyes opened wide. 'By all the gods! I'd recognize that ugly mug anywhere. Nobu, young Nobu. I can't escape you. Wherever I go, there you are. You bring bad luck wherever you go.'

He shoved Nobu to the ground and kicked him hard. Nobu screwed his eyes shut and rolled into a ball as the foot slammed into his ribs again and then again. He heard shuffling. The men had closed in and were watching, waiting their turn.

The onslaught stopped abruptly. 'Eijiro-*dono*. We're not thugs. We're samurai.' Nobu uncurled cautiously and opened his eyes. The officer with the amulet on his belt had gripped Eijiro's arm and pulled him away.

'If you knew this fellow you'd kick him too. Bastard was a servant in our house. What do you mean by coming here, you traitor?'

Nobu took a breath, grimacing, and licked the blood from his lips. Nothing he could say could make things any worse. 'I have a message for your father.'

'My father?' Eijiro scowled. 'I'm a sentimental man, I'm too soft-hearted, that's my trouble. I remember now, the Yoshiwara, you helped me out that time. I should spare you for that. But you're a soldier now, we're enemies. You'd kill me too if you had the chance. I'm afraid I have no choice.' He shook off the officer's hand and took his dagger from his belt.

'This is not a time for personal quarrels,' snapped the officer. 'The man is a samurai. He deserves respect.'

'A samurai? He's an Aizu and a servant. Insolent bastard. He behaved badly. I had to dismiss him. He was spending too much time with my sister.'

'Your sister?' There was an odd inflection in the officer's voice that made Nobu look up. A dark flush had spread over the man's stern face all the way to his ears. His eyes shifted and he looked away uncomfortably. Nobu stared, puzzled. It meant nothing, he told himself. Taka must have known many Satsuma officers and how could anyone fail to admire her beauty?

Eijiro looked from one to the other and began to grin. It was not a pleasant grin.

'If he dishonoured her, he must be killed,' said the officer coldly. He'd regained his composure but a trace of colour still tinted his cheeks.

'She's a foolish girl but not that foolish, though the gods know what he would have got up to if I'd let him have the chance,' Eijiro conceded with a grimace. 'General Kitaoka's daughter – that would have been an excellent revenge. No, I kicked him out before anything terrible happened. He's a pathetic creature, can't even read. My sister felt sorry for him. I know you have a soft spot for her, Kuni-*don*.'

The amulet on the officer's belt glittered in a stray shaft of sunlight. It was a small brocade pouch, red embroidered with gold.

Nobu stared at it, mesmerized, as it swung back and forth. He felt as if he were standing on the edge of a high crag, leaning further and further over while a sinister voice urged him to jump. He could almost see the ground rushing up to meet him.

The amulet. It was horribly similar to the one he'd bought for Taka at Sengaku Temple. That didn't mean anything, he told himself desperately. Anyone could have an amulet from Sengaku. It was a very popular temple. But the suspicion had taken hold. It gnawed at him, burrowing deeper and deeper until he no longer even felt the pain in his ribs.

Then the amulet and the officer's confusion and

Eijiro's gloating face snapped into place like pieces of a puzzle and he shut his eyes and groaned aloud. He'd seen men die by the hundreds, trampled over corpses, heard horses screaming as they were blown apart by cannon – yet nothing had shaken him like this. It felt like the end of everything he'd ever lived and fought for. All this time the thought of Taka had kept him going, given him hope that there could be an end to the fighting, a future. But now he was lost in a fog with nothing to hold on to, no direction, nowhere to go.

Somewhere close by, Eijiro and the officer were arguing but all he could hear was the blood thundering in his ears as the rock walls closed in around him. He slumped forward, gasping for breath. The heat was unbearable. An image floated into his mind – a dingy upstairs room, afternoon sunshine on a spring day in Kagoshima, her soft skin and slender waist, the taste of her lips, her long black hair hanging loose in tangled strands, her musky perfume. If this officer, if he . . .

The thought was more than he could bear. He wished Eijiro would cut his throat right then and put an end to the clamour in his head. But no, first he would have his revenge. He braced himself, ready to spring on the man with his bare hands and grip him round the throat, no matter that he'd be beaten to death before he could do any damage.

A hand grabbed his hair and pulled him to his knees and Eijiro's swarthy face swam into view. 'Nobu, old friend,' he said with exaggerated politeness. 'Will you do us the honour of preceding us to the western paradise and sweep the path for our arrival?'

Nobu wanted to spit in his face but his mouth was

dry. Eijiro raised his dagger, grinning, and pulled his head back. Nobu struggled fiercely. He was not ready to die.

Suddenly Kuninosuké's hand gripped Eijiro's wrist. His thin face was dark with fury.

'Enough,' he bellowed. 'We're not executioners. We kill in combat, not cold blood. Let's see what your father has to say.'

The foot of the cliff had been hollowed into caves, each large enough for a couple of men to sleep in. Some looked natural, others as if they'd been carved out of the rough rock. Injured men lay in the shade, staring around, eyes glittering with fever. A musician sat on a large stone, strumming a *biwa*, and a few men were bent over games of *go*, using stones as pieces. A large fire was burning where the rebels smelted down metal for bullets. In the glare of the flames the ragged men and overhanging branches cast long shadows that flickered across the rock wall. Dogs roamed about, turning to snarl at the new arrivals.

Vines dangled in front of the largest cave, forming a curtain. Eijiro pushed them aside and went in. Nobu could hear his drawl and another, lower voice answering. Then the vines parted and a man came out.

Nobu's ribs and shins were so bruised he could hardly stand, but he also felt an unexpected surge of awe. He dropped to his knees. The voices echoing around the cliff fell silent as one by one men turned and bowed.

So this was Taka's father, the famous General Kitaoka. He towered over Eijiro like a tree over a lowly shrub. He was not just tall, he was huge. His chest, as big as a barrel of sake, bulged through the thin cotton of his striped kimono, his belly swelled over his low-slung obi and his massive calves were clad in blue leggings. It was strange, rather incongruous to see this imposing personage in the garb of a humble peasant. His eyes sparkled like black diamonds. He was a man who was not afraid of anything.

He looked at Nobu as if he could see into his soul. He had a long-stemmed pipe in one hand. He tapped it out slowly against a rock, as if he had all the time in the world, then cleared his throat. 'My son tells me they caught you climbing around the hillside, spying.' Nobu stared at the dusty ground, expecting a blow or to hear an order for his execution. Instead there was a soft chuckle. He raised his head, startled. The general had a kindly, almost fatherly look in his eyes. 'Brave fellow. Too bad you're not on our side. We could do with men like you.'

Eijiro was turning his dagger over and over in his hand. 'Shall I interrogate him, Father?'

'What could he possibly tell us? That we're foxes in a trap, that we have no further to run? That the army's encamped at the bottom of the hill, determined to starve us out? We know all that already.'

'Shall I kill him?'

'Leave him be. He's just doing his job.'

'He's an Aizu, Father. He's our enemy. He'd kill us if he could.'

'He feels loyalty towards his clan, just as we do towards ours.' He turned to Nobu. 'What's your name, boy?'

Nobu licked his lips. 'Nobuyuki Yoshida, sir.' His voice was a croak.

'Give this lad a drink.' The tall officer appeared beside Nobu and put a flask in his hands. He took a swig, thinking it was water, and choked as fiery liquor coursed down his throat. He coughed convulsively.

'You're not used to our local brew, I see. We don't have any water, I'm afraid, only shochu.' The general laughed. 'I understand you have a message for me.'

Nobu felt himself coming back to life as the liquor reached his empty stomach and radiated out to his fingertips. He fumbled inside his jacket and found the letter, crumpled but intact. He half rose and put it into Kitaoka's hands.

The general smoothed it out and held it away from his eyes. He scowled, squinted, held it a little closer then slowly read it. 'Do you know what it says, young Yoshida?' Nobu bowed respectfully. Of course he didn't.

'"Aritomo Yamagata, your intimate friend, humbly addresses this communiqué to his honoured comrade, Masaharu Kitaoka,"' he read. He looked at Nobu with his large black eyes. 'It's true, Yamagata and I are old friends. We fought in the northern wars and served in the government together. I doubt if he wanted to lead the army against me but he's a man who knows his duty. This is what he writes. "How worthy of compassion your position is! I grieve over your misfortune all the more intensely because I have a sympathetic understanding of you."' He read out the rolling phrases in sonorous tones.

'He couldn't have written this himself. He had a good education, our Yamagata, but he was never a stylist. This is the work of a professional.' He turned to the letter again. ' "For several months we have been embroiled in warfare; both sides daily suffer many hundreds of casualties; friend kills friend, kinsman is pitted against kinsman yet the soldiers fight without malice. The imperial troops are carrying out their military obligation while the Satsuma men loyally fight for Kitaoka." This is all true. "An end to all this is in your hands only. I beg you to take all necessary measures to end the fighting, both to show that the present situation is not of your making and to bring an end to casualties on both sides as quickly as possible." '

He paused, frowning. ' "Take all necessary measures to end the fighting . . ." What do you think that means, young Yoshida? He's far too cunning to say it in so many words but he's giving me a chance to surrender with honour, is he not? Tell me, what would you do? Would you surrender?'

With every mouthful of shochu, Nobu was growing bolder. He looked at the general. With his frank eyes and all-knowing gaze, it was hard to imagine such a man being anyone's enemy, let alone condoning the violence and bloodshed of the last months – and yet he had. Nobu could see how men could worship him like a god, follow him blindly, do whatever he ordered. But he also saw that he was human. Maybe other men had lit the flame that had set these dreadful events in train, maybe he'd been caught up in them and been unable to stop them.

There was only one answer that any self-respecting samurai could give to the general's question: 'No, sir, no surrender. To surrender is dishonour. There's no such thing as surrender with honour.' But to say that would condemn these men to their deaths. Maybe General Yamagata really did want to give his old friend a last chance to save all their lives.

Nobu stared at the ground. 'There's no loss of honour, sir, if you surrender now,' he muttered. There was a long silence. He quailed. At this moment, he knew, he was in more danger of losing his head than he had ever been.

'My life's worth nothing,' Kitaoka growled. 'My men have not fought their way across Kyushu to lose their heads like common criminals. They deserve to die on the battlefield. We fought to uphold the samurai way of life and we failed. But we can still show the world how samurai die.'

'Is that your answer, sir?'

Eijiro gave a snort. Nobu heard the scrape of metal on rock. He was honing his dagger. The odds of making it safely back to the bottom of the hill were slight if Eijiro had anything to do with it.

'No need for an answer,' the general said. 'Stay a while. Relax, cross your legs, enjoy the view.' It was true. They could see the volcano from here. 'I'm sorry we can't give you proper hospitality befitting the envoy of my old friend General Yamagata. We'd offer you food but we don't have any. But share some shochu with me before you go. I can see you're a drinking man.'

The general sat down on the ground opposite Nobu and crossed his large legs. The tall officer with the amulet hanging from his belt brought a tray of chipped glasses. Kitaoka took the flask and filled Nobu's glass, then handed the flask to Nobu to fill his. They clinked glasses.

Eijiro squatted by his father's side, his swarthy face sullen. He twisted his dagger in the ground. 'Don't let him worm his way into your confidence, Father.'

'My obstinate son sees death looking him in the face. You must excuse his behaviour. Eijiro, my boy. So you know this lad?'

Eijiro growled, 'He worked for us in Tokyo.'

'Tokyo.' Kitaoka heaved a sigh and gazed into the distance, his big eyes wistful. 'So you knew our Tokyo house. You knew my Tokyo family – my geisha, Fujino, whom they called Princess Pig. She was the most beautiful woman in all Kyoto, the home of beautiful women, and in Tokyo she was supreme. Did you know that, young Yoshida?' Nobu was amazed to see that the general had tears in his eyes. 'Women, that's what I miss most. Women, to make life sweet, to bring beauty and tenderness. My wife is a good woman. I wear the obi she made for me. But when I wanted to ease my heart I went to Fujino. You've brought good memories, Yoshida. I'm happy to have such memories the day before I die.'

Men had gathered around them and sat silently cross-legged. Kuninosuké handed around glasses and they poured each other shochu. The shadows were getting longer. The sun was about to disappear behind the crags.

The general emptied his glass. 'A lot has happened since then,' he said. 'Too much. Nothing matters now except to die well. I've written my death poem, Yoshida. Before you leave, let me tell you it.'

He adjusted his legs and took a breath, as if he were in a Zen monastery, preparing to meditate. The setting sun lit his heavy-jowled face. He fixed his eyes on the stony ground and said the words softly, as if to himself:

'If I were a drop of dew, I could take shelter on a leaf tip,
But being a man I have no place in this whole world.'

A shudder ran down Nobu's spine. It was eerie, sitting with these men who all expected to die. It was like being at a convocation of ghosts. Eijiro's hatred, even Kuninosuké and his amulet – none of it mattered in the all-consuming face of death.

He nodded. There was nothing to say in answer to such a poem, at such a time. Kitaoka raised a large hand. 'We're all dead men here, Yoshida, except you – you and your friend there.' The general gestured towards Sakurai, squatting morosely against the cliff face, cradling a glass of shochu. 'You belong in the land of the living. It's not often that men visit the western paradise and are permitted to leave again – but you will.' Somewhere an owl hooted, a long-drawn-out melancholy cry, and branches snapped as a monkey swung through the trees. 'I wasn't expecting a visitor but now that you're here, I have a message for you to take back; but not to Yamagata. You're an Aizu man. I didn't see the fall of Aizu – I wasn't there – but I heard about your women, how bravely they fought and died.'

Nobu flinched, but time had softened the pain.

Kitaoka's voice was a rumble. 'This is my request. Find my family – my wife, my geisha whom you worked for in Tokyo, and my daughter. Give them this.' He took a fan from his obi. Kuninosuké was at his elbow with a brush and a flat stone with a drop of black ink on it.

The general unfurled the fan, wrote a few words on it, waved it in the air to dry, then furled it and held it out to Nobu. 'Tell them that you saw me and I was in good spirits. Tell them we died bravely.' He paused again and looked at Nobu. 'I fear that if we die, my womenfolk will kill themselves too. They may have done so already.'

The rocky cliff with its dense covering of trees and bamboo and lichen and vines swayed as if it was about to topple on Nobu's head. The ragged bearded men with their glasses full of colourless liquor swam in and out of focus. There was a roaring in his ears as if the ground was about to open beneath him and swallow him up. He stared at the general, blinking hard. He couldn't have heard correctly. Surely it was the shochu befuddling his mind.

Kitaoka had spoken of his own death lightly but now his face was drawn and ghastly. His eyes were huge as if he was already searching the underworld, looking for his women. His words hung in the air. 'They may have done so already . . .'

Nobu took a shuddering breath. His mother and sisters and grandmother had all killed themselves rather than be dishonoured by the victorious Satsuma. Surely it couldn't happen again. Surely the Kitaoka women wouldn't do the same. But they were as proud and fierce as the women of his family had been. And if they did kill themselves, if they had killed themselves, that meant Taka . . . Taka . . .

'I thought there was nothing I could do but now I see there is. Save them, Yoshida. There's no one else who can. Try and find them, try and stop them.' The general's voice was urgent, pleading. 'If they're dead, please make sure they are cremated with the proper rites. We men may feed the crows but I want my women to rest in peace.'

Nobu stumbled blindly to his feet, his mind reeling. He'd forgotten the beating, he no longer felt any pain. There was only one thing that mattered now. Taka.

'I must go,' he gasped, his voice a thin whimper of horror. 'I must go immediately.'

'Kuninosuké,' said the general. 'Escort these two back to their own lines. Remember, if any harm comes to them you answer to me.'

But Nobu hardly heard as he plunged down the hill. Branches reached out to block his path, roots and stones rose up to trip him, but nothing could slow his pace. His mind seemed to fly ahead, leaving his body behind. He was gripped by a deadly certainty that squeezed his heart till he could hardly breathe and turned the blood in his veins to ice. He dared not even frame the thought. If the gods had any mercy, let him find her in time. Let it not be too late.

38

The sun had already set and it was nearly dark. Behind the trees a deep red glow streaked the sky as Taka scrambled up the stony path to the clearing at the top of the hill. She stood on tiptoe and pushed aside branches and ferns and clumps of swaying plume grass. The city lay below her, though it could hardly be called a city any more – an uninhabited plain of rubble, with nothing to indicate it was once a human habitation, dotted with lights and cooking fires marking the army camps.

A dark crag rose alongside it – Castle Hill. There were fiery dots there too, blazing bravely halfway up the slope. A little while earlier the watchman from the Bamboo House had come hobbling up the trail to their farmhouse at West Beppu to break the news that at dawn next day the army would attack her father and his rebel band and wipe them out. Maybe they'd fail, perhaps he'd drive them off, but none of them really believed that. At most there were only a couple of hundred rebels left and thousands upon thousands of soldiers, all armed to the teeth with the latest weapons.

Taka had rushed out straight away and climbed up to the clearing to gaze across at the hill where his camp was. It was strange and terrible to know her father was so close, yet so far away. She narrowed her eyes, imagining she might be able to see him if she peered hard enough. Gunfire rumbled like thunder through the valley, sending a jolt of fear through her with every explosion, and flashes lit the distant slopes. Then for a while it stopped. Bats squeaked and foxes rustled through the undergrowth and leaves shivered in the breeze.

She stared dry-eyed into the night and tried to picture her father, large and imposing, the twinkle in his eye, the ponderous way he used to speak, weighing every word. She remembered him in Tokyo, pacing the grounds with his beloved dogs, talking to the great men who gathered to pay their respects and ask his opinion, on his knees in his study in his kimono, working. Even when he'd gone to see the emperor he'd dressed like a farmer in kimono and leggings and straw sandals that he wove himself. Then she thought back to that last night, when he'd come to their house in the geisha district.

Everyone loved and respected him. He was the greatest, most principled, most honest and true man in the entire country. The emperor too had loved him. How could they send troops to kill such a man?

Every day all of them – she and her mother and everyone in the farmhouse at West Beppu – struggled to be cheerful, to keep each other's spirits up. But there was another grief eating away inside her that she couldn't share with anyone.

She gazed up at the sky, arching vast and mysterious above her. It was nearly dark now and the stars were beginning to twinkle. The River of Heaven swirled from one side to the other, a myriad pinpricks of light. She picked out a bright star on one side of it, then a second on the other. Every night she looked for those stars and tonight they were particularly clear – the tragic lovers, the weaver princess and the cowherd, doomed to be apart for ever except on that one day of the year, Tanabata, the seventh day of the seventh month, when the magpies built their bridge.

Nobu. She thought of him every moment of every day and every night, when she saw those stars, she prayed to the gods to keep him safe and bring him back to her. Perhaps she hadn't prayed hard enough. Perhaps if she prayed more fervently they would listen.

She pictured his aristocratic nose, his sudden sweet smile, the intense way he looked at her. Tears sprang to her eyes and she fell to her knees and buried her face in her hands. Ever since he had left her standing alone at the gate of the Bamboo House, there had been silence. She'd waited and waited and heard nothing. He hadn't written, he hadn't sent a message. Every time the watchman came she thought he might have a letter for her, but he never did.

And the worst of it was she couldn't even talk about it. She couldn't confide her doubts and sadness and fear and anger to anyone. It was only alone on this hilltop that she could let her feelings out. Her shoulders heaved and she sobbed bitterly.

Why did he not write? Hideous suspicions ran through her mind. Maybe it was not that he didn't want to be in touch; maybe that was not why she hadn't heard. Maybe it was because he couldn't, because something dreadful had happened. Maybe he was wounded or maybe he'd found someone else or maybe, maybe . . .

She dared not put her worst fear into words even in her mind, terrified that if she even thought it, it would make it happen. She groaned and pressed her forehead to the cool earth, then slowly sat up and heaved a shuddering sigh. Her whole life stretched ahead of her, bleak and empty. She dried her cheeks with her sleeves and tried to compose her face. She would have to run down the hill back to Madame Kitaoka and her mother and Aunt Kiharu. She had to smile and look cheerful, even though she'd lost everything.

But now the war was ending. Nobu had said he'd come and find her when it was over and soon – tomorrow – it would be. Then she'd know for sure. Either he would come or he wouldn't and, if he didn't, she would know he was dead and she'd be able to mourn. Because if he was alive, even if he was dreadfully wounded, he would come, she was sure of that.

And if he did come back, she thought, he wouldn't even recognize her. She was no longer the white-skinned young woman he remembered. Instead of full-skirted western gowns or embroidered silk kimonos, she now wore baggy hempen trousers and a wide-sleeved indigo-dyed jacket of coarse cotton, like a peasant. She dug and planted and harvested, she chopped wood and built fires, she could trap rabbits and pigeons and find mushrooms and wild berries and even spread nightsoil. Her soft pretty hands were calloused now and engrained with dirt. But no matter how hard they worked, none of them had enough to eat. When she looked in her mother's tarnished mirror, she saw a hungry ghost, brown and wiry, all skin and bones and wide staring eyes. She'd become a daughter her father could be proud of, she thought ruefully. Farming was the life he loved.

The moon was rising huge and round behind Sakurajima, a haze of black ash veiling its white face. Taka tried to make out the rabbit pounding rice cakes on its surface. Two days to go, she thought, before it would be a perfect circle, like the mirror in a Shinto shrine. She remembered how they used to celebrate the harvest moon in Tokyo, admiring its reflection in the pond, writing poems and feasting on fat white yam cakes while musicians played elegant music on flutes and kotos.

This year there'd be no celebration. Here in their mountain hideout, the only lights were the menacing red dots of the army fires and the only noise was gunfire.

Booms shook the air and flashes lit up the dark hillside where her father's camp was. The shooting had started again.

Then the guns fell silent and in the lull she thought she heard a distant unexpected sound. She held her breath and listened. Nothing. Then she caught it again.

It couldn't be – but it was. Far away someone was playing the *biwa*.

There was no mistaking now – music, drifting across the valley through the still night, faint but clear. She heard men's voices singing and picked out the tune – 'The Autumn Moon', full of sweet regret for the passing of summer. They used to sing it when her father was in Tokyo. Then she heard the thin pipe of a flute and the rhythm changed to a sword dance, wild and defiant.

She leapt to her feet and laughed aloud as she realized.

It was not the soldiers in the army camp preparing for the final assault, or the people who'd started to move back to their devastated homes, anticipating the end of the war. It was not from the city at all. It was coming from Castle Hill.

Tripping over stones and roots in her haste, Taka raced back to the small thatch-roofed farmhouse halfway down the hillside. Usually there were voices talking and silhouettes of people moving about inside, but tonight it was strangely silent. Candles flickered behind the paper screens.

'They're playing music on Castle Hill,' she called. 'And dancing!'

An owl hooted and bats flitted out of the trees. It had been spring when she'd arrived and now the leaves were beginning to turn and flocks of geese had appeared, flying south.

After so many months the wooden walls and cramped rooms, the rickety sliding door and earthen-floored kitchen area had come to feel like home. She no longer noticed the woodsmoke that permeated their hair and bodies and clothes, or the hardness of the floor where they laid reed mats to sleep. She'd almost forgotten she'd ever lived anywhere else. Apart from the old watchman, they never saw a soul, as if everyone in the whole wide world had perished and they were the only ones left. They squabbled, they bickered, but they knew they needed each other to survive.

She burst through the trees and ran around to the front of the house. They were all standing outside, eight adults and seven children, their faces rapt. Taka's half-brothers and sister – Madame Kitaoka's three youngsters – and the children of Taka's two aunts frowned solemnly, their small heads tilted, cupping their ears.

'I hear music, I hear it!' shouted Kentaro, Aunt Kiyo's son, a four-year-old with huge eyes and a thatch of thick black hair, jumping up and down in excitement.

In the moonlight they looked like a gathering of ghosts. Madame Kitaoka's skin was stretched tight over her gaunt cheeks and Aunt Fuchi and Aunt Kiyo, the wives of Taka's father's brothers, were bony skeletons while Uncle Seppo, the elderly calligrapher who had lived at the Bamboo House and came with them to the farm, was as bent as a dried-up old stick. Okatsu had lost her pretty plumpness and Aunt Kiharu had shrunk so much that Taka could hardly see her. Taka's mother's full white flesh hung loosely on her arms and belly. No one would ever guess she'd once been the famous Princess Pig, celebrated across Kyoto for her glorious round body.

Fujino had told Taka what happened when she, Aunt Kiharu and Okatsu first arrived at the Bamboo House. They'd sold the few kimonos they'd managed to bring with them from Tokyo to send the money to the Satsuma army and were all three modestly dressed, but it was perfectly obvious none the less exactly what they were – two ladies from the Kyoto pleasure quarters and their maid.

Nervous about how she'd be received, Fujino had knelt when Madame Kitaoka came out. 'So sorry to intrude,' she'd begun, putting her hands on the ground and bowing as low as she could. 'I'm not sure if you've ever heard mention of this humble person, my worthless self. Your honourable husband once graciously . . .'

Madame Kitaoka seemed entirely unsurprised to see her. She bowed briskly and held up her hand. 'Of course. You're welcome, Sister. We are alone here, my husband has gone, all the men have gone. I'm glad to see you. You bring brightness into my life.'

That same day she'd dismissed the servants. They'd wept and begged to go along with her to the farm but she'd told them they should return home, that they'd be in danger if they stayed. Then they'd all – Madame Kitaoka, the two aunts, Uncle Seppo, Fujino, Aunt Kiharu, Okatsu and the seven children – set off for West Beppu.

Taka had arrived later that evening. The watchman had pushed open the gate and taken her to the door and she'd stood on the threshold feeling angry and resentful and utterly defeated. She'd sworn she would never come here, never meet Madame Kitaoka and now she had, only because she had nowhere else to go.

But Madame Kitaoka had received her graciously and she'd felt unexpectedly at peace, no longer trapped in the tiny geisha house but part of this big family with children running around. They all had the same fears, waited anxiously for the watchman to come and tell them what was happening, realized they had to work really hard just to survive. They'd buckled down at once.

Grudgingly Taka had to admit that her mother had coped better than anyone. In Kyoto and Tokyo Fujino had always behaved as if she was entirely spoilt and helpless, but the moment she'd arrived at the farm she'd taken a quick look around, seen what needed doing, tied her sleeves back and got down to work. Madame Kitaoka was the head of the house and everyone deferred to her, but Fujino made sure everything ran smoothly – precisely the division of roles one would expect of a man's wife and his geisha.

And every day Taka climbed to the clearing at the top of the hill. She saw the smoke of battle and heard the gunfire as the rebels took the city and then as the army drove them out again. After that there had been silence, with just the wreckage of the city shimmering beneath them all through the long hot summer.

A burst of gunfire drowned the distant music. In the silence that followed they heard the defiant piping of the flute again, floating across the hills. Madame Kitaoka drew herself up. She was probably the same age as Taka's mother but her greying hair pulled back in a severe knot made her look older. Over the months Taka had come to admire her, even to like her. She was not easy to get close to, but she had a pride, an iron in her, a refusal to be beaten down that Taka envied.

'They're saying goodbye,' Madame Kitaoka said quietly. 'They're celebrating their last night on earth.' A smile flitted across her pinched cheeks, the first Taka had seen in all these months. She was usually silent and self-contained but the music had brought her to life. 'We'll have a glorious last night too. We'll build a fire on the hilltop, a huge bonfire, so they can see it across the valley. Masa knows where the farmhouse is. He'll know it's us.'

Taka stared at her in shock. Madame Kitaoka was supposed to be the sober, thoughtful leader of the group, yet here she was coming out with the most outrageous, ill-considered idea she'd ever heard. They were in hiding. If they lit a beacon on top of the hill, it would be a signal to the army – to everyone – that they were there. She wasn't even sure her father would see it. How would he know they were all at West Beppu? And if he did, would he think it was a good idea to light a beacon and summon the army? She felt a great spasm of loneliness. She missed him so much. She wished he were there to tell them what to do and, looking around at the hollow faces, she could see that everyone else did too. His absence was palpable.

Besides, they didn't have any firewood to spare. They needed it all for cooking.

She twisted her fingers in frustration and turned to her mother, silently begging her to intervene. She was young still. It was not her place to speak. But Fujino was beaming with excitement.

'We'll sing so loudly they'll hear it right across the valley,' she cried, clapping her hands. They were no longer smooth and plump but brown and bony, with broken nails, like Taka's.

'If it's the end for them, it's the end for us!' declared Aunt Fuchi, her thin, pretty face alight. Taka admired her aunts. They must be only a few years older than her, they hadn't been married for long, and they couldn't have expected to lose their husbands so soon. They hadn't seen them for more than half a year, they had no idea what had become of them, but they never revealed a hint of despair. They were proud of them. They worked hard, quiet and uncomplaining, always ready with a smile.

'We'll mark the occasion,' added Aunt Kiyo, nodding. Of the two she was the more aware of her rank. She was as weather-beaten as a farmer's wife but she still carried herself proudly like a samurai.

Taka couldn't believe she was the only one who saw the folly of it. She glanced desperately at Uncle Seppo but he was leaning on his stick, his eyes closed, pretending to be asleep, as if to shut out the women's shrill voices.

'We must start right away,' urged Madame Kitaoka. They all – women, children, even Uncle Seppo – lined up at the woodpile at the side of the house and picked up as much firewood as they could carry. Okatsu staggered under a huge bundle, Uncle Seppo carried a few sticks, and even the children, laughing as if it was a game, dragged branches manfully up the slope.

'Okatsu, Taka, take that log up,' said Madame Kitaoka. 'It'll burn for a good while.' It was as big as a small tree trunk. The two of them found stubs of branches at the sides to take hold of, gritted their teeth and heaved it to the bottom of the path then dragged it up the hill together. Their hands were raw and torn by the time they got it to the top.

Taka ran back down to the farmhouse. Madame Kitaoka was holding a large shapeless bundle. 'Taka, carry this up for me.' Her eyes gleamed in the darkness. Taka took it in both arms. It was soft and bulky and heavy, as if it contained clothes of some sort.

It was many journeys before the precious firewood they'd collected with such effort was piled at the top of the hill. They gathered brushwood for kindling and heaped it into a huge pyre.

Madame Kitaoka went to the edge of the clearing and stood, a thin commanding figure against the black sky, gazing across to the dot of light on Castle Hill that was blazing out like a beacon. 'Our men.' Her voice was choked. 'Our brave men.' She lowered her head and Taka heard her swallow.

Gunfire shook the air. Taka buried her face in her hands. They were on a boat spinning along a roaring river, rushing towards the rapids, disaster coming up to hit them, but there was nothing she could do to stop it. Hoping and praying made no difference. The gods were indifferent to their fates.

When she looked up Madame Kitaoka was still gazing across to the distant hill. The wind blew her hair and rippled her baggy trousers. Clouds rushed by as the world revolved beneath them.

With slow deliberate movements, as if performing a tea ceremony rather than lighting a fire, Madame Kitaoka knelt beside the pile of wood and struck a flint. It took a few attempts before one branch, then another smouldered and took light until the whole pyre was ablaze. Taka wondered if her father on Castle Hill was looking across and seeing it too.

'Let it spread,' said Madame Kitaoka. 'It will make it brighter.'

She brought out the last flasks of shochu. When they drank in the evenings, Taka's mother and Aunt Kiharu always led the singing and dancing. They were geishas, experts at making people laugh and forget their troubles. But tonight Madame Kitaoka led the revels.

Taka's mother and Aunt Kiharu covertly tipped their drink on the ground and Taka did the same. Their men were going to die and nothing they could do would stop it. Rather than bewailing their fates, it was better by far to see them off in style. Nevertheless there was something about the reckless burning of the firewood that made her uneasy. She wanted to keep her wits about her.

The seven women, seven children and Uncle Seppo raised their cups. 'To victory! To Masa, our beloved master! To the beautiful land of Satsuma!'

'To Father,' Taka whispered.

'To the next world,' Madame Kitaoka added softly.

'The next world!'

A chill ran down Taka's spine. She wished there was somewhere she could run but she couldn't think of anywhere. She could hardly remember the world outside their little hill any more, but she knew there was no help to be found there. She thought of Nobu and wished he would come. But if he was alive at all he was with the enemy forces, preparing to close in on her father. She shuddered. There was nothing for it but to stay and go through with whatever Madame Kitaoka had planned for them.

Soon the roaring and crackling of the flames and the spitting and banging as the wood split drowned the distant music and even the bursts of gunfire. The heat grew more intense and they moved further and further back until they were pressed up around the edges of the clearing. The firelight sent shadows flickering across their faces, carving dark hollows around their eyes and sharpening their cheekbones, transforming them into demons.

Madame Kitaoka refilled everyone's cups. 'Sister,' she said. 'Will you dance?'

'It's our last night,' the aunts pleaded. They meant it was their last night at West Beppu, not their last night on earth, Taka told herself. She mustn't let her imagination run away with her. 'Won't you do "Dojoji"?' they chorused. Taka's mother bowed gracefully and rose to her feet.

'Musume Dojoji' was the most beautiful and dramatic of all the dances in the geisha repertoire and the dance her mother was famous for. Fujino smiled and in the firelight Taka could see the contours of the face her father had loved so much. 'I'm out of practice,' she murmured. 'It's years since I've performed. I don't have my wide-brimmed scarlet and gold hat or my nine kimonos and snake-scale robe, so you'll have to imagine them all. We don't even have a shamisen; but at least we have a *biwa*.'

Kiharu folded her tiny legs under her, picked up the *biwa* and plucked out a melody. Her plaintive warble filled the still air. Fujino was in baggy trousers and a coarse hempen jacket but as she began to move, tilting her head and moving her hands with spellbinding precision, everyone forgot the shapeless clothes. All they saw was a beautiful maiden in love with a temple acolyte.

Kiharu's voice, soft and seductive, grew strong and dramatic, breaking with emotion as, spurned by the priest, the maiden's thwarted passion transforms her into a fire-breathing serpent. Fujino's dance grew wilder and wilder and Taka could almost see her throwing off her nine kimonos one by one, like a serpent shedding its nine skins.

Taka had seen her mother perform 'Dojoji' many times but never as she danced it that night. She was on fire, whirling and turning, throwing her hands high. She was not dancing for them but for her lover, Taka's father, imagining him watching from the distant hill. It was her gift to him, the last thing he would see before he died.

At the end of the dance the terrified priest has hidden under a bronze temple bell. The vengeful maiden, now fully transformed into a serpent, coils around it and breathes fire on it, melting it and incinerating him.

As Fujino struck the last dramatic pose, poised atop the imaginary bell, Kiharu took two sticks and beat them on a rock in a drum roll. Taka was startled to see a look of pain cross Madame Kitaoka's face, as if it was the first time she'd realized the depths of emotion that bound Fujino and her husband.

In the silence that followed, an owl hooted, long and low. Everyone sat transfixed then one by one began to clap.

The moon had reached its zenith. The trees loomed over the clearing like shadowy sentinels. Taka felt as if she had lost control of her limbs. She rose to her feet as if lifted by some force more powerful than she. Everyone else was standing up too, forming a circle around the fire. They started to sing and clap, swaying to the left, then to the right, moving faster and faster. Caught up in the rhythm, Taka forgot who and where she was, even the dreadful events that were to come. She moved in a trance, dancing round and round, feeling only the rhythm, her body turning and the heat of the fire.

She had often danced at seasonal festivals, forgetting everything, losing herself in the crowd of sweating, weaving bodies. But this felt more like loosing the bonds of life.

In the firelight their shadows danced too. Anyone watching would have thought they were not human at all but fox spirits who'd taken the shape of women.

The fire blazed higher and the heat grew more intense. Aunt Kiharu threw off her jacket, then her drawstring trousers, and Taka threw hers off too until they were all dancing naked, a circle of whirling skeletons. Samurai, geisha – without clothes there was nothing to show their status, no barriers between them, like people at the bath or at the great naked festivals that filled the streets in summer. Even Uncle Seppo stripped down to his loincloth and joined in. They'd become part of an ancient ritual back at the beginning of time, dancing madly like the Dread Female of Heaven to lure the Sun Goddess out of her cave to bring light back to the world.

39

The gunfire stopped and an eerie silence settled over the clearing. The moon had set and the fire had died down but in the darkness a red dot still glowed on the slopes of Castle Hill. Tiredness descended on Taka like a fog and she was suddenly aware how much her legs hurt. They'd been dancing all night, she hadn't slept a wink. She dragged herself round in one last twirl then let her arms fall and stumbled to a halt. She stood very still and listened. There was something important she'd forgotten. Feet still churned the charred ground but of the distant music there was not a trace.

One by one the dancers broke off, panting, and looked around for their clothes and pulled them back on. The children had long since left the circle and were huddled under the trees, sleeping. Taka gazed across the valley to the volcano, a vast triangular hulk in the black sky with a plume of fire spurting from the crater, blotting out the stars. She scoured the horizon for traces of light, praying that dawn would never come. She wanted to hold it back, not just for her father but for herself, too.

'It's nearly time.' Madame Kitaoka had been watching the dancing like a priestess at a mysterious rite. She pulled the bundle Taka had brought towards her and untied it. A pile of smooth flat garments gleamed snowy white in the flickering light of the candles. Taka squeezed her fists until her nails dug into her palms and tried to quell the panic that surged in her chest. She felt her heart thumping, her skin prickling with sweat.

She knew what the garments were: burial robes.

'Our vigil is nearly over,' said Madame Kitaoka. 'When the gunfire starts again, it'll be time.'

Taka's mother sat up abruptly. 'Time? For what?' she demanded, drawing in her breath sharply.

'For our journey to the other world. It's what Masa would expect.'

'Not the Masa I know.' Fujino's eyes were huge and her face dark with fury.

'My dear sister. Please don't spoil the beauty of the occasion.' The two glared at each other, then Fujino lowered her eyes. Formidable though she was, Madame Kitaoka was more so.

Starch crackled as Madame Kitaoka unfolded one of the garments, slipped her arms into the wide sleeves and tied the robe in place with a white sash. The two aunts shook the older children awake and they put on robes on top of their clothes, shivering in the pre-dawn chill. Madame Kitaoka glanced enquiringly at Taka. Her eyes bored into her as if she could see right through her and read her innermost thoughts – her shameful desire for an enemy soldier, her cowardly fear of death.

One robe still lay flat and white on the open wrapping cloth. Madame Kitaoka lifted it and held it out to Taka on both hands. It smelt of starch and mildew, as if it had been stored away throughout the hot steamy summer.

Taka stared at it, petrified. Her heart was pounding so hard she could hardly breathe. Her instincts had been right. It had been a terrible mistake for all of them – her mother, Aunt Kiharu, Okatsu and her – to throw in their lot with Madame Kitaoka. She belonged to that world of samurai and swords and death that Taka's father had gone to war to defend. But Taka didn't. She'd come to West Beppu to find sanctuary, not death. The war was nearly over. Now if ever was the time when – if her prayers had been answered, if the gods chose to be kind – Nobu would come. The last thing she wanted was to die.

There had to be somewhere she could go, something she could say, some argument she could drum up so she wouldn't have to go through with it. But she couldn't see any way out. She was like a fox with its foot caught in a trap. Looking around in panic, her eyes went to the red dot on Castle Hill. Her father was there, large and calm. She could feel his presence. He too was facing death.

Suddenly she was filled with shame at allowing such cowardly fears, unbefitting a samurai's daughter, to enter her mind. She owed it to him to die gladly and with dignity. It would be a small atonement for having betrayed him, for having bound herself in her heart to his deadly enemy, not just a soldier but a member of the Aizu clan.

She saw it all now. This was how it had to end. It was the logical conclusion to the last few months – learning the halberd, getting to know and admire the samurai women, coming to live with Madame Kitaoka. Death was the apotheosis of the samurai way her father was fighting to preserve. She remembered the forty-seven ronin and the way Nobu's eyes had lit up when he told her their story, and of how they had all gone gladly to their deaths. This was what her father would want and Nobu too – that she should go out in a blaze of glory.

Madame Kitaoka looked at her through narrowed eyes as if to say, 'I knew you'd do the right thing.' Taka wriggled one arm, then the other, into the sleeves of the crisp white robe, easing apart the starchy cotton. Her fate was decided, she would accept it with grace. But despite her efforts rebellious thoughts still crowded her mind. There had to be some way she could escape. She took a deep breath. She must not go to her death with her mind in such turmoil.

Taka's aunts had lit incense sticks. Smoke perfumed with aloe, cloves, camphor and ambergris coiled into the air. It was the heady scent that filled Buddhist temples, the aroma of funerals, of monks sitting in meditation. As she breathed it in, Taka felt her mind becoming calm, her heart pounding less fiercely, the mad whirl of thoughts growing quieter. There was no reason to cling on to life, she could see that now. To die when she was young, when life was before her – surely that would be truly beautiful.

Madame Kitaoka, the two aunts and the three older children knelt in a circle in their white robes. The children scowled proudly like little samurai.

Madame Kitaoka took out her dagger and adjusted the silken cords that bound the hilt. It was an exquisite piece of workmanship with a metal scabbard sheathed in doeskin decorated with a cherry blossom design. As she drew the weapon from its scabbard, the candles sent shards of light glancing off the blade. The hilt was marked with the Kitaoka crest. Taka's heart surged with pride at being part of such a noble family. Madame Kitaoka's cheeks were flushed and her face alight, as if she really was eager to take death as her lover. Her thin pinched face looked fuller. She was quite beautiful.

Taka's mother, Aunt Kiharu and Okatsu were watching with barely concealed horror. Madame Kitaoka turned to them. 'Fujino, my sister. Kiharu. I have one last request. Please ensure that Masa receives a proper cremation with all due rites. The army will try to stop you but do your best.'

'It's too soon to speak of last requests,' Taka's mother protested. Her voice was shaking and her breath coming in gasps. 'There's no need for you to die, no need for anyone to die.'

Madame Kitaoka spoke calmly. 'The victors will have no mercy on samurai women. They'll violate us and turn us into slaves. They've already arrested some of the rebels' wives and taken them to Tokyo to work. There's only one path for us.'

'The emperor will pardon Masa,' Fujino wailed.

Madame Kitaoka shook her head and smiled pityingly. 'You geishas will never understand. He won't live out his life in prison. He'd rather die.'

Fujino's eyes flashed. She was trembling. She looked as if she was going to explode. 'We are modern people,' she shouted. 'We eat beef, we wear western clothes. We don't kill ourselves. You expect us to sit and watch while you perform this barbaric ritual?' She grabbed Taka's sleeve. 'You're not dying,' she said, gripping her arm. 'You're not a samurai, you're my daughter.'

'She belongs to her father's house,' Madame Kitaoka said quietly.

Taka hesitated. She didn't have to do this, she realized. No one was forcing her. It was up to her whether she took part in this drama. She was mortified at her mother's behaviour. Fujino was braver than anyone. She'd seen the Kyoto streets running with blood, she'd faced up to the shogun's police, and the greatest samurai of them all – Taka's father – was her lover. She knew men killed themselves rather than be captured. But their life of luxury in Tokyo had made her forget all that.

Taka shook off her hand and joined the circle. 'I'll make my own decision, Mother,' she said. She took out her dagger, feeling the silken binding of the hilt against her palm. The cool metal reconnected her with something she'd lost touch with, something ancient and real and powerful.

Of course she didn't want to die; no one did. But being a samurai meant being prepared to do things you didn't want to do. She would die willingly and proudly. Her rank required it and she would go through with it with dignity.

Her father was not afraid of death and neither would she be. She too would embrace it like a lover.

Sakurajima loomed into view, black against the first flush of dawn. Streaks of pink and orange spread across the horizon and a ribbon of ash streamed from the crater's mouth. Tears sprang to Taka's eyes. She couldn't think of anything more perfect than to die with this glorious sight before her.

Suddenly the rattle of rifle fire broke out, like beans popping in a pan. It was louder, more concentrated, more intense than ever before. Flashes like lightning sparked across the dark flanks of Castle Hill, shooting towards the place where the red dot should have been.

'It's started,' said Madame Kitaoka. Her words hung in the air.

Taka fingered her dagger. How could she ever have thought of betraying her father by not dying with him? She'd had a good life, she'd known love and happiness. Now was her chance to have a good death too.

Voices echoed from the past. She remembered her childhood in Kyoto, the narrow streets of dark wooden houses, the bamboo blinds over the upper floors flapping and clattering in the breeze, her mother bewitching everyone with her dancing, her father rising ponderously to his feet and dancing too, the games, the laughter, the tiny old geisha who played the shamisen cackling and rubbing her gnarled hands. Then she thought of the fighting, the heads on poles along the riverside, the shogun's police marching stern-faced, shoulder to shoulder, hands on their sword hilts.

Then she was in their Tokyo house, sitting quietly in one of the huge breezy rooms, reading or sewing. She saw Nobu's face, remembered those innocent days, walking in their beautiful gardens, leaning against him as they sat in their secret place in the woods, picking wild vegetables, writing on the veranda. She smiled to herself as she remembered their secret meetings last summer and then in the spring, and thought of his touch, of being close to him. She wished they could have died together, that would have been the perfect way to consummate their love. But it was not to be.

She felt as if she was floating, already on her way to the western paradise. The roar of gunfire grew faint. There was a silence around her. The world was beginning to fade. A halo of light swam before her eyes, growing brighter, summoning her. She could almost see Amida Buddha smile as he held out his hand to greet her.

She put her fingers to her throat and felt for the throbbing vein just under her ear, then raised her dagger and drew back her hand, concentrating with all her might. She took a breath. She would only have one chance. She must stab hard and true.

Suddenly, above the gunfire, she heard a shout. 'Stop!' A shadowy figure was charging out of the woods at the top of the hill, racing towards them. She glimpsed a uniform, a thin body and spiky hair and her heart leapt.

Nobu! Of course. Who else could it be? Who else would go to the trouble of finding them, if not him?

The spell was broken. The dagger fell from her fingers.

The volcano was framed in light. Taka gasped for breath, so flooded with joy she thought she would faint. The hilltop and shadowy trees and sky growing brighter by the moment tilted crazily around her and she closed her eyes and put her hands over her face. There was a roaring in her ears. A field lark began to sing and she felt the first warmth of the day touch the back of her hands. She smelt bush clover and carnations and gentians and heard a cricket chirrup.

He was here now. Everything would be all right. No one would die.

She could hardly wait to be alone with him. There was so much she had to tell him. She wondered what he would feel when he saw her. She'd changed so much. Would he still feel the same? She couldn't believe she'd doubted he would come. She should have had more faith in him.

For now she would have to hold herself back, stop herself from looking up, from shouting and laughing with joy, running to him and throwing her arms around his neck. She would have to sit, very calm and quiet, somehow hiding her feelings from her mother's and Madame Kitaoka's hawk-like gaze.

Yet he was here, he was here. He had come at last. The thought was unbearably sweet and poignant and wonderful.

She couldn't restrain herself any longer. Trembling, she peeked through her fingers.

Above the firing she heard scuffling and Madame Kitaoka's voice. 'Get away from me. Get your hands off, I order you. Toyoda-*sama*. Kuninosuké!'

Kuninosuké . . . ?

Taka crumpled, breathing out hard, as if someone had hit her with all their might, knocked the wind out of her. The rosy flush had faded and in the dawn light she saw a tall pale man with coarse black hair and a straggle of beard gripping Madame Kitaoka's arm. It looked as if he was attacking her but then he grabbed her hand and wrestled her dagger away. He turned and looked at Taka, his eyes wild, and she noticed something swinging on his belt, a small red bag with threads of gold that caught the first pale rays of light.

Everything seemed to crumble around her. It all made terrible sense. She'd set up a karmic chain that could never be broken. The gods were punishing her – for allowing him to get close to her, for opening her heart to him, for giving him the precious amulet, her only link to Nobu. She'd lost everything and it was all her own fault. Despair swept over her and she closed her eyes and slumped forward, letting her head fall on the ashy ground, too overcome even to cry. Her shoulders heaved and dry sobs shook her body. All she wanted was to be left alone to slip away into nothingness.

'No deaths, Master's orders. Put away your daggers,' the man barked. 'Thank the gods I got here in time.' His voice was shaking. Taka shuddered. It was the voice she had heard that winter's evening in Kagoshima, the night before her father left.

'You . . . you've ruined everything, everything,' Madame Kitaoka screeched. She gave a howl of despair that sounded as if it couldn't have come from a human throat. A boom from across the valley shook the air and birds flapped out of the trees, cawing.

Slowly Taka raised her head. An acrid smell stung her nostrils. Mounds of ash and charred lumps of wood filled the clearing. The rocks and stones were blackened and the grass burnt to nothing. Even the trees were scorched.

The two aunts, Uncle Seppo and the older children were still in a circle in their white robes, staring blankly at their daggers. Taka knew she must look as crazed as they did. They had all been halfway to the other world, seen things they could never forget. Madame Kitaoka's hair hung in strands around her shoulders. Her face was sagging and her eyes dull as if she'd already left this world, as if it was agony to be forced to return. There was a trickle of blood where she had touched her blade to her throat. A moment later and it would have been too late.

Kuninosuké was looking around at them all, his eyes wide. He was panting. 'I'm sorry,' he said brusquely. Beneath the scraggly beard his face was thinner than before and there were dark hollows around his eyes and under his cheekbones. He had rags wrapped around his feet, Taka noticed, with tattered straw sandals tied on top. His voice softened. 'The master orders you not to kill yourselves. He doesn't want you to die. He begs you not to accompany him to the other world.'

Madame Kitaoka was visibly struggling to compose herself. 'Not accompany him to the other world?' she repeated as if she didn't know what she was saying. Her teeth were chattering. 'How can that be what the master wants? Why should he tear me away from death? Why should I want a life of dishonour? Why are you still alive, Kuninosuké, after all these months away? You should be on Castle Hill with your master, facing death, not arguing like a woman.' Words tumbled from her lips but there was no spirit behind them. Taka felt just as empty. Suddenly her life stretched before her again and she too could see no purpose to it at all. Aunt Fuchi started crying in great convulsive sobs.

Kuninosuké had turned even paler but he held his

ground, breathing hard. No one was going to kill themselves while he was there.

In their indigo farming clothes, Fujino, Kiharu and Okatsu were the only ones who hadn't taken leave of their senses. They were picking up the children, shaking them, hugging them, prising their hands open, taking their daggers and putting them back in their scabbards. The children stared around, dazed.

Fujino went to Madame Kitaoka. She put her arms around her and held her and the two women knelt, Madame Kitaoka's bony shoulders shaking, Fujino stroking her hair and murmuring as tenderly as if she was a child. It was a sight so extraordinary it almost shook Taka out of her stupor. She would never have dared hug Madame Kitaoka. No one would.

Still on her knees on the ashy soil, Fujino turned to the newcomer. 'Toyoda-*sama*, we're in your debt. You came just in time. I'm Fujino, the master's number two wife.'

He bowed. 'Forgive me, Madame. I should have recognized you. I often visited your house in Tokyo.'

She held her hands out pleadingly. 'Please tell me. My son, my Eijiro. How is he?'

He shook his head. 'I can't lie to you. When I left they were preparing for death. We have no ammunition, no food. But I promise you one thing. You can be proud of him. Rest assured he will die like a warrior.'

His eyes fell on Taka and she realized she was staring stupidly. He'd risked his life to come down from Castle Hill and cross this city crawling with hostile troops to find them. She wondered how and why he, her father's right-hand man, came to be here, not on the opposite hill at her father's side. He'd said her father had sent him but she wondered if that was true or if he'd come, in part at least, because of her.

But seeing him just made her disappointment all the sharper. It was unbearable that it should be him here and not Nobu. She turned away and swallowed hard, trying to stop tears welling up. If she once let them flow, she thought, she would never stop, she would cry until the end of time.

Her mother took her arm and shook her. 'Taka, you remember Toyoda-*sama*. He's a hero. He's one of your father's most loyal men. He's brought an important message from your father.'

Taka could hear the eagerness in her mother's voice. She couldn't bring herself to look at him. 'I heard his message,' she said, her voice thick. 'If it's my father's wish, I'll obey.'

She kept her eyes fixed on the ground. Suddenly she saw her life taking a different, unexpected turn. Her mother would want her to marry Kuninosuké – not now, not at this terrible time, but later, when everything was over. The hero who had braved enemy gunfire to deliver her father's message, the man her father had loved and would have wanted her to be with, who would remind them all of their beloved master whenever they saw him and who, as her mother knew, Taka had admired when she was a little girl – it was the perfect match. Madame Kitaoka would want it too. Taka groaned and shook her head. If she had never known Nobu, if he had not reappeared in her life, she might have gone along with it. But now it seemed the grimmest of futures.

'Give her time, Fujino,' said Aunt Kiharu. 'The poor girl's been to the other world and back. Children, run down to the well and fetch water and food. Bring up as much as you can find.' The children had thrown off their white robes. They trooped off into the trees as if the night's events had never happened.

'More people coming up,' one shouted back. 'The watchman's here.'

The rifle fire was more intense than ever. 'I saw that blaze of yours from down in the valley.' Straw-sandalled feet crunched across the stones. The watchman's voice was stern. 'What can they be thinking of, using up all their firewood like that, I asks myself?'

The footsteps stopped and Taka heard wheezing. The watchman gabbled on, half audible above the guns. 'I came up here as fast as I could on these old legs. Had to make the journey in the dark. Fellow won't take no for an answer. Hammering on the door in the middle of the night, wouldn't even let me stop for a drink or a bite to eat. "Hurry, hurry," says he. "What's the rush?" says I. "It's urgent," says he. And there I'd been thinking all along he was deaf and dumb.'

40

Somehow Taka managed to struggle to her feet and stumble towards the gap in the trees, scuffing through fallen leaves, breathing the sharp sweet smell of sap and pine needles as she pushed aside bushes and swaying plume grass. She had to get to the edge of the clearing, see what was happening on Castle Hill. Holding on to a branch to steady herself, she stood swaying, gazing out across the valley. Lights glowed and the shadowy ruins of houses were beginning to take shape. Behind the volcano, layers of pale gold, amber and violet streaked the sky. A bird sang and others answered its dawn cry.

Smoke hung like a shroud over Castle Hill. Flashes ripped across it, close to the place where the red dot had been. There was no red dot now. Rifle fire echoed round the hills, rattling her brain, making it hard to think. It was best that way. Thinking hurt too much. Surely no human being could survive such a relentless barrage.

She heard Madame Kitaoka's voice behind her. 'What have you done, old fool? You've betrayed us! You've brought the army down on us!'

How unfair, Taka thought, when it had been

Madame Kitaoka's own idea to light the fire in the first place. Now everyone knew where they were.

'But . . .' It was the watchman.

'Silence!' shrieked Madame Kitaoka.

Taka's legs felt as if they didn't belong to her. Slowly she turned her head. It made her dizzy to move too fast.

So their hiding place had been discovered. It was no surprise that Kuninosuké knew it. He must have come here many times with Taka's father, he knew Madame Kitaoka, the aunts, Uncle Seppo. There was nothing to worry about in that.

But if the army had found them, it was the end for all of them. They'd thought soldiers wouldn't bother with mere women but they'd been wrong, it seemed. Armed men – maybe hundreds – could have crept up the hill in the darkness, taking advantage of the gunfire to mask the crunch of feet and crack of branches. Madame Kitaoka must have caught a glimpse of movement or of rifles glinting in the trees. The woods were probably full of them, lurking behind every tree and bush, waiting for the signal, ready to burst out. Maybe they'd shoot them but more likely they'd beat them, rape them, take them away and make them into slaves, just as Madame Kitaoka had said.

Taka wished she'd listened to her. She'd been right. They should have killed themselves then and there before such humiliation could overtake them, before Kuninosuké had a chance to stop them.

The watchman had taken off his conical straw hat and was turning it round and round in his thick brown fingers, his head bowed and his shoulders hunched. Madame Kitaoka's eyes blazed. She was on her feet, her arm raised, holding her dagger. She must have snatched it back from Kuninosuké. Her taste of death had turned her into a fearsome warrior.

Fujino, the other women and Uncle Seppo were staring wide-eyed towards the far side of the clearing. Taka drew in a breath sharply as the first soldier limped out of the trees, a rifle slung over his shoulder. His uniform was ripped and dirty and his face bearded. His eyes were dark hollows. He looked a battle-hardened veteran, as if he'd been fighting for years.

She peered into the woods behind him. It was too dark and she was too far away to see much but she was sure she caught a glimpse of figures in the shadows. Any moment now there'd be uniformed men pouring out. There was a sudden movement and she started violently but it was only a deer bounding away. Monkeys shrieked. A crow landed on a branch, sending leaves showering down, and gave a caw. It sent a shudder along Taka's spine. It was an omen of death.

The soldier stared wildly at the mound of ash and the heap of white robes lying in the dirt then turned towards the women in their indigo work trousers and jackets and started to run, half limping, towards them. Taka shrank as deep as she could into the bushes, trembling, praying to the gods he wouldn't notice her.

Kuninosuké was crouching at the edge of the clearing, watching the soldier steely-eyed. He glanced at Taka as if to check that she was well hidden, then leapt up and charged towards the man, shouting, 'Stop! That's far enough!' The soldier started and swung round. Even in the dim light Taka could see his eyes, wide open as if he'd seen a ghost. Kuninosuké darted into his path, the veins in his neck standing out, blocking his way like a fierce guardian deity outside a temple, his hand on his sword hilt.

Taka turned away and gazed at the smoke billowing over Castle Hill. It made no difference what befell a few women compared to the massacre taking place there. Her head was throbbing and there was a fiery pain pressing behind her eyes. She wanted desperately to lie down, curl up and sleep and never wake up again.

'It's not the army, Older Sister.' Aunt Kiyo's dry tones were barely audible against the rattle of gunfire. She was the only one who dared stand up to Madame Kitaoka. 'There's only one of them. He could be a new recruit. Thousands have joined our cause. We couldn't possibly know them all.'

'I don't think we have to worry with Kuninosuké here.' It was Uncle Seppo's voice. He'd been the first to put away his dagger.

She peeked through the leaves. The men were squaring up to each other like a couple of sumo wrestlers before a bout, neither taking his eyes off the other. If she hadn't known it would have been impossible to tell which was the Satsuma rebel and which the soldier. They were both as thin and wiry as skeletons, in faded, filthy uniforms with shaggy hair and beards. Kuninosuké was bigger and burlier and his square-jawed face was paler, while the soldier's was bruised and blackened. Their eyes blazed like coals.

There was a fan poking from the soldier's belt. He put his hand on it and tried to sidestep Kuninosuké but Kuninosuké was too fast. 'Go back. There's nothing for you here. Go back where you came from.'

The man scowled and opened his mouth but Kuninosuké held up his hand. 'You're too late. The job is done. I've carried out my master's command. You kept your word, you're a man of honour, but you're not needed now. There's nothing more to do.'

The soldier lowered his eyes to Kuninosuké's waist where the amulet swung. He brought his eyebrows together in a grimace, gripped his sword hilt and took a step forward.

Taka distinctly heard the whisper of metal and saw a flash of steel as Kuninosuké slid his own sword a hand's span from its scabbard. The women and Uncle Seppo had drawn back into the trees. Madame Kitaoka was poised, blade in hand. The samurai aunts too had their daggers bared. Fujino, Aunt Kiharu and Okatsu held back the children, who scowled as fiercely as their mothers.

'This is Satsuma territory,' said Kuninosuké. His voice was soft and menacing. It carried right across the glade to where Taka crouched. 'You're not welcome. Your men have killed enough of ours. Our women are alive, that's all you need to know. Now leave them to mourn. Go. I don't want to kill you but I will if I have to. You're young. Save yourself, get out of here.'

The soldier took his hand off his sword hilt, pulled out the fan and held it up. He gave a grunt of laughter. His beard made him look old but he had a young man's laugh. He shook his head and threw up his hands. 'You know why I'm here, Toyoda-*sama*,' he said. 'Your master sent me. And I know why you're here. We have no secrets from each other.' Taka started and rubbed her eyes. She knew that voice. 'You gave me the slip, you cheated me. I should have guessed that was what you were planning when you disappeared at the bottom of the hill. You're right, the job's done. But I can't fight you. I won't, I refuse. You saved my skin on Castle Hill and I'm in your debt for that. You're a good and honourable man.'

Taka listened open-mouthed, feeling as if she was waking from a dream. Nearly half a year had passed and it was hard to hear above the rattle and clatter of gunfire but she recognized the intonation, the accent. She didn't have to see his face to know. On the other side of the clearing Okatsu gasped and clapped her hands to her mouth. She'd recognized him too.

'I won't fight you,' the soldier said again. 'Kill me if you want, if you care to kill the bearer of your master's fan. But before you do, I need to know one thing – that Madame Fujino and her daughter are alive and well.'

Taka had been too shocked and dazed to move before but now her heart gave a leap. She scrambled to her feet, pushed aside the branches and bushes, rushed out of the trees and flew towards the soldier. Her legs wouldn't carry her fast enough, they gave way with every step. He turned and saw her. His face lit up and he straightened his shoulders, no longer worn out and beaten down but young and full of joy. She couldn't believe she hadn't realized who it was before.

He had taken his eyes off Kuninosuké. There was a glint of light. Kuninosuké was drawing his sword, not swiftly, as samurai usually did, but slowly, stealthily, his eyes narrowed.

Taka screamed, 'Kuninosuké, no!'

He froze, swung round and stared at her as if she'd gone mad.

Madame Kitaoka gave a shout. 'Aizu.' She'd recognized the accent. The word echoed around the glade like a battle cry. 'Kill him, Kuninosuké, cut him down, or I will.'

In her peasant's trousers, unencumbered by kimono skirts, she flew across the clearing with shocking speed, her eyes blazing as if she carried the vengeful spirit of the entire Satsuma clan in her thin frame. Nobu's eyes were on Taka. He was running towards her, careless of the middle-aged woman bearing down on him.

Taka's heart was pounding. She wasn't going to lose him now. She plunged through the mound of ashes, sending cinders and chunks of charred wood flying and threw herself in Madame Kitaoka's path. The thin face loomed towards her, grey hair whirling, lips drawn back, eyes huge and fierce.

Taka threw out her arms. 'Kill me first,' she panted.

Madame Kitaoka was almost on top of her when she saw her and stopped, gasping for breath. 'Idiot child! Out of my way!' For a moment Taka thought she really would stab her.

She held her ground. The others were running towards them. She screamed, 'Mother, it's Nobu! Don't you recognize him? Nobu!'

Nobu pushed himself between Taka and Madame Kitaoka. He turned to face Madame Kitaoka. 'I'm not your enemy, Madame.' He thrust the closed fan towards her. 'I carry a message from General Kitaoka.'

Madame Kitaoka pulled back as if she couldn't bear to be so close to the hated enemy. She drew herself up like a serpent about to strike, her arm raised.

'Aizu,' she hissed.

Kuninosuké was standing like a statue, his shoulders slumped. Slowly he put his sword back in its scabbard. A look of pain crossed his face as if everything had suddenly become horribly clear.

Taka felt a pang. This was the man she'd embraced that winter night in Kagoshima, her father's right-hand man whom he'd loved and trusted. She felt sure that he was the man her father would have wanted her to be with and she could see too that he was a fine, upright man. Now when her family were facing ruin she owed them even more of a duty than ever, not just her mother but Madame Kitaoka too. It would be so simple to do what they wanted and make them all happy.

But her heart belonged to Nobu. It wasn't reasonable or dutiful or right but it was the way it was.

She looked into Kuninosuké's pale eyes and for a moment felt that she could see into his soul. There was so much that she wanted and needed to say – that she was sorry she couldn't give him what he wanted, that she was grateful he cared for her and had given up so much to come to their rescue and that she'd always admire him. But words seemed hopelessly inadequate.

Kuninosuké's thin cheeks flushed. He swallowed and lowered his head, then drew himself up and thrust out his chest, as if mortified that he might have shown even a trace of weakness.

He seized Madame Kitaoka's wrist, holding it so tight his knuckles were white. 'Enough killing,' he muttered. Madame Kitaoka seemed to shrink. She stumbled back and meekly let him take the dagger from her.

'Forgive me, Madame,' Kuninosuké said, addressing her in formal language. 'In the heat of the moment I didn't recognize this man. I know him and can vouch for him. He came to our camp last night to deliver a letter from General Yamagata and our master requested him to find you. He carries our master's fan as authorization.'

Madame Kitaoka bowed and reached out with a look of distaste and took the fan from Nobu. She slowly unfurled it. She closed her eyes and held it to her face, breathing the smell of it, then read the message, running her finger down the scrawled, smudged characters. She bowed her head and held her sleeve to her eyes. 'Masa's writing, Masa's last command.'

Taka hardly heard her. There was a roaring in her ears. She'd dropped her arms. She was shaking. Nobu turned towards her. She saw the face she'd pictured so often, the slanted eyes and full mouth and shock of black hair, and the knowledge that everything was going to be all right was so strong it made her knees buckle. She tottered and started to fall and he caught her and held her tight.

Her eyes filled with tears and she flung her arms around him. 'You're alive,' she whispered. 'I prayed so hard for you to come. I'll never let you go again, never.'

She could feel Madame Kitaoka's eyes boring into her. She was breaching the rules of propriety by touching any man, let alone an Aizu. The general's wife for one would certainly do all she could to make sure she never saw Nobu again. But having been so close to death put everything into perspective. Taka didn't care what anyone said or thought any more.

Then all the pent-up feelings of the last months and years, the yearning and sadness and disappointment, swept over her like a flood and she clung to him, buried her head in his chest and sobbed. He was there at last. She remembered the first moment she'd caught sight of him, when he'd come to their rescue in Tokyo, a skinny urchin with big eyes and clothes that didn't fit properly, and the last, when he'd walked away from the gate of the Bamboo House and left her behind. So much had happened since then. She wondered where he'd been and what he'd seen and if they'd ever be able to tell each other even a little of all that they'd been through.

A wind blew across from the opposite hill, rustling the trees and prickling her nose with the hot tang of gunpowder. The noise of firing was louder than ever. Nobu couldn't save her father, he couldn't ease the pain of that loss, but to have him there, alive and real, was a comfort. He bent his head to hers and she felt safe and home.

The watchman cleared his throat. 'I was trying to tell you, Madame,' he said timidly. 'It wasn't the army coming up the hill, it was the young lady's servant. I thought he was deaf and dumb but he isn't, not at all.'

Fujino was gazing across at Castle Hill with a look of horrified fascination, as if she couldn't pull herself away. Her face was haggard.

She turned to Nobu. 'Well I never,' she said, trying to smile. 'Young Nobu. You've turned into a man.' The sun had coloured her skin but beneath the tan her face was ashen, not an opalescent white as it had once been but pale like a ghost. She looked worn and faded and exhausted.

Taka stroked her arm. She was afraid she might die too along with her father, not by her own hand but simply slip away. 'Have something to eat, Mother,' she said.

The children had returned with flasks of water and cooked sweet potatoes they'd managed to find. Madame Kitaoka and the samurai aunts, the two geishas, Okatsu, Uncle Seppo, the young men in their ragged uniforms, even the watchman, sat down on the ground in a circle with the boom of rifle fire echoing in their ears. Taka felt as if she was at a wake, as if the world really was coming to an end and they were the only survivors.

She tried to eat but it was hard to swallow. She couldn't think about anything except her father. She couldn't bear to imagine what was happening on the opposite hill.

But even as Taka thought about death, she couldn't help feeling perversely, exhilaratingly, joyously alive, more alive than she had ever felt before. With every breath she was aware of Nobu next to her. His closeness made her tingle. She reached out shyly and touched his foot gently with hers. It was all she dared do with Madame Kitaoka and the others around.

She looked at his face with concern. When she'd hugged him she'd been shocked to feel his ribs poking out under his uniform. He was holding his hand to his side as if he was in pain and there were dark bruises around his eyes.

He gave a wry smile. 'It's nothing,' he muttered.

'Yoshida braved our camp,' said Kuninosuké. 'Some of our boys were a little enthusiastic.'

'So you met my father,' Taka whispered.

'I had that honour.'

Taka's mother leaned forward, clasping her dirt-stained hands. 'Did he look healthy?' she asked softly, looking up at him with big eyes. 'Was he in good spirits?' She was no longer gloriously plump but her voice still had the husky notes that had bewitched Taka's father in Kyoto all those years ago.

'The last thing he spoke of was you.' Nobu hesitated. Fujino bowed her head and wiped her cheeks with her sleeve. Flies buzzed around the remnants of food and a wind sent the ashes whirling. 'He said how beautiful you were and how he missed you. And then he said he was afraid you . . . you might take your own lives. He wanted to be sure you lived. When he said that, I couldn't stop myself, I just ran as fast as I could. Kuninosuké came with me, on the general's orders, to make sure none of his men took a shot at me. We carried a white flag. He protected me on Castle Hill and I protected him when we reached army territory. He disappeared into the woods before we reached the checkpoint, otherwise he would have been shot himself. But when I got back to base, I had to report. I only managed to slip away as the army was advancing up the hill. I thought Kuninosuké had gone back up the hill but he'd delivered the general's message himself. He knew I wouldn't make it in time.'

He turned to Kuninosuké, put his hands on the ashy soil and gave a formal bow. 'Toyoda-*sama*. I'm in your debt. We all are. You carried out your master's orders and saved everyone's lives here. I know our people – yours and mine – are enemies, and have been for generations. You have every reason to hate me, especially now.' He gestured at Castle Hill where gunfire continued to roar. 'I know you're close to General Kitaoka. He's a great man. I revere him too. It's terrible that things have to end this way. It's too soon to speak of such things but once this is all over I hope the old enmity can come to an end and we can be friends. You're a fine and honourable man and a true samurai. I have nothing but respect for you.'

He hesitated and gave a wry, embarrassed laugh. He suddenly looked very young. 'I know you have another reason too to hate me.'

Taka stiffened and her eyes went to the amulet on Kuninosuké's belt. So Nobu knew. He hadn't said anything but he couldn't have avoided seeing it and he must have guessed Taka had given it to him. But there was nothing to say, no need to explain. It was already in the past.

Kuninosuké was on his knees, pale and stern, his back very straight. The Satsuma clan had lost everything but he'd lost more. He'd given up the chance of a glorious death, shoulder to shoulder with his beloved general, Taka's father, to save her and now he'd lost her too.

He returned Nobu's bow. 'If we'd had it out on the battlefield I would have killed you,' he said quietly. 'But this is a different sort of battle. I let myself be distracted from my duty. I disobeyed my master. My orders were to escort you back to your lines, not to carry out your mission for you. I behaved like a woman. I'll have to live with that for the rest of my life.'

But he'd also saved them, Taka thought. A flicker

crossed his face and she remembered the hug and the warm words they'd exchanged. Now his eyes were hooded, all feelings concealed beneath the stern exterior.

'We've been living like nuns here,' said Fujino. 'The watchman brought us news, but – forgive me, my good man – he hasn't told us the worst. Nobu, Kuninosuké, you must tell us everything, everything.'

Taka looked at the two young men, crouched side by side on their haunches, one committed to one side, one to the other. There was a look in the dark recesses of their eyes as if they had done and seen things too terrible ever to tell.

Suddenly there was an unearthly silence. Taka held her breath, waiting for the next explosion, but there was nothing. The gunfire had stopped.

One by one they stood up and went to the edge of the clearing and looked out across the valley. A pall of smoke hung over Castle Hill. Crickets began to chirrup and birds to circle again. The first rays of sunlight were peeking from behind the volcano.

'It's over,' Fujino said hoarsely.

She fell to her knees and buried her face in her hands and her shoulders heaved. 'Masa, Masa,' she cried, her voice choking. 'Eijiro, my boy!' Taka put her arms around her and wept too. There was an emptiness in her life that could never be filled. Even when her father had been far away for years at a time she'd always known he was there and that one day she'd see him again. But now, now . . . Aunt Kiharu and Okatsu knelt together, sobbing.

Kuninosuké was striding towards the edge of the clearing.

Nobu raced after him and took his arm. 'Where are you going?'

'To my master.' His face was grim. 'I betrayed him by coming here. I betrayed them all.'

'They'll arrest you. They'll kill you,' said Aunt Fuchi. Taka suspected that that was exactly what he had in mind.

'My place is with my master,' he said. 'Whatever has befallen him I will share his fate. If he's dead already I must deal with the consequences.' The amulet swung on his belt. It had given him a cruel kind of protection, kept him alive when all his comrades were dead.

Madame Kitaoka rose to her feet. She'd pinned her hair back up and only a few greying strands hung loose to remind everyone of the warrior beneath the prim exterior. She flourished the general's fan imperiously. 'For better or for worse you brought us back to life. We're bound together by karma now, all of us. We'll go down together and identify the bodies and make sure our men are properly and respectfully buried.'

'You'll be arrested too. Everyone in Kagoshima knows Madame Kitaoka,' said Aunt Kiyo.

'Let's not assume the worst,' Fujino said breathlessly. She was panting in distress. 'We don't know what's happened. There's always hope till we know for sure.'

'You mustn't have false hopes,' said Nobu. 'The army would only stop firing once General Kitaoka was dead. You must prepare yourselves.'

'It's over for us all. We'll give ourselves up and they can kill us.'

Nobu turned and faced the women. 'There'll be no more killing.' His voice was quiet and firm. He took a breath. 'If Kuninosuké had been seen coming down from Castle Hill they'd have shot him, but he's with us. We're in the same uniforms, we look the same. No one will even realize he's a rebel. I mourn General Kitaoka and his men, we all do. General Yamagata was his friend, he'll mourn him more than anyone. But the killing's over now. I'm an officer of the Imperial Army. I will protect you all. You can be sure of it.'

Madame Kitaoka was holding the fan in both hands. She bowed her head. The samurai aunts followed suit. Okatsu was silent. She couldn't say a word in front of Fujino, but she gazed at Nobu and smiled.

Taka looked at Nobu. With him here she could face anything, she thought, even this most terrible moment in their lives. If anyone could make things better, he could. He could take care of everything, take care of all of them. They had nothing to fear.

It was the end of their lives but also the beginning of a new life.

Like a party of wraiths, thin and ragged and brown, they set off down the hill. Madame Kitaoka strode in front and the others straggled after her. Fujino stumbled along at the back, dragging her feet as if the fire that had kept her going all that time had finally gone out.

As they passed the farmhouse, Taka took a last look at the smoke-blackened walls and thatched roof of this place that had been home for five long months. She was going back to a world which she knew had been totally changed, which she could not even imagine any more. The city had been destroyed and even the Bamboo House had burnt down.

Walking behind the others where no one could see

them, she took Nobu's hand and held it tight. As she felt the touch of his palm on hers, she knew that so long as he and she were together, everything would be all right. Perhaps this was where the new Japan really started, with them – north and south, Aizu and Satsuma – together. She thought of her father, big and bluff, and suddenly was totally sure that wherever he was, in whatever world, he would approve.

Afterword

Taka and Nobu are products of my imagination but the world they lived in and the historical events they lived through – the war known in Japanese as the War of the Southwest and in English as the Satsuma Rebellion – are all true and as accurate as I could make them.

General Kitaoka is modelled on the real 'last samurai', Takamori Saigo (Saigo Takamori, to put his name in the Japanese order, surname first), who is as famous and beloved in Japan as Winston Churchill or the Duke of Wellington in Britain, and whose name and exploits and tragic end are known to every Japanese schoolchild.

On 24 September 1877 – the year that Edison invented the phonograph, *Anna Karenina* was published and *Swan Lake* had its debut in Moscow – Saigo and some three hundred of his most devoted and loyal followers were holed up on Castle Hill. The Imperial Army, some 35,000 strong, was encamped at the foot. The army began shooting at 3.55 a.m. By 5.30 they had destroyed the rebels' fortifications and closed in on them. At 7 a.m. Saigo and a ragtag band of forty men, who had all made the decision to die with their master, charged down the hill, swords drawn. They had no ammunition left.

Saigo made it 650 metres. Just above the school where the rebels had trained, he was hit in the groin by a bullet. He turned to his trusted lieutenant and appointed second Shinsuké Beppu (Beppu Shinsuké in the Japanese order) and said, '*Shin-don, mo koko de yokaro.*' 'Shin, my good friend, here is as good as any-where.' According to legend, he then cut open his stomach (though in reality he was probably in too much pain to do so and there was no abdominal wound on his corpse) and Beppu cut off his head. Then Beppu shouted that the master was dead and that the time had come for those who wished to die with him. They rushed towards enemy lines and were mown down by rifle fire.

The sound of guns stopped the moment Saigo's body was found.

When the bodies were laid out and identified, one, of a strikingly large, powerful-looking man, was headless. An American ship's captain, John Hubbard, was present. He wrote to his wife that while he was looking, 'Saigo's head was brought in and placed by his body. It was a remarkable looking head and anyone would have said at once that he must have been the leader.'

According to legend his head was washed in spring water and carefully dried and taken to General Yamagata (Aritomo Yamagata, commander of the government forces and Saigo's old friend and colleague), who stood in silent tribute, then bowed respectfully and said, 'Ah, what a gentle look you have on your face.' He is also quoted as saying, 'Takamori Saigo was a great man. It is a matter of regret that history has forced him to die like this.' The surviving rebels were killed or overpowered and disarmed.

Saigo was fifty years old.

Saigo and his men were buried in the grounds of a nearby temple, overlooking the city, the bay and the volcano. Three years later memorial stones were erected and the bones of some of the other rebels – 2,023 men in all, including two aged only thirteen – brought there too and marked with 755 memorial stones. Right in the centre of the graveyard is a huge stone which reads simply 'Saigo Takamori'. There are always fresh flowers in the stone vases in front.

Saigo was officially rehabilitated in December 1898 when a bronze statue of him striding along with one of his dogs, kimono flapping, was erected outside Ueno Park in Tokyo. Yamagata was one of the dignitaries who attended the unveiling. Saigo's widow did not like the statue. She said he always dressed with great care. She had never seen him so poorly dressed.

In Kagoshima I climbed Castle Hill, a tangled impenetrable mass of green, dense with trees and bamboo, and visited the cave where he holed up, barely a cave, more a hollow in the rock, and the site where he was killed. The black lava-stone walls of the school are still there, pocked with bullet holes. There are memorial stones in each of these places. I went to the site of the castle in the shadow of Castle Hill, to Iso where the ammunition works were, to Daimonguchi where the geisha district had been, to West Beppu, and to the cemetery. Towering above the city like a gigantic backdrop is the spectacular cone of Mount Sakurajima, spouting ash. Black dust swirls in the wind, gathering in every corner, and cats lounge and stretch.

Madame Kitaoka is entirely my fictional creation. In photographs the real Madame Ito Saigo looks beautiful, dignified and refined. She lived on quietly for many years after Saigo's death and (apart from her comment on the statue) kept her opinions to herself. As was usual at that time the marriage (Saigo's third) was a union of families, not love.

There really was a Kyoto geisha called Princess Pig – Buta-hime – who was famously fat and whom Saigo acknowledged was his real love. He said she was the only person with whom he could ease his heart. Nothing more is known of her (geishas are famously discreet) and her story and family by Saigo are my invention.

History is written by the winners, and never more so than in the case of the civil war that came to be known as the Meiji Restoration. The Aizu were very definitely on the losing side and, as a result, their stories are far less widely known than the exploits of their southern contemporaries.

The hatred of the northern and southern clans is true, as are the atrocities meted out to the northerners by the southerners and the hardships suffered by the northerners in the years after the civil war.

Early on in the Satsuma Rebellion the government realized that conscripts were not effective against the battle-hardened Satsuma warriors and that they would have to oppose samurai with samurai. They put out a call to unemployed samurai. Many Aizu joined up, seeking to avenge their earlier defeat at the Satsumas' hands, and fought with extraordinary courage, wielding their swords with abandon at close quarters. Almost 25 per cent of police casualties were Aizu, though Aizu men comprised fewer than 10 per cent of all mobilized police.

Nobu and his story are much inspired by the wonderful memoir of Shiba Goro, *Remembering Aizu: The Testament of Shiba Goro*, the true and terrible tale of what happened to him and his family during and after the battle of Aizu Wakamatsu. I'd like to acknowledge my considerable debt to this beautifully translated and very moving book, listed below, and urge everyone touched by Nobu's story to read it.

Bibliography

The story as I tell it is largely based on research and historical fact, though I've tweaked dates and other details here and there in the interests of telling a good story. The main books I used are listed below; there are many more. Besides books, my primary resource for the story of the Satsuma Rebellion was the accounts in the *Japan Weekly Mail* of 1873, 1876 and 1877, all stored in the Diet Library in Tokyo. There are also accounts in the *Illustrated London News* with illustrations by the artist Charles Wirgman.

Except for the poem on page 15, all translations are by me.

Aizu

Ishimitsu Mahito (ed.), *Remembering Aizu: The Testament of Shiba Goro*, translated by Teruko Craig, University of Hawaii Press, Honolulu, 1999

Saotome Mitsugu, *Okei: A Girl from the Provinces*, translated by Kenneth J. Bryson, Alma Books Ltd, London, 2008. Novel set at the time of the fall of Aizu.

Wright, Diana E., 'Female Combatants and Japan's

Meiji Restoration: the case of Aizu', *War in History*, 2001: 8: 396.

Satsuma

Black, John R., *Young Japan: Yokohama and Yedo, A Narrative of the Settlement and the City from the Signing of the Treaties in 1858, to the close of the year 1879. With a glance at the Progress of Japan during a period of twenty-one years*, Vol. II, Trubner & Co., London, and Kelly & Co., Yokohama, 1881; reprinted by Elibron Classics, 2005

Booth, Alan, *Looking for the Lost: Journeys Through a Vanishing Japan*, Kodansha International, New York, Tokyo, London, 1995. Witty and well-informed account of a journey in Saigo's footsteps through Kyushu.

Buck, James H., 'The Satsuma Rebellion of 1877. From Kagoshima through the Siege of Kumamoto Castle', *Monumenta Nipponica*, Vol. 28, No. 4 (Winter 1973)

Cortazzi, Hugh, *Dr Willis in Japan, 1862–1877, British Medical Pioneer*, Athlone Press, London and Dover, New Hampshire, 1985. Dr William Willis, a brilliant surgeon who saved many lives, worked in Aizu and later lived in Kagoshima from 1870 to 1877, right up until the Satsuma Rebellion.

Huffman, James L., *Politics of the Meiji Press: The Life of Fukuchi Gen'ichiro*, University Press of Hawaii, Honolulu, 1980. Fukuchi, the pioneering Japanese journalist, went to the front line to cover the Satsuma Rebellion.

Man, John, *Samurai: The Last Warrior*, Bantam Press, London, 2011

Morris, Ivan, *The Nobility of Failure: Tragic Heroes in the History of Japan*, Secker & Warburg, London, 1975

Mounsey, Augustus Henry, *The Satsuma Rebellion: An Episode of Modern Japanese History (1879)*, first published John Murray, London, 1879; reprinted by Kessinger Legacy Reprints, 2011. A wonderfully detailed and accessibly written contemporary account.

Ravina, Mark, *The Last Samurai: The Life and Battles of Saigo Takamori*, John Wiley & Sons, Inc., Hoboken, New Jersey, 2004. The most up-to-the-minute scholarly work.

Yates, Charles L., *Saigo Takamori: The Man Behind the Myth*, Kegan Paul International, London and New York, 1995

Books and articles that deal with the period in general

Bennett, Terry (ed.), *Japan and the Illustrated London News: Complete Record of Reported Events, 1853 to 1899*, Global Oriental, Folkestone, 2006

Keene, Donald, *Emperor of Japan: Meiji and His World*, Columbia University Press, New York, 2002

Meech-Pekarik, Julia, *The World of the Meiji Print: Impressions of a New Civilization*, Weatherhill, New York and Tokyo, 1987

Mertz, John Pierre, *Novel Japan: Spaces of Nationhood in Early Meiji Narrative, 1870–88*, Center for Japanese Studies, The University of Michigan, Ann Arbor, 2003

Roberts, John G., *Mitsui: Three Centuries of Japanese Business*, Weatherhill, New York and Tokyo, 1973

Seidensticker, Edward, *Low City, High City: Tokyo from Edo to the Earthquake, 1867–1923*, Alfred A. Knopf Inc., New York, 1983

Acknowledgements

I owe a debt to the Japan historians whose work I've drawn on to write this book, though I've taken the odd liberty in the interests of telling a good story. As always, all mistakes, misinterpretations, etc., are my own.

In Kagoshima I'd like to thank Professor Haraguchi Izumi, the pre-eminent expert on the period, Satsuma history and Saigo, who, far from disapproving, as I'd feared, embraced the concept of fictionalizing Saigo and his life with great enthusiasm and joie de vivre and offered many brilliant suggestions. He introduced me to Higashikawa Ryutaro and his wife, Miwa, who showed me around the key sites very knowledgeably. I had expert guidance too on all matters Saigo from Fukuda Kenji of the excellent and comprehensive Museum of the Meiji Restoration and Matsuo Chitoshi of the Shokoshuseikan Museum at Iso. Heartfelt thanks to Morita Mikiko of the Kagoshima Prefectural Visitors' Bureau not only for her help and introductions but also for a memorable night out in Kagoshima. Many thanks too to Kylie Clark at the Japan National Tourism

Organization in London for introductions, maps and enthusiastic support.

I was fortunate to be able to use the resources of several wonderful libraries, including the Diet Library in Tokyo, where I pored over newspapers of the period, and the library of the School of Oriental and African Studies in London (SOAS). I also appreciated the superb Reimeikan Museum in Kagoshima and the Saigo Nanshu Memorial Museum. In Tokyo I stayed, as always, at the International House and enjoyed all its resources including its excellent library.

Huge thanks to my agent, Bill Hamilton, who as always provided brilliant ideas, wise advice and sterling support, above and beyond, and to Jennifer Custer and everyone at A. M. Heath.

My thanks to my two editors – Selina Walker, with whom I discussed the book in its early stages; and Catherine Cobain at Transworld, who was my careful, thoughtful and supportive editor for the later stages. I'm much indebted to her and to her team – Deborah Adams, Lisa Horton, Phil Lord and all at Transworld. My appreciation too to Sakiko Takada for the beautiful calligraphy on the cover of the hardback, which reads 'The Floating Bridge of Dreams'. Thanks to Suzanne Perrin, Heidi Potter of the Japan Society and Rupert Faulkner of the V&A for help in tracking down the right kimono for the cover and to Jonathan Rich and all who worked on it. And 'Merci' to Claude Grangier for the French proverbs and tongue twisters!

Thanks too to Kuniko Tamae for her advice on all things Japanese, including very important matters like whether a name was suitable for a first, second or third son, and much else.

As always, last but most important of all is my husband, Arthur, without whose love, good humour and excellent cooking I couldn't possibly have written this book. He read each draft carefully and made sure I got the rifles and cannons right and that the men talked like men and not like sissies. We visited Japan together in 2011 right after the huge earthquake and tsunami of 11 March (which struck very close to Aizu Wakamatsu). We visited Meiji Village, where I was able to step inside a Meiji-period beef restaurant and barracks, went to Sengaku Temple where the forty-seven ronin are buried and in Kagoshima soaked in the steaming waters of an outdoor hot spring overlooking the sea at the foot of Sakurajima volcano.

This book is dedicated to him.

Lesley Downer

The Last Concubine

Lesley Downer

Japan, 1865, the women's palace in the great city of Edo.

Bristling with intrigue and erotic rivalries, the palace is home to three thousand women and only one man – the young shogun. Sachi, a beautiful fifteen-year-old girl, is chosen to be his concubine.

But Japan is changing, and as civil war erupts, Sachi flees for her life. Rescued by a rebel warrior, she finds unknown feelings stirring within her; but this is a world in which private passions have no place and there is not even a word for 'love'.

Before she dare dream of a life with him, Sachi must uncover the secret of her own origins – a secret that encompasses a wrong so terrible that it threatens to destroy her . . .

Epic history and romance combine in a passionate, exotic novel featuring the mysterious concubine of the last shogun

The Courtesan and the Samurai

Lesley Downer

1868. In Japan's exotic pleasure quarters, sex is for sale and the only forbidden fruit is love . . .

Hana is just seventeen when her husband goes to war, leaving her alone and vulnerable. When enemy soldiers attack her house she flees across the shattered city of Tokyo and takes refuge in the Yoshiwara, its famous pleasure-quarters. There she is forced to become a courtesan.

Yozo, brave, loyal and a brilliant swordsman, is pledged to the embattled shogun. He sails to the frozen north to join his rebel comrades for a desperate last stand. Defeated, he makes his way south to the only place where a man is beyond the reach of the law – the Yoshiwara.

There in the Nightless City where three thousand courtesans mingle with geishas and jesters, the battered fugitive meets the beautiful courtesan. But each has a secret so terrible that once revealed it will threaten their very lives . . .

An epic story of forbidden love in a time of war